Praise for *I Have Some Questions for You*

"A twisty, immersive whodunit perfect for fans of Donna Tartt's *The Secret History.*" —*People*

"[Makkai's] prose is lean yet lush, with short, incantatory chapters and sentences as taut as piano wire." —*The New York Times Book Review*

"Rich in incident and alive with expressive imagery." —*The Wall Street Journal*

"A great accomplishment. [*I Have Some Questions for You*] is at once a campus novel, a piercing reflection on the appeal and ethics of the true crime genre, and a story of Me Too reckoning. It is also the most irresistible literary page-turner I have read in years." —Priscilla Gilman, *The Boston Globe*

"A fully immersive, addictive whodunit." —*San Francisco Chronicle*

"[*I Have Some Questions for You*] embraces the intricate plotting and emotional heft that made [Makkai's] previous novel, *The Great Believers,* a Pulitzer finalist. . . . Makkai sharply conveys the insidiousness of misogyny . . . [and] deftly explores how remembrance can melt into reverie. . . . Her patient, evocative character work prevents Omar and Thalia from becoming types. . . . The result is not a book that leers at a discrete and unfathomable act of violence but one that investigates . . . 'two stolen lives.'" —*The New Yorker*

"Vastly entertaining . . . Both a thickly plotted, character-driven mystery and a stylishly self-aware novel of ideas . . . In a twist worthy of Poe, Makkai suggests that the truth alone may not set you free or lay spirits to rest."
—Maureen Corrigan, NPR's *Fresh Air*

"Bewitching."
—*Vanity Fair*

"[An] addictive page-turner."
—*O Quarterly*

"As we race through [*I Have Some Questions for You*], we're pulled into playing much the same role as Bodie does: trying to piece together the various stories, eagerly awaiting a verdict. . . . [Makkai] leaves us to fill in the gaps, to conjure the lurid details from scraps and rumors—trapped in a quest, her agile book reminds us, that should always leave us second-guessing."
—*The Atlantic*

"Makkai's powerhouse novel has all the draw and momentum of the wildly entertaining mystery that it is, but lurking behind the plot is a series of escalating existential questions about trauma, memory, and the ever-shifting terrain of the past. . . . Makkai brings to the story a vertiginous sensation of falling again and again into new doubts and desires, one that brings to mind Hitchcock at his best and forces the reader constantly to double back and wonder where the story has taken them, really. *I Have Some Questions for You* is a smart, sophisticated mystery, crafted with verve."
—*CrimeReads*

"A sleekly plotted literary murder mystery . . . Makkai has written a complicated whodunit fueled by feminist rage as Bodie relentlessly interrogates her past and recalls the countless murders of girls and women whose stories have been all but lost in our collective memory."
—Associated Press

"*I Have Some Questions for You* asks us to examine many things: high school, the '90s, privilege, justice, sexual harassment, what we owe the dead. Like the true crime podcasts it's modeled on, it's addictive, well told, and a little bit unsettling."   —*Los Angeles Times*

"Gripping . . . A damn good story . . . [Makkai turns] abstractions of personal, social, and cultural politics into a practical, deeply felt, and occasionally even thrilling reality."   —*Star Tribune*

"Makkai combines skilled storytelling with abundant human insight. [*I Have Some Questions for You*] is so well plotted and thought-provoking that readers may struggle with conflicting impulses to keep turning the pages to find out what happens next or to stop and think about what it all means."   —*St. Louis Post-Dispatch*

"[Makkai's] writing is witty and knife-sharp."   —*Condé Nast Traveler*

"Hits all the high notes, complete with at least a few revelations you won't see coming."   —*Good Housekeeping*

"[*I Have Some Questions for You*] calls into question our relationships to memory and power while also challenging readers to reconsider how we think about race, sex, and class."   —*Time*

"Makkai has crafted an unputdownable, captivating boarding school mystery novel with podcasting, teaching, race, divorce, parenting, professional drive, and teen dynamics as undercurrents. . . . The writing in this book is absolutely A+ sensational. Pure perfection."
                    —Zibby Owens, GoodMorningAmerica.com

"Makkai's sleek, beautifully crafted prose and sharp sense of character make *I Have Some Questions for You* a pleasure to read even as its twisting plot propels us into darkness."   —*Tampa Bay Times*

"[A] deft murder-mystery . . . Makkai's poignant mediation on memory and loss is distinguished by clear prose [and] memorable (and flawed) characters."   —*Pittsburgh Post-Gazette*

"Perfectly illustrate[s] the present mood."   —*Dallas Voice*

"*The Secret History* meets *Serial* [in this] modern campus novel."
     —*Lit Hub*

"Makkai's triumph of a novel mixes clever storytelling with an exploration of consent, control, and memory. . . . Satisfying and cleverly multi-layered . . . Combines the smarts of literary fiction with the thrills of a whodunit, topped with all the divertissements of the best boarding school–set dramas."   —*Financial Times*

"[A] skillfully crafted academic mystery."   —*POPSUGAR*

"Dark academia meets state of America in this brilliant, original novel."
     —*Daily Mail*

"An enthralling mystery, an interrogation of the past, an entrancing campus novel, *I Have Some Questions for You* is a propulsive page-turner."
     —*B&N Reads*

"Clever and deeply thoughtful . . . A deliciously complex reckoning . . . [*I Have Some Questions for You*] is sure to be a hit."
     —*Publishers Weekly* (starred review)

"A thought-provoking and delicious tale of life and death and justice that very well may have gone sideways." —*Library Journal* (starred review)

"Engrossing . . . A well-plotted indictment of systemic racism and misogyny craftily disguised as a thriller and beautifully constructed to make its points." —*BookPage* (starred review)

"A beguiling campus novel . . . Chilled as the deep New England winters during which it takes place and twisty with the slowly found and then suddenly illuminated branches of memory, Makkai's rich, winding story dazzles from cover to cover." —*Booklist* (starred review)

"Every year, I look for the novels that truly respect their victims, and think carefully about the tropes of true crime; for 2023, [*I Have Some Questions for You*] is that novel." —Molly Odintz, *CrimeReads*

"Makkai's novel takes on some of the defining issues of its time . . . without battering readers with them. Instead, Makkai carefully winds her themes around her story's scaffolding, which strengthens her masterly plot even more." —*Shelf Awareness*

"[Makkai adds] intriguing layers of complication. . . . Well plotted, well written, and well designed." —*Kirkus Reviews*

"Part boarding school drama, part forensic whodunit, *I Have Some Questions for You* is a true literary mystery—haunting and hard to put down."
—Jennifer Egan, Pulitzer Prize–winning author of
A Visit from the Goon Squad and *The Candy House*

"One of the things I love most about Rebecca Makkai's writing is her absolutely engaging voice; reading her books feels like hearing a well-told story by a longtime friend. This book—through the voice of its beautifully complex narrator, Bodie Kane—brings readers along on a journey they won't forget."   —Liz Moore, *New York Times* bestselling author of *Long Bright River*

PENGUIN BOOKS

I HAVE SOME QUESTIONS FOR YOU

Rebecca Makkai is the author of the novels *I Have Some Questions for You*, *The Great Believers*, *The Hundred-Year House*, and *The Borrower*, and the story collection *Music for Wartime*. A finalist for the Pulitzer Prize and the National Book Award, *The Great Believers* received an American Library Association Andrew Carnegie Medal for Excellence in Fiction and the Los Angeles Times Book Prize, among other honors, and was named one of the Ten Best Books of 2018 by *The New York Times*. A 2022 Guggenheim fellow, Makkai is on the MFA faculties of the University of Nevada, Reno at Lake Tahoe and Northwestern University, and is the artistic director of StoryStudio Chicago. She lives on the campus of the midwestern boarding school where her husband teaches, and in Vermont.

Penguin Reading Group Discussion Guide
available online at penguinrandomhouse.com

ALSO BY REBECCA MAKKAI

The Great Believers
Music for Wartime
The Hundred-Year House
The Borrower

I HAVE
SOME
QUESTIONS
FOR YOU

Rebecca Makkai

PENGUIN BOOKS

PENGUIN BOOKS
An imprint of Penguin Random House LLC
penguinrandomhouse.com

First published in the United States of America by Viking,
an imprint of Penguin Random House LLC, 2023
Published in Penguin Books 2024

ISBN 9780593490167 (paperback)

THE LIBRARY OF CONGRESS HAS CATALOGED THE HARDCOVER EDITION AS FOLLOWS:

Names: Makkai, Rebecca, author.
Title: I have some questions for you / Rebecca Makkai.
Description: [New York] : Viking, [2023]
Identifiers: LCCN 2022032713 (print) | LCCN 2022032714 (ebook) |
ISBN 9780593490143 (hardcover) | ISBN 9780593654729 (international edition) |
ISBN 9780593490150 (ebook)
Subjects: LCGFT: Novels.
Classification: LCC PS3613.A36 I33 2023 (print) |
LCC PS3613.A36 (ebook) | DDC 813/.6—dc23/eng/20220711
LC record available at https://lccn.loc.gov/2022032713
LC ebook record available at https://lccn.loc.gov/2022032714

Printed in the United States of America
1st Printing

BOOK DESIGN BY LUCIA BERNARD

for CGG
in joyful memory

"You've heard of her," I say—a challenge, an assurance. To the woman on the neighboring hotel barstool who's made the mistake of striking up a conversation, to the dentist who runs out of questions about my kids and asks what I've been up to myself.

Sometimes they know her right away. Sometimes they ask, "Wasn't that the one where the guy kept her in the basement?"

No! No. It was not.

Wasn't it the one where she was stabbed in—no. The one where she got in a cab with—different girl. The one where she went to the frat party, the one where he used a stick, the one where he used a hammer, the one where she picked him up from rehab and he—no. The one where he'd been watching her jog every day? The one where she made the mistake of telling him her period was late? The one with the uncle? Wait, the other one with the uncle?

No: It was the one with the swimming pool. The one with the alcohol in the—with her hair around—with the guy who confessed to—right. Yes.

They nod, comforted. By what?

My barstool neighbor pulls the celery from her Bloody Mary, crunches down. My dentist asks me to rinse. They work her name in their mouths, their memories. "I definitely know that one," they say.

"That one," because what is she now but a story, a story to know or not know, a story with a limited set of details, a story to master by memorizing maps and timelines.

"The one from the boarding school!" they say. "I remember, the one from the video. You *knew* her?"

She's the one whose photo pops up if you search *New Hampshire murder*, alongside mug shots from the meth-addled tragedies of more recent years. One photo—her laughing with her mouth but not her eyes, suggesting some deep unhappiness—tends to feature in clickbait. It's just a cropped shot of the tennis team from the yearbook; if you knew Thalia it's easy to see she wasn't actually upset, was simply smiling for the camera when she didn't feel like it.

It was the story that got told and retold.

It was the one where she was young enough and white enough and pretty enough and rich enough that people paid attention.

It was the one where we were all young enough to think someone smarter had the answers.

Maybe it was the one we got wrong.

Maybe it was the one we all, collectively, each bearing only the weight of a feather, got wrong.

I HAVE
SOME
QUESTIONS
FOR YOU

Part I

I first watched the video in 2016. I was in bed on my laptop, with headphones, worried Jerome would wake up and I'd have to explain. Down the hall, my children slept. I could have gone and checked on them, felt their warm cheeks and hot breath. I could have smelled my daughter's hair—and maybe the scent of damp lavender and a toddler's scalp would have been enough to send me to sleep.

But a friend I hadn't seen in twenty years had just sent me the link, and so I clicked.

Lerner and Loewe's *Camelot*. I was both stage manager and tech director. One fixed camera, too close to the orchestra, too far from the unmiked adolescent singers, 1995 VHS quality, some member of the AV club behind the lens. And my God, we knew we weren't great, but we weren't even as good as we thought we were. Whoever uploaded it two decades later, whoever added the notes below with the exact time markers for when Thalia Keith shows up, had also posted the list of cast and crew. Beth Docherty as a petite Guinevere, Sakina John glowing as Morgan le Fay with a crown of gold spikes atop her cornrows, Mike Stiles beautiful and embarrassed as King Arthur. My name is misspelled, but it's there, too.

The curtain call is the last shot where you clearly see Thalia, her dark curls distinguishing her from the washed-out mass. Then most everyone stays onstage to sing "Happy Birthday" to Mrs. Ross, our director, to pull her up from the front row where she sat every night jotting notes. She's so young, something I hadn't registered then.

A few kids exit, return in confusion. Orchestra members hop onstage to sing, Mrs. Ross's husband springs from the audience with flowers, the crew comes on in black shirts and black jeans. I don't appear; I assume I stayed up in the box. It would have been like me to sit it out.

Including the regrouping and singing, the birthday business lasts fifty-two seconds, during which you never see Thalia clearly. In the comments, someone had zoomed in on a bit of green dress at one side of the frame, posted side-by-side photos of that smear of color and the dress Thalia wore—first covered in gauze as Nimue, the enchantress, the Lady of the Lake, and then ungauzed, with a simple headdress, as Lady Anne. But there were several green dresses. My friend Carlotta's was one. There's a chance that, by then, Thalia was gone.

Most of the discussion below the video focused on timing. The show was set to begin at 7:00, but we likely started our mercifully abridged version five minutes late. Maybe more. The tape omitted intermission, and there was speculation on how long the intermission of a high school musical would last. Depending on what you believe about these two variables, the show ended sometime between 8:45 and 9:15. I should have known. Once, there would have been a binder with my meticulous notes. But no one ever asked for it.

The window the medical examiner allowed for Thalia's time of death was 8:00 p.m. to midnight, with the beginning of the slot curtailed by the musical—the reason the show's exact end time had become the subject of infinite fascination online.

I came here from YouTube, one commenter had written in 2015, linking to a separate video. *Watch this. It PROVES they bungled the case. The timeline makes no sense.*

Someone else wrote: *Wrong guy in prison bc of racist cops in schools pocket.*

And below that: *Welcome to Tinfoil Hat Central! Focus your energies on an ACTUAL UNSOLVED CASE.*

Watching the video twenty-one years after the fact, the memory that dislodged from my brain's dark corners was looking up *lusty* in the library dictionary with my friend Fran, who was in the show. To quiet our giggling about "The Lusty Month of May," Mrs. Ross had announced that "*lusty* simply means *vibrant*. You're welcome to look it up." But what did Mrs. Ross know about lust? Lust was for the young, not married drama teachers. But ("Holy apeshit," as Fran would have said, might have said), look, according to Webster, *lusty* indeed meant *healthy and strong; full of vigor*. One of the examples was *a lusty beef stew*. We fled the library laughing, Fran singing, "Oh, a lusty stew of beef!"

Where had I kept that memory, all those years?

The first time through the video I skipped around, really only watching the end; I had no desire to listen at length to teenage voices, poorly tuned string instruments. But then I went back—the same night, two a.m., my melatonin tablet failing—and watched all the parts with Thalia. Act I, Scene 2 was her only scene as Nimue. She appeared upstage in a dry ice fog, singing hypnotically behind Merlin. Something bothered me about how she kept glancing away from him as she sang, looking offstage right, as if she needed prompting. She couldn't have; all she needed to do was sing her one repetitive song.

I climbed carefully over Jerome to get his iPad from his nightstand and brought the video up there, this time zooming in on her face, making it larger if not clearer. It's subtle, but she looks irritated.

And then, as Merlin gives his farewell speech, bidding goodbye to Arthur and Camelot, she looks away again, nearly over her shoulder. She mouths something; it's not my imagination. Her lips start to close and then part, a formation that makes a W sound when I replicate it. She's saying, I'm almost sure, the word *what*. Maybe just to a stagehand, one of my crew holding up a forgotten prop. But what could have been so important in that moment, right before she exited?

As of 2016, no one in the comments section had fixated on this. They only cared about the timing of the curtain call, whether she was indeed onstage for that last minute. (That and how pretty she was.) Fifty-two seconds, their reasoning went, was enough for Thalia Keith to meet someone waiting backstage, to leave with that person before anyone saw.

At the very end of the tape: Our illustrious orchestra conductor–slash–music director, bow-tied, baton still in hand, begins an announcement no one's listening to: "Thank you all! As you leave—" But the video cedes to a buzz of gray lines. Presumably something about dorm check-in, or taking your trash with you.

Check out Guinevere the last two seconds, one comment reads. *Is that a flask? I wanna be friends with Guinevere!* I froze the video and yes, it's a silver flask Beth's holding aloft, maybe confident her friends will recognize it but any teachers in the audience will be too distracted to notice. Or maybe Beth was already too buzzed to care.

Another comment asks if anyone can identify the audience members passing the camera as they leave.

Another reads, *If you watch the 2005 Dateline special, don't listen to anything they say. SO many errors. Also, it's THA- like the beginning of "thatch" or "thanks" and Lester Holt keeps saying THAY-lia.*

Someone replies: *I thought it was TAHL-ia.*

Nope, nope, nope, the original poster writes. *I knew her sister.*

Another comment: *This whole thing makes me so sad.* Followed by three crying emojis and a blue heart.

I dreamed for weeks afterward not about Thalia's head turn, her mouthed question, but about Beth Docherty's flask. In my dreams, I had to find it in order to hide it again. I held my giant binder. My notes were no help.

The theater crowd had begged for that show—had brought it up constantly the year before, whenever Mrs. Ross had dorm duty. There'd been a Broadway revival in '93, and even those of us who hadn't seen it had heard the soundtrack, understood it entailed medieval cleavage, onstage kissing, fabulous solos. For me, it meant castle backgrounds, thrones, trees on casters—nothing tricky, no flesh-eating houseplant, no Ford Deluxe convertible to roll onstage. For the journalists of the future, it would mean endless easy metaphors. Boarding school as kingdom in the woods, Thalia as enchantress, Thalia as princess, Thalia as martyr. What could be more romantic? What's as perfect as a girl stopped dead, midformation? Girl as blank slate. Girl as reflection of your desires, unmarred by her own. Girl as sacrifice to the idea of *girl*. Girl as a series of childhood photographs, all marked with the aura of *girl who will die young*, as if even the third grade portrait photographer should have seen it written on her face, that this was a girl who would only ever be a girl.

The bystander, the voyeur, even the perpetrator—they're all off the hook when the girl was born dead.

On the internet and on TV, they love that.

And you, Mr. Bloch: I suppose it's been convenient for you, too.

Against all odds, in January of 2018, I found myself hurtling back toward campus in one of those good old Blue Cabs that had picked me up so many times, so long ago, from the Manchester airport. My driver said he'd been making runs to Granby all day.

"They all went on vacation somewhere," he said.

I said, "They were home for holiday break."

He snorted, as if I'd confirmed his rotten suspicions.

He asked if I taught at Granby. I was startled, for a moment, that he hadn't taken me for a student. But here was my reflection in his rearview: a put-together adult with lines around her eyes. I said no, not really, I was just visiting to teach a two-week course. I didn't explain that I'd gone to Granby, that I knew the route we were traveling like an old song. It felt like too much information to lay on him in casual conversation. I didn't explain the concept of mini-mester, either, because it would sound twee, the exact kind of thing he'd imagine these spoiled kids getting up to.

It was Fran's idea to bring me back. Fran herself had barely left; after a few years away for college, grad school, time abroad, she returned to teach history at Granby. Her wife works in Admissions, and they live on campus with their sons.

My driver's name was Lee, and he told me he'd "been driving these Granby kids since their granddaddies went there." He explained that Granby was the kind of school you could only get into through family connections. I wanted to tell him this was dead wrong, but my window for correcting his assumption that I was an outsider had long passed. He told me that "these kids get up to trouble you wouldn't believe" and asked if I'd read the article "a few years back" in *Rolling Stone*. That article ("Live Free or Die: Drink, Drugs, and Drowning at an Elite New Hampshire Boarding School") came out in 1996, and yes, we'd all read it. We emailed each other about it from our college dorms, livid over its errors and assumptions—much as we would all text each other nine years later when *Dateline* dragged everything up again.

Lee said, "They don't supervise those kids a bit. Only thing I'm happy about, they have a rule against Uber."

I said, "That's funny, I've heard the opposite. About the supervision."

"Yeah, well, they're lying. They want you to come teach, they'll say whatever."

I'd only been back to Granby three times in the nearly twenty-three years since graduation. There was one early reunion when I lived in New York; I stayed an hour. I returned for Fran and Anne's wedding in Old Chapel in 2008. In July of 2013, I was in Vermont for a few days and came to see Fran, to meet her first baby. That was it. I'd avoided our tenth and fifteenth and twentieth, ignored the LA alumni meetups. It wasn't till that *Camelot* video surfaced and Fran looped me in on a subsequent group text, which devolved into theater memories, that I grew genuinely nostalgic for the place. I thought I'd wait for 2020, a reunion my classmates would show for—our twenty-fifth as well as the school's bicentennial. But then, this invitation.

It was convenient, too, that Yahav, the man I'd been having a dragged-out, desperate, long-distance affair with, was just two hours away, teaching for the year at BU Law. Yahav had an Israeli accent and was tall and brilliant and neurotic. Our relationship wasn't such that I could simply fly out to see him. But I could find myself in the neighborhood.

Plus I wanted to see if I could do it—if, despite my nerves, my almost adolescent panic, I was ready to measure myself against the girl who'd slouched her way through Granby. In LA I knew in theory that I was accomplished—a sometime college professor with a lauded podcast, a woman who could make a meal from farmers' market ingredients and get her kids to school reasonably dressed—but I didn't particularly feel, on a daily basis, the distance I'd come. At Granby, I knew it would hit me hard.

So there was the money, and the guy, and my ego, and—below it all, a note too low to hear—there was Thalia, there was the way that ever since I'd watched that video, I'd felt just slightly misaligned.

In any case: They asked, I said yes, and here I was, buckled into the backseat letting Lee drive me to campus at ten miles over the speed limit.

He said, "What are you gonna teach them, some Shakespeare?"

I explained that I was teaching two classes: one on podcasting, another on film studies.

"Film studies!" he said. "They watching movies, or making them?"

I felt there was no answer that wouldn't make Lee think worse of both me and the school. I said, "The history of film," which was both correct and incomplete. I added that until recently I'd taught film studies at UCLA, which had the desired effect—I've used this trick before— of getting him straight onto Bruins football. I could make noises of agreement while he monologued. We only had twenty minutes left in the drive, and the odds were low now that he'd either ask me about podcasts or mansplain Quentin Tarantino.

The school had invited me specifically to teach the film class, and I'd volunteered to double up because it would mean twice the money—but also because I've never known how to sit still, and if I was leaving my kids and heading to the woods for two weeks, I didn't want to just sit around. The need to keep busy is both a symptom of high-functioning anxiety and the key to my success.

My podcast at the time was *Starlet Fever*, a serial history of women in film—the ways the industry chewed them up and spat them out. It was going as well as a podcast reasonably could, occasionally hitting top slots in various download metrics. There was a bit of money in it, and some- times, thrillingly, a celebrity would mention us in an interview. My cohost, Lance, had been able to quit his landscaping gig, I'd been able to turn down the adjuncting crumbs UCLA threw my way, and we had a couple of literary agents offering representation if we wanted to cowrite a book. We were knee-deep in prep for our upcoming season, centered on Rita Hayworth, but it was research I could do from anywhere.

We followed another Blue Cab down Route 9, one with two kids in the back. Lee said, "See, there's some of your students, I bet. None of these kids are from around here. They're from other countries, even. This morning I drove some girls coming back from China, and they didn't say a word. How can they do classes when they don't speak English?"

I pretended to take a call then, before the racism turned more overt.

"Gary!" I said to the no one in my phone, and then I spaced out a series of *uh-huh*s and *okay*s for ten minutes as the frozen woods blurred past. Without Lee's distractions, though, I was unfortunately free to feel the nerves I'd been ignoring, free to feel the woods swallowing me toward Granby. Here was the little white union church I always took as the sign that I'd be there soon. Here was the turnoff to the narrower road, a turn I felt deep in my muscle memory.

As if the turn had brought it up, I remembered the too-long jean shorts and striped tank top I wore on my first drive to Granby in 1991. I remembered wondering if New Hampshire kids had accents, not understanding how few of my classmates would be from New Hampshire. I restrained myself from telling this to Lee, or saying it into my phone.

The Robesons, the family I lived with, had driven me most of the way from Indiana in one day, and the next morning we woke with just an hour to go. The backseat windows down, I sat with my face in the rushing air watching the scroll of calendar-pretty farmland and woods you couldn't see into, just walls of green. Everything smelled like manure, which I was used to, and then, suddenly, like pine. I said, "It smells like air freshener out there!" The Robesons reacted as if I were a small child who'd said something delightful. "Like air freshener!" Severn Robeson repeated, and gleefully slapped the steering wheel.

On campus that first day, I couldn't believe the density of woods, the way the ground was somehow the woods, too—rocks and logs and pine needles and moss. You always had to watch your feet. The only woods I'd known in Indiana stood between rows of houses or out back of gas stations—woods you could walk through to the other side. There were cigarette butts, soda cans. When I'd heard fairy tales as a child, those were the woods I pictured. But now the stories of primeval forests, lost children, hidden lairs, made sense. *This* was a forest.

Outside Lee's cab: the Granby Post Office, and what used to be the video store. The Circle K was unchanged, but it was hard to get nostalgic over a gas station. Here was the campus road, and here was a wave of adrenaline. I ended my fake phone call, wishing Gary a great day.

When all the leaves fell that first November, I expected to see the houses and buildings that had been waiting, all along, through the trees. But no: Beyond these bare branches, more bare branches. Beyond them, only more.

At night, there were owls. Sometimes, if the dumpsters hadn't been latched, black bears would take entire garbage bags, drag them across campus to open like party favors.

The car we'd been following took the fork toward the boys' dorms, but Lee opted for the long route around Lower Campus so he could give me a tour, and all I could do now was listen politely.

He said, "Where you have me dropping you, that's Upper Campus, above the river, the fancy new buildings. But down here, this is the old part, going back to seventeen-something."

The 1820s, but I didn't correct him. It was midafternoon, and a few kids trudged out of Commons and across the quad, hunched against the cold.

Lee pointed out the original classroom building, the dorms adolescent farmer boys used to freeze in, the cottages where bachelor teachers of yore passed solitary lives, Old Chapel and New Chapel (neither a real chapel anymore, both impossibly old), the headmaster's house. He pointed out the bronze statue of Samuel Granby and said, falsely, "That's the guy who started the school with just one classroom."

As a student, I couldn't pass Samuel Granby without rubbing his foot, a tradition shared by no one. I also couldn't pass a pay phone without flipping the receiver upside down. This was incredibly witty and rebellious; you'll have to believe me.

When Lee finally circled to the bottom of Upper Campus and stopped the car, I opened the door onto a wall of cold. I paid him and he told me to stay warm, as if that were a choice—as if it weren't the absolute pit of winter, everything locked in ice and salt. Looking at buildings that hadn't changed, at the thin ridge of White Mountain crest rising above the eastern tree line, it was easy to imagine the place had been cryogenically preserved.

Fran had offered me her couch, but the way she said it—"I mean, there's the dog, and Jacob's always at volume eleven, and Max still doesn't sleep through the night"—made it seem more gesture than invitation. So I'd opted to stay in one of the two guest apartments, located right above the ravine in a small house that used to be the business office. There were a bedroom and bathroom on each floor, plus a downstairs kitchen to share. The whole place, I found, smelled like bleach.

I unpacked, worrying I hadn't brought enough sweaters, and thinking, of all things, about Granby pay phones.

Imagine me (remember me), fifteen, sixteen, dressed in black even when I wasn't backstage, my taped-up Doc Martens, the dark, wispy hair fringing my Cabbage Patch face; imagine me, armored in flannel, eyes ringed thick with liner, passing the pay phone and—without looking—picking it up, twirling it upside down, hanging it back the wrong way.

That was only at first, though; by junior year, I couldn't pass one without picking up the receiver, pressing a single number, and listening—because there was at least one phone on which, if you did this, you could hear another conversation through the static. I discovered the trick when I started to call my dorm from the gym lobby phone to ask if I could be late for 10:00 check-in, but after I pressed the first button I heard a boy's voice, muffled, half volume, complaining to his mother about midterms. She asked if he'd been getting his allergy shots. He sounded whiny and homesick and about twelve years old, and it took me a while to recognize his voice: Tim Busse, a hockey player with bad skin but a beautiful girl-friend. He must have been on a pay phone in his own dorm common, across the ravine. I didn't understand what rules of telecommunications allowed this to occur, and when I told my husband this story once, he shook his head, said, "That couldn't happen." I asked if he was accusing me of lying, or if he thought I'd been hearing voices. "I just mean," Je-rome replied evenly, "that it couldn't happen."

I stood in the gym lobby mesmerized, not wanting to miss a word. But eventually I had to; I called my own dorm, asked the on-duty teacher for ten extra minutes to run across campus and get the history book I'd left in Commons. No, she said, I could not. I had three minutes till check-in. I hung up, lifted the receiver again, pressed one number. There was Tim Busse's voice still. Magic. He told his mother he was fail-ing physics. I was surprised. And now I had a secret about him. A secret secret, one he hadn't meant to share.

I had a sidelong crush after that on Tim Busse, to whom I'd never previously paid an ounce of attention.

In the following months I tried every pay phone on campus, but it was only the gym one that worked, and only if someone happened to be talking on a phone (maybe one specific phone) in Barton Hall.

Most of what I heard was indecipherable mumbling. Once I heard someone order pizza. Sometimes people spoke Korean or Spanish or German. Once I heard "Rhapsody in Blue," the hold music for United Airlines. Sometimes I heard more interesting things, bits of information I held close. I knew that someone—I never figured out who—would be home for Passover but refused to go to Aunt Ellen's house. I learned that someone else missed his girlfriend, no, *really* missed her, really, and no, he wasn't seeing anyone else, he loved her, why was she being like that, stop being like that, didn't she know he missed her?

We're granted so few superpowers in life. This was one of mine. I could walk the halls knowing things none of those Barton Hall boys would voluntarily tell me. I knew Jorge Cardenas didn't let himself drink when he was sad, because that was how alcoholism started, and he didn't want to be like his father.

It would be convenient if I'd picked up that phone one day and heard something useful, something incriminating. Heard someone threatening Thalia, for instance. Or heard something about you.

But it was simply part of a broader habit: I collected information about my peers the way some people hoard newspapers. I hoped this would help me become more like them, less like myself—less poor, less clueless, less provincial, less vulnerable.

Every summer, I'd bring home the yearbook and mark each student's photo with a special code of colored checkmarks: whether I knew them, considered them a friend, had a crush. Sometimes, in the depths of summer isolation, I'd look up people's families in the school directory to learn their parents' first names, with the sole purpose of lifting me, for a minute, out of a bedroom I hated in a house that wasn't my own in a town where I didn't know anyone anymore.

This doesn't make me special, and I knew that then, too. I'm only saying it by way of explanation: I cared about details. Not because they were something I could control, but because they were something I could own.

And there was so little that was mine.

Fran and Anne had invited me for a late dinner, so I put on the snow boots I'd purchased for the trip and headed across South Bridge to Lower Campus. It was nine degrees out, the snow hard enough to walk across without sinking. I wondered if I'd pass people I knew, but I seemed to be the only living thing outdoors.

When I'd been back before, it was to limited parts of campus. I hadn't crossed the bridges, entered academic buildings. The dimensions seemed off now; my memory, and my frequent Granby dreams, had moved things inch by inch. The statue of Samuel Granby had somehow moved ten feet uphill, for instance. I passed close, touched his foot with my glove for old times' sake.

That fall, right after I'd accepted the invitation to teach, I woke thinking about the main street through town, the one with all the businesses, but couldn't remember its name, so I googled *Granby School map*.

What I found, beyond the answer (Crown Street!), were detailed maps of campus as it was in March of 1995, maps people had marked with dotted lines representing their theories, the routes they'd charted through the woods. I knew Thalia's murder had caught and held the public's attention, but I hadn't understood the sheer amount of time people were putting in.

Diving down online rabbit holes was not great for my mental health. (The night after I watched the *Camelot* video, I stayed up googling Granby classmates and faculty, and I googled facts about drowning, and I rewatched part of the *Dateline* episode. Finally Jerome woke up and saw my eyes and made me stop, told me to take a NyQuil and spend the morning in bed.) So I allowed myself only an hour to stare at the maps, to read what people were saying.

The term *rabbit hole* makes us think of Alice plummeting straight down, but what I mean is an actual rabbit warren, the kind with endless looping tunnels, branching paths, all the accompanying claustrophobia. It blew my mind how much people cared. To them, Thalia was a face from a few well-shared photos: a life barely sketched out, rather than a girl who smelled like that Sunflowers perfume, whose laugh sounded like hiccups, who'd toss herself onto her bed like a hand grenade.

But I've cared as much, I admit, about people I haven't met. I care about Judy Garland and Natalie Wood and the Black Dahlia. I care about the lacrosse player murdered by her ex at UVA, and the girl whose boyfriend was definitely not working at LensCrafters that day, and the high school student killed in her boyfriend's Shaker Heights backyard while everyone slept, and poor Martha Moxley, and the woman in the hotel elevator, and the only Black woman at the white-lady wine party, dead on the lawn, and the woman shot through the bathroom door by her famous boyfriend, who claimed he thought she was a burglar. I have opinions about their deaths, ones I'm not entitled to. I'm queasy, at the same time, about the way they've become public property, subject to the collective imagination. I'm queasy about the fact that the women whose deaths I dwell on are mostly beautiful and well-off. That most were young, as we prefer our sacrificial lambs. That I'm not alone in my fixations.

Fran and Anne's combined seniority at Granby meant they'd been promoted from dorm apartments to a house, one of the three old stone ones down by the front gate. I felt bad ringing the bell empty-handed—I'd forgotten to have the Blue Cab stop at the wine shop—but it was their son Jacob who opened the door, letting the golden retriever out to bruise my thighs and slobber on my jeans.

I hope you remember Fran, because Fran deserves remembering. Fran Hoffnung—although now it's Hoffbart, since she and her wife combined their last names. You at least remember the Hoffnungs: Deb Hoffnung taught English, Sam Hoffnung taught math, and Fran and her three older sisters grew up in the front apartment attached to Singer-Baird, the girls' dorm with that funny steep roof. She was the loud kid who'd emcee Lip Sync, the one whose hair was always pink or purple with Manic Panic. Nowadays it's brown with streaks of gray, somehow as cool as the pink once was.

Their Christmas tree was still up, and after I hugged his moms, Jacob needed me to come admire it—big, old-fashioned colored bulbs and sparse ornaments from Fran's and Anne's own childhoods: a painted Snoopy doghouse, a tiny silver cup with Anne's name, a needlepoint owl. One obviously newer addition, an RBG figurine with lace collar.

Jacob, whom I'd met as a red-faced and colicky newborn, was nearly five, and had a little brother I'd seen only online, a two-year-old who kept staggering up to drive his trains down my leg until Anne bribed both boys with *PAW Patrol* on the iPad. Anne made us vegetarian tacos. I ate more than I normally would just because Fran was always worried I didn't eat enough. Fran mixed a pitcher of margaritas, and we listened to Bob Marley, which didn't match the food but still came from a warm place. Fran couldn't let go of the fact that I'd arrived from LA right as it had gotten so cold. "You're gonna resent me," she said. "I'll be a constant guilt puddle."

I said, "A frozen guilt puddle. A tiny skating rink of guilt."

Anne asked if I'd need extra socks, extra blankets, extra anything.

"Maybe a couple sweaters?" I said. "I forgot it gets cold *inside*."

Anne scuttled off and reappeared with a whole reusable grocery bag of sweaters and sweatshirts and a pair of Granby green-and-gold-plaid pajama pants.

Fran herself had mini-mester off; she'd taught her Vietnam War class three years in a row and it was her turn for "professional development," which meant reading books and catching up on email and drinking with me. "We don't have to hang *every* night," she said, "but if you aren't over here I'll assume you're laid up in that guest suite watching sad straight porn and thinking about work." Fran had dorm duty on Wednesdays, but "every other night," she said, "we're gonna party like it's 1995."

"With Zima and SnackWell's?"

"I was thinking *Sassy* magazine and lukewarm Natty Light."

I said, "I'll have grading," but Fran knew she didn't have to talk me into it.

"Every *other* other night, at least. And Friday there's this party, so you have to come. Everyone wants to meet you. We call it the Midi-Mini because, you know, halfway through mini-mester."

"We can't resist wordplay here," Anne said.

Anne had long blond curls, and a runner's build that made Fran look squat in comparison. Anne coached cross-country in the fall and track in the spring and was, in general, the perfect combination of audience, straight man, and manager for Fran. If you needed an idea for a party, Fran would have twenty. If you needed someone to order the pizzas and buy ice and clean the living room while Fran was making the playlist, that was Anne. They'd met here at Granby, Anne having started in Admissions while Fran was off having her brief life outside the boarding school world. When Fran came back they were friends, resisting everyone's urge to set them up, commiserating about the impossibility of meeting anyone. Then they rode down to Boston together one long weekend, and came back in love.

And now Anne was the one shuffling the boys off to bed, telling them they could skip their baths if they were quiet, while Fran leaned across the table and said, as if we'd only been waiting for her wife to leave the room, "Tell me everything."

She meant everything about Jerome, because I'd mentioned, when we emailed a few weeks back, that Jerome had moved out and was living next door. And now Fran needed all the information, including why I hadn't told her already. "We're still married," I said. "It's just not what our grandparents would have considered marriage." It happened so slowly that it didn't seem a thing to announce on social media, text old friends about.

"We went through a rough patch," I said, leaving out that this was two years ago, when the kids were five and three, that their loud ubiquity was part of the stress. We got to the point where everything I said to Jerome was the wrong thing, came out in the wrong voice. Everything he said to me was worse. We'd slowly grown allergic to each other, eventually realized we were each unfairly shackled to a person who was sick of our face. "And right around then," I did tell her, "Jerome's mom went into hospice. She'd been in the other half of our duplex, so he moved over there." He's a painter, and the decision was partly practical: He could use the second bedroom as a studio and stop paying rent on the one downtown. We could stay married, with one address, for tax reasons and convenience—and, honestly, out of sheer laziness. The kids could go back and forth, we figured, but really Jerome ended up going back and forth, and so, for instance, while I was at Granby he stayed in my bed, which was our old bed, which occasionally he also stayed in when I was in it, because he was good at sex and now that we didn't see each other all day, we didn't hate each other. I was actually enormously fond of him: grateful when he took the kids, nostalgic when we slept together, bemused by his dating life, equal parts flattered and revolted and possessive when he came to me for romantic advice. I found everyone he dated borderline crazy, couldn't figure out if that was on him or on me.

Fran said, "You know I love how you never give up on people, but it's kind of hilarious that your way of breaking up involves him still living in your house."

"Well, next door."

"So the upshot is," she said, "you're single?"

"Essentially. Married but single."

"It's funny that my marriage is more traditional than yours."

I hadn't told her about Yahav, maybe because I didn't want to jinx it. Yahav was skittish and unpredictable, a handsome Israeli bunny rabbit, equally likely to drive straight here as to vanish into the woods forever. I'd texted him from the airport that afternoon: *As warned, I've invaded New England.* He texted back only an exclamation point.

I had not yet been sleeping with Yahav when I split from Jerome, but his friendship then had been a helpful reminder that not everyone was tired of me, not everyone blamed me for the weather. Yahav had enormous, warm hands. He had dark stubble so thick it consumed his chin and neck, more darkness than light, more night sky than stars.

Anne returned and we poured new drinks and the evening turned to a sort of retroactive gossip session. (Wait, remember Dani Michalek? Remember how she tried to pierce her own nose and it got so infected? Yeah, and she had to go home for a month. We were paired for lab and I didn't do a thing. She hated me. Me too. Whatever happened to her? Didn't I *tell* you? She's a Lutheran minister!)

Anne's encouraging laughter, her bewildered questions, egged us on. If she hadn't been there, we might've said "Remember the Kurt shrine?" and left it at that. But with Anne present, we wound up describing for her sake (and really each other's) the elaborate shrine we'd built to Kurt Cobain in the woods junior year, and tended from the time he overdosed and was hospitalized (early March, when we wore thick gloves to tack cutout magazine photos to the frozen tree) to the time he died by suicide in April. By then other people knew about the shrine, and the day after his body was discovered, Fran and I found messages and more magazine photos and a Mylar heart balloon and what looked like a leftover Spring Dance corsage stuck to the tree as well.

"We were so in love with him," I said, and then it occurred to me that Fran probably hadn't been, actually. "Or I was."

"Oh, I loved him," Fran said. She was drunker than me. "But I was *in love* with Courtney. Kurt was my beard."

Dessert was caramelized bananas with vanilla ice cream—Anne still sober enough to manage things at the stove, to ignore our demands that she light the bananas on fire—and the more into arcane details we got, and the more lost but patient Anne was, the more hilarious everything became.

I was always my funniest self around Fran, or at least she found me funny. We met in world history our freshman year, and didn't talk at first, just flopped into adjacent desks most days out of seating inertia. I'd squirmed through September without any real friends, eating my meals at the corner of a long table of assorted freshmen, watching them splinter off into actual friend groups and knowing I'd soon be alone. There was a kid named Benjamin Scott who'd established himself early as the genius of our grade—a tall blond kid who, from the way he referenced books none of us knew, seemed to have arrived at Granby following a couple of PhDs. Someone must have made a joke in class about killing Benjamin, or Benjamin dying, because what I said, under my breath, was "If you die, can I have your grades?" Fran was the only one who heard me. She snickered and looked around and said, loudly, "Yeah, Benji, if you die, can I have your grades?" And (a miracle!) the class cracked up. Even Benjamin Scott laughed sheepishly. After class, Fran ran up beside me in the hall. "Don't hate me," she said. "It was too good a line to waste."

From then on, I made sure Fran could hear my asides, the things I usually wouldn't even have said aloud. She never repeated me again, but she'd smirk or cover her laughter with coughing. Because Fran had claimed the classroom's only left-handed desk, our writing surfaces abutted and we didn't have to pass notes, could just scribble in our own textbook margins.

Where are you even from? she wrote once, and I wrote back *West Bumblefuck*, which was original enough to us at the time to be amusing. No one had ever found me particularly entertaining before. It was intoxicating.

Fran had a different lunch block than me and lived with her parents rather than in a dorm room, played field hockey while I rowed crew, so it took a while for us to become friends outside of class. When we did, though, it was natural. We could already read each other's handwriting.

She started coming to my room to study for our history midterm, and then for other exams. And then she was shrieking at me because I didn't know who the Pixies were, and then we were best friends.

Neither of us dated anyone the whole time at Granby—Fran because she was closeted and assumed she was the only lesbian in New Hampshire; me because I had a pathological aversion to risking rejection and humiliation in a place where I was already only hanging on to the edge. I needed to keep Granby pristine. Indiana was the place where bad things happened; Granby had to be a place where nothing could hurt me. The second my heart got broken in New Hampshire, the whole place would crumble. In the summers, I dated a few guys. But not at Granby, not even for a dance. Fran would gather a group for Homecoming, a phalanx of the dateless, and I'd join, wearing Chucks with my dress so everyone knew I wasn't serious. Because neither of us dated, we didn't have those months apart when one person eats lunch only with her boyfriend. When Fran and I got bored of each other, we'd just add another friend to the inner circle. Carlotta French, Geoff Richler, a Polish student named Blanka who was glued to our hips for the entirety of her one semester in the US.

For some reason, that night we started listing classmates who'd died since school. We didn't do this with the gravitas it deserved—but remember that we were drunk, and it was part of the general reminiscing.

Zach Huber, a year above us, crashed in a helicopter in Iraq. Puja Sharma, who fled Granby a few weeks before graduation, died of a pill overdose two years later in her Sarah Lawrence dorm. Kellan TenEyck, just that previous spring, had been found in his car at the bottom of a lake. He was divorced and alcoholic and had, generally, a terrible life. He'd seemed so happy at Granby, so unremarkable. He had red hair that would flop in his face when he ran for the lacrosse ball.

We'd counted eight of our classmates dead, and then Fran said, "But three kids dying senior year has to be the record."

"Except maybe in, like, World War II," I said. But no, I was thinking of college. High school students didn't go to war. Maybe I was trying to change the subject. I hadn't told Fran the extent to which Thalia had been on my mind, how talking every week for my podcast about dead and disenfranchised women in early Hollywood, about a system that tossed women out like old movie sets, had helped bring back Thalia's death: the way her body had been cast aside, the way Granby distanced itself from the mess, the way her murder had made her public property.

"Wait," Anne said. She was at the sink, already scrubbing dishes. "*Three* died, out of the whole school, or only your year?"

Only our year, we confirmed. "It's not like there were other dead kids in other grades," Fran added. "Three died, and they were all our class."

"Three out of a class of, what, a hundred twenty? That's absurd."

"Two together," I said, "just a month before graduation. Two guys drove up to Quebec to drink, and they went off the road on the way back. And of course Thalia Keith, a couple months earlier."

"Jesus," Anne said. "I knew about Thalia, but not the others. Hell of a senior year."

"Graduation was weird," I said. And for some reason, Fran and I both found that hilarious, both lost it while Anne stood watching, soapy scrubber in hand.

4

The lights of the Old Chapel tower illuminated long, geometric patches of snow on the quad—the opposite of shadows. They were so beautiful that I avoided stepping on them. The tequila maybe helped my appreciation.

I didn't recall being this enchanted by the snow as a student, but then my primary memory of winter here was of being cold, so cold. When I'd seen the catalogue, I thought all the photos of the ski team and snowshoeing students were for effect. I hadn't understood somewhere could be so much colder than southern Indiana, for so much longer. I didn't understand how the skiers—both the athletes and the kids who'd just grown up taking ski vacations—held social dominion over the school, as if this additional form of locomotion made them a superior species. I hadn't understood how thin my socks were, how inadequate my hand-me-down coats.

I passed Couchman, which I remembered as the grimmest, grungiest dorm, but it must have gotten a recent face-lift. The stones looked shockingly clean in the floodlights, the fire escape new and sleek. Early freshman year, I used to sit on the lip of the old rusty one to get afternoon sun and study in peace. Maybe it was odd to perch on an appendage of a boys' dorm, but it seemed logical at the time. This was where, late that fall, Dorian Culler shouted down from his window, asked if I was there to stalk him. He thought it was so funny that it became the theme of all our interactions, the next three and a half years. In front of his friends he'd say things like "Bodie, I got your letter, but it was weird. Guys, she wrote me this ten-page letter about how she wants my man meat. Her phrase, not mine. Bodie, you need to get it together." Needless to say, I'd never done anything to Dorian other than get involuntarily paired with him a few times in French class. Or he'd say, "Bodie, it was not cool of you to follow my family to London. I'm in my hotel bed and I hear this *moaning* from underneath, and everything smells like tuna fish, and I look under the bed and there's Bodie pleasuring herself."

It was the kind of joke that left no room for response. I could never figure out if he thought he was flirting, or if I was so far below him on the social scale that this was pure mockery. I tried to play along once— said, feebly, "Yes, I *did* crawl in your window; it was to ask you to Spring Dance, and I'll die if you don't say yes"—but he only laughed bigger and said to his friends, "*See?* I should report her! Jesus, Bodie, this is textbook sexual harassment."

I was halfway across South Bridge when I slipped, found myself plunging forward, knew how hard my chin would hit the ice—but then it was my elbows and forearms that hit instead, and I lay facedown for a second, my brain jostled, my bones shaken. I felt, oddly, humiliated, even though no one had seen. Only all the specters of my youth.

It jarred me for another reason, too, a stupid one: I was supposed to have come back to Granby invulnerable. Fifteen-year-old Bodie might have fallen on the ice, might have been breakable or broken, might have drunk herself to sleep one night by the Kurt shrine and woken up half-frozen, terrified she could have killed herself, wondering if this had actually been her intention. But forty-year-old Bodie had her act together, had long been in control of her body and mind. And here was the hard, cold ground, rising up to remind me how easy it was to slip.

I was more careful after that. I had to remind my spoiled LA self to pitch my weight low and slightly forward. I turned on my phone light and watched for black ice.

I opened the guesthouse door to find the guy staying downstairs— a young man in skinny jeans—just arrived after a delayed flight from Newark. He was here to teach two weeks of web design. He offered me a beer and I got a water instead, plus one of the oranges from the thoughtful fruit basket left for us on the counter.

He'd never seen a place like this, he told me. He wanted to know if the kids were all geniuses or what.

"They're *smart*," I said, thankful he hadn't asked if they were all wealthy orphans, "but they're normal teenagers. You'll get some international kids. American kids from places where the schools aren't great. Plenty of kids whose parents went to boarding school, so it's just the thing they do."

The guy, whose name I'd already lost, blinked. He gripped his craft beer in front of his chest.

I used to try, home on break, to explain Granby to my old friends in Broad Run. The worst thing I could do was make it sound fancy, so I unwittingly made it sound more like a correctional facility. A good number of them believed I'd been sent away against my will.

"Think of it as a small liberal arts college, but for younger kids. Or— did your high school have honors classes? Pretend it's an honors class."

"But in the woods," he said, smiling faintly. "An honors class in the woods."

I told him we didn't have mini-mesters in my time; we'd trudge from holiday break straight back to precalculus, verb conjugations, pH levels. These kids got winter forestry, textiles, abnormal psychology, Shakespearean soliloquies, the history of rap.

Skinny Jeans shook his head. "My high school didn't even have a choice for foreign language. It was Spanish for everyone. Even the Puerto Rican kids."

I laughed, said, "Gotta love an easy A."

I might have been honest about how equivocal I felt toward Granby, how rough my time there was—but I was sobering up a little and something protective had kicked in, a familiar need to prove this wasn't an entirely elite place and I was not, myself, an elitist to regard warily. So I said next what I usually say: "It's an amazing school. Coming here on scholarship changed my life." Note my careful wording, the way I worked in that of all the privileges I've had in life, wealth wasn't one. The scholarship was a lie, but only technically.

"I was a fish out of water," I said, "but it got me out of a tiny town in Indiana and into a place with students from all over. People sometimes think boarding school is all white kids named Trip, but it's not." I'd polished that speech to a gloss. I could even deliver it drunk.

"I mean," he said, "they were literally *from* Puerto Rico. What does a Puerto Rican kid get from Spanish 2? That's as far as we went, Level 2. Like, *Yo tengo que comer manzanas.* Level 2."

I lay a long time in bed the next morning—hard mattress, soft pillows—trying to think where I was, what hotel. It clicked when I saw, on the wall opposite, a black-and-white photo of Old Chapel—and a moment later heard the distant bell from that same chapel chime eight. Only two hours before class, and one hour before the journalism teacher overseeing my visit would scoop me up and take me to HR to sign some last things.

I sat up and was flooded with hangover bile. Appropriate: I'd had my first hangovers at Granby. I once left physics to vomit in the hallway trash can, and Miss Vogel walked me to the infirmary, where I feigned food poisoning for a nurse who surely was onto me.

I texted Jerome and asked how the kids were, something I hadn't managed yesterday. They were so used to my traveling that we'd long ago abandoned the *Here safely!* text.

I checked that I hadn't drunkenly texted Yahav last night; I hadn't, and he hadn't written anything else. I wrote: *Get together this week? Wednesday?*

As I let the shower steam the small bathroom and brushed my teeth, my hangover started to clear; and underneath was just nerves. I was nervous not only about teaching but—it took a minute to put my finger on it. It was the feeling I still got when I walked into a suburban shopping mall, despite it being decades since groups of teenagers roved the food courts looking for people to ridicule. I was scared like a dog is scared of the spot where a walnut once fell on his head. Irrationally, viscerally, in a way tied more to memory than possibility.

I put on the newest clothes I'd brought: crisp dark jeans, a red sweater, and a gold bangle an online stylist had picked for me that fall.

The fall of senior year at Granby, I'd been thrilled to inherit a long, crinkly J.Crew skirt from one of Fran's sisters. The J.Crew label inside was as good, in my mind, as Armani. I wore it with Birkenstocks and a white T-shirt and hemp jewelry. I had already lost some weight—I'd lose far too much that year—and my hair was newly longer, and I felt, for the first time, that I was passing as somewhat attractive. I'd even toned down the eyeliner, barely. I was crossing the quad when a sophomore, crossing the other way, said to me, her voice squeaky as if talking to a child, "Oh my God, I remember those skirts! Those are from, like, eighth grade!" The skirt was indeed probably two years old. It was one of the newest things I'd ever worn. Apparently it was safer to wear things from Sears and thrift stores—things the kids at Granby had never seen, couldn't date to some past catalogue, some discount sale.

Petra, the journalism teacher, met me outside the guesthouse and presented me with a Granby tote containing a Granby fleece and a water bottle and a copy of the *Sentinel*. She was strikingly tall with a soft German accent and chicly short hair, a curtain of blond over her left eye. She asked if I'd slept well, if I needed a coffee.

I skimmed the paper as we walked: dorm renovations, sandwich delivery options reviewed, an ongoing lawsuit from a former art teacher.

We stepped off the slushy road and onto the frozen planks of South Bridge and I tucked the paper away, ducked my head against the wind so the freezing air hit my hat and not my face. The last of my hangover evaporated in the cold.

Someone called out behind us and we waited for her to catch up. Good Lord: It was Priscilla Mancio, who was still teaching French. "*Bodie Kane*," she said. "Unbelievable. I *never* would've recognized her," she told Petra, "if they hadn't run her picture in the magazine." She was walking her bulldog, a delicious beast she introduced as Brigitte, and whom I squatted to scratch.

Petra said, "You've changed since eighteen." I find it hard to tell if people with German accents are asking questions.

"Sure," Madame Mancio said, "but—well, most alums, they either look the same, or worse. You know, it's the boys. They go sloppy in the middle. But you look so much prettier, Bodie! Was your hair always that color?"

I said, "Yep, this is my hair." It was still dark—just no longer stringy and self-cut and ruined by cheap shampoo.

"Well, I've listened to your podcast, and I suppose I was picturing your old face." To Petra she said, "She had such a round little face!"

Madame Mancio, meanwhile, looked shockingly unchanged. If she'd been thirty when I was at Granby, she was maybe in her early fifties now, but with the same androgynous haircut, the same tall, bony frame. She still dressed as if she might head off at any moment to hike the mountains.

She said, "We were always so worried about her, especially at the end there. There are those students you just *worry* about. And look at her, turning out so successful, so put-together."

I was glad to be on Brigitte's eye level rather than hers. The dog licked my face, and I marveled at the little pocket her wrinkles made between her eyes. You could stash a spare piece of kibble in there.

We walked toward campus, the two of them discussing the lawsuit in the paper, the details of which I couldn't grasp.

Petra said to me, "Granby is always being sued. So is every other school in the country."

"For what?"

"Oh God," Madame Mancio said, "anything. Mostly it's families *threatening* to sue. Suspensions, grades, negligence, the kid didn't get into the right college, a coach didn't put the kid on varsity. I wish I were kidding. All those lawyers the school pays? They're *busy*."

I said, "I didn't know."

Beneath the bridge, the Tigerwhip was surely frozen solid under its blanket of snow. I could see boot prints heading down the ravine slope and across the flat surface that was, now, only a suggestion of water. (We'd sat on those slopes during junior year bio, Ms. Ramos making us each sketch ten plants. I wore a sweater long enough to hide my backside, and it got ruined in the dirt.) Fifteen miles away, where the creek emptied into the Connecticut River, the ice would be looser, chunkier, yielding to slush and running water.

"Has the campus changed much?" Petra asked me.

Madame Mancio, whom I ought to be thinking of as Priscilla if I were to have any chance of a normal conversation with her, said, "Not as much as Bodie! I remember when I saw your picture on that cover. I thought, my God, she's gone and done something! I don't remember everyone that well, but I had you all four years, didn't I?"

I nodded, although it wasn't true; I'd had Mr. Granson freshman year.

Then she said, with sudden urgency: "Who's watching your kids while you're away?" As if I might have overlooked this detail.

"Their father."

"Oh, good. They must miss you so much!"

Brigitte panted casually, and I got the impression this was a dog who never retracted her tongue.

When Lance and I toured for *Starlet Fever*, people would often ask me where my children were, how they felt about my absence, how my husband felt about it—but they never asked Lance, who had three kids.

We stepped onto Lower Campus, onto the quad path, its snow packed down to gray ice.

Priscilla said, "Now, who are you still in touch with?"

"More faculty than students. Mostly through Facebook."

"Oh, Facebook, pffft." Priscilla dismissed it with the hand that wasn't holding the leash. "I believe in phone calls and letters. I'm out there every reunion weekend. You know who I still exchange Christmas cards with, is Denny Bloch and his wife. Weren't you an orchestra kid?" She said to Petra, "I remember her up there playing the flute. It was flute, wasn't it?"

I said, "You wouldn't want me anywhere near a flute. You're remembering me doing backstage stuff."

"You were in the orchestra, though!"

"No. I just ran lights for them."

She said, "He transformed that music program in such a short time. You know they're still good. It's so hard to get boys to sing, though, isn't it? They have to make girls sing tenor."

But: Now that she'd brought you up, you were the fourth person in our group, a phantom crossing Lower Campus to the teachers' lounge.

As a child, I'd often compulsively imagine someone watching me. I knew it wasn't true, I wasn't paranoid, but I'd pretend, for instance, that my third grade teacher could see everything I did without seeing anything else around me. So as long as I stepped naturally over the junk piles on my floor, she'd never know my room was messy. As long as I brushed my teeth long enough, she wouldn't know I hadn't used toothpaste. The habit still crops up in adulthood, particularly when I can't believe where I am, when I need to process myself from the outside.

And as soon as Priscilla mentioned your name, as soon as she summoned you, the person I imagined watching me was you.

In the lounge, you watched me pour chemical creamer into my coffee, stevia from a little green packet.

I wasn't furious with you yet. That would come later. For now, you were simply an audience.

Don't be flattered.

I didn't understand yet that I was there on your trail, that I wanted answers from you. But the subconscious has a funny way of working things out.

6

After HR, Petra walked me into Quincy Hall, swept me upstairs and down a corridor that still smelled exactly like itself, like the dark, ancient wood of its windowsills. Only—what used to be the darkroom was a 3D printing lab; the water fountain was now a bottle-filling station with a digital counter. In the corner classroom where I once took art history, my five podcasters waited.

They were the most adorable, wide-eyed babies. There was a tall, skinny boy with an old-school high-top fade and a David Bowie shirt. There was a pale kid with purple hair who looked like Lillian Gish. They were all beautiful, in a way we never were. I don't mean this on some profound spiritual level. It took a few minutes, but then I had it: It was their skin and teeth. Not an acne mark among them. No one wore braces, but their teeth were straight, already aligned in middle school. The dermatologists and orthodontists have finally solved it.

We went around the table doing names and pronouns and home-towns and aspirations, but I couldn't stop fixating on their youth. Unlike my UCLA students, these were children. Seniors, all but one (the guy in the Bowie shirt, an ebullient half-Ghanaian, half-Irish junior from Connecticut, wanted to work in public radio), but so dough-faced, so unformed.

You would have loved these kids, Mr. Bloch. They would've been yours for the molding.

The Bowie kid was named Alder ("like the tree," he clarified) and he kept apologizing for his sneezing, getting up to grab Kleenex from the chalkboard ledge. Eventually I handed him the whole box, and he looked mortified. "I want to make something about the 1930s," he said. We were going around a second time, spitballing podcast ideas. "But I want to do it like it *is* the 1930s."

In the email I'd sent the week before, I'd asked them to brainstorm topics related to the past or present of Granby. *This way,* I wrote, *you'll have easy access to interview sources and archives.* It also meant I wouldn't have to deal with video game fancasts or vampires. I included a list of ideas, with links. The fire that destroyed the original gymnasium in 1940. The 1975 murder of a Granby teacher by her drug-addled boyfriend in her apartment in Kern, a story I'd been obsessed with as a student. The hazing situation in the late aughts, and the resulting expulsions. The recent fallout from the school ending its football team. The debate about AP classes. The 1995 death of Thalia Keith.

If you'd asked me at the time why I included Thalia I'd have said I was just trying to get them thinking, trying to lay out as many different points on the Granby timeline as I could. I'd have believed it, too.

Alder said, "My concept is, like, what if they'd had podcasts back then, so, sort of a cross between old radio and podcasts. So I'm a Granby student from the '30s, talking about life. I'm basically the only Black kid at Granby and then there's the Great Depression and, like, Roosevelt—"

A girl named Jamila interrupted. "You'd have to pick a year," she said. "There's a huge difference between 1930 and 1939."

Alder nodded slowly, rolling a tissue to a point in his hand. "1938," he said. "It's 1938, and I'm a podcasting kid sending messages into the void, and I'm inventing podcasts as I go."

"1938 was the year that *War of the Worlds*—" I started, but Alder slapped the table, grinned, pointed at me.

"Yes!" he said. "You *get* it!"

Jamila planned to do a series on financial aid and race at Granby. That sounded like a tough job reportorially, as I couldn't imagine the admissions office being terribly open on the subject, but Jamila seemed determined and well-informed.

I'd hoped they'd at least read my email, but I hadn't dreamed they'd come with notes, with research already done, some with backup proposals, too. By the time we got around the table, I wouldn't have been surprised to learn they had grant money secured. The kid with purple hair, Lola, who used they/them pronouns and had spoken at length about their passion for elephant welfare, wanted to interview restaurant workers in town. Alyssa Birkyt, a quiet skier who'd already committed to Dartmouth, had settled on the complicated legacy of Arsareth Gage Granby.

Only one demurred: Britt, an intense girl with long caramel hair, who would have struck me as a typical golden-child Granby student of my own era (loose cashmere sweater, cute jeans, genetically blessed cheekbones) if it weren't for the ankh tattoo on her inner wrist and the way she talked with no embarrassment about clinical depression when we first went around. Her voice was dry and deep, somewhere between a smoker's and a fifty-year-old lawyer's.

She shrugged when it was her turn. "I'm torn between a few ideas."

After class, she hung back near the door, waiting out Alder's monologue about the links he planned to send me to his favorite music criticism podcasts and his favorite documentary series, and also a podcast where the earliest blogs of the late '90s were read aloud. He blew Britt a kiss as he left, an actor floating out of a party held in his honor.

"I, um," Britt said, looking at the floor and then over my shoulder. "Okay, this is no offense, but, like, I know you do a lot of true crime on your podcast, and I think it's a problematic genre."

She waited, as if I were supposed to repent. I said, "That comes up. But we're following the workings of the studio system, not chasing gore."

"I'm concerned about the tropes of true crime, the way it's turned into entertainment."

"That's sharp of you," I said. "It's definitely a matter of approach. When we fetishize things—"

"Right, no. I listened to your podcast, and I get, even when you did the Patricia Douglas thing, or the Black Dahlia thing, I get that you're doing—it's more about structures and—like I said, no offense. I just, I see so much fetishizing, and I don't want to be another white girl giggling about murder."

I said, "Most violent crime is remarkably boring." I pulled out a chair and sat back down, gestured to Britt to do the same, but she didn't, just stood tugging her backpack straps. I went into my panelist answer. "The vast majority of murders are two young men getting into an altercation; one kills the other. You dig deep on *unsolved* crimes, or quote-unquote interesting crimes, and most of what you find is a man killing his partner. So either you talk structural racism, domestic violence, policing issues, or you end up picking one story that's interesting in specific ways. Usually in ways that break those molds. One concern is that those cases are misrepresentative. And sure, there's a temptation to sensationalize things. Are you—" I expected to find her glazed over, but she wasn't blinking. "Are you interested in pursuing this as a subject?"

Britt said, "Like, also, me as a white person, if I wanted to tell the story of a white person's murder, then I'm ignoring the violence done to Black and brown bodies. But I can't tell a story of violence against people of color, because I'm white and that would be appropriation." She sounded frustrated. I shouldn't have been surprised that she talked like an Oberlin freshman who cared deeply but hadn't fully worked things out—I used to teach undergrads, after all—but it felt so incongruous here at Granby, where we'd all once spoken with such blithe, hurtful carelessness. And hadn't that been just yesterday?

I said, "I really don't think that's appropriation. And honestly, this is for a small audience." I gestured at the bare trees outside the window, hoping Britt would see what I did: that we were in the woods, not—as it certainly felt to a twelfth grader—at the center of the universe.

She said, "In that email, you had two murders. The one from the '70s and the one from the '90s. I was thinking I'd do one of those. But—"

I could feel my pulse in my neck. It was like being a child in an audience as the magician asked for volunteers, utterly terrified he'd pick you but also thrilled he might. Whether I could admit it or not, I wanted this girl to look directly at Thalia's death in a way I myself couldn't (out of closeness, out of trauma, out of the irrational fear that my former class-mates would think me presumptuous—no, that Thalia *herself* would somehow find me presumptuous); and at the same time, and for some of those same reasons, I wanted to stop her. I regretted putting Thalia on the list. I thought I could maybe steer Britt toward Barbara Crocker and 1975, the boyfriend they found hiding in the woods right near campus, his remarkably light sentence.

But Britt said, "I know you were friends."

"I'm sorry?"

"You and Thalia Keith. Okay, so I take journalism, and we have access to the *Sentinel* archives. I got into the story last year, and I read everything from the paper, and I did the deep dive online, all the Reddit boards."

"You found my name on Reddit?"

"No. I mean—you were quoted in the *Sentinel*, and I googled every-one quoted there, to see what had happened to them, and you were easy to find. And then they announced you were coming here, and I was like—*whoa*." Britt began chewing the cap of her green pen.

I said, "We were assigned as roommates for most of junior year, but we weren't friends."

Britt said, "If you're okay with it—of the two cases, I'd want to do Thalia Keith. It would be easier. I mean, there's teachers I could inter-view. And maybe you? But, like, I still wonder how problematic that is."

I said, "The fact that you're asking is a sign you'd do this thought-fully and responsibly." I was just self-aware enough at this point to clock that I was talking Britt into it, and to wonder why.

She nodded, chewed the pen cap.

I said, "It's up to you. But remember to consider scope, what you can do in two or three episodes."

Britt extricated the pen cap and said, "I think the wrong guy is in prison."

"Interesting." I nodded, noncommittal. I should have guessed this was where she was headed. I said, "I'm looking forward to this."

7

Petra had said I could find her at lunch, but I discovered I was neither hungry nor ready to face the dining hall, where I might run into my own awkward ghost—so I opted for another coffee and a few minutes to spend on my own podcast research. In the library, the light sliding yellow through those tall, warped windows to illuminate the circulating dust, I sat doing homework once again. This was the place where I'd looked up vocab words at ten p.m., the place I'd smuggled magazines out from, under my shirt. There were fewer books now and more tables, more kids with laptops and headphones. But a boy near me held a covert bag of chips in his lap; that hadn't changed.

During World War II, Rita Hayworth was the most popular pinup for GIs. (There's a reason that's her poster on the wall in *The Shawshank Redemption*.) She'd been forced into show business (by her vaudevillian mother, her dancer father), and she was introverted, reluctant, dogged by her public persona. She was born Margarita Carmen Cansino, with dark hair. They turned her into a redhead. They did electrolysis to raise a hairline they considered too ethnic. They posed her in her underwear. She gave good face.

Lance wanted to center each episode on a man in her life—her father, then each of her five husbands. In one sense, it was fitting, since her life was defined by men. Almost always terrible men, ones who took her money or asked her to leave Hollywood or used her children as pawns. Her fourth husband hit her in the face at the Cocoanut Grove. But it seemed unfair to organize her life around the people who controlled it. I said I'd consider it.

Research has always been my happy place. It might be related to my sometime collecting of facts about my peers, an attempt to feel safer by mapping the world. If I can chart everything around me as far as I can see, then I must be in the middle of it all, real and in one piece. *You are here.*

Rita was a pinball, bounced from one spot to the next. I related; what had my childhood been but a constant ricochet from one place and one disaster to the next? But to be fair, that's many childhoods. I have to resist the urge to self-mythologize, to paint my own journey as harder than everyone else's just so I can give myself credit for getting out. I'm allowed to take that credit regardless. So declareth my shrink.

There were kids who came to Granby from housing projects, kids who came as a custody compromise. I wasn't the only one with a less-than-romantic origin story.

Jerome texted, asking if I'd gotten the email from Leo's class mom about tomorrow being the hundredth day of second grade. It seemed impossible, but the year had flown by. The kids were to bring one hundred of something, and to dress like old people. Lest any twenty-first-century mother find a moment not devoted to proving maternal devotion through crafts.

Jerome wrote: *Leo on his own or you want me going over the top?*

I was torn. Teach Leo independence and thereby give the middle finger to a school that demanded this, in addition to Heritage Week and Crazy Hair Day and Historical Figure Day and Cupcake Day and Funky Socks Day—or let Leo's artist father spectacularly outdo the Pinterest moms. We tended to vacillate between the two responses, our kids sometimes walking masterpieces, sometimes DIY messes.

I wrote back: *Your call.*

Although Jerome was fully prepared to glue one hundred gummy bears into the shape of the *Mona Lisa*, he still wanted me directing the show from New Hampshire. From hotel rooms on podcast tours, I was happy to run things. But even one day into Granby, it felt absurd.

I stood to walk around the library at my Fitbit's insistence, and as I circled I remembered, Mr. Bloch, how you used to nap in the big leather chair by the periodicals, how some of us thought it was funny to leave a magazine in your lap as if you'd fallen asleep reading it. *House & Garden* or *YM* or *Glamour.*

I reached up to check the window above the reference books, just in case its sill had gone undusted and undisturbed for a few decades.

My brother, Ace, died two and a half years before I started Granby. On campus, I'd mark certain spots on certain days (his birthday, the anniversary of his death, the day I wanted him to know the Pacers won the division title) by peeling off a swath of tree bark or stepping a stone hard into dirt—leaving some mark that would be there later. I'd check it weeks or months on. Sometimes I'd carve his initials, but more often I'd just slightly alter the world.

My son, Leo, might call these marks Horcruxes, and he wouldn't be far off. I was planting a ring of protection around myself. There wasn't much I wanted to think about from home, but if Ace could be all around me, I wouldn't *have* to think of him, wouldn't feel guilty when I didn't.

Anyway: One time, I took the broken arch of a plastic coat hanger hook—a perfect half circle—and hid it on that library windowsill.

It was impossible that the coat hanger piece would still be there, but some credulous fragment of my brain still expected it, was still disappointed to find nothing at all.

8

There was so much I never told you about myself, even as you asked, sincerely; even as the entire school played endless get-to-know-you games every August.

I believed people would like me most for being average, an amalgam—so I sanded my history down to the generic. I told them my mother was a dentist (she was really a dental *receptionist*) and my late father had been a businessman (he'd owned a failing bar). That I had an older brother. That I grew up in southern Indiana.

The short version of the truth, the version I give every new therapist in the first five minutes, then wait to see which bait she takes:

When I was eight, my brother, who was fifteen, accidentally killed my father by pushing him off a porch with a spatula.

I always end on the word "spatula," just to dare people to laugh. It's not so much a test of the person I'm talking to as a way to take control of the conversation before they pin me down to the pity mat.

Later that year, my mother, midbreakdown, let Mormon missionaries into our house, and they kept returning, bringing cookies and crafts. They helped me make a bottle of layered colored sand. Within a few months we became Mormon, or my mother did, and Ace and I tagged along, eager to keep her whole. I still remember some of the Mormon stories I paid half attention to in youth Bible study (Lehi's dream of a happy fruit tree, some other guy's two thousand invincible soldiers) and often can't remember if something is from the Book of Mormon or the Bible I'd previously grown up with.

Not quite four years later, the April I was eleven and he was eighteen, my brother, high on more than one thing, either jumped off the roof of a shoe store or fell off, but in any case he lasted three days in a coma and then he left us. Then my mother fully lost it.

She—for example—would set the microwave to five minutes with nothing in it and sit in front of the door, watching the glass plate spin and spin. She didn't notice when I cut my hair to ear length in the bathroom, didn't notice when I stopped doing laundry, or began wearing Ace's old clothes. She didn't notice if I stayed home to watch *Days of Our Lives*, didn't notice when the groceries expired, didn't notice when I took cash from her purse to buy Wendy's. She stopped showing up for work and from what I understood, we were living off my father's life insurance.

In retrospect, I wonder how much the Mormons were helping. We were an easy sell, a sob story. A wealthier Mormon couple, the Robesons, had taken special interest in us, picking us up every Sunday for church, having us over for Monday-night dinners. They told me I should call them aunt and uncle, so I avoided saying their names at all. The Robesons had grown children, a house full of artificial flowers and little bowls of potpourri, soft pastel carpets in every room.

My mother needed to be hospitalized. It was obvious, and it was obvious I was the reason she wasn't going. Not that her being home was healthy for me, either; by the beginning of eighth grade, my schoolwork had slipped along with my friendships and hygiene. I don't know if I was clinically depressed, but the best way to survive my mother's depression was to go numb, to match her silence and her disregard for cleanliness, for answering the phone, for making meals.

Severn Robeson had grown up outside Boston and attended Granby in the '50s, sent his son and daughter there, too, and sponsored the occasional scholarship. The Robesons had a proposal: I would come live with them for the rest of eighth grade, pulling my grades up, while my mom got treatment. Then, as long as I could get into Granby—and they were certain I could, wink wink—they'd pay for tuition and room and board and books. I'd stay with them on breaks, until my mom was stable and home. Severn sang me "You Can't Beat the Granby Dragons" to the tune of "You Can't Ride in My Little Red Wagon." He told me about the teacher who made him memorize ten Shakespeare soliloquies.

My idea of boarding school was mostly bits of *The Facts of Life* plus a dim impression of something gothic and fancy. The brochure, though, showed kids laughing over plates of fries. It showed tan, muscled teenagers playing tug-of-war, as if that were a regular pastime rather than (as I would learn) a forced orientation activity. Granby looked a lot better than Indiana. It looked like a school where people wouldn't stick gum on your locker, where they wouldn't find it hilarious to ask if your brother killed himself because you were fat.

When I left for school in the fall of '91, my mother was in a residential program. She and two roommates had their own little house with a tiny kitchen. By Thanksgiving, she'd left for the Arizona desert with a man she'd met in group therapy. They made wind chimes and handbound books together. She flew back to Indiana and we had Thanksgiving with the Robesons and their kids and grandkids, and she talked the whole time about the Arizona sun, how the gloom up here was half her problem.

I stayed with her near Sedona that June, but I hated her faux-hippie boyfriend and the Airstream we were crammed in. She and I fought viciously, and I returned to Indiana a month early. By the time you got to know me, sophomore year, I fully lived at the Robesons', spent vacations hiding in my room or perched with a book on their velveteen sofa hoping no one would make small talk. I'd go to church with them because I felt obliged. They pressured me only gently to get baptized, and didn't disown me when I declined. They'd ask about my mother as if I were in touch with her beyond the occasional postcard. *You're so much better off with me out of the way,* she wrote on one of them.

To other students, I called the Robesons my aunt and uncle; for more official purposes I called them foster parents. But neither term covered the guest room aspect of the whole thing, the way Margaret Robeson would slip in to make my bed when I was in the shower, the relief we all

I HAVE SOME QUESTIONS FOR YOU

felt when their son, Ammon, came home with his twins and I had a role to play, corralling them in front of Disney movies for five dollars an hour.

Fran knew all this; I told her in pieces as our friendship jelled over the course of freshman year. First I told her my father and brother were both dead, one death causing the drug problem that caused the other, tragedy breeding tragedy. Fran's older sister Liza, who'd just spent a year in Japan, had taught us to make matcha with a bamboo whisk, and we'd sit in the Hoffnungs' kitchen (stacks of ungraded tests, the fish tank right on the table surrounded by ancient *New Yorkers*, a half-finished cake always on the counter) getting caffeinated until my check-in. This was winter, when I didn't have to rise at four a.m. for crew. I told Fran the details of my father's death, playing with the whisk as I answered her follow-up questions. I'd never answered anyone's questions before, not even the gentle Mormon therapist the Robesons had found me.

I told her he'd been drunk that night, not a typical state of affairs. The bar he owned was generic, neon-signs-in-the-windows, and my brother worked for him that summer, serving fried onions and fried cheese in red plastic baskets. My brother asked for an advance on his pay, and my father refused—although he'd granted the same to other employees. They argued out on the back deck after closing as Ace cleaned the grill. My father, not falling-down drunk but drunk, said things that triggered a fifteen-year-old with temper problems, and my brother yelled and my father yelled and my father pushed my brother and my brother jabbed him with the grill brush he was holding—not a spatula, forgive my poetic license—and my father fell back over the low railing and down eight feet to the rocky slope below, his head landing hard. An inch to the side and he'd have been fine, but as things were, he was knocked unconscious— and Ace was not yet panicked enough, when he phoned 911 from behind the bar, to merit the paramedics hurrying. By the time they arrived, my father had hemorrhaged beyond saving. He died in the ambulance.

Fran didn't share any of her own confidences in exchange for mine, but listened attentively and formed opinions about things like my mother's boyfriend's horrible ponytail and the Robesons' family game night and whether I could avoid church that summer and whether my mother would melt down further in Arizona (I thought so) or heal (Fran's optimistic take). Fran didn't come out until freshman year at Reed, so she wasn't about to tell me about her burning crush on Halle Berry, or the turmoil she endured at a school where even her second ear piercing was nonconformist.

By 2018, my mother and I were on decent terms, although since she'd missed most of my adolescence and only reentered my life in my twenties (the Robesons supplementing my aid package for IU, too, only slightly disappointed I didn't follow their kids to Brigham Young), we had a stiff, cordial, adult relationship. She was still in Arizona, divorced from the hippie, keeping books at a resort-cum-ashram. She loved her grandkids, which was something. Severn Robeson had died in 2009, and Margaret Robeson was someone I sent an extra Mother's Day card. When there were wildfires anywhere in California, Margaret emailed asking if I was all right in LA.

I quite like most Mormons as people, even if I settled into solid agnosticism at Granby, even as I take great issue with the church's history of bigotry. I at least owe them my fondness. But I was always a guest in the Robesons' home, and the more I changed at Granby—such a different Granby than the coat-and-tie all-boys school Severn attended in the '50s—the clearer it became that their support of me was rooted in their values, rather than attachment.

I don't believe the adults at Granby knew any of this, except the Hoffnungs, and perhaps Mrs. Ross, since as my advisor she communicated with the Robesons.

I got so good at answering those generic orientation questions. *Favorite vacation?* Arizona! I love the sunlight! *How many siblings?* One. My dad's golf friends joked that since my brother was Ace, I should be Birdie. So they named me Elizabeth and tried to call me Birdie. And what did my brother do, with his lisp? Called me Bodie. Closer to bogey, yes, ha ha ha! *How did your parents meet?* Blind date! *Name one food you miss from home!* Brownies, I always said, because the Mormons make excellent brownies.

9

I autopiloted my afternoon film class, launching into my standard first-day Intro to Film Studies lecture, movie clips cued up. I had twelve kids, three of whom named *The Godfather* as their favorite film. I told them we'd start at the beginning. We'd talk orientation and disorientation.

I couldn't help checking my phone as the first clips played; Yahav still hadn't written back.

On-screen, the Lumière brothers' train pulled into its 1895 station. A space capsule hit the moon right in the eye.

A firefighter carried a woman from a burning building.

There was one kid in that class, a jetlagged white girl from South Africa, who was brand new to Granby. She'd arrived on the continent only the day before, and I felt guilty keeping the lights off. The girl was not cute enough to warrant a swarm of attention, but not awkward enough that other kids kept their distance. When we took a break halfway through the period, a boy kept giving her words to repeat ("Say *milk!*") then trying to match her accent. She found it funny, or pretended to.

How strange that this girl, a sophomore, had known the people around her for all of an hour, and yet soon they'd wind up deep in her psyche. They'd pop into her dreams thirty years from now, unbidden.

On-screen, a silhouette with a knife, Janet Leigh's face in close-up, her fingers on the tiles, the shower curtain rings in close-up, the drain. "Let's talk about what he doesn't show," I said.

There had always been kids who arrived at Granby a semester in, a year in. Some left again right away, a rejected organ transplant. Others stayed and you couldn't remember a time before them.

Thalia was one of those, arriving two years late and in a fog of rumors.

A junior transfer, so there had to be a *story*. Sophomore transfers made sense—their middle school had run through ninth grade, or they'd found another school wanting, or failed to make friends, or plain failed. Senior transfers were all like Parkman Walcott, whom I doubt you knew—nineteen at the youngest, graduates of other high schools, public or private, brought in as fifth-year football or hockey ringers with hopes of a better shot at a better college. An acne-riddled defensive lineman with a Kentucky accent that grew more pronounced the longer he spent in New Hampshire, Parkman Walcott was called, with unsubtle irony, Peewee, and I have a particularly unpleasant memory of him I'll save for later. Those were the senior transfers: four or five Peewees a year. There were no junior transfers, unless you counted the Nordic or Brazilian exchange students who'd come for nine months to date everyone hot and break our swim records and shake their heads at our college process, then leave.

Then, out of nowhere, came Thalia Keith. (Theme music! Follow spot! All heads turn.) Black curls down her back, clear olive skin, eyes people reverently described as *aqua*. Flat-chested, which helped explain why rather than killing her on sight, a high-status group of junior girls instantly adopted her. Chief among them were Rachel Popa and Beth Docherty, who looked like negative images of each other. (The Pantone Twins, Fran called them. "I wonder if they come in blue," she said. "Maybe I'll order one in lavender.") Rachel was glowingly tan with long straight dark hair, Beth glowingly fair with long straight blond hair—both of them petite and pretty and athletic and rich enough to spend their days sparking social drama rather than dodging it. They scooped Thalia right up. So did Sakina John, who, along with Beth, was one of Granby's musical theater stars. She embraced Thalia once October Follies rehearsals began and Sakina realized Thalia was good, but not better than her. Puja Sharma met Thalia on the tennis team and glommed on hard. Puja was from London and a bit socially desperate but adept at buying friends with vacations and gifts. Thalia was not the queen bee of the class (that would be Beth), but she was central, beloved.

And she was new meat for the boys, could have been half as pretty and still held their interest with her newness alone. I know now that for straight boys at that age, it's less about the girl than the competition. Just as soccer isn't about your love of the ball. And once she was declared the object of collective interest, she became the ball.

A Thalia-specific bingo card started making the rounds of the boys' dorm bathrooms—a sheet on which they could initial squares that said things like *touched outside clothes*, or *under clothes above waste* (this spelling error gleefully reported to me by Geoff Richler), or *asked out*, or *fucked*. The only initials he believed, Geoff said, were the five guys who claimed to have already asked her (in September!) to Homecoming. But I saw what was happening: boys running up to Thalia and poking her arm so they could sign the *outside clothes* square. Thalia laughed so confidently that she managed to own the joke, laughed so beautifully and so well that it was clear to anyone watching that these boys were her *friends*, whether or not they'd ever spoken to her. She laughed like someone who'd known them for years. An "Oh, Marco, that's how you've always been" laugh, when—did she even know that was Marco Washington running up to stroke her hair?

You might not remember Marco. He wasn't exactly signing up for your opera seminar. Do you remember Peewee Walcott and Dorian Culler and Mike Stiles? Don't worry about it. They were the foundational souls of my adolescence, but to you they were faces passing through. You've had a new crop every year since. Thalia meant enough to you that I'm sure you remember the kids right around her—Robbie Serenho, Rachel, Beth—the ones who orbited her like moons.

On-screen, a house fell around Buster Keaton, and he stood there unharmed—bewildered, blessed.

The rumors, in case you never heard them: That she'd been engaged to a boy back home and her parents sent her here to separate them. That she'd had an abortion and everyone at her old school found out. That she was anorexic, and her parents traveled too much to supervise her, so they sent her here where she was subjected to daily weigh-ins with the nurse. That she'd had a nose job, wanted to start over where no one knew her old face.

It isn't hard to guess how the rumors started—girls angry that their boyfriends and crushes trailed Thalia that first week, drooling after her curls in the August heat. She played tennis, and suddenly tennis practice had spectators.

We weren't roommates at first. My ninth and tenth grade roommate, a quiet girl named Diamond, dropped out just before the start of the year. My new assigned roommate, Ji-Hyun, spent preseason curled in bed with menstrual cramps that turned out to be appendicitis. She went from infirmary to hospital, and a week after her surgery I returned from class to find her things packed; she was flying home to Seoul. Thalia and her first roommate, a dour Ukrainian girl, never got along. One day in late September, after wondering for days what had happened to her purple bra, Thalia saw a purple strap peeking out at Khristina's shoulder. Word got around in hours, and we all assumed Khristina would be expelled (a *bra thief*!), but the student discipline council forgave her. After all, maybe they didn't have great underwear in Odesa. Thalia requested a room change, though, and after three weeks solo, I had a roommate.

I was under no illusion that Thalia and I would become friends—she had already ascended into the social stratosphere—but I was secretly thrilled to see the other side of the room occupied again, despite my brief and unprecedented luck at having scored a single as a junior. The half-empty room had felt aseptic and haunted.

Thalia brought actual decorations—a string of tiny white lights, an aloe plant, a fuzzy green bean bag chair—and she was friendly enough, joking with me as she dumped onto her bed the clothes and books she carried down the hall one armload at a time. When she found out I was from Indiana, she asked what it was like and I told her it was like hell, but boring. "Don't worry," I said, "we have our own bras at least." She laughed at that.

Before long her friends, her real friends, came to help her move in. Beth Docherty and Rachel Popa stood on her bed to reach the long, high shelf above it, a shelf I used for the books we wouldn't read till next semester. But Thalia had *sweaters*. Piles of sweaters, Fair Isle and merino and cashmere. They lined her shelf like flavors in an ice cream shop. I estimated five sweaters to a pile, six piles. She'd brought *thirty* sweaters to school. I felt a pang of empathy for Khristina, who must have assumed one purple bra couldn't be missed.

Thalia sprang around decorating, in shorts and a tank top, hair in a ponytail she'd never have worn to class. They put on Janet Jackson, and soon I was forgotten. Puja Sharma showed up with muffins she'd bought in town, and which the four of them ate in little pinches, squealing about the calories. I lay on my own bed, a notebook on my knees, and soon decided it would be better to put my earphones on than risk looking like I hoped to be included. I wasn't lurking awkwardly, I was *studying*.

I was always good for a defensive move.

But I'm making this about me, and I was talking about Thalia. And here's what I wanted to say: One of the rumors that fall was that she'd left her last school after she was caught sleeping with her math teacher. That he, in fact, was the one she was engaged to. That *all* the rumors were true: He'd gotten her pregnant, paid for her abortion, left his wife for her, helped her through her eating disorder. I'd bought into some stories but dismissed this all-in-one rumor off the bat, coming as it did from Donna Goldbeck, our class gossip and a highly unreliable source.

In the darkened classroom, the memory started to roil, to trouble me. We were so quick to spread lurid gossip, but so void of concern. Perhaps because we believed we were adults. If she'd slept with a teacher, that was on her. We were scandalized or even impressed, but not worried.

On the screen: A narrow cloud crossed the moon; a man slit a woman's eyeball. The students covered their faces.

10

Alder found me outside Commons on my way to dinner and asked what I thought of his project, if he should stick with the 1930s or do this thing about comparing the dorm rooms of Virgos and Libras. Or he had a third proposal, about how far Black students had to travel for a haircut, waiting for monthly Dragon Wagon runs to Manchester. (In my day, that wasn't even an option; kids set up in dorm rooms with clippers or in common rooms with bottles of relaxer whose smell made me ask, one humiliating and probably hurtful time, who was using Nair.) Alder struck me as a hugely creative kid who'd gotten the unfortunate message early on that there was always a right answer.

"It's about committing to something," I said. Here was Fran, waving at me from inside the doors, where she said we'd meet. "And making the best version of that thing." Alder nodded. He had a habit of looking up and past you, moving his eyes back and forth as if he were solving equations above your head. "Just—it's about confidence. If it helps, imagine I'm grading you not on the podcast but on your confidence."

I gestured vaguely at his chest, which was weird of me, as the Bowie shirt was now covered with a gray parka.

Alder said, "Confidence," and he laughed, blew out a flat whistle. "I mean. I'm not great at that."

To me he seemed spectacularly confident, in that he talked all the time and the other kids seemed to love him, but I suppose no eleventh grader has ever felt confident on their wobbly fawn legs. Had any of my classmates? Dorian Culler, maybe, who made his own warped reality, announcing that I was stalking him or that Thalia was his secret fiancée or that poor Blake Oxford had asked to be his prison bitch. Maybe Mike Stiles, our King Arthur, who wore his charisma like a custom-tailored suit.

Alder must have taken my staring into space for the end of the conversation. He thanked me too many times and pawed his way through the door.

Fran swept me past the mailboxes and into the dining hall, just as she'd done a thousand times—and the bandage was off, I was under that unchanged vaulted ceiling in a room that still smelled like bacon and coffee and disinfectant. She shepherded me through the salad bar line and to a table where Anne, the boys, and a bunch of young faculty sat under the Asian batch of international flags. But goddamn it, the whole time she introduced me around, I seethed, thinking for the second time in two days of all the things Dorian Culler had gotten away with. And I seethed at the realization that I had accepted this as normal, that I could only now calculate the full, ugly weight of it.

No more trays in the Granby dining hall, an environmental measure that also made the place classier. It probably meant fewer opportunities for kids to drop their entire meal with a spectacular crash.

What if, a year from now, Dorian Culler ran for office? Would I feel obliged to come forward? Would I need, for my own conscience, to say something, even if no one listened?

I was delighted when Mr. Levin joined us. He still taught geometry (still nerdy and gentle and kind), and his son Tyler, in Pull-Ups when I graduated, was doing a postdoc in entomology at Cornell.

I managed to talk to Mr. Levin, but listen: Dorian used to do it in *class*, for Christ's sake. I came into world history one day, soon after he started the whole gag, to find that he'd written *I'm so wet for you, Dorian—BK* on the board. "Bodie!" he said. "Bodie, why would you do that? You know you could just slip a note in my backpack. I feel violated, Bodie." When Mr. Dar arrived, Dorian said, "Mr. Dar, Bodie's sexually harassing me. Look what she wrote." His voice made it clear he was joking, so Mr. Dar chuckled, and the note stayed on the board most of class until he needed room for his notes on Suleiman the Magnificent. He turned to me, eraser in hand, and said, "Mind if we scrub your love letter, Miss Kane?" I can't remember what I did—grimace and give a thumbs-up?—but I remember the writing remained visible, ghost words behind the history notes.

Mr. Levin confirmed that Granby's admissions standards had risen. "The top kids were always bright," he said. "Like you. But the bottom—there were kids who foundered." It was kind of him to forget I'd nearly failed geometry, spent class typing notes into my TI-81 and passing it to Geoff Richler as if he needed to borrow my calculator, whereupon he'd delete my message, enter his own, hand it back.

If you don't remember, Geoff was the kid who'd get up at colloquium and juggle oranges as he made announcements about yearbook, ignoring the catcalls. On the short side, with freckles and, by junior year, thick chin stubble he called "a gift from my Semitic and prehistoric forefathers." His dad was significantly older than his mom (Geoff had stepsiblings old enough to be his parents), and after they'd dropped Geoff off freshman year, they left New York for a retirement community in Boca Raton. Geoff seemed vaguely humiliated by the situation, even as he played up his stories of four p.m. social hours, bland barbecues with ancient neighbors. He'd caddy in the summer and write masterpiece letters to his Granby friends, cartoons in the margins.

Since Geoff was on my mind, I asked if Mr. Levin remembered him. I brought him up partly as an antidote to Dorian Culler, a reminder to myself that not every boy at Granby had been a jerk. "We struggled through geometry together," I said, when really Geoff swung an A despite our note-passing, and grew up to be a noted economist.

Geoff essentially lived in the Granby darkroom. The nearest Rite Aid was in Kern, so Geoff processed film not only for the yearbook and the *Sentinel* but had a side hustle for kids who wanted personal shots developed. Even photography students had to sign up on the darkroom schedule, but Geoff finagled a key and unlimited use in exchange for maintenance. I'd find him there during free periods or after dinner. I'd perch on the table and we'd talk, red light illuminating our faces like campfire.

Mr. Levin said, "I remember every student. You'd think my brain would be full after thirty years, but no."

"I don't even remember *last* year's students," Fran said.

"Quiz him!" called one of the young teachers from the end of the table. "We should go get, like, the 1970 yearbook!"

Mr. Levin cleared his throat and asked exactly how old they thought he was. A ruckus, then, of laughter and teasing. Mr. Levin was born in 1962.

One woman at the table coached crew, and was thrilled to learn I'd rowed. "I wish you were here in warm weather!" she said. "We'd get you out with us!"

It was in that same dining hall that Karen King and Laura Tamman had stopped me with a survey, the first week of school. They asked how much I'd grown in the past year. "Not much," I said, bewildered, and they seemed unduly pleased. They asked if I considered myself a leader or follower, if I was a morning person. Then Laura said, "You'd be *perfect* for crew." I hadn't arrived early for preseason—had signed up for PE instead, not understanding that PE was for hard-core smokers and kids with heart issues, that preseason was when everyone bonded and forged friend groups. I told them I'd never been in a boat and my arms weren't strong. I didn't add that crew seemed like something for girls named Ashley. I didn't add that I was overweight (only a bit, but enormously so in my mind) and worried I'd tip the boat.

"*No one* has experience," Karen said. "That's the beauty." She said I'd have a year to row novice, with and against girls who'd never rowed before. She explained it was about your core and legs. She got me out of PE that afternoon to try the erg, which turned out to be a rowing machine like the one in the Robesons' basement. The crew girls were hilarious and tough, kids who made fun of the sports where you hopped around in a tiny skirt. Within the week, I found myself rising at dawn to ride the

Dragon Wagon to the boathouse down at the wider, deeper part of the Tigerwhip, found myself holding my breath as I climbed into the boat with eight other girls, wondering how easily this thing could capsize, found myself rowing three seat and then, as they discovered I had rhythm, four seat.

Part of what I loved was the escape from campus. A boat was a place where no one could reach you, a place where some boy couldn't slide into your path to make you a prop in his joke. Even when the boys rowed past us, all we'd do was holler or chant; we didn't have to drop everything to watch them, which was the usual expectation. (Do you remember, for instance, the fake Woodstock that Marco Washington and Mike Stiles set up on the quad? They hauled couches from the dorms, used extension cords for guitars and stand mics. I joined the audience to listen to their terrible playing because it was the thing to do. Just as Open Dorm nights were for girls to feign interest in boys playing video games. Just as the only sporting events with full stands were for boys' teams. At the time, what rankled was the idea that we were supposed to see these boys as the stars, to fall at their sweaty feet. What bothers me now is those boys internalizing *girls as audience*, there only to act as mirrors, to make their accomplishments realer.) But out on the boat, we were neither watchers nor watched; there was only the sound of water and of our cox's voice calling for a power ten, only the muscle burn, only cold air on wet skin.

By spring I was signing up again, this time for sprint season, and then I was in it for life. Or at least till senior year, when I flaked out in every way—when I quietly dropped to 115 pounds, when I stopped going to calculus, when I smoked ten cigarettes a day and started mixing Tylenol and vodka. I got in the boat that first week of sprint season and couldn't do it, quite literally couldn't pull my weight. I dropped off the team, blamed it on senioritis. But in college I sometimes subbed in for practice, and in New York and LA I joined rowing clubs. When I think of Granby, I see the Tigerwhip and the Connecticut before I see campus itself. I see Robin Facer's back, her braid swishing as she rows. I see us celebrating at Stotesbury for not embarrassing ourselves, pelting each other with M&M's in the hotel hallway.

This current-day coach pointed out all the crew girls she could see in the dining hall. "There's one," she said, indicating a tall girl by the sandwich station. "There are three, those three together."

I said, "I love them at first sight."

I did. They seemed utterly themselves, laughing loudly, filling tall glasses with chocolate milk. The Dorian Cullers of 2018 would be out of their minds to mess with them.

As we stood with our dishes, Mr. Levin said, "You know, I always knew you were going to be okay." I felt like crying—out of bitterness? out of tenderness?—because if that was true, he was the only one who'd ever thought so. I certainly hadn't thought it myself. He said, "You were always going to be just fine."

11

That night, I told Fran about Britt's podcast.

"I don't want people thinking it was my idea," I said. Anne had taken the boys home for their bath; Fran walked me back to check out the new guesthouse, stayed for wine.

"Nah." She was opening and closing each cabinet, each drawer. "No one would even, like, put it together that you knew Thalia." She was talking about what the faculty would think, when I meant everyone: our classmates, Thalia's family, the world. "If you'd been best friends with Thalia, maybe they'd remember. If you were Robbie Serenho or someone. But like I was saying at dinner—what kids were here together, it's a blur."

My housemate came out into the kitchen and introduced himself to Fran. Oliver Coleman. I was grateful for the reminder, repeated his name in my head. Oliver-Oliver-Oliver. I asked how his first day went.

"They're smart," he said. "You were right. And *respectful*. I kind of thought—I don't know. I thought they'd be more entitled."

"They're plenty entitled," Fran said, sitting down at the island with her wine. "Most of them. They just hide it."

"I thought there would be more sweater vests involved." He said it deadpan, but then he grinned—dimples and eye crinkles.

Oliver clearly wanted to hang out. He got a box of crackers from the cupboard and poured them into a bowl, asked Fran what it was like living here, if kids came knocking at all hours with their problems. He was cute, and if I'd been closer to his age, I'd have eyed Oliver as more than an interloper.

"I'm only on duty one night a week," she said. "They knock at my door any other time, I spray them with a hose."

I got the feeling these were the small-talk questions Fran fielded constantly, so I changed the subject.

"One of my students," I said, "wants to do a podcast about a girl who died when Fran and I were seniors. I think she sees 1995 as ancient history. Like, old-time spooky."

Fran asked Oliver how old he'd been in 1995.

"Um—" He thought a second. "Six."

Fran said, "Good *God*."

"I was doing the math," I said, "and we're as far from 1995 now as 1995 was from 1972."

Fran shook her head. "That's just rude."

"You know what's weird," I said, "is the memories don't dim. I have *fewer* memories. But the strong ones don't go anywhere."

Oliver said, "Wait, was this the swimming pool thing? The one—when I googled Granby after they invited me, I saw there was a whole *Dateline*."

I said, "That's the one."

"Should I watch it?"

"It's cheesy," Fran said. "Every time they cut to commercial they have her picture floating underwater."

I'd only seen it twice: in 2005, when it first aired, and then again during my rabbit-holing episode. What had seemed clichéd in 2005 was downright cringeworthy more than a decade later.

Let's pause and acknowledge that in my twenty-four hours at Granby, I'd had three separate conversations about Thalia Keith. Last night and just now, I'd brought it up myself. And while Britt had found the story on her own, that didn't change the fact that I'd put it right in that emailed list. If Thalia was following me around, it was in the way bees follow someone who happens to have slathered their hands in honey.

I managed to wonder why I was doing this.

Maybe because that mouthed *What?* kept replaying in my head, a question with no answer. When Jerome got stuck on a painting, I'd ask what exactly he was stuck on and he'd roll his eyes. "If I knew," he'd say, "I wouldn't be stuck. If I knew, I wouldn't have started this painting to begin with, because there'd be no sticking point."

Thalia's question seemed not just for the person offstage, but for me: *What? What's your problem? Why are you back here? What's bothering you so much? Why now? What? What? What?*

My phone buzzed with a text, not from Yahav but Jerome: *You haven't been on Twitter, have you?*

If he was asking, it was likely because some news story I wouldn't handle well was making the rounds. He was good at hiding specific issues of *The New Yorker* from me, telling me not to click certain links, getting me to stay offline for a day or two. My insomnia still affected him, even if we lived on opposite sides of a wall now. If it were good news—the resignation of a loathsome politician—he'd have led with that.

I texted back a question mark.

"Is it unsolved?" Oliver was asking.

"No," Fran said, "they caught the guy right away. Omar Evans, this athletic trainer. He worked in the weight room, and he was the guy who'd tape your ankle if you twisted it. He'd been kind of stalking her. Or they'd been dating. Or both."

"She was *not* dating him," I said.

"True," she said. "She was too busy. She was hanging around Mr. Bloch all the time."

"Right, but that wasn't—"

"Mr. Bloch was a *creeper.*"

I didn't remember Fran talking about you that way, back then. She sang for you in Choristers and musicals and Follies. She won the arts department award for overall involvement, hugged you onstage when you handed it off.

I said, "Wait, hold on, that's not true."

Fran rolled her eyes and said to Oliver, "Bodie is fiercely loyal. Like a cute pit bull. It's her best and worst quality. And Mr. Bloch was her favorite. But Bode, he was a creeper."

Maybe it hit me harder because you'd been on my mind. I didn't object again, because I didn't want to hear her double down.

Fran said, "She had a real boyfriend, a student, and Omar was, what, twenty-three?"

"Twenty-five," I said.

"Did he seem like the type?" Oliver asked.

"No," we both said.

"He hung around the students a little too much," Fran said, "but in retrospect I think that's because as a Black guy, like—this is a white-ass town in a white-ass state. He maybe felt more comfortable with the Granby football team than at some bar down the road."

"We really liked him," I said. "He kept trying to teach us all yoga."

Fran said, "He was a Pisces. You can *never* read them."

"So wait," Oliver said, "should I watch it or no?"

I said, "Only for fun. Don't take it seriously."

That was essentially the end of the Thalia conversation. Oliver wanted to go into *Dateline* fresh, so the only other thing we told him was that Lester Holt mispronounces her name.

"Oh," Fran said, suddenly beaming, "and near the beginning, when they show a guy in a white shirt writing on a chalkboard? That's my dad."

We stayed up late talking, my phone resting on the island as my kids sent animal emojis and close-ups of their nostrils, and I sent back hearts and asked if they'd remembered their inhalers. Leo was seven that winter and Silvie was five. Leo was into sharks and LEGO Star Wars and baking, and Silvie was in a horse phase—as in, constantly pretending to be a horse.

Yahav texted, finally finally finally, about Wednesday: *I have to see. I'll let you know. Please believe me that I want to!*

After Fran left I asked Oliver, "Do you check the news? Was there anything big today?" I was itching to check Twitter, but if Oliver could just tell me what had happened it would be better. It was important that I got sleep. Instead, though, he scooped up the remote and turned on the big TV in the seating area.

And there it was, the reason Jerome had warned me off the internet: Anderson Cooper with new developments on a story I'd found particularly disturbing.

It doesn't matter which story.

Let's say it was the one where the young actresses said yes to a pool party and didn't know.

Or, no, let's say it was the one where the rugby team covered up the girl's death and the school covered for the rugby team.

Actually it was the one where the therapist spent years grooming her. It was the one where the senator, then a promising teenager, shoved his dick in the girl's face. She was also a promising teenager. It was the one where the billionaire pushed the woman into the phone booth, but no one believed her. The one where the high school senior was acquitted of rape because the sophomore girl had shaved her pubic region, which somehow equaled consent.

Oliver asked if I was hungry, and I shrugged.

It was the one where the woman who stabbed her rapist with scissors was the one who ended up in jail. It was the one where the star had a secret button to lock the doors.

Oliver called Foxie's and ordered us a white pizza with sage, and a mushroom and onion pizza, and extra packets of red pepper flakes. I decided I was allowed to eat one slice of each.

It was the one where the harasser ended up on the Supreme Court. It was the one where the rapist ended up on the Supreme Court. It was the one where the woman, shaking, testified all day on live TV and nothing happened.

Anderson had moved on to other topics, but Oliver asked if I minded his switching over to MSNBC. I didn't. I said, "I can't believe there's finally cable on campus. We used to get three channels." Just to watch *Beverly Hills, 90210*, we had to have Dani Michalek's mom tape it every Wednesday in Darien and mail it to us on VHS.

The story was on MSNBC, too. The one where the judge said the swimmer was so promising. The one where the rapist reminded the judge of himself as a young rapist.

It was the one where her body was never found. It was the one where her body was found in the snow. It was the one where he left her body for dead under the tarp. It was the one where she walked around in her skin and her bones for the rest of her life but her body was never recovered.

You know the one.

The pizza was at the door. Oliver found us plates. He said, "So who's watching your kids while you're here?"

12

I took forever to fall asleep, and then woke too early, stewing over whether you'd in fact been a "creeper." The idea bothered me, and I needed to weigh it—a strange marble I found I was holding in my hand.

There were kids who thought you were cute, or at least you were the answer if they had to confess a teacher they crushed on. The girls loved that your cheeks blotched red when you got up at colloquium to make announcements, and some boys did, too, I'm sure. Red cheeks and dark hair are a compelling combination.

And you certainly had your cult, the kids who wouldn't only stop by your classroom but would sign up to carol with you on the town green or to watch the screwball comedies you screened. Occasionally they'd save you a seat at their dinner table, convince you to eat with them. This was a subset of the choir and orchestra kids, the ones who took private lessons, the musical theater divas like Beth and Sakina and Thalia who thought they could flatter their way into a lead. I'd never have gone caroling, wasn't part of the group that got up onstage to surprise you with that German drinking song on your birthday—but I did feel free to stop by just to talk shop, as if we were colleagues. I felt you were *my* teacher, in a way Mr. Dar, for instance, whose history teaching seemed secondary to his hockey coaching, was not. Mr. Dar belonged to the hockey players, but you, you were mine and Fran's and Carlotta's, you belonged to the music kids and the speech geeks and the Italian club, to these tiny pockets of the school, not to everyone.

I'll never know why, when you arrived my sophomore year, Mrs. Ross decided I was the tech kid to throw your way. Maybe she could spare me to work October Follies when she couldn't spare her juniors and seniors, already busy building the set for *Our Town*. Follies was just a variety show, after all; it only needed to entertain families at Parents' Weekend and pad a few seniors' college portfolios.

Because you were new and I'd at least *seen* Follies the previous fall, I found myself in the odd position of explaining things to you. I saw it as my choice, the way we talked as friends. I was the one who teased *you*. I was the one filling you in on relevant theater gossip: who couldn't memorize lines, who used to date and shouldn't be onstage together, who was likely to miss rehearsals.

But things looked different in 2018. We were, all of us, casting a sharp eye back on the men who'd hired us, mentored us, pulled us into coat closets. I had to consider now that perhaps you were skilled at subtly eroding boundaries, making adolescent girls feel like adults.

We did spend a lot of time together—but no, you never stuck a sweaty palm to my knee. In college, a professor once felt the need, in his office, to tell me that the most erotic experience of his life had involved watching a French woman soap her unshaved armpits. You never said things like that, never invited me to sit in your desk chair to look at something on your computer while you breathed on my ear. Thank God.

Although, I reminded myself, the fact that you didn't cross boundaries with me doesn't mean you didn't do it with girls less guarded, less wrapped in barbed wire.

More than once, before the curtain rose on opening night of a show, you looked at me and said, "You hold my career in your hands."

You thought it was hilarious to write my name on rehearsal schedules as *Body! Bodi! Bodé!*

You told me, your first year, about the tiny public high school you'd attended in Missouri, and what I remember you saying—as we sat in front of the TV cart on that little brown corduroy couch in your office-slash-choir-slash-orchestra room watching old videotapes of previous Follies—was that some people are meant to travel beyond where they're from. You didn't mean the wealthy two-thirds of Granby, the kids who'd seen Europe as toddlers. You meant people who had to get themselves out of small towns, people with ambitions too big for where they'd been born. This wasn't quite true of me; Severn Robeson was the one who'd sprung me from Broad Run, Indiana. But I loved that you assumed I'd fled on my own. For a teenager, being seen a certain way is as good as being that way—and soon your vision became part of my self-image. On first dates in my twenties, I'd talk about leaving Broad Run as a choice. I believed it.

Later, I was more honest: My ambitions didn't precede Granby, didn't get me to Granby. My ambitions were born at Granby. They grew in the mossy woods like mushrooms.

You said, "This is the first place you've gotten yourself. That means it belongs to you."

I was silent, not because I disagreed, but because I wanted to weep with gratitude.

You said, "You might think Granby belongs more to some kid whose grandfather went here. But you *chose* it, and that makes it yours."

During the second Follies we worked together, you asked why I preferred being backstage. I said, "Oh God, *no one* wants to hear me sing!"

You said, "I'm talking about more important things. Directing. Writing. Aren't you into film? I don't think you're destined to be a backstage girl. I think you'll wind up in charge of it all."

I can look back and see how that might have made a certain kind of kid fall in love with you. But I got something completely different from it. A new vision of myself, for one. A sense of possibility. Ultimately, a career.

And what about someone like Thalia, so clearly smitten with you from the moment she stepped onto campus? I don't know if she talked about you to everyone else, but with me she brought you up constantly. I was, after all, someone who must have inside information. Or at least my connections to you were a convenient excuse for her to say your name.

That fall, there was a joint choir concert with Northfield Mount Hermon in New Chapel. A mass, or something else long and classical, and for whatever reason—maybe because, as Priscilla Mancio pointed out, there was always a dearth of singing boys—you not only conducted half the concert but also performed as a soloist when the NMH guy conducted. You swayed your whole height with the music, an oscillation that started at your wide-open mouth and ended at your feet. You were so lost in it, so exaggerated in your rapture, that I thought at first it was a joke. But Thalia, behind you in the soprano section—I saw the look on her face. It wasn't just admiration; she looked nervous for you, deeply invested in your success.

Naturally, the rumors about Thalia and some teacher transferred onto you. They also transferred onto Mr. Dar, and onto Mr. Wysockis, her tennis coach. Perhaps because Thalia was the kind of person to touch *any* man she was talking to on the shoulder. We believed it all, if only so we'd have gossip. (I certainly contributed to it, sharing with Fran and Carlotta every time I came to your classroom and found her already there, sprawled on the couch with her shoes off.) It was for the social clout of gossip that we also spread—and even believed—stories about teachers with crushes on students, teachers who'd check out girls' legs. But they couldn't all be true, and as the years passed I came to understand they'd been immature fantasies, related to our certainty that the world revolved around us.

I thought of the Follies rehearsal senior year when we were all called out of the theater by Bendt Jensen, our Danish exchange student. You might not remember Bendt, who was only there one year; the reason I remember him myself is that he was gorgeous, an unquestioned fact. A swoop of blond hair that looked drawn on, a *chin cleft*.

Bendt was late to rehearsal that night, and when you asked why, he'd stood there, embarrassed and wide-eyed, and explained that there were, he didn't quite know how to say, but there were . . . lots of little UFOs outside? And as soon as the words were out he reddened, but everyone was ready to believe him, already out of their seats, already jumping off the stage, you calling after us with fake upset that masked your real upset.

We tumbled outside and stood on the steps, on the sidewalk below, staring out at the empty hill behind the theater, the one where the off-season baseball boys would play Wiffle ball. It was still the tail end of summer, but late enough that full New Hampshire dark had descended.

"There were—" Bendt said, and he seemed to try, unsuccessfully, to laugh at himself. "There were like a hundred little—I don't know what—*there*!"

And he pointed in triumph to the sudden illumination of dozens of tiny flickering lights at the forest's edge.

"*Dude,*" someone said. "You've never seen fireflies?"

Apparently he hadn't. Poor Bendt had never even *heard* of them, was completely new to the idea that a living thing could illuminate like that. I remember, in the hilarity that followed, thinking that I understood. That, my God, if you'd never known something like this existed, yes, your mind would jump to the nearest, strangest, most terrifying associations.

"They light up to attract mates," someone said, and explained that what we were seeing was essentially a firefly nightclub. We ran around until we caught a few that we could show Bendt up close. Max Krammen smashed one on the sidewalk and spread the glow with his sneaker as we all screamed at him to stop.

We filed back in to find you still at the piano, which Thalia leaned on like a torch singer. She alone had stayed back. Carlotta was in Follies that year, singing "Adelaide's Lament" in a campy New York accent undercut by the Virginia one she couldn't shake. She whispered, before I went back up to the booth: "Someone was doing a mating dance of her own."

Back in the dorm later, the story stretched to include (had we seen it or not?) the details of your cheeks burning red, you wiping at your neck as if to rub lip gloss off.

If we believed at all that you returned her affections, why didn't we tell some adult? The truth is that even if you'd kissed Thalia right there in rehearsal it never would have occurred to us to say something, just like we never would have turned in Ronan Murphy for having more coke in his room than a Colombian drug lord. Not because we were honor-bound, but because it seemed like just one of the many secrets of the world to which we were now privy, secrets we were supposed to be cool about. And because maybe we knew, on some level, that our assumptions would melt away under examination.

When I still taught at UCLA, I used the firefly story in lectures as an example of the uncanny valley—although I have to admit it's a terrible one. Sometimes I used it to illustrate the way our brains fill gaps, the way we use what references we have. Sometimes it was about false assumptions.

It wasn't lost on me—though I never included this detail—that Carlotta and I had done the same thing, looking at you and Thalia and filling in the lurid details that would make the best story later.

We thought we knew, so we became certain we knew. It became as real to us as those lightning bugs, their mating dance at the tree line, our laughter, Bendt's good-humored relief, our feet hitting the earth as we raced to catch them for him, bringing him miracles in our cupped hands.

13

My students were supposed to show up the second day with plans for their first episode—an idea of someone to interview, a couple of paragraphs of introductory script, names for their podcasts. They'd all done more than enough work. Plus, they were awake and hydrating: entire bottles of water on the table! It struck me that while I might have been happier going to school with this sweet band of Gen Zers, I'd likely have failed out, the only kid showing up fifteen minutes late with wet hair, mouthful of bagel, term paper lost in her computer. Even today, after my bad night's sleep, I felt two steps behind them all.

Jamila's intro for her financial aid podcast was the strongest, although she talked at warp speed, would need to slow down for recording.

I said, "They still do senior convocations, right? Are you working with a coach for that?"

"Not till spring term."

"Didn't they used to be, like, half an hour?" Britt asked.

"Yes," I said, "and we worked on them all year. What are they now?"

"Ten minutes."

I stopped myself from gasping. I didn't want to be the old lady who couldn't stand change. Instead I told them my convocation was on veganism.

"Are you still vegan?" Alder seemed excited, and I hated to disappoint him.

"I'm still vegetarian," I said. "Which, let me tell you, the dining hall has improved a *lot* on that front. On everything, really. That omelet station this morning? We'd have died. They promised one vegetarian option every meal, but half the time it was fried fish."

I can't fathom what I ate for a whole year of veganism in the New Hampshire woods. I know I found vegan cream cheese at the health food co-op in Kern, stored it in the minifridge Donna Goldbeck was allowed in her room because she was diabetic. I'd dip vending machine Fritos in the fake cheese. In the dining hall I ate salads, PBJs. I'd take white rice, add soy sauce, dump on scallions, microwave it, call it stir-fry.

Do you remember how you thought it was funny, sitting at your desk while I practiced my speech, to eat your pilfered dining hall cookie in front of me? "Mmmm, Bodie, you know what makes this so good? The eggs and butter."

When it was Britt's turn to present her intro, she sat forward, scanned the room to make sure everyone was listening.

"In 1995, Thalia Keith died on the campus of the Granby School in Granby, New Hampshire."

I did admire the ambition inherent in her framing, the idea that this would reach some national audience in need of orienting.

"Her body was found in the campus pool on the afternoon of Saturday, March fourth. Although the cause of death was drowning, Thalia also had open fracture wounds to the back of her skull plus bruising on her neck and damage to her carotid artery and thyroid cartilage, as if she'd been choked. She was a star in musical theater and tennis, a senior who'd been admitted to Amherst College. Suspicion soon settled on Omar Evans, a twenty-five-year-old Black man who worked as head athletic trainer at the prestigious boarding school. He was the only official suspect in the case. Evans falsely confessed under extraordinary pressure after fifteen hours of interrogation, a confession he recanted the next day. He was a victim of an inexperienced and racist small-town police force and a racist school that wanted to close the case quickly. Omar Evans was convicted of second-degree murder and sentenced to sixty years. He has now been imprisoned nearly twenty-three years for a murder he did not commit. This is the story of two stolen lives: those of Thalia Keith and Omar Evans."

Lola whistled. Alder said, with no apparent irony, "Oh, *snap*."

Jamila said, "You really just called us *prestigious*?"

I said, "That was well done, Britt. I have a small correction, which is that the case was handed to the State Police. They might've been racist, I don't know, but they weren't inexperienced. I like how you've laid out not just the subject but a thesis statement, too. One danger with that—" I sipped my coffee, buying time. I felt adrenal, wondered what on earth I'd started. "One danger is that if you lay out your theories at the beginning, and then change your mind as you investigate, you'll be stuck."

"I won't change my mind," Britt said. "I've already done a ton of research. The case was *so* flaky." I assumed she meant flimsy. She asked if I'd seen the Diane Sawyer interview with Omar's mother. I hadn't; she told me she'd send it. "When you hear her speak you'll understand," she said. I was sure his mother believed with every cell of her body that he was innocent. I was sure that came through on camera.

I said, "Maybe there were flaws in the case. But they had his DNA on her swimsuit. One of his hairs was in her mouth. They had him in the building when she died, and they can't put anyone else there. They had a confession. They had the motive, at least according to her friends. They had that noose he drew in the directory. People get convicted on *much* less." I heard myself, a parrot. But Britt was only parroting the Reddit boards. I didn't want her to swing into obstinacy in either direction. I wanted her to do a good job, to wake all the sleeping tigers and ask all the questions I couldn't wrap my own head around. Because there were things I could never quite reconcile. In real life, you don't get the murderer telling you exactly what he did and why he did it. Even Omar's confession, taken at face value, left major gaps. What I wanted, but could never get, was to go back and see it happen. Not the grisly parts, not the death, but every step leading up to it, every moment when fate could have stepped just an inch to the side and left Thalia intact.

"What does everyone think?" I asked the group. "In general, is it better to go in asking questions, or positing answers?"

"But I listen to your podcast," Jamila said, "and you're, like, *Everything you know about Judy Garland is wrong.* That's how you hook people, right?"

I said, "Sure, and I did a year of research on Judy Garland before we started. I wasn't still learning as we produced."

Alder said to Britt, "Okay, so who did it? Isn't that the unanswered part? Or do you know?"

She shrugged. "There's a ton of people it *could* be, but no one obvious. Like, her boyfriend was this guy Robbie Serenho, but he was at a party in the woods with tons of witnesses, but if the time of her death is wrong that doesn't matter. And also, it might not have even been murder. There's a theory that she jumped into the pool from the observation deck, and she hit her head and then she bruised her neck on the lane line. Because for one thing: How do you get someone into a swimsuit against their will? Like, I've babysat and I can tell you it's impossible. So if she put her own suit on, maybe she dove."

Anyone who knew anything about forensics had dismissed that theory—a lane line couldn't leave finger marks around your neck—but I didn't say so.

We moved on. Or the class, at least, moved on.

One of the more provocative pieces of evidence against Omar was the *Faces of Granby '94–'95* they found in his desk. I can't imagine they still make physical versions of what we used to call "face books," but you'll remember them—the little spiral-bound directories with black-and-white headshots of each student.

Omar had written under every picture. He later claimed this was a mnemonic device, to recognize who belonged in the gym—as if local interlopers might try to use the bench press. An article Fran sent me the next year—her parents would mail her extra *Union Leader*s at Reed and then she'd send the relevant pieces back across the country to me at IU—showed the page Thalia was on. On two of the photos, he'd drawn in details. Glasses on Daphne Kramer. And around Thalia's neck and extending up to the top of the photo: a noose. Omar claimed he hadn't drawn it, had never seen it before, but it was in the same ink as the writing, which was provably his.

I was on that same page, our names separated alphabetically only by Hani Kayyali, now a major restaurateur. *Wednesday Addams*, Omar had written below my photo. It could have been worse; I looked like an angry chipmunk. He'd written *kebab breath* under Hani. Under Thalia, he wrote *jailbait*.

Jamila was calling her admissions and financial aid podcast *Admit It*. Lola's restaurant worker one was *Served*. Alyssa's piece on Arsareth Gage Granby was *Founding Mother*. Alder couldn't settle on a name, had seven contenders. Britt had wanted to call the Thalia podcast *False Confession*, but by the end of class settled on *She Is Drowned*, a *Hamlet* reference Alder confirmed on his phone. It seemed melodramatic, but this wasn't something headed out to the wider world. It was just for us. Two or three episodes, just for us.

14

That afternoon's film class: Eisenstein's baby carriage tumbling down the Odessa steps. I had the kids time the average shot length. Three seconds, practically a strobe effect for its time. Then, in color, sixty-two years later, De Palma's baby carriage descending the steps of Chicago's Union Station, the mother's silent scream. Eisenstein again, De Palma again, Eisenstein again, both babies plummeting, both cameras blinking fast, fixated but refusing to focus. I wrote on the board, *Montage of Attractions*. I wrote, *movement → concentrated attention → "moved" emotionally, mentally, politically.*

There was one particularly bright bulb in the class, a boy who tilted permanently forward in his desk. He said, "It feels—okay, so scene replicates lived experience? But montage replicates memory, the way memory is fractured."

A boy and a girl whispered in the back. To stop them, I asked if they had any thoughts. The girl said, "We were wondering what happened to the babies. Like, do we ever get a follow-up?"

After class: Three texts on my phone, all from Jerome. A question about the dog's flea pill; a picture of Leo headed to school with white hair and a cardigan; and then, *Stay away from Twitter. Find a cute teacher to fuck. Hope you're getting rest.*

I was happy being separated, and was indeed sleeping with other people, or at least with Yahav, or at least I had been—and I had little issue with Jerome seeing other women. But when he talked like that, it made me sad in a way I couldn't articulate.

I had time before dinner for the fitness room, which I found newly renovated and only half full of teenage weight lifters. I'd brought my swimsuit and goggles just in case, and was hot enough after twenty minutes on the elliptical that what I remembered as frigid water began to seem appealing.

If you can believe me: I told myself this was why I wanted to go to the pool. To cool off. That I'd packed my swimsuit because I liked to swim.

I changed in the locker room and jumped in the shallow end, making a noise I wasn't proud of. I wondered if my legs' sudden blue tint was a reflection of the pale blue pool walls, or if I'd gone hypothermic. I hadn't bothered turning the lights on; I liked how things looked in the half dark, the late sun shining through high horizontal windows in soft, heavy beams. I'd forgotten about the light at Granby. It was different there, older, passing through centuries before it reached you. Outside in winter, it came down in needles; inside, it fell like soup.

Little about the pool had changed. There were records on the board from the early '90s, a couple from one kid in the '70s, additions for Stephanie Pasha, class of '16, who'd shattered nearly every girls' record. Two big equipment lockers still stood in the corner, kickboards spilling out. The lane lines still alternated bands of Granby green and gold. The same colored league banners from Holderness, Brewster, Proctor adorned the wall.

Fortunately, swim season was over when Thalia died, with only an away meet left. Could you imagine swimmers getting back in the pool, even with the water replaced?

I'd meant to think through lesson plans as I swam, but (shocker) it wasn't where my mind went. It didn't help that the space was vast and empty, or that my goggles messed with my peripheral vision and made me imagine movement beside me in the water.

The day I looked at the campus maps online, I'd found obsessively detailed calculations: The observation deck is twenty feet up and eight feet back from the lip of the pool, and the deck railing is three feet high, which means someone traveling from the top of the railing would have to travel twenty-three feet down and over eight feet out to reach the water. People had applied complicated geometry involving the arc of a jumping body. There were diagrams.

The reasoning went: If Thalia jumped, she might have come up short, twisted, grazed her head on the pool's lip—or she might have gone long and landed neck first on a lane line. She couldn't have done both at once, was the problem. The damage to her carotid artery suggested choking; and the injuries to the right side of her face, in addition to the damage to her brain stem and the back of her skull, were inconsistent with a single fall onto the pool deck or a lane line. Plus there had been no sign of impact at the pool edge.

My only experience in the pool as a student was the swim tests we had to pass before each fall and spring crew season. The first time, I'd barely gotten to know my teammates over a few days of erg training. It was a particular humiliation to stand there with my chubby, pale legs, the borrowed Granby swimsuit noosing my thighs.

Thalia wore one of those same green school-issued suits when she drowned, suggesting she'd either found it at the pool or borrowed it from someone on the team. It was size Large, and Thalia was a small person. No swim cap, no goggles. Trace DNA from Omar Evans was found inside the suit crotch—one of the main pieces of evidence against him. Although: One of the articles Fran sent me the next year had mentioned the instability of DNA in water. While water couldn't put Omar's DNA there, it could have washed someone else's away.

Then there was the piece of his hair in her mouth. Well, there were actually two hairs in her mouth. A two-millimeter piece consistent with Omar's DNA, and a three-centimeter strand from someone else, someone unidentified. A swimmer, the police had posited, another student who'd recently used the pool. I imagined what Britt would argue: Either hair might have been in the water already, inhaled as Thalia drowned.

I was out of breath. I didn't swim often, and although my limbs were in shape, my lungs were not. I draped my arms over the lane line, hung there by the armpits. How many pieces of lint, fiber, hair speckled the pool's surface? If I lowered my sight line exactly so, the water seemed covered in dust.

Those Reddit detectives would have had a field day in here. They'd have whipped out their measuring tapes, their calculators.

For years, I'd assumed Thalia was found in the deep end (isn't that where one drowns?), but then I learned from *Dateline* that it was the shallow end, her hair so tangled around the lane line that a Campus Security officer, called by the teacher who discovered Thalia, had to jump in the pool and cut her free while the EMTs were on their way. I'd also assumed she was floating, but when my son was in his gory-and-disturbing-facts phase I learned that bodies don't float for a few days. If Thalia's head was near the surface, it was only because she was held there from above, her hair turned to puppet strings.

It wasn't obvious that the cause of death was drowning. There was water in her lungs, but all that meant was *either* she took several breaths in the water, *or* water—maybe water already in her mouth—entered her lungs during the EMTs' attempts to revive her.

They weren't able to perform the autopsy until the day after Thalia was found, almost two days postmortem—a lapse that would erode many positive signs of drowning, such as (I was horrified to learn) froth in the upper airways. The medical examiner ended up having to look at tissues on a microscopic level, where the results were solid if not iron-clad. The official cause of death was "drowning precipitated by injury."

Britt had pointed out in class that the crime scene—which wasn't considered a crime scene for days—was a mess. Water everywhere, mud tracked in, Thalia's arm scraped as they pulled her out. The traces of blood they found later on the concrete by the shallow end, even the blood on the emergency exit doorframe—those were likely enough to have been smeared there by uncareful paramedics that no one could draw conclusions. Plus, who knew what had been washed away by the chlorine. No one came in with a luminol test for days.

There are two doors to the pool. In other words, two ways in and out—both down by the shallow end, directly opposite each other. One opens to the hallway full of trophies—the shiny new ones and the desiccated 1890s footballs—which in turn leads to the gym, the locker rooms, the lobby, the front entrance. Omar's office was off that hallway—twenty-six feet from the pool door, according to the internet. The other door is the emergency exit, with its giant Alarm Will Sound sign, not meant to open from the outside.

Omar had a key not only to the gym's front door (the same master key that opened most doors on campus) but one for the pool itself (a unique lock). So did the athletic director, Mr. Cheval. So did poor Mr. Wysockis, the assistant athletic director, who first found Thalia on Saturday afternoon, heading in for his swim. The swim coaches—Fran's mother, Mrs. Hoffnung, among them—had keys, as did the custodians. There were a lot of spare master keys floating illicitly among the students—but not pool keys. Why risk it all for a pool key?

When first questioned, Omar said he'd had his office door open that night. (His office was where kids got their shoulders examined, their wrists taped. A desk, an examination table, a couch to wait on, a noisy ice machine.) Anyone entering the pool, therefore, would cross his line of vision. Unless perhaps someone got straight into the pool through the emergency exit, or had been in the pool already for hours. But Thalia couldn't have been there for hours; Thalia was onstage.

Omar would have heard someone screaming in the pool, even with the pool door closed. On *Dateline*, Lester Holt had stood inside what used to be Omar's office while a woman stood next to the pool and screamed. He could hear her loud and clear. I'd always found that convincing. (But Britt's imagined voice in my head, again: Did they try it with an ice machine running?)

According to Omar's later statements, before he left, at 11:18 p.m., he checked the building as usual, even tugged the glass-paneled pool door to ensure it was locked; it was. No, he said, he hadn't peered through it. It would've been dark in there. I would remind Britt of that in the morning: If Thalia intended to swim, she'd have turned the lights on.

I switched to backstroke, slowed my breathing, watched the ceiling go by. The even slats of wood, the flags. I wanted my muscles to burn. I wanted to exhaust every thought I had about Thalia, everything I'd learned, and I wanted to exhaust my quads and hamstrings and arms. I wanted to emerge drained. Then, that night, I could sleep dreamlessly and wake up sore.

The prosecution's theory of a motive was that Thalia was having sex with Omar in exchange for drugs—which was ludicrous, because Thalia had enough money to buy pot for the whole school. She might well have been *buying* drugs from him, that might have been how they knew each other, beyond his taping her elbow, but she wouldn't have needed to barter. The state argued that as Omar and Thalia slept together, he associated her more and more with his ex-wife (he'd had a ten-month marriage) and transferred his anger onto Thalia. A great deal was made of the fact that his ex, like Thalia, was white. They posited that one night, high on drugs and jealous over her ongoing relationship with Robbie Serenho, he lost it—and everything about his ex came flooding back until in a fit of rage he strangled Thalia, bashed her head on something hard, changed her into that swimsuit, threw her unconscious body into the pool.

Displaced anger had always seemed an odd motive, though, even at the time—and by 2018 I knew more about the way prosecutors weave narratives from scraps. I certainly knew more about how rage gets ascribed to Black men.

I tried to think, in the pool, about the actual Omar I'd known, rather than the version rewritten on top of him from the moment he was arrested, the one that invited me to look back on every memory as tainted, a conversation with a murderer. He had green-flecked eyes and very white teeth. He'd bounce around the weight room like he was on springs.

I told him once that he reminded me of Tigger. He'd lie down for crunches between the ergs, talk without getting winded. He seemed curious about the students, asking us not about ourselves but each other: *What's up with that kid?* he'd ask. *Are those two dating? Is she really the Anheuser-Busch heiress or was someone yanking my chain?*

There were other scenarios, of course. Thalia and Omar scuffling at the pool edge—maybe he'd caught her sneaking in and confronted her, or maybe they'd fought about sex, or money—and, what, she fell and hit her head? And he tried to cover it up by drowning her? Or they'd been swimming together, they'd been wrestling in the water, and things got out of hand? Although you'd think, then, that this would be what he'd confessed to, rather than the story he'd told, and then recanted, about attacking her in his office and carrying her in here.

I turned it over, lap after lap, the cold of the water settling deep in my joints. The story I knew felt a lot like the stories Lance and I examined on our podcast, the ones passed down through decades of misinformation and bias. The truth was in there, but you had to dig.

There had to be something I'd missed about their relationship, or about that night. I wanted Britt to take me there. I wanted second sight. I wanted the ability to remember things I was never there for.

Someone else entered the room, a young man barely old enough to be faculty. He stepped up on a starting block at the deep end and launched himself into the water, sleek as a dolphin.

15

I had promised Britt I'd watch Diane Sawyer's interview of Omar's mother before our next class, so I pulled it up on my laptop as I brushed my teeth that night.

Sheila Evans was prim—small and contained as a wren. I'd learned after Omar's arrest that his mother was a department secretary at Dartmouth, that his father died young. She struck me as old-fashioned, with her tidy hair and her clipped, careful diction. Behind her, framed family photos lined the top of an upright piano. Diane Sawyer leaned in, her face a spectacular blend of compassion and skepticism.

"When my husband passed," Sheila said, "it was like losing the bookend to a row of books. We all tipped over sideways. But losing Omar, the shelf itself went. He was pulled out from *under* us."

Diane nodded, oozing sympathy. I preferred Lester Holt, his frank blinking. You never felt he was putting on an act.

The camera zoomed in on one of the photos: a teenage Omar, smiling like he'd just heard a joke. He looked like the guy I'd known, only with a lot more hair. When I first got to Granby, Omar had his head shaved—and because he was light-skinned and because I thought people with Arabic names must be Middle Eastern, I didn't realize Omar was African American until late sophomore year, when he grew his hair out. I asked some teammates if they'd known, and they looked at me like I was an idiot. Angie Parker, who was Black, found it hilarious the rest of the year to point out random blond people and say, "Whatcha think, Bodie, Asian? Jamaican?"

We learned now, through Diane Sawyer's voice-over, that Omar had gotten his BS in athletic training at UNH, where he was a track star, and while he was at Granby he'd enrolled in part-time classes there again, working toward his MS. None of that had made it onto *Dateline*. Omar lived in an apartment in Concord above an independent pharmacy—an hour-long commute from Granby in his rusted-out Grand Am. UNH would have been another hour from Granby, and not toward home.

Sheila said, "His little brother was lost for so long. Malcolm was only six when his father died but Omar was fifteen and I told myself, okay, my husband raised up one man, now Omar can raise his brother. But the year Malcolm's sixteen, his brother is ripped away, too. I try to hold things together, but I'm busy fighting for Omar. We have the trial and the appeal. I got shingles from the stress, and that was debilitating. All my support team, my sister, my own mother, we're consumed with this. What's left for Malcolm? And we live in a small community. You can imagine how he was treated after this, even by his teachers. He's finding his way now, but only through the strength of his character."

I felt gut-punched—the way she articulated something I'd never been able to. My own father's death destabilized us, but Ace's was a life yanked from the center of us all, the last pin holding anything in place. One loss wasn't worse than the other, but it was the second that did us in.

I found that I'd finished brushing my teeth, that I was flossing them again even though I'd already flossed.

She said, "They made Omar out to be a bad person all-around. This one accusation wasn't enough, they have to say he was dealing drugs, he was a violent man, he was sleeping with students. They paint a whole picture. They talk about him as if he came from nowhere, as if he had no family."

It was true that the prosecution and the papers made him out as a full-on drug dealer, implied he was selling to students, which was news to me. In fact, he *talked* a lot about pot, would go on about the difference between indica and sativa, would tell injured athletes who returned from the hospital with narcotic painkillers that they should chuck them all, that pot was healthier. It seemed part of his being into meditation, breathing. He got the football team doing vinyasas. The pot talk never felt like a big deal. And even if it was more than talk: Every other kid on campus had a Ziploc of weed, or at least of oregano they'd been sold as weed. Ronan Murphy, that slick little kid from Bronxville, was the one everyone actually bought from, and he sold much more than pot.

After Omar's arrest, I certainly believed he was selling to students, if only because everyone else said so. I'd wondered in the years since why he would jeopardize his career that way—but then, why would he jeopardize his career by stalking a student?

"I do think my mother would have lived longer," Sheila Evans said, "were it not for the stress. She had deep vein thrombosis, and that's not helped by worry. He was her first grandbaby. She used to get mad if I'd bathed him before she came over, she was so eager to do it." She swallowed in a way that dimpled her chin; she was holding in so much it was a wonder she didn't implode, turn to a tiny pebble of grief. "My mother left us in 2008," she said.

I took my laptop with me into bed.

"My own sister fell out with all of us. She wasn't sure of Omar's innocence. We haven't spoken in years. I started with a family," she said. Her voice had started cracking, and she paused until she had control. "A healthy, functional family, and—you know, I ended with a shambles. It's the ruins of a family."

The dosage of my antidepressant is such that I haven't cried actual tears in a decade, but there are times when I want so badly to cry that I make all the noises of crying, press my fists into my eyes so I feel something similar. The absence of tears hurts more—or makes whatever hurts hurt more—than if I could just sob. In any case: That's what I was doing, on my bed. There was a childish bitterness to it all that I only slowly identified beneath the sympathy: Sheila Evans, unlike my own mother, hadn't abandoned her remaining child.

I hated that I was thinking about myself rather than becoming a pure vessel to absorb Sheila's grief, but the truth is that while anyone with a heart would have felt it break right then, my heart cracked along familiar fault lines.

Since I shouldn't be thinking about myself, I stuffed the recognition down into the subterranean, into the dank, loamy places where it might take root.

Instead of working it all out, I went to sleep.

In the morning I couldn't remember what I dreamed, except that it was troubling, that it was about water, that I dreamed about texting friends about the dream. I didn't feel rested in the slightest. I knew, as the sun finally came through the blinds, that I couldn't get up until I'd stayed there with my eyes closed fully picturing the night Thalia died. If I could do that, if I could think it all the way through, I could get up and leave behind me whatever had tangled these sheets into a sweaty mess.

So—may the universe forgive me—that's what I did.

Thalia changes from her costume, the tulle smelling of sweat and sawdust. She puts on the jeans and sweater that will later be found neatly folded on the pool deck bench. They never found a shirt, just a green cashmere sweater, so let's assume this is all she has. Hiking boots. No coat; the more foolhardy of us are done with them.

She grabs her backpack (reported contents: hairbrush, lipstick, tampons, calculus book, Toni Morrison's *Beloved*, Granby-issued weekly planner, assorted pens and scrunchies, mini deodorant, dorm room key), slips past the other changing girls, exits via the backstage fire escape. No one will miss her: All her friends in the cast and a lot of other kids, Robbie among them, are heading to the woods to drink by those two disgusting old mattresses.

Her footprints melt into others', and in any case, they're rained away by the next night, the soonest anyone would think to look.

She avoids the floodlights till she's behind the gym where there's no light at all, her fingers on the building's bricks to guide her. At the emergency exit she knocks three times, and Omar disables the alarm. He's been waiting right there, impatient. They go to his office couch.

Thalia's still in her stage makeup, the green eyeshadow that matched her dress. Omar says she looks hot.

Or no—he says she looks slutty, and she bats her eyes, pouts.

Maybe he asks if the makeup was for Robbie. He asks why she needs to look trampy for the play, asks if she's looking for more boyfriends, because he knows she doesn't care about him, she's probably fucking Dartmouth guys, too.

Sometimes this is foreplay for them. Sometimes she says, *What if I went to a frat party and saw how many guys would screw me?*

But he's not in the mood, and he stands over her, still high on whatever he took while he waited for her, and he grabs her throat and maybe he didn't mean it till this moment. If her face hadn't seized with terror, he could still play it off as a joke, but it's too late; she's seen what's in him, and the only way he can fix things is to stop her from seeing him and judging him and remembering this. He slams her head against a new CPR poster taped to the cinder-block wall above the couch. She claws him, makes the deep scratch the police will find nine days later behind his right ear, down to his collarbone, the one he'll say he got from his neighbor's dog. There was no skin found under her fingernails, but hours in chlorinated water could account for that. He chokes her harder, and when her arms go limp he steps back.

No. This couldn't be it.

This was the version we were all handed—this was what he said in his confession (drugs, his office, the couch, the wall, a poster no one ever remembered seeing), but I couldn't make it work. The movie director who lived in my brain wanted to scrap it, send the actors home for the day.

Omar was someone who noticed the stress in your shoulders before you felt it yourself—not someone who bottled up rage till it exploded.

So maybe instead—maybe there's someone else there. Maybe Omar has a violent friend, one whose temper erupts. And Omar decides, later, to take the fall for them both.

Maybe Omar has taken tainted drugs, ones that make him hallucinate.

I had to leave it at *something happens*. Because it did. Because there was no other explanation. Because there was no one else in the gym that night. Something very bad happens, and he can't call for help.

She's breathing still. He has enough medical training to know, even in his haze, what he's done, and also to know she could still survive this. But if she survives this, he won't.

He checks the hall, carries Thalia over his shoulder the twenty-six feet to the pool.

He strips her rag-doll body on the pool deck, wrangles her into a spare suit from the equipment locker. He's reminded of dressing his little brother, pushes down the thought. Her breaths: ragged but steady. He rolls her into the water, doesn't notice till she's in that there's blood on the pool deck cement. This must mean there's blood on his wall, blood on the hallway floor. Her dark curls had been hiding the wound.

Omar grabs the pool net, uses the handle end to hold Thalia's body a few inches below the surface. She doesn't struggle. This is what he said in his confession, a detail that always destroyed me: the idea that someone who'd been so alive could be killed—so gently, so slowly—by a pool net.

Omar racks his brain to think who's seen them together, who might know. He can't deny being here in the gym; he's been making calls all evening from his office phone. He'll have to say he saw nothing, heard nothing. (So why, then, when they first questioned him, did he volunteer that his door was open?)

He waits ten minutes, longer than anyone could possibly survive without air. To his surprise, she sinks a little. Her feet lower than her head, but both below the water's surface. He folds Thalia's clothes, puts them on the bench. He knows where the maintenance guy keeps the bleach, industrial strength, and he goes to the cabinet, uses his shirt cuff to lift the bottle, to pour it onto the bloody pool deck. He watches it fizz white. He scrubs with a forgotten towel, and it's a long time before he can step back and not see a pinkish blur. He turns on the lights for a second, to check. He uses the same bleach and the same towel on the drops that dot the tiled hallway. He's lucky: In his office, there's blood visible only on the CPR poster. Still, even after he peels it off, folds it, stuffs it in his backpack, he scrubs the wall. He returns the bleach to the maintenance closet. To do this, he has to reenter the pool, has to see Thalia bobbing below the surface.

He's sobered a bit, and it's harder now to look. The smell of chlorine starts to sicken him, and the last thing he needs is his own vomit at the scene. The water keeps moving her. Her arms don't stay by her sides, her head hits the lane line. She's close enough to his end of the pool that he can reach one lock of her hair to pull her closer. He rubs the hair in his fingers, because oh God, what has he done, such a beautiful girl—he ruins everything. He breaks things. He broke his own marriage. This is who he is, and he hates who he is, hates that he's the same boy who once broke his grandmother's crystal hummingbird. Look at him. Look at her. He wraps her hair around the lane line, getting his sleeve wet. He wraps it around five, six, seven times, to anchor her in place, to keep her from— what? He doesn't even know.

He locks the pool door behind him; maybe it will buy him time, delay the moment her body is found. He takes the towel, to burn with the poster.

All that night, all the next day, his hands smell of chlorine.

(Was I satisfied with my story that morning? I told myself that despite the missing pieces, I ought to be. Perhaps the dull nausea I felt had something to do with last night's dining hall lo mein. In any case: I was able to get out of bed. I was able to start my day.)

16

Before class, Britt asked if she could interview me later. I told her I'd talk, but that mine shouldn't be the first interview she played on the podcast. "It might seem sloppy," I said, "using your teacher as your first source."

I said it partly out of an instinct to disavow responsibility. If the podcast somehow got out into the world, I didn't want it to look like I was steering the ship. I wasn't someone who'd decided that despite being utterly peripheral to this story twenty-three years ago, I was the one to tell it now. (Everyone shut up and listen to me, a girl who wasn't even friends with those people!)

I warned Britt that I didn't have a lot to say, that all I could do was describe Thalia as a person. And that I might not even be free that night; I was trying to meet up with a friend from Boston. But by class break, I hadn't heard from Yahav. I texted him—because if I didn't, I'd wait around like an idiot. *Sthg came up for tonight, but lemme know if you have time in next few days!*

I don't need you to care about Yahav. It would be odd if you did. But he's part of the story, and he was a big part of my mental state those two weeks. Lest I sound clueless and desperate: This was someone I'd been seeing for two years, someone who would, when things were working, text me just to say good morning. When we got together he, too, was separated and starting the divorce process. We were already friends— both teaching at UCLA, both enjoying rapid-fire conversation and politics and tapas bars. I don't believe in soul mates, and that's made life easier; we were simply good together.

I'd met him at a potluck thrown by a psychology professor friend, in a house full of spider plants—a remarkably unsexy party if only because the place smelled of cat litter. Yahav had piled his plate with so much food that I found myself scoping his physique to see if he was all muscle or just an ectomorph. The answer turned out to be both, I confirmed two years later when we finally slept together, when I ran my hand down his ribs and his long, ropy quadriceps. But in the moment, I apologized for staring at his plate, the mountains of orzo and chicken and veggie lasagna. I said, "You have literally everything, so tell me what ends up being best." He took the request seriously, and kept reporting back throughout the night, advising that the brownies on the far end of the table were the superior ones. "The key is salt," he sotto-voced into my hair. "The others lack sufficient salt."

Still married to Jerome, I considered my coffee dates with Yahav simply, if thrillingly, social. We shared an interest in Israeli cinema, and he wanted help finding some early Uri Zohar movies, which led to us watching *A Hole in the Moon* in his office. I was more taken with the books on his shelves than the film, doubly so because he was a law professor and I hadn't expected to find David Mitchell and Audre Lorde in lieu of anything leatherbound. I understood that because we were becoming friends, we would never sleep together. Specifically: Because I'd opened myself up to him in unflattering ways, because I'd worn glasses and no makeup on our walks, griped about Jerome's anxiety, even moaned to him about the stretch marks my kids had gifted me, I'd taken sex off the table.

And then, at a wine bar late one night after we discussed our foundering marriages and the panic attacks Yahav was getting in traffic, he looked at me with such imploring eyes that the future rolled out in front of us, soft and green.

We'd only been seeing each other six months when his wife was diagnosed with severe chronic fatigue syndrome and he realized he needed to stay with her, take care of their daughter, live in the house. Her illness put us on hold, turning a legitimate relationship into an illegitimate one.

I found myself in an affair by default, not because I chose to transgress but because I was unwilling to cut off a full-throttle romance just because circumstances had changed. We saw each other, we didn't see each other, we were together, we were undefined, he emailed, we texted, he begged me to send nudes, he said he needed me, he went silent, we met in hotels, we met at my place, he felt guilty, he felt relief, she was getting better, it was back, she had heart issues, I was the only thing keeping him together, I was the reason he was falling apart. He took the BU post that fall—a yearlong sabbatical from UCLA, but he'd be teaching a couple of classes in addition to writing his new book—and his family came with him. His wife was doing better, somewhat. They were still talking divorce, but I was in no position to rock the boat. I couldn't fault him for any dismissive action, because he was doing the Right Thing when he ignored me. And I couldn't advocate for myself without being wrong.

So: Here I was, giving him the easy out. Reduced to the girl I'd always refused to be, happy with crumbs.

After the break we were supposed to talk about editing, but the other kids had grown interested in Thalia's case, had started googling things, developing their own theories, and wanted to talk about it.

Lola forked fingers through their purple hair and said, "The guy who killed that Spanish teacher in the '70s, he was out of prison by then. There's this whole thing about how he might've been living in the *woods*. Just hanging out by campus. And they never look into him?"

"That was only something we said to freak each other out." The rumor must have come from an alum, someone who'd heard four years of tall tales—how an old jacket found hung on a branch clearly belonged to Barbara Crocker's estranged boyfriend, who now lived in an old lacrosse goal he'd tied blankets over, or maybe he lived in the clock tower, watched us all with binoculars. "There's no substance to that."

Jamila said, "Those mattresses in the woods? I read he was supposed to live there."

"Oh, God no. It was where students went to drink. That was where Thalia's friends were that night."

And then they wanted to hear about the mattresses instead, and whether I used to go there, but I wasn't falling for the distraction.

"My friends and I smoked more than we drank," I said. "It was all pretty regrettable."

In any case, I never attended an *actual* mattress party. But I passed the mattresses many times, and once you knew they were there, you couldn't miss them, just a few yards off the Nordic trail that the cross-country skiers used in winter and the cross-country runners used in fall. The media took the presence of mattresses to be a sex thing, when really it was just two disgusting old dorm mattresses that marked a meeting spot, and anyone having sex there would risk tetanus and fleas. Senior spring, when I dropped crew and smoked half a pack a day, Geoff Richler and I would walk there during our empty third and fourth periods, stepping over broken bottles to sit not on the mattresses, which were always wet, but on the logs people had dragged into the clearing. I'd smoke, and Geoff would entertain me. Sometimes Carlotta would ditch her unsupervised studio art time to join us and smoke half a cigarette, and Geoff would watch like that was his actual cock she was putting to her lips.

Half an hour sounded right for the walk—that's what I'd seen quoted online, as people questioned whether someone could have left the party, killed Thalia, and returned—but it took longer in snow and ice, longer in the mud. I can tell you with certainty that we couldn't have walked to the mattresses and back in one class period. The mattresses were, as we now all know, 1.4 miles from both the theater and the gym. It was a bit farther than that from the darkroom in Quincy, which was where Geoff and I would start our trek.

I tuned back in to Britt, preaching to her choir. "Plus," she was saying, "the only evidence that Omar ever even *talked* to her was student gossip. She'd told a few friends she was having trouble with some older dude. And her friends look around for someone older and creepy, and they settle on the Black guy."

"That's not quite how it happened," I said.

There was chatter in the room, but it only swam around me. It was the word *creepy*, an echo of something just out of reach.

And then—I wonder if I actually sat there slack-jawed, or if I managed to keep my face composed—it was as if the hemispheres of my brain jolted out of decades-long disconnection.

The time the two of you stayed behind and missed the firefly show. The days I'd waited endlessly outside your door while Thalia's convocation coaching ran overtime. Low rumbling when you talked, the sound of Thalia projecting her voice across the room, long periods of silence. I'd seen her turn red, junior year, when she talked about you. I'd seen you sitting too close. I'd seen her stay late after Follies practice.

We had talked about it, me and Fran and Carlotta and Geoff. We joked that she was obsessed with you, we joked that you were sleeping with her. Wasn't it a joke? Or, it was something we only believed for fun. The same way we chose to believe in dormitory ghosts.

And what if—

You didn't even seem that shaken up after Thalia died, at least not more than other teachers. You asked again and again at our convocation practice if *I* was okay, talked about how your kids, who'd known her as a babysitter, were so shaken. By then, I must have abandoned any notion that something illicit was going on.

Back in '95, I'd learned first that there were rumors about Omar, then that he'd confessed, then—after we graduated—that he'd been convicted, and only *then* that part of the evidence against him was Thalia's alleged statements about some older guy.

It had thickened the air in the classroom: Thalia having trouble with an older guy.

Not that you would hurt her; this wasn't what I was thinking. Your hands were so thin. You were scared of bees. I couldn't imagine you bashing someone's head. I reminded myself of the DNA evidence against Omar. And you had an alibi: You'd stayed behind at the theater, making sure instruments and sheet music got packed up, wheeling the timpani back into the closet. *I* was your alibi, for Christ's sake. I told the police how we'd chatted about *Braveheart*. And then you went home to your wife and kids.

But still: How disconcerting that this one piece of information, these rumors about Thalia and someone older, had been what started the police looking at Omar to begin with.

It hit me with the weight of twenty-three years.

The older guy was you.

If Thalia was having trouble with an older guy, the older guy was you.

17

Here's what I thought about as I climbed uphill through the wind to my guesthouse, skipping lunch:

Opera class, and New York City, and Bethesda Fountain.

There were only six of us in your opera seminar, fall of senior year: three who'd squeeze onto your couch and three who pulled over padded orchestra chairs. It was me, Thalia and her boyfriend Robbie, Beth Docherty, Kwan Li—who went and became an actual opera singer—and Robbie's friend Kellan TenEyck, the one who drank himself to the bottom of a lake twenty years later. It's hard to look back and see us as we were, rather than who we would become, hard not to see text bubbles floating above our heads: "Murdered Girl" and "Opera Star!" and "Sad Drunk."

I wonder if they let you add the class to the elective schedule just so it'd sit, forever, in the list of courses sometimes offered at Granby. "Wow!" the moms of bored eighth graders have said every year since, leafing through the viewbook in the admissions office. "History of opera! That's like a college course!"

Robbie Serenho was only there because Thalia was, and Kellan was only there because Robbie was. A ski star, Robbie oozed privilege. And he had swagger: the way he wore shorts even in snow, his floppy hair, the way he'd show up late to class, chewing gum, and no teacher called him out. Dating Thalia certainly bolstered his status. I hadn't had class with Robbie since ninth grade English, and was mildly surprised now to find him insightful. He'd be picking at a hole in his khakis like he wasn't listening, then pop in with "Beethoven was the Miles Davis of his time. Like, constant reinvention." Robbie might not have come in an opera fan, but he was at least a casual music geek, knowledgeable about any-thing he deemed cool enough; he'd go on about laser tag or World Cup soccer in the same way. He'd sit with his arm slung around the back of Thalia's seat, keeping her anchored to the floor of the classroom.

I'll forever remember the operas we saw that October at the Met. Three operas in three days, missing our other classes. *Le Nozze di Figaro*, *La Bohème*, *Tosca*. I owe you that: A girl from southern Indiana got to see three operas at the Met. It was exhausting, but it rewired my brain.

Thalia was dating Robbie, and Beth was all over Kellan, and all four were friends—which left me and Kwan the odd ones out. The trip was unstructured; we had nothing to do between waking up and meeting for dinner. Kwan and I were both awkward enough that we weren't going to suggest exploring the city together—so I set out alone every day, seeing how far I could walk, doing mental math on calories burned per block.

The biggest city I'd seen was Indianapolis. Well, and I'd flown through O'Hare, which didn't count. I didn't mention this, not wanting to seem like a rube. I'm sure if you'd known you'd have given me more direction, at least taught me how to hail a cab.

Everything was enormous, and the sidewalks were broad, and I loved it all, even the way the streets started smelling like garbage at five p.m. when the trash came out. I was terrified the whole time of pickpockets, of crime, of wandering into a gang war (ah, the notorious gang wars of Lincoln Square), but otherwise it was heaven.

I had thirty dollars for the three days, and while Granby covered our Met tickets and dinners, those thirty dollars needed to get me through breakfasts and lunches and transportation. I'd rise early (my body woke at four a.m. for crew, even here in New York), sneak out of the room without waking Thalia and Beth, and buy a small bagel with jam and an orange juice from the deli across from our hotel. That was $3.75. I'd have $6.25 for the rest of the day. I had sorbet for lunch once, which would have broken my diet if it hadn't been the only thing I ate. Another time I got a pretzel from a cart.

I sent a postcard to my mother in Arizona—letters spelling *NEW YORK*, each filled with a photo of the city. She didn't know I was there, and I wanted to casually surprise her. In retrospect, it wasn't a kind thing, sending that postcard. The back might as well have read, *Look how little you know about me.* Or *You've never been here, have you?* It's possible I was taking the opera class for the same reason. How much farther could I get from Broad Run, Indiana?

Not long after we arrived, I was walking down Columbus Avenue when a man who was clearly mentally unwell swerved at me and made like he was grabbing enormous breasts on himself, shaking them in the air. I sidestepped him, hurried down the sidewalk hating the rush to my limbs, my stomach. He called, "Run, little bunny rabbit! Hoppity-hop!" I felt I'd done something wrong and embarrassing, hadn't been tough enough.

On the second day, I ran into Kwan as he returned to the hotel with poster tubes under his arms. "I was at the Met!" he said, and I was so confused, because weren't we going to the Met every night? He said, "You only pay what you want." Further confusion. But then he popped open one of the tubes to show me Van Gogh's self-portrait in a straw hat, the words *Metropolitan Museum of Art* across the bottom.

So on the morning of the third day, our last full day, I set out from Lincoln Square through the park to the museum I'd circled on the free hotel map. I made sure to pass a landmark my map called "Beth. Fountain" because a fountain would be good for photos.

I assume you remember what happened next. I saw you and Thalia sitting way too close—legs toward each other, touching at the ankle—on the lip of what I now know is Bethesda Fountain. If I'd been far enough away I'd have stopped, hidden behind other tourists, watched to see what happened next. It would be something to tell Fran when we were back—how Thalia was *throwing* herself at you. But by the time I saw you, I was five feet away, and you also saw me. You and Thalia jerked your legs apart. Thalia looked like she was trying not to laugh; your cheeks were forest fires. You said, smoothly, "Bodie! Small city, huh?" You said, "Thalia just talked me into being her convocation advisor. Do you have an advisor yet? You need one?"

Whatever else I'd been thinking was subsumed by my enormous relief at what seemed like, and indeed was, your offer to work with me. They'd just posted the list of the ten or so faculty who'd be advising convocation speeches, and they expected us to simply *approach* someone. That was easy for most kids—the hockey players went to Mr. Dar, the skiers to Mr. Granson—but the thought of walking into someone's classroom, even yours, and asking them to advise me felt egregious.

So I said, "I—yeah, I guess I do need one."

You seemed genuinely overjoyed, and I was starved enough to take it.

You asked where I was going, and I said "the Metropolitan Art Museum" and you gently corrected me, told me to be sure to find ancient Egypt.

That night at *Tosca*, Kellan TenEyck, a row ahead, turned as we stood for intermission. He stretched his arms overhead, oxford shirt rising to expose a pale stomach. He said to me, out of nowhere, "So you and Fran Hoffnung are dykes together, right?"

And that was the thing I went to bed angry about, the thing I stewed over. Not what I'd seen in the park.

18

When did you first notice her? She'd have been in Choristers from the start of junior year, one of many sopranos. Then she joined Follies, one of four girls spinning in black dresses to "I'm Every Woman." By mid-September, you'd picked her for parts in the opening sketch and given her a solo in the closing number.

By the time we roomed together, she'd definitely noticed you. She kept asking how long I'd been stage managing, what your kids were like when I'd babysat, if I knew what kind of bagel you liked, what kind of soda she should bring you if she stopped by the snack bar before rehearsal.

Aside from this grilling, our interactions that year were oddly formal. Right before bed, the only time we were consistently alone together outside the merciful silence of study hours, Thalia always hit me with a polite conversation starter. It might have come out condescending—might have *been* condescending—but at least she tried. "Does your family have any special Christmas traditions?" she might ask, or "Have you seen any good movies recently?" She rarely just *said* things, didn't complain to me about homework or tell me about her day. It was as if her grandmother were watching, and she needed to prove she'd been well raised.

That spring, she asked my summer plans. I said, "Maybe I'll work at Burger King," and she clearly didn't know if she was meant to laugh. I was kidding, but barely; I hoped to land the swing shift at Baskin-Robbins again.

She said, "Back in Idaho?"

I wondered if she'd been picturing Idaho this whole time, or was picturing Indiana but didn't know its name. I said, "The thing about Burger King in Idaho is our fries are local. We harvest them ourselves."

That was junior year, of course. Senior year, after Thalia died, Asad Mirza said, kindly and with interest, "Bodie, is it true you live on a potato farm?"

Thalia's friends spoke to me, in contrast to her studied politeness, with barely concealed distaste. Beth once told me that I should try a bronzer, that it would slim down my face and make me look "less angry." Even something like "Nice top" was a baited hook, a feigned act of generosity played for the rest of the audience as pure joke. Its success relied on the assumption that while everyone else would hear the ironic edge, I wouldn't. The irony being: I was steeped in irony. I was the one whose entire attendance at Granby felt ironic. I was the one whose clothes and posters were ironic. Whereas they (I believed) sailed through life sincerely, with their layered haircuts and North Face and plaid miniskirts. So when I replied with *"Oh my God, you too,"* even though the girl in question was wearing her lacrosse uniform, I enjoyed the look of confusion, then the unsubtle roll of eyes Beth would share with Rachel.

Beth was the star of that pair, the singer, a blonde Christy Turlington, the one who'd made flirting an art form. Rachel's mother was the daughter of a former Connecticut governor, and her father owned commercial real estate in Manhattan. This seemed to compensate for her lack of personality. Rachel followed Beth like a shadow, and they made each other more attractive by proximity.

(Is it strange that I knew what random classmates' parents did? Remember: Every detail I overheard made the world more navigable.)

Beth Docherty was responsible for my greatest humiliation at Granby. That year, I'd started bleaching the dark hair on my upper lip, using a little pot of stinging cream and powder you mixed in with a stick. It just gave me yellow fuzz, but I didn't know what else to do. I had no idea this was something most women dealt with; I assumed it was an ignominy only a few dejected girls knew.

I took care of it every few weeks, in the time after school when Thalia walked Robbie to the gym and waited with him for the ski van. I had locked the door and spackled the stuff on my face one afternoon, when someone knocked. I looked for my washcloth and realized I'd left it in the bathroom. I made the mistake of asking who was there; Beth called that Thalia needed her music folder. If I'd known where Thalia's folder was, I would have handed it out the door, but I didn't—and now I was looking for something to wipe my lip on, something that could get bleach on it, but all my clothes were black, my sheets dark blue.

Beth wiggled the knob, said, "Would you just please let me in?"

I grabbed a white T-shirt from Thalia's laundry and wiped my face, opened the door. I must have been flushed, out of breath. Beth looked me up and down and said, "Why was the door locked?"

The next day, Dorian Culler came up to me at breakfast. He said, "I heard you were letting your fingers do the walking."

I didn't understand until Puja Sharma, who had no filter, found me in the Singer-Baird laundry room and said, "Ohhh, you know, I don't think Thalia hates you, everyone is just worried about her." I asked what she meant, and she said, "They're saying, like, oh, she has to live with a masturbator."

I wonder if you can understand, as a man, the stigma around this at the time. It was one thing to be called a slut; that was half-good, half-bad. This was entirely bad.

Mike Stiles stopped me in the hall that week. He said, sincerely, "I'm sorry they're being shits to you." It was a lovely gesture, but the fact that he knew made it worse. Along with everyone else, I had a crush on Mike Stiles, our eventual King Arthur; I was infatuated in the purest way. Pure because I never really talked to him, and because he seemed genuinely nice. He had a sloped, ridged brow, a broad chin, Elvis-thick hair. ("He's like a hot Neanderthal," Fran had said once, although I'd thought he looked old-fashioned in other ways—like a Union soldier, maybe.)

When I signed Thalia's yearbook that May, I opened to the back and saw that Jorge Cardenas had ended his message with *Enjoy your summer free from the Masturbator!* On the previous page, Beth had made a list of inside jokes (*Bunny???* and *That's not ping pong* and *Mr. WHATNOW* and *The Masterbator*). Thalia was packing, her back to me, and I flipped to the *Little Shop of Horrors* page and signed my name—only my name—under the cast and crew photo that included us both.

But Thalia never mentioned it, was never unkind for a moment. She was mature—which I'm sure made her more appealing to you. If you'd been interested in someone *truly* mature, you wouldn't have spent time with a teenager, but her maturity was probably a convenient excuse. Maybe you told yourself she was an old soul. I'm sure you told yourself she knew what she was doing. I bet you felt, when she brought you bagels and soda, that she was mothering you.

It was to my advantage that Thalia and I had no past together. These other girls had seen me come in freshman year trying earnestly, wearing knockoff Laura Ashley hand-me-downs from the Robesons' daughter, my bangs teased and sprayed—still the fashion in Indiana but definitely not at Granby. They saw me join yearbook in a fit of school spirit (where I didn't last long but took Geoff Richler's friendship as a souvenir). They saw me try to befriend people like them, before I found my way to Fran.

From the perspective of girls like Rachel and Beth, having lost track of me around November of freshman year, my transformation over the next summer must have seemed abrupt. I cut my hair chin-length, chopped my bangs Bettie Page–style. I left my hand-me-downs in Indiana and, when I got back to campus a week early to stay with the Hoffnungs, went thrifting with Fran in Hanover, spending my Baskin-Robbins wages on dark, oversized clothes, fishnets I carefully ripped, a fake army jacket. We went through her sisters' closets for things they hadn't been back to claim. I cultivated a look I'd now call goth grunge, designed to hide my weight: all black, a flannel shirt either tied around my waist or flung on open like a coat. At Clover Music in Kern, I bought chokers made of hemp and Fimo, black-light nail polish. Fran gave me her old Doc Martens, duct-taped at the toes and a size too big. I plucked my eyebrows into sharp little checkmarks. Everyone was doing this, but mine were extreme. I learned to apply thick black eyeliner. I'd spent the summer shedding what I'd seen as pathetic artifice, ready to return as my true self.

Sophomore year was when Carlotta French showed up, a refugee from an all-girls' school in Virginia, and all but announced that Fran and I were her new best friends, positions we happily accepted because Carlotta was cooler than either of us. Carlotta wore ankle bracelets and no bra. When she played guitar on a blanket under trees, boys who theoretically were interested only in preppy girls out of shampoo commercials would move their Frisbee games closer, end up lying on their stomachs to talk to her. She found them ridiculous. She sang "Rhiannon" for Follies, an ethereal version that made me want to *be* her. Her hair was wild, the color of sand. She was reed-thin, but I didn't hate her for it. She seemed to have sprung from the earth that way, rather than crafting herself from the pages of a magazine.

That winter, Fran pulled out the previous year's *Dragon Tales* and showed Carlotta, in the freshman section, how I used to dress, and Carlotta let out her most frog-like laugh. "Were you kidnapped into a cult? It's like—if JCPenney was a cult!" And I was able to laugh with her, grateful she saw the girl in the picture as the fake me, the one who'd gotten something terribly wrong.

But most people that fall greeted my transformation with concern.

Karen King saw me on move-in day and said, "Oh God, does this mean you're quitting crew?"

Poor Ms. Shields tried to suss out if I was okay. Before practice one morning, as we waited outside the gym for the Dragon Wagon, she started asking about my summer but within two minutes was listing resources: people I could talk to, appointments I could make. I stammered something nonsensical, didn't understand till later that I was radiating damage. Of course, that's exactly what it *was*—I was damaged, and must have subconsciously wanted to dress the part. But since the damage was only newly visible to everyone else, they assumed it was fresh. The whisper was I'd discovered drugs that summer, or witchcraft. If I'd gone to any public high school in 1990s America, I'd have blended in, at least with a certain crowd. But at Granby, land of Ralph Lauren and duck boots, I was seen for the wreck I actually was. It was only the fact they got the details so wrong—heroin! occult! wrist-cutting!—that allowed me to shrug off the gossip.

After Kurt Cobain died junior year, Clover Music sold copies of his suicide note. It was a Xerox of a Xerox, Kurt's handwriting blurring at the page edges. The pages were double-sided, and I bought two copies so I could tape the whole thing above my bed, each page facing out.

I was in the dorm hall, returning from the bathroom, when I overheard Rachel reading the note aloud to Beth and Thalia in a stoner voice.

Thalia said, "I think it's sweet. He was her hero."

Beth said, "You say that now, but wait till you find her hanging from the ceiling."

Shrieks of laughter till I opened the door.

In any case: To Thalia's friends, I was the girl to whom *something had happened* over freshman summer—or, at best, a girl playacting various roles and never getting it right. To Thalia, though, I was myself, unchanged. A tidy and considerate roommate who was deeply uncool but at least wouldn't steal her bras.

And I was someone who knew all about *you*.

RC Cola, I told her, was your favorite soda. I said it because you'd found that six-pack in the greenroom fridge and announced that you hated them. You'd been trying to offload them ever since, offering me one every day until I finally started accepting them just so I could hide them, unopened, around your office. If Thalia gave you an RC Cola, you'd know it was really from me.

19

When Yahav hadn't answered by Wednesday night, I told myself it was a relief that Britt wanted to meet. It would distract me from thinking about him, and from thinking about you, grasping for tiny moments I'd missed.

I'd given Britt a list of other people to talk to (Fran, and various teachers still around), so I wouldn't be the only other voice on her show.

We met at seven in an empty study room in Dwyer Hall, a sleek, glassy Upper Campus dorm that hadn't existed in the '90s. I sat on a plush couch under a whiteboard, and Britt set her phone on a table in front of me, opened to the recording app I'd had the kids download.

Britt wore a creamy fisherman's sweater and skinny jeans and what looked like the same Frye boots Fran had in 1994. She said, "I'd love to start with the timeline."

I went through the basics. Thalia and I were roommates from 1993 to 1994. She died in March of '95. Omar was arrested that spring, but the details of the case didn't come out till summer, when we were all spread back out across the country, packing for college. The internet was nascent; I didn't have my first email account till that September. I told Britt about the snail mail news clippings, feeling ancient. Omar's trial was '97, his appeal '99. After the appeal failed, a lot of nothing. The occasional mention on true crime shows, because, you know, *dead white girl at a boarding school*. More than that: pretty, rich, dead white girl. If only she'd also been blond. Each story a recap: *Remember this gruesome case?* The details hazier with each retelling, the verdict more obvious. *They caught the guy who did it, thank God. Look at this photo of him after years and years in prison, bulked up and dead in the eyes. Doesn't he look like a murderer?* Then, in 2005, the *Dateline* special, the occasion for which was the tenth anniversary of Thalia's death and a growing Free Omar movement online.

Dateline gave some time to his defenders—particularly the actress I remembered for her smallish role in *Spider-Man*, who'd briefly made it her pet cause—but mostly focused on the pile of evidence: The DNA, his pool access. His confession, even if retracted. That drawing in the directory. Even if he hadn't been the "older guy" Thalia mentioned to her friends: Three skiers claimed they'd heard Omar joke about a fantasy of tying Thalia to the weight bench.

"Omar was fun," I told Britt. "He'd blast music in the weight room and then he'd run around holding his fist out like a microphone to get you to solo." This wasn't relevant to the timeline, but it felt important. "He didn't have the same boundaries a teacher would have. I guess when you're icing people's groins things get a little personal."

Britt nodded as I talked. Then she said, "I was actually wondering about the timeline of *that night*."

"Oh." I was relieved, because I hadn't known what I'd say next. I wasn't about to mention you—certainly not on the record—but my mental deck was getting shuffled in uncomfortable ways. Why, for instance, had I thought so much about Thalia over the years, but so little about Omar? I wanted to defend myself from the very question.

I said, "Okay. That Friday. I was stage managing, we ended the show, I went back to my dorm, and I learned about everything the next evening. Which was Saturday."

"Right. But what do you remember? About Saturday?"

One wall of the room we sat in was glass, and girls passed occasionally, still in sports gear or already wrapped in towels to grab the nighttime shower spots. They gazed in with mild curiosity.

I said, "I had a single, senior year, and I would've slept in. This isn't a major part of the story, but the dorm smoke alarm had gone off Friday around midnight, just a microwave incident, so we were all standing outside till pretty late. Are kids still burning popcorn?"

Britt laughed. "Oh my God. I don't understand why there's a *specific popcorn button* on the microwave, when pressing it is, like, nuclear meltdown."

"*Exactly!* Okay, so—as you know, a bunch of kids were drinking in the woods Friday night at the mattresses off the Nordic trail. It was warmish for March, so they were taking advantage. I mean, it was probably thirty-three degrees, but you know that first day when the air doesn't hurt your face?"

Britt said, "I have so many notes on this. It was nineteen students total."

"I'm pretty sure it was all kids who'd been at the musical," I said, "or in it. Not Thalia, but most of her friends, and her boyfriend, so it was a little odd she wasn't there. My point is, a lot of kids were hungover Saturday. Not me—I mean, I wasn't virtuous, but—that wasn't my friend group. So between the smoke alarm and the drinking, people were tired, sleeping in. And Thalia had a single, so no one missed her for a while."

What had happened was that Jenny Osaka, our senior class president, had been invited to the mattress party—she played flute in the pit orchestra—but stayed back for prefect duty in the dorm where Thalia and I both lived. When the Singer-Baird contingent of the mattress crew was late for check-in (11:00 p.m., the weekend curfew), Jenny stalled, did room checks slower than usual. Jenny didn't drink, would never break curfew, but wasn't about to rat them out. She knew where they were, she explained later, so she wasn't worried. Then at five after, a handful of girls poured through Beth Docherty's ground floor window and scurried to their rooms. Jenny clocked that they were back, quickly checked off the rest of the names, and handed the sheet in to Miss Vogel. Jenny assumed Thalia was among them; those were her friends, so where else would she be? The fire alarm business was after all that. Miss Vogel followed protocol then and went through the dorm to make sure every room was empty—but because we were all standing together in the cold, what looked like forty of us, and no one was left inside, she didn't take attendance, didn't bother checking us back into our rooms at 12:30 as she was supposed to.

Jenny had been racked with guilt—maybe still was. She went on to ski in the actual Olympics, the first of our classmates to do something huge. But how do you move on from a mistake like that? After Thalia's body was discovered, Jenny was the one to go to Miss Vogel and tell her about the mattress party. Not that the others wouldn't have, soon enough; after all, it was the alibi for everyone there. Jenny resigned as class president, resigned as prefect. I'm sure Miss Vogel faced quieter, more serious repercussions.

I wasn't about to tell Britt all this. To name poor Jenny Osaka, of all people.

Britt said, "Were you in the same dorm? Singer-Baird?"

"Yep, all four years."

"Oh my God!" Britt sounded like the cheerleader she might have been in some past era of Granby. "I lived there my first two! I haven't been able to figure out what room she was in."

I was glad Thalia's room wasn't some haunted shrine. "I don't remember the number," I said, "but it's the single at the left end of the upstairs hall, the one with the window seat."

Britt shuddered, pleased. "I know who has that room! Should I tell her?"

"Probably not."

Britt looked a little dreamy, like she was planning a reason to stop by this girl's room, to check the inside of her closet for Thalia's initials. "But upstairs means she couldn't have left her room in the middle of the night."

"Not unless she went out through a ground floor room. But even so, the latest time of death they gave was midnight," I said. "And no one *ever* saw her back in the dorm, or outside after the fire alarm."

"But no one noticed she was missing till they found her?"

"Right. And that was Saturday afternoon." I was pleased that I had something firsthand to relate now. "I rowed crew, and we had our pre-season swim test, so a few of us were walking together toward the gym. It would have been around four o'clock. Suddenly this police car and ambulance come barreling down the access road. They must've been the first ones."

"Did you see anything?" Britt affected calm professionalism, but her eyes glowed.

I shook my head, then remembered to say "no" aloud for the podcast. I was usually holding a script for these things. "Eventually there was a crowd outside. The crew girls, some volleyball players, teachers. At some point, we heard it was a drowning. There was a fire engine, too, by that point. I guess they sent the whole emergency squad."

"When did you know it was Thalia?"

I tried to remember. Maybe an hour later, I told her, a stretcher emerged from the pool's side door, the figure on top covered with a white sheet. It was dark by then, everything glowing in the gym floodlights. But we had no idea who it was yet, and somehow I didn't think it was a Granby student. It must have been one of those white-haired ladies from the local swim club, suffering a heart attack mid-lap. Or it was a janitor, or maybe that creepy townie who liked to watch basketball practice. Even when whispers started in the crowd that it was a student—it was Hani Kayyali, it was Michelle McFadden, it was Ronan Murphy—that seemed too dramatic to be true.

I said, "They sent us away, and we still didn't know. By the time I got back to the dorm they'd already put up signs that we had mandatory dorm meetings before dinner and *Camelot* was canceled. We met in the common room and there were already girls crying, ones who'd figured it out." Fran had come out of the Hoffnungs' apartment, which she didn't do for most dorm meetings. I remember her sitting with me on the coffee table. Her parents came out, too.

I knew who it was before the teachers spoke; word had spread through the room, and, of course, Thalia was the only one missing.

"Who announced it?" Britt asked.

"Miss Vogel. She was young. I don't think she stayed much longer. She taught physics and coached girls' skiing." It occurred to me that

Angela Vogel must, as dorm head, have been the one to clear out Thalia's room, after the police went through it. It would have fallen to Dr. Calahan, as headmistress, to call the Keiths. I couldn't imagine breaking that news to anyone, ever. It wasn't like being a surgeon, someone who'd trained for this moment and expected it. And then, my God, two other kids the same year. It was a miracle Dr. Calahan had stuck around another decade, hadn't run off for some cushy fundraising job at a museum.

I said, "They ordered pizza for anyone who didn't want to go to the dining hall." Fran and I absconded to my room with our slices, sat cross-legged on my bed. I remember Fran saying she knew it wasn't the point, it wasn't the main thing, but it sucked that we'd only had two of four performances and now the show was over. Fran had been playing Mordred, putting on a husky tenor and a swagger. I said, "Jesus, Fran, she was my *roommate*." Fran said, "I thought you hated her." If this hadn't been my room, I'd have stormed out. Instead I just stared at her, dead in the eye, until she looked mortified and hugged me and I started sobbing on her shoulder.

"At that point," I said, "we still thought it was an accident. That either she'd been swimming drunk at night, or she'd gone over in the morning to exercise and—who knows."

Britt said, "When did it become clear they were investigating the death as a murder?"

"Not for a few days. They did an autopsy, which I guess is standard for accidental deaths, and after that the State Police showed up."

Britt referred to her notebook. She said, "So, the State Police came on Tuesday, and the family's own investigators did, too. That's three full days after the body was found, and meanwhile the Granby police hadn't even secured the scene."

I said, "Well, they thought it was an accident."

"You're supposed to secure the scene, but apparently they just *left*. They didn't even take good pictures. And the school didn't keep kids out of the gym."

I nodded slowly. "They actually drained the pool. You knew that, right?"

Britt hadn't known. Her eyes went wide and she covered her mouth, but she ought to say something, for the sake of the podcast. I nodded at her phone.

What she said was, "Holy wow."

"What I remember," I said, "was Alumni Weekend was coming up, I think that next weekend. The last thing they wanted was yellow tape around the gym."

Leave it to Granby to schedule Alumni Weekend not for a gorgeous spring day but for the end of ski season, so alumni could day-drink at the Granby Invitational.

I said, "You'd think they might have canceled the weekend, but they went right ahead. They strung up those Welcome Back banners. I remember they had the State Police park behind the gym so no one would see." We'd rolled our eyes at the time, but saying it aloud in 2018, I found myself kind of shocked. By the school's callousness, but also by the way the police apparently just did whatever Dr. Calahan asked.

"So that same weekend," Britt said, "that's when they started interviewing students. A whole *week* after her death."

Was that right? I remembered people missing class right away, but maybe that was to meet with counselors rather than detectives.

I wouldn't have dared to sign up for counseling on the bulletin board. Nor was I one of the girls with just enough claim to Thalia that I could walk around the next few weeks collapsing whenever I wanted out of a test. Perhaps that's unkind, but really—there were a few girls vying for Oscars that spring.

I was on the detectives' list, though, and one night I was called into Miss Vogel's apartment to sit at her table with two men from the Major Crimes Unit, Miss Vogel's parakeet chirping in a cage over the sink. The detectives were both tall—one beefy, one gray-haired. They were far too loud for that little kitchen.

I told Britt, "They interviewed me for maybe ten minutes. I remember they asked if I knew of anyone she was fighting with. In the past few days I'd heard other kids talk about Omar, but it was secondhand so I didn't bring that up. I did tell them this random story, and I thought it was surreal how they wrote down whatever I said. It made me feel important."

I'd felt at the time like it was at least *something* to give them, and I felt the same way with Britt now. At least I had one story no one else would have.

I said, "That past September, I was babysitting for a family in one of those stone houses." It was the one to the right of Fran and Anne's. The Pelonis' house, if you remember them. Three obnoxious kids who thought it was funny to spin each other in Mr. Peloni's desk chair till they were sick. "There were a couple dumpsters behind those houses, between their backyards and the loading dock of the dining hall."

Britt nodded. "That's all still there."

"So the kids had gone to bed, but it was still light out, and I was on their back porch doing homework. I looked up and Thalia was by the dumpsters, wearing pajamas. I mean, bare feet, boxers, a T-shirt. She didn't see me. There were shrubs between us." I hadn't wanted to be seen, didn't want Thalia to feel obliged to make patronizing small talk. "She started circling this one dumpster. Just walking around and around it, but like something was wrong. Every once in a while she'd jump up, trying to see in. It was weird."

Britt looked confused. I wasn't telling it right.

"What I'm saying is, something was off. At first I thought she was sleepwalking, and then I'm like, it's eight thirty p.m. I wondered if she was on drugs. I mean, something serious. Something that made the world not totally real."

Britt was excited now, leaning forward. "Something that could make you try to jump into the pool from the observation deck!"

I said, "But they did toxicology on her, and she was only a little drunk, right?"

"What's weird," Britt said, "is there was *some* alcohol in her bloodstream, but there was lots in her stomach that hadn't been absorbed yet. So, like, she drank a lot but she died before she was drunk."

I said, "Oh, right." I had known this at one point—it was probably in one of the articles Fran had sent—but I hadn't put it together with—with what? There was a word-on-my-tongue feeling, some Jungian breakthrough that wouldn't break through.

Britt said, "You know they used that in the trial? Like, if she was drinking right before she died, but she wasn't in the woods with those kids, she somehow got alcohol at the *gym*. So the prosecution decides it must have come from Omar. How naïve is that? Like only an adult would have booze?"

The flask. The flask in the video, in Beth Docherty's hand.

I didn't say anything. Because I was still piecing it together, and because I was being recorded.

They'd probably passed the flask backstage as the show wound down, as they pre-gamed for the mattresses.

There were kids who, if they'd been asked the right question soon enough, if they'd been honest enough, might have said they saw Thalia drink. They might have seen her come back after her last scene and gulp down whatever was left.

I said, "Could they tell what kind of alcohol it was?" and Britt shrugged.

It would have been vodka in that flask, for sure. Beth always drank vodka and still sprayed her mouth with Binaca after, would breathe in your face and ask if you could smell anything. Or rather, she'd do it to boys she liked, an excuse to breathe on them.

If it was vodka in Thalia's stomach—well, that wouldn't prove anything. But it might *suggest* she died soon after the end of the show.

And what would that mean? That she went straight to Omar's, that he killed her almost immediately? That he was waiting backstage, even, and whatever she mouthed into the wings was to him?

It certainly wasn't to you; you were down in the pit.

Britt said, "Do you think?"

"I'm sorry?"

"That the police got it from you?"

I looked at her, baffled; I'd missed a few sentences.

"The idea that she was on drugs. That was what the prosecution argued, that she'd been sleeping with Omar in exchange for drugs. Do you think they based that on the story you told them?"

My mind pinwheeled, and then my guts did. That couldn't be it, couldn't be the only reason.

They had to know I wasn't even in that crowd. But did they? Were they actually tuned in to the fact that my too-old J.Crew skirt meant I wasn't *really* friends with Thalia?

I could see how dots would get connected, how the detectives would write the word *DRUGS* on their yellow pad, circle it, how they'd start asking where Granby kids got drugs, how they'd form a theory that looped in Omar—the same guy Thalia's friends were saying had followed her around, the same guy who'd been in the building. I could see how this theory would get handed to prosecutors as gospel. Thalia was on drugs; Omar sold the drugs. Thalia had romantic trouble with an older man; Omar was an older man. Thalia was sleeping with Omar, an older man, in exchange for drugs.

But other people must have said similar things. Because if her friends had insisted that she never touched a joint, the police would have listened, wouldn't they?

"It's possible," I said, and I hated how my voice sounded. Like a trapped animal.

"Anyway," Britt said, "I don't believe the toxicology report. It sounds like she *was* on something. Maybe she thought she could fly."

#2: THALIA

The products of that night's insomnia:

Half-dreams about you and Thalia, you looking into the dumpster, you keeping Thalia hidden in your house all these years. You morphing into the guy who assaulted me in college. Me trying to put my contacts in, but they were the size of dinner plates, stiff, wouldn't fit in my eyes.

An itching on my thighs that worsened the harder I scratched, an itch that arranged itself in long, hot welts.

Another story, another film reel I made myself watch all the way:

Thalia takes off alone.

She wants to get away from Rachel and Beth, who pretend to be her friends but aren't, and from Robbie, who's bound to be drunk and insufferable in the woods. She wants to get away from you, wants to make sure you don't find an excuse to keep her back as everyone leaves, that you don't look at her with puppy eyes and tell her she's the one with all the power, she's the one who has your heart in her fist. So she changes quickly, slips out the back.

Earlier, she took a few tokes off Max Krammen's joint, a soggy thing he kept in the pocket of his Merlin robes. And late in the second act she sipped from Beth's flask—but she isn't wasted, just lighter, full with her own ideas.

She floats to the gym and finds the front door unlocked. She finds the pool door unlocked, too, and locks it behind her because she can change right here on the deck into the spare suit she's found, one Omar spotted the last time he passed through, scooped up wet from the floor—and what, sneezed into? wiped across his sweating forehead? would that be enough?—and dropped on the bench with his DNA in the knit.

She knows if she gets in slowly it'll be too cold; she'll chicken out. So she climbs to the observation deck, because if she can fly in—and she's seen people do it, knows it can be done—she'll be irrevocably in the water.

She climbs over the two bars of the rail, painted Granby green, holds the top bar behind her, stands with only her heels on the edge. It's a matter of force; the only danger is not jumping hard.

She used to have conviction. As a ten-year-old, grass-stained and sunburnt, swinging from branches; as a twelve-year-old athlete, diving racquet-first for the ball. But something has happened to her lately, even on the tennis court, a failure of the body to go full bore, to surrender to her will. It's an instinct, perhaps, for self-preservation, but one that always betrays her.

And how does a seventeen-year-old girl lose that control? Did it crack the moment the bingo chart went up in the bathroom? If a thirty-three-year-old music teacher takes possession of a teenager's body, does he take agency from her muscles as well? Does he fray the line between body and mind? Perhaps not entirely. But enough to make an inch, three inches, five inches of difference?

She springs, but she hesitates slightly, doesn't push off with the legs of a ten-year-old but with legs that have been told what they are until she believes it.

She knows, in the way you always know, in any bad fall, that the earth is rising for you, and she manages to twist. Not to right herself, but to turn like a barbershop pole so it's the back of her head that hits the pool rim. And not even the outer rim, but the inner one, the one under a few centimeters of water. Her head leaves no dent; her blood billows through the water in faint pink clouds.

She struggles a minute, drifting in and out of consciousness. She can't pull herself out but she follows the lane line to the shallow end, draping herself on the green and gold rings, nestling them under her chin, slipping under, coming up, slipping under, coming up on the far side, but now something has her hair, something's pulling her head back and down, and the easiest thing, the only thing, is to sleep.

20

After our interview, Britt had sent me a link to a YouTube video from a man named Dane Rubra. He had a whole channel, in fact, that seemed to be ninety percent about Thalia. At two a.m., suddenly wide awake, I decided I could enter this particular rabbit warren for exactly one hour, after which I'd sleep.

Dane Rubra looked, and I'm putting this gently, like he hadn't seen the sun or eaten a vegetable or gotten laid in a decade. A pastier Norman Bates with stringier hair and doughier cheeks. According to his first video, which I had to scroll to find, he was "between jobs" when he first saw the *Dateline* special, and he had an epiphany, felt he could contribute.

When he said Thalia's name, oozed over the vowels, I felt the skin on my neck tighten. He was about my age, and I imagined he fancied that if only he and Thalia had crossed paths, he could have saved her, bedded her, won her love.

He showed a yearbook photo of Puja Sharma and said, "This one wasn't as pretty as her friend, and you have to think, that could have been a source of jealousy. Miss Sharma is a real possibility here. Someone we can never question, unfortunately." I nearly slammed my laptop shut at that one, at the gall, the wrongheadedness, the slime. Puja might have been a hanger-on—might have used Thalia's kindness as entry into the crowd that spent Feb Week at Mike Stiles's ski house, that went to the Vineyard on long weekends—but she was devastated by Thalia's death. Two weeks afterward, Puja took off on foot in the middle of the night, walking the roadsides until police picked her up two towns over, muddy and disoriented. She was sent home to London, and we never saw her again. Her overdose two years later at Sarah Lawrence—I always wondered if it was related.

Every time this guy said Robbie Serenho's name, jealousy crossed his face like a moth. He believed Robbie knew something, thought Robbie was "an entitled boarding school prick" with a "suspiciously airtight alibi."

In one video, he manages to get Robbie on the phone. Calling his office, he pretends to be a Granby alumni liaison looking for updated information. He gets Robbie to give his home address, which he's mercifully bleeped out of the video. Then he asks Robbie who else from the class of '95 he's in touch with. "We have so many missing addresses," he says. "Would you still be in communication with someone named Angela Parker?" Robbie says no. "How about"—and here Dane pretends to struggle with the pronunciation—"Thalia Keith?"

Robbie says, "Ah, she—Thalia Keith passed away in 1995."

"Oh!" Dane says. "I'm sorry to hear that. I just started working here, and that's not in our records."

Robbie says, "That's odd. Yeah, you should cross her off your list."

Dane says, "Can you tell me more about that? More details? I'd love to update our files."

There's a pause, Robbie catching on. He says, "I'm hanging up now."

I first met Robbie when we were put in the same freshman orientation group, playing games on the quad in groups of twelve, trying to knock pegs down with Frisbees. There were kids who made Frisbee look like ballet. I didn't know how to throw one (who would have taught me?) and was initially mortified. But Robbie, with no patronizing, showed me how to throw the disc. He was patient, called me by my name, which no one else had bothered learning yet.

You have to understand: He wasn't a ski star till it snowed. In August, he was just another new arrival—a semicute one, symmetrical and clear-skinned in the manner of adolescent TV stars. Dark hair, nose upturned, chin sharp. That tattered Red Sox cap. The only way to see the ski team compete was to take the fan van and stand for hours in the snow, which would be awkward if you weren't dating a skier. But we all absolutely knew who was good, and by winter of freshman year we'd seen Robbie's picture in the *Sentinel*, goggled and helmeted, shredding the mountain.

By the time Thalia started dating him, late in the fall of junior year, he had a reputation for being a player, for callously breaking hearts, for drunkenly crashing Ronan Murphy's car over Thanksgiving break.

He wasn't a perfect boyfriend. He sat back and laughed as Dorian Culler told "Thalia jokes," which were retellings, essentially, of dumb blonde jokes, but with Thalia as the punch line. ("What did Thalia say when she found out she was pregnant? *I wonder if it's mine.*") Thalia screamed at Robbie one night, in the dining hall, for not stopping his friend, not standing up for her.

Robbie wasn't mean to anyone; it was more that he tended to pass through the halls like a Zamboni, gliding straight ahead and expecting everyone to move out of his way.

It made me proud that he'd been kind to me right off the bat, that we'd always been cordial. He didn't have time for everyone. But once, unprompted, he'd been kind to me.

I left a comment under the video: *Robbie was nicer than you think. And Thalia never would have dated you.*

21

I'm not sure I fully slept after that. My phone pinged with a text from Jerome at seven (the crack of dawn in LA) asking the dosage for Leo's anxiety medicine. I had the CVS app, so I brought the prescription up and screenshotted it back to Jerome, who absolutely had the same app and could have done this himself.

A minute later he FaceTimed from his laptop. I was ready to answer some question about where the pharmacy was, but the Jerome on the screen was a mess. His eyes were red, his silver hair sticking up in sweaty sprigs.

I said, "Have you not even been to bed yet?"

I watched him sink into his giant leather chair. If he'd been about to give me bad news about the kids, he'd have been panicked, not resigned. This was something else—but still, I climbed back in bed, pulled the covers over my bare legs. I said, *"What?"*

Jerome said, "You really haven't been on Twitter, have you. Oh, Jesus. So, I think I've been, ah—I got canceled, as they say."

It took a moment to register, and I doubted he was using the term correctly. I asked where the kids were (still asleep) and then I said, "What did you do?"

"Well. Fifteen years ago." His eyebrows rose, as if this detail alone should get me on his side. "When I was living in Denver."

This was right before we'd met. I nodded, wished he could simply hand me a write-up of the whole fiasco so I could skim to the end.

"I was showing at Peter's old gallery."

Peter Boll was someone I could see getting canceled. He had a *vibe.*

"And there was—you know, we used to call them gallery girls.

Probably not okay to say anymore. There was a young lady working as Peter's assistant."

I said, "Jerome, what did you *do*?"

"I dated her! We dated! Consensually!" He threw his arms up. "We dated for, I'd say six months. On and off. Casually, but—well, casually as in not committed. It was tumultuous. She was twenty-one."

I did the math. Fifteen years ago, Jerome would have been thirty-six, because right now I was forty, and Jerome had eleven years on me. When we met, I knew Jerome had dated women my age before, but I also knew his longest relationship had been with a woman eight years his elder, and I figured it balanced out. He wasn't only interested in power, or in girls with no body mass. He was a flirt, I knew that and liked it. But never creepy. His method was to grin, crinkle his eyes, bite his lip, caress the bowl of his wineglass. Not to rub shoulders or talk to boobs or hover with onion breath.

He said, "I'm sure I still have amorous emails in my old Yahoo! account."

"Jerome," I said. "What *happened*?"

He sighed and brought a coffee cup into view, stared into it without drinking. "This woman, her name is Jasmine Wilde. Real name. She's a performance artist in Brooklyn now. And her, ah—apparently her new piece is about me."

"What do you mean 'piece'?"

"A performance piece. She sits on a park bench and starts talking, just to anyone who'll stop and listen. She goes for a couple hours."

"That's the plot of *Forrest Gump*."

He looked blank for a second and then started wheezing with laughter. Far more than my observation merited.

When he stopped, I said, "Should I google this, or what's the gist?"

"Ah. Okay." He wiped at the tears he'd laughed out. "I mean, what she's accusing me of, is dating her. When I was thirty-six and she was twenty-one."

"There's got to be more to it."

"Sure. Sure. She's saying that because I was a successful artist, which—was I successful, fifteen years ago? I suppose in her eyes, but I was broke, I was just starting out. To me, the gallery is the power! They handle the sales and money and I'm the monkey in the cage! Anyway, she's saying I had power, because she worked at the gallery and I was successful. So even if she didn't see it at the time, apparently that means the relationship was predatory."

"Was it?"

"I just told you it wasn't!" Jerome's voice could go startlingly shrill. "I broke up with her a few times, and finally she broke up with me. I introduced her around, I got her some connections, which I saw as being a good boyfriend, but apparently now that's *grooming*."

"Grooming, like a pedophile?"

Jerome flinched. "Jesus, Bodie. I guess, yeah."

"And she's . . . talking about this on her park bench?"

He started laughing again, desperately. He said, "I'm sorry, I'm just—"

"You're picturing her with the white suit, aren't you. And the box of chocolates."

Still laughing, he put on his reading glasses, pulled out his phone and thumbed around. He said, "I'm texting you a link." It descended with a vibration from the top of my screen, and I clicked through to Twitter, a tweet with a video thumbnail. A svelte woman with light, long tangled hair sat on a bench, hands frozen midgesture. The tweet read, *I'm watching the genius @wilde_jazz and blood is BOILING. Listen to what predator Jerome Wager put her thru. @CGRgallery plz don't provide a platform for this man's spring show.* It was dated two days ago.

"So I have to watch," I said. "I'll have to answer for this myself. This isn't the kind of thing to spare me from."

I knew better than to expect an apology for not alerting me sooner. He said, "Once you watch, tell me what you think. Honestly. I—you know I was never perfect. I was drinking more back then, and I think she expected me to be faithful when that wasn't my understanding. But these people are trying to get me fired."

"From the college?" I asked—a dumb question, because although most of Jerome's income came from commissions and sales, teaching one class a term at Otis College was his only actual job.

"I guess because she was college-aged?" he said. "Although she wasn't *in* college! And I wasn't teaching yet."

I said, "Jerome, this doesn't make sense." He nodded, but I meant it more as a question. There wasn't enough there to make the story work. Either he wasn't telling me everything, or he was missing the point, oblivious—like so many men had proven themselves over the past year of reckoning—to what he'd done.

Now that I was on Twitter, Jerome's face floated in a postage stamp in my screen's corner. I typed his name into the search box and found dozens of similar tweets—a stack of the same video thumbnail, frozen in the same moment.

And several results down: my own Twitter handle. After the 2016 election I'd decided to detox by checking my account only once a week, mostly to schedule promotional posts for *Starlet Fever*. But someone was tagging me, writing, *Hey @msbodiekane, when will you address your husband's predatory behavior? More and more allegations coming out. Now is NOT the time for silence.*

"What other allegations?" I asked, as if he could see my screen. "They're saying—"

"I interrupted someone on a panel once," he said. "A Black woman. I don't remember, and it's probably true, but—I don't know. That kind of thing. Listen, you should just watch the video."

"Will this affect the kids?"

"It's the art world," he said. "Some people are talking, but it's not school parking lot fodder. I don't think. Is it? Jesus."

I asked what time it was, even though I knew; I just wanted him to realize.

"Oh, Bo, I'm sorry. I—you were right, I have not actually slept. I'll get the kids to school and then I'll sleep."

"You're okay, right?" I said. "You're not, like—"

"You don't need to rush back and hide the sharp stuff. But I can't imagine I'll keep the job. I'm not worth the hassle. What sucks is once they fire me it'll all sound more legitimate. *Artist canned after allegations.* That's so concrete."

I told him I'd text later, and I told him I loved him—something we did so rarely since he'd moved next door that now it carried more meaning. But it came out strange. I had questions. Over the past few years, I'd pulled away from the current iteration of Jerome, the Jerome whose shine had worn off. We'd grown apart: This was easy and socially acceptable to say. But that morning, my legs cold in the bed, I felt myself pulling away from even the earliest version of him I'd known. What did I not know, and when did I not know it?

It was an uncomfortable echo of the way I'd had to recast every memory of Omar, twenty-three years back. And the way, over the past day, I'd been turning memories of you in the light, looking at their ugly backsides, the filthy facets long hidden.

I'd love to be one of those people who complain when things change. But no one around me was changing; here was my entire high school, preserved in amber. The only thing changing was my vision—like the first time I put on glasses and looked in wonder at the trees, and felt inexplicably betrayed. Those clearly delineated leaves had been there all along, and no one ever told me.

In the bathroom, I scrolled through the tweets again, saw that the only one he seemed to have replied to was the one tagging me. *Bodie Kane and I separated a few years ago,* he wrote. *Please leave her out of it.* He was classy. Or at least I'd always thought so.

I needed something stronger than dining hall drip coffee, and so I walked, hair damp, to the Lower Campus entrance and down Crown Street, whited out with salt. There's a newish indie place there that smells like toast and displays Granby student art. I'd been relying too much on caffeine that week, but how else would I stay upright?

I sat at the counter and put on my giant headphones and started the video on my laptop. Jasmine Wilde was luminous, a forest nymph walking under trees in a flowing brown dress, hair like the Millais painting of Ophelia. She approached a bench in a city park, the surrounding trees not casting enough shade to suggest that we'd stumbled upon her in a clearing, but still telegraphing woods, nature, purity. The first full minute was just her circling the bench and finally sitting, each sound so crisp that it felt intimate, the brush of a lover's clothes next to your ear. A lanky, graying man eventually perched beside her. He looked self-conscious, as if someone off-screen had just invited him to sit, made him sign a consent form, and he had no idea what he was in for.

She said, "Do you remember what it is to be twenty-one?"

The man said, more to the camera than to her, "Uh, yes."

And then the video froze to buffer. I skipped back, but this time it wouldn't even start.

"Yeah," said the same server who'd given me the wi-fi password, "it works but it's real slow. I'd just let it load awhile."

The video was forty-eight minutes long, and I still had two hours till class. I'd already ordered a latte and a croissant so I stayed and waited for the video and tried to compartmentalize, halfheartedly drafting part of a Rita Hayworth script.

The satin negligee she wore in her famous *Life* pinup photo sold from Sotheby's in 2002 for nearly twenty-seven thousand dollars. I hadn't been able to find anything on the buyer, hoped it was a lovely gay man with an Old Hollywood collection, someone who'd appreciate it in the least creepy way.

A *USA Today* lay on the counter, smeared with someone else's coffee, the front page devoted to the same story that had been on the news the other night. The one where the men finally told about the priests, decades later, and everyone lauded their bravery. The one where the women came forward after five years, and everyone asked why they hadn't spoken sooner.

The waitress saw what I was reading. She said, "You'd think if she was all that troubled, she'd have told the producer."

It was the one where fifteen women accusing the same man of the same thing was too much of a coincidence; they must have coordinated their stories.

It was the one where the witness wasn't considered credible because six years earlier, she'd accused another man of the same thing, and it was easier to believe she was lying than that lightning loves a scarred tree.

I flung the paper down, went back to Rita, but I couldn't focus. I could walk to campus and use Granby wi-fi to watch the video, but the combination of dread and cold—every time the door opened a polar draft found me—made that prospect less than appealing.

The croissant they'd warmed for me was astonishingly good. Sourdough with a crackly crust. I dropped crumbs in every direction.

I decided to google you.

Such a riddle, why I'd think to do this right when I'd had proof of slow internet. Why wait so long and then finally look you up when I was most likely to get a 404 error? Almost as if there were things I didn't want to deal with.

But, lo: Google worked fine. It was only video the wi-fi couldn't support.

I'd searched you two years back, the night I stayed up googling everyone. Because yes, there you were on the website of a private day school in Providence, and I'd already seen that picture. You looked the same. Perhaps wider in the face. Your hair had lightened, as if someone had dusted you with powdered sugar. There was little else, other than articles from that school's student paper on the Gilbert and Sullivan shows you'd done, the student trip you'd led to Chicago. It was unsatisfying. No mug shot, no halo, no wedding announcement for you and a former student. I searched for your name plus Thalia's, but the only results were the *Camelot* video and a few archived *Sentinel*s.

I tried googling your wife and got nothing—maybe she had a different last name?—so I looked for your kids. From the few times I babysat Natalie and Phillip, I remembered the dark hair and rosy cheeks they'd gotten from you, the electric blue eyes like their mother's. (We didn't particularly know your wife, except from afar, wrangling the kids into dining hall booster seats. She was young and pretty—enough so that I imagine Thalia was jealous.) I was fairly confident the Natalie Bloch I found on Facebook, a striking, dark-haired woman in Boston, was your daughter. I felt predatory going through Natalie's profile. She looked athletic in a bathing suit, in love with the guy next to her.

I clicked out and rescued myself by texting Carlotta: *I am in Granby Fucking New Hampshire!* She'd known about my trip, had made me and Fran promise to send a selfie. Carlotta, who lived in Philly now, had married the sweetest man you could imagine—the head sommelier for a restaurant group—and they had three perfect children, the youngest a boy with Down's whom I loved overwhelmingly. I'd been back in close touch with Carlotta since the advent of social media. My generation only missed each other's twenties.

I wrote: *Remember how we always said Denny Bloch was involved with students? Do you think that was true?*

She responded a moment later: *Haha, we thought so, but probably not? I mean, we thought lots of stuff.*

For some reason, this stung. I didn't want it to be true, but her answer felt dismissive.

I wrote: *You don't think he and Thalia had a thing?*

She sent a shrug emoji. Well, okay then.

I had a flash of Carlotta eating with me and Fran every meal sophomore year, but then suddenly that February eating with no one but Sakina John, or, later, sitting for a week with a bunch of girls from the spring hiking trip, her colossal laugh reaching us across the dining hall. Then she'd be back like nothing happened, flirting with Geoff and coming to my room for *Cosmo* sex quizzes. Then she'd do it again. She didn't mean to hurt us; she was just a flake.

I tried the video one more time and, to my surprise, it had gathered all its strength, was ready to roll.

Jasmine said, "I was twenty-one, and Jerome Wager walked into the gallery and before his meeting with my boss he wanted a glass of water."

She explained that she'd felt herself to be a child, she was a child, she was naïve, so young. And Jerome, aged thirty-six, had been a full-fledged adult. Having married Jerome when he was thirty-nine, I can attest that he was still in most ways a child, as he continues to be. At thirty-nine, the only dinner he could make was eggplant parmesan. He would ruin suede sneakers in the washing machine. He'd never registered to vote. I'm wary of the narrative that suggests men mature so slowly that they pair best with younger women; I just mean that Jerome in particular was not terribly grown-up in his thirties.

Jerome took an interest in her work, Jasmine said to the next person who sat down, a woman with a squirmy toddler. He asked Jasmine about her own art over dinner, told her it sounded exciting. They began sleeping together, he introduced her to friends in the art world, he was a shitty boyfriend. For instance: He broke up with her on her birthday, begged her forgiveness the next morning. He left used condoms on her floor. He told her he hated wearing condoms at all. He ordered a pizza for them, but it had pepperoni, because he'd forgotten she didn't eat pork. He told her he couldn't be monogamous. She didn't like having sex in the morning, but he did, so she agreed to it but didn't enjoy it as much, and he knew she didn't enjoy it as much but he still asked for it, and she obliged. Once, he woke her at four in the morning and they had sex because he asked, but she kept drifting off and so he stopped.

I kept waiting for the bombshell, the moment when he would pin her down or hit her or threaten to ruin her career—the thing I wouldn't recognize as Jerome, that would forever change my sense of him; the thing that would make me divorce him for good and get custody of the kids; the thing that would derail his career and lead to his unanimous public censure. But forty-five minutes in, she was wrapping things up (circling the bench again like a lioness) and it had gotten no worse than undesirable—but consensual—morning sex.

She looked at the camera for the first time, and she said, "Have you ever lost something somewhere, a book or a necklace, and you—it feels like you left an arm back there, or an ear? You're missing a part of your-self, and—I left a part of myself in Denver in 2003. I left parts of myself all over this country. What I left back there, it was—" And here she made a fist in front of her stomach, and I understood it as a pit, a missing pit in her core. "—I can't ever find it."

Fair enough. Her trauma was real. (This was, incidentally, what so many of the Twitter comments said. *I see you, Jasmine, and I see your trauma.*)

I felt ancient, from some elderly generation that didn't understand the basics of the twenty-first century. If she'd been my friend back then, I would have coached her to break up with him. I'd have recited a list of his wrongs. I'd have told her she was better than that.

But good God.

I tried to assess if my rage—because it was indeed rage I felt, at Jas-mine rather than Jerome—was personal (the loyal pit bull in me) since she'd attacked the father of my children, or if I'd feel this way about any woman who claimed abuse when, Christ, she'd been a consenting adult, she'd had agency, she hadn't been assaulted, hadn't been coerced. This didn't do great things for those of us who'd been through worse. Forget the guy who had sex with me when I was unconscious in college: I could make a better case against Dorian Fucking Culler than she was making against Jerome. I could find Dorian Culler's wife and demand she denounce him.

I checked Twitter, and there didn't seem to be much new, but then I checked the *Starlet Fever* account, and someone had posted Jasmine's video under every one of the past twenty or so tweets. I wouldn't be able to ignore this much longer. I texted Lance and told him I'd explain later.

My stomach was a mess. It was time to get to class, time to talk to these kids like I had any idea how the world worked.

Since I'm relating what happened those two weeks at Granby pretty much in order, I'm going to tell you something now that I didn't learn till much later. That morning—as close as I can tell, right around the time I was dropping my plate in the coffee shop's dish bin—Omar Evans, fifty miles away at the New Hampshire State Prison for Men, was stabbed in the side by a fellow inmate with a four-inch shard of broken glass. It was most likely a case of mistaken identity; Omar didn't know the man who did it.

The glass entered below his right ribs, and as I walked back up the hill to campus worrying about myself and Jerome and griping about the cold, Omar was taken by prison ambulance—meaning two inmates dispatched with a gurney—to the infirmary.

Around the time I opened the doors to Quincy and felt the blast of the radiator heat, they were examining him visually, probing the wound with instruments. They did no scan to check for organ laceration, no X-ray to check for remaining glass. They cleaned out the cut, sutured him, gave him a tetanus shot and a topical antibiotic and not enough gauze. They told him he'd be allowed 600 milligrams of ibuprofen every eight hours.

Sometime late that morning, as we sat in class discussing him like a character in a movie, he tried to sit up in his infirmary bed and passed out from the pain.

In class that day, purple-haired Lola announced, "My uncle says he knows you."

"Yeah?"

"He was your year. His name is Mike Stiles."

"Your uncle is *Mike Stiles*?"

I wondered if Lola had looked through the 1995 yearbook, found the hottest guy there, and was messing with me.

"He's my mom's little brother."

They didn't appear to be joking. I said, "No *way*."

"He said you were cool but scary."

"Scary! I mean—I wore a lot of black, I guess."

"Anyways, he says hi."

I wondered what was happening to my face. It felt hot.

"What's he up to now?" I asked, although I already knew from the internet—the same google spree that had led me to your Providence school that first time—that he was a professor at the University of Connecticut, specializing in US foreign relations, and that he hadn't even had the courtesy to grow a dad bod.

Mike hadn't stood out academically at Granby; either he'd been hiding it, or something clicked in college. Until he joined *Camelot*, we'd all assumed his brain was made of snow.

He came back from senior Thanksgiving in a full-leg cast, femur shattered in a bike accident, and chose to do the winter musical rather than endure the indignity of PE. It turned out he could sing and act; he beat out the regular theater boys for King Arthur. And he came in humble and sweet, not mugging from the stage, like most jocks did, so everyone knew this was a joke.

His cast came off a week before opening night, and backstage he showed us the pale, hairless skin of his left leg, dared people to touch it.

But by that point, my official crush on Mike Stiles was already over. It had come to an abrupt halt one night the previous spring on an Open Dorm night in Lambeth when Fran and I passed his room (door open the regulation ninety degrees). He sprawled on his bed, long legs toward the door, feet bare. Above him, posters of Kate Moss and Winona Ryder. Waifish girls with hollowed cheeks and plumped lips, girls whose elbows were the widest part of their arms. He wanted a girl he could carry on one shoulder. I understood I was no longer allowed to like Mike Stiles. I was too fat, too messy, too chipmunk-cheeked to like Mike Stiles.

I wasn't about to tell my students any of this, but for the rest of class I kept looking for any resemblance between Lola's soft, full face and Mike Stiles's chiseled one.

Mike Stiles had been prominent on the Dick List, the document Carlotta and Sakina John had started junior year. Carlotta had drawn a remarkable likeness of his face next to the entry about his dick.

I recognize my hypocrisy. I still seethe when I think of Thalia Bingo, but I laugh unguiltily when I remember this document that detailed everything we knew about any guy's junk. It didn't matter if the boys went to Granby; if any of us (me, Carlotta, Sakina, Fran, Sakina's friend Jade, Carlotta's roommate Dani, who'd pierced her own nose) had any intel, it went on the grid. There were boxes for length, girth, curve, balls.

I contributed details about Brian Wynn, the boy I'd quasi slept with in Indiana that summer, and his rodent-like penis, which lay on his stomach half-hard and pulsing. Carlotta messed around with a few Granby boys but was always still dating one or two from home. Sakina—to the distaste of her father, the first Black Granby alum on the Board of Trustees—spent all four years attached to Marco Washington, who was always in trouble. Marco filled her in on the dick of every boy in

Lambeth, since the boys in the dorms saw each other not only in the shower but also, apparently, on not infrequent occasion, fully erect—a joke, a performance, a threat. So Marco shared that Kellan TenEyck was hung like a Coke can and Blake Oxford, who had it bad enough already, was tiny and uncut. *Pinky finger,* Sakina wrote on the list, and drew a picture of what she imagined. Under Mike Stiles's name, Sakina wrote, *Even Marco is jealous.*

I wasn't particularly friends with Sakina, who played Morgan le Fay in *Camelot* and Chiffon in *Little Shop* and Rizzo in *Grease* and seemed destined for Broadway fame—though in reality she wound up an ob-gyn—but when Carlotta started a band and got Sakina involved, they ended up close, and she would join us in the Singer-Baird common for *My So-Called Life.* I was always worried she was judging me, and she probably was, yet later she ended up one of the people I kept in closest contact with—at first because we were both in New York, and then because our oldest kids were born the same day.

The list lived in Carlotta's dresser. No one else was supposed to know (not even Marco; he told Sakina about everyone's dick just for fun), but senior year, on our morning walk to the mattresses, I filled Geoff in. Geoff seemed only amused, especially once I assured him he wasn't on it. He said, "You need to add me. *Please.* Can you make me nine inches long with the balls of a god?" For weeks, he'd mouth it to me in the hall or the dinner line: *balls of a god.* Is it wrong if that still cracks me up? Unlike the bingo sheet, our list didn't put anyone in danger, didn't turn anyone into a ring to be grabbed.

Plus, dicks were in our faces, figuratively or literally, whether we wanted them there or not. I never sought out a dick, hoping to see it, until college. But here they were. Even nervous Brian Wynn, that summer, had been the one to undo his belt, push my head down with his sweaty hand. Dorian Culler exposed himself to me three times. Once was in the back hallway of the gym. He'd passed where I sat on the floor studying, then returned with a couple of friends, already laughing. He said, "Bodie, when you snuck into my room last night you left a bite mark on my cock." He pulled it out the top of his gym shorts and managed a confused, wounded look. Instinctively, I held my hand up to block my view—he was only a few feet away—and he said, "God, Bodie, look at you reaching for me again. You're insatiable. And when I'm wounded! I need medical attention." I chastised myself for doing the wrong thing. What would the right thing have been? They left, but I had a feeling they'd be back so I scooped up my books and found another floor to sit on.

Which is all to say: Documenting the dicks of Granby felt more like revenge than predation.

I tried to imagine Jerome whipping it out in front of Jasmine Wilde. But no, Jerome was not Dorian. I tried to imagine Jerome pulling her onto his lap at an after-party. I tried to imagine him saying, "You should come by my studio tonight; I'll give you some pointers." Or "You know I can make or break people in this world."

Just because you can't picture someone doing something doesn't mean they aren't capable of it.

All of this went through my head in the time it took Lola to find a photo of Mike on their laptop—his official shot from the UConn website—and show the class.

Britt was bouncing in her corner seat. "Can I interview him? Lola, can I interview him?"

Lola shrugged.

I said, "He knew Thalia pretty well. He'd know Omar, too. He was an athlete."

Mike would have more to say than I had: Another ski star, he was one of Robbie Serenho's best friends. He'd been both in the show and at the mattresses. He'd likely spoken to the police at much greater length than me. Plus, if he talked to Britt he'd see how obsessed she was, and, if news of the podcast got out to my classmates, he could maybe vouch for the fact that I hadn't put her up to this.

Lola said to Britt, "I mean, I can give you his email."

We caught up on everyone's projects and talked editing, since the first of their first episodes would be due the next morning.

Alder had a convoluted idea about convincing listeners his podcast consisted of rediscovered tapes from 1938, tricking them the way *War of the Worlds* had tricked people. Alyssa, the one covering Arsareth Gage Granby, kept falling asleep. I couldn't blame her: She sat in front of the radiator, framed by a window that bathed her in morning sun. I was jealous.

Britt had tried reaching out to Omar himself, through his lawyer, but hadn't heard back. She'd decided to structure the podcast around unanswered questions. How exactly did that emergency pool exit work, in 1995, and who else might have had access to the building? What influence did the school have over the State Police? What were the circumstances of Omar's confession? Was Thalia sleeping with her music teacher? Okay, no, not that last one. Not yet.

That afternoon, I had the film kids think about flashback. I showed them, to start, the wavy-screen memory intros from the *Wayne's World* sketches of my own adolescence. Then I showed cheesy jump cuts from *Lost*. Also before their time, as ancient to them as the clips of *Rashomon* I showed next.

We talked about the difference between a character remembering, and the camera as impartial eye on the actual past.

Jimmy Stewart was dreaming, falling, his head floating in fields of vertiginous color.

Fellini's traffic jam gave way to flight.

Their assignment that night was to watch *Memento*, to come in with notes and thoughts.

"You're going to watch it on your phones, aren't you," I said as they stood to leave.

They shrugged. My bright-bulb kid said, "When you hold it close to your face, it's as good as a theater."

I was scared to check my phone, didn't want more bad news about Jerome coming through the screen. But I looked, and it was worth it: Yahav wrote that he could come up Saturday—the day after tomorrow. I'd been thinking I wouldn't see him, steeling myself with a lifetime's accrual of getting-over-men skills. But yes, he could drive up Saturday, and "maybe walk around" and had "three hours at most."

I could sense my proximity panicking him. Since August, I'd been just my electronic self, nudes in his phone, words and pixels. And now here I was, shaking him from his moorings. But I found myself uncharacteristically helpless to leave him alone. It had something to do with Yahav being the only man with whom I'd ever first been friends and *then* lovers—so I was stuck to him on two levels, which hadn't even happened between me and Jerome. Jerome and I met when he shot me sexy-eyes at a friend's gallery opening. Our first conversation was loaded with innuendo, him teasing me for eating the olive out of my martini before it had time to soak up the vodka. I wonder now how I'd have felt about that encounter had I been a young artist, had I already known Jerome's work and worried about impressing him. Wasn't my notion of him the purer one, though? I'd seen him for what he was: a wildly confident, wildly insecure flirt.

But with Yahav: It was like we'd been scored open and *then* stuck together, and his absence was a raw wound.

The need I felt would have been fascinating, were it not so painful.

I wrote back: *I will take you on a tour of my adolescence. Beware.*

Following his failed appeal in '99, Omar's family had launched the Free Omar website. I'd seen it briefly years ago, after *Dateline* discussed it; when I pulled it up in my darkening guest room before dinner, I found it relatively unchanged. It seemed that after that initial flood of publicity, online interest had drifted from activism into true crime gossip. The *Spider-Man* actress left to chase new causes, and the Dane Rubras of the world stepped in.

The home page led with childhood photos of Omar: ears too big for his head, toes buried in sand, smile a yard wide. In Web 1.0 neon purple on a black background, his family stated their case: Omar was coerced into a false confession. The evidence against him was questionable. Other suspects weren't investigated.

There was a link for donations, an email address for tips.

There was a page labeled "A Prayer for Thalia." It read: *We pray for the soul and family of Thalia Keith, beloved daughter and treasured child of God. She left earth too soon. We pray for her spirit to guide us to truth, and to justice for herself and Omar.* There was that same photo of her, the one cropped from the tennis team shot.

Another page gave the details of the case. I hadn't gotten this far last time, but I had an hour till Fran would pick me up—we had plans to eat out, while Anne stayed home with the boys—and I'd rather read the website than the seven texts Lance had sent since he'd written me back that morning asking if we should block all the Jasmine supporters tagging the podcast.

I started clicking, skimming. Here were transcripts of the initial trial, made in preparation for the failed appeal. Here was Omar's recanted confession, with footnotes pointing out inconsistencies.

After a short list of evidence entered by the defense in court—you could click through to see Omar's office phone records, for instance—came a much longer list of documents and items entered by the prosecution, plus ones handed over during discovery. This included all the photos from the mattress party—presumably proof that nineteen of Thalia's closest friends were accounted for all night and didn't need looking into. What horrible photos. Red-eyed students washed out by flash. The kind of shots that, these days, you'd instantly erase from your phone. But here these kids remained, forever drinking in the woods, forever overexposed. I couldn't imagine what good the shots did Omar's case, why his family would put them up online, but then this archive seemed comprehensive.

I recognized almost all the kids.

Robbie Serenho. He's in many of the night's photos, in his gold Granby Ski sweatshirt, jeans, Red Sox cap.

Bendt Jensen, our Danish exchange student, Lancelot to Beth's Guinevere. Everyone was in love with him.

Vishwas Singh, the kid we called Fizz—so named because freshman year he'd shaken a bottle of wine, like salad dressing, before opening it. When people laughed, screamed at him to stop, he said, confidently, "No, it's *beer* you don't shake." He somehow still became popular, got elected class president our sophomore year. In one photo he's holding a cigarette in each hand, arms out like a scarecrow.

Rachel Popa, Beth Docherty, and Donna Goldbeck, posing like Charlie's Angels. Beth, like Bendt and Sakina John and Mike Stiles, is fresh from the *Camelot* stage. Sakina still wears her Morgan le Fay makeup, the long wings of eyeliner. The fact that Mike's cast had just come off put a speed limit on the night; the group couldn't have run down the trail either there or back.

Dorian Culler. There's a shot of just him, leaning against a tree, eyes closed, long eyelashes against pale cheeks, mouth open to talk. He might have been good-looking, if he weren't so terrible.

Asad Mirza—a devout Muslim back then, so there was at least one sober account of the mattress party.

A few other skiers and ski-adjacent people whose faces didn't mean much to me anymore.

The kid taking the pictures was Jimmy Scalzitti—a skier who'd used one of the expensive yearbook Pentaxes for curtain-call shots of *Camelot*, also unhelpfully shown on the website. He then used most of the rest of the film in the woods. He must have started shooting only once he was drunk enough not to think twice about documenting underage drinking with a school camera.

The kids had built a flashlight bonfire, meaning they'd turned on their Granby-issued pocket lights and some bigger heavy-duty ones and arranged them like kindling in a big pile, illuminating the clearing.

I'd seen one of these shots before, the one they showed on *Dateline*: Robbie looking over his shoulder at the camera, Sakina and Beth leaning together laughing in the background, Dorian twisting his hands into some joke approximation of a gang sign. There are beer bottles in that shot, a few cigarette glows: the perfect visual encapsulation of mild teenage debauchery.

I remembered that the film was still in the Pentax, and still in Jimmy's dorm room, when the State Police started nosing around; that was when Jimmy brought the film to Geoff and asked if he could develop it before his interview. "I just want to clear the air for Serenho," Geoff told us he said. He asked Geoff if there was a way to cut any alcohol and cigarettes from the shots—but then the school promised disciplinary immunity for anyone forthcoming about drugs or drinking that night, so it didn't matter.

Geoff told me he was keeping the negatives and making duplicates to hang on to. "Like—of course I keep them, right?" he said, and it seemed perfectly logical: What if Scalzitti threw it all away, and it turned out to be important? "Plus," Geoff said, "it's yearbook film."

For some reason, Jimmy Scalzitti had turned on the timestamp, rendering the *Camelot* photos useless for yearbook unless Geoff cropped them, but making the shots of the mattress party tremendously helpful for establishing a timeline of the night. Or, more specifically—and a dozen online theories sprang from this, I already knew—Jimmy had only the *date* stamp on during the show, but somehow, by the first party shots, had toggled the timestamp on as well. *A little too convenient*, some people's thinking went. Others argued that a drunk kid taking photos in the woods, in the slush and cold, had probably just messed up the switch.

I found myself leaving the Free Omar site and looking on Reddit for threads about the roll of film.

(If you care, Mr. Bloch: Fifty miles away, Omar was only then being allowed his second dose of ibuprofen. They finally changed his soaked gauze. It was too early for any signs of infection. He had not yet developed a fever.)

There were so many Reddit threads. I found, among other things, a theory that Thalia had been murdered at the mattresses by all nineteen kids, a satanic sacrifice. Another poster noted that Tim Busse's eyes were buggy and bloodshot. *That kid is coked out of his mind*, NotYoPaulie82 wrote. *Capable of anything.* But that was just how Tim looked.

There was a long thread just about the splatter of mud up the back of Robbie's ski sweatshirt, some people insisting it was blood. *So you're saying*, reads a reply with hundreds of upvotes, *that he not only killed Thalia and threw her in the pool in the TEN MINUTES between the musical and the party, but he did it BEHIND HIS OWN BACK? Ginger Rogers has nothing on this guy.*

This was all based on the second party photo, a candid, poorly composed group shot. Most threads were obsessed with the timing and order of the pictures. The first photo from the mattresses, stamped 9:58 p.m., is of the ground, a blurred coat, some legs. After the mud splatter one, a 10:02 shot shows Robbie with his arms around Beth and Dorian, tongue out, a mad devil grin. In that one Robbie has his hat on, but in others you can see his hair shaved up the sides, long and floppy on top, parted in the middle. ("The penis cut," Fran had called it. But in 1995 it was on trend.)

The show had ended by 8:45 at the absolute earliest. Let's say fifteen minutes for the *Camelot* kids to shed their costumes; for Mike, at least, to wash the makeup off. A few minutes to gather friends who hadn't been in the audience, for Beth to stuff a backpack with bottles from under her bed, for others to grab flashlights, cigarettes, lighters. Everything procured from the girls' dorms, because the boys' dorms were down on Lower Campus. The boys stood outside waiting for the girls. They headed the 1.4 miles from the theater up the Nordic trail to the mattresses no faster than Mike could hobble—about a half-hour trek. Then the first photos around ten p.m., party already in full swing. That's where the Reddit responder got his "ten minutes" thinking. Someone might have had a few minutes to run off and do *something*, but not enough time to critically injure someone, change her clothes, get her into the water.

According to the state, within the time of the party Thalia had headed from the theater to the gym to meet Omar, to wait for him until he got off his office phone at 10:02 p.m. They believed she was dead before curfew. And I agreed: If she wasn't back in the dorm by eleven, something had already happened. Thalia might have broken rules, but never something she'd automatically get caught for. She wouldn't have missed check-in.

Most of the rest of the photos (twenty-one of the thirty-six shots were taken in the woods) were spread out over the next forty minutes; the last of these, at 10:39, shows Fizz downing a can of Pabst.

The kids who were there said in their statements that that's when someone noticed the time. They scrambled back down the trail, Jimmy Scalzitti falling and twisting his ankle. The girls made it back to the dorms at five after, and the boys, who had to cross to Lower Campus still, and had an injured Jimmy and a still-fragile Mike with them, were twelve minutes late. They got heat from Mr. Dar, but they all checked in together.

Another Reddit theory went that Robbie killed her later that night, that the two of them sneaked out of their dorms to meet. *He just seems the type,* one person wrote. *Spoiled kid, has a tantrum when something goes wrong. He finds out she's screwing Omar, flips out.* There were reasons this was impossible, one of which was that Mr. Dar, who'd been on duty in Lambeth, vouched that after checking in, Robbie stayed in the common room playing Madden Football till midnight, when he had to be upstairs in his room. And Mr. Dar wasn't one to go to bed early and rely on the door alarms to keep kids inside. He would famously set up a card table on the stairway landing and sit grading history papers in his little panopticon till two in the morning.

The last three shots were from the next Tuesday: Jimmy's dorm room floor—laundry and textbooks and pilfered dining hall dishes—as he quickly finished off the roll.

I'd missed a text from Fran: *Where are you?? I'm outside.* Another: *Are you sleeping with that guy? Get your ass down here.* I leapt up to brush my hair. It was a quarter past. I had lost myself.

#3: ROBBIE SERENHO

He has split himself in two.

There's a Robbie Serenho who goes to the mattress party, who's captured on film, seen by friends, who checks in only twelve minutes late, who shows up at breakfast the next morning and jokes around and finds out that afternoon with the rest of us that Thalia's dead. This is the Robbie who loves Thalia, the Robbie who'll be a decent father and teach his kids to ski.

But there's a second Robbie, the entitled jock, the one who's gotten everything the easy way, the one who can't control his anger or his fists, the one whose hard edges come out when he drinks. This is the Robbie who meets Thalia outside the theater.

The first Robbie takes off with his friends while the second Robbie needs to ask Thalia about all the time she's been spending with you. He noticed something tonight, when he snuck backstage before the show. He saw you leaning too close to Thalia, your hand on her elbow. He noticed the way she looked at you, tilting her face down, her eyes up. He lingered backstage, tried to get her attention during her scene, which made her turn her head to the wings and mouth *What?* He goes to sit in the audience then and seethe. Dorian leans over to tell him one of his Thalia jokes. "Your girlfriend's not a slut," he says. "She's just a volunteer prostitute."

Robbie's backstage again at curtain call, beckoning her into the wings.

He says, "Let's go for a walk."

He interrogates her, won't stop asking about you. He's drunk. There were Poland Spring bottles full of cheap vodka floating around the audience, and Robbie, for all he drinks, can't hold his liquor. While the other Robbie sips his first beer at the mattresses, flashing the camera a peace sign, this Robbie is wasted.

They end up behind the gym, and Thalia tells him she has to leave because she needs the bathroom. But there's a bathroom in the gym, he tells her. He has a master key in his pocket, because he always does—and this back door accepts it, doesn't need the special pool door key. The exit alarm doesn't sound. (Things always work out for Robbie.) They go through the pool, quietly, quietly, and down the hall—not past Omar's office, where the door is open and the light is on, but just into the girls' locker room, where Robbie won't stop asking questions even while she pees.

She takes so long that he steps into a shower stall with his clothes on, turns on the water. He must have fallen asleep for a second, leaning against the wall, because she's in here now with him, slapping his cheek, telling him to wake up.

If they're in the shower they might as well have sex, and he tries to take her wet clothes off.

She gets mad and yells, pushes him away. She's making too much noise. He asks why she won't have sex, asks if it's because she already had sex with someone today, asks if that person was you.

She tells him he's an idiot and tries to leave the shower stall.

This Robbie grabs Thalia's neck, shakes her, just wants to shake sense into her, needs to shake her against something hard, against this wet and slippery wall, and he feels like an animal, feels like when he's flying down a hill in snow, when the fire flows into his muscles, when his body is a machine. He doesn't tell his body what to do because it knows, it follows the hill, it follows gravity, and that's what he's doing now, following gravity, until Thalia starts seizing, her eyes rolling back. She slides to the bottom of the stall, the water washing the blood on the wall from red to pink to nothing.

He sobers up, or at least the things in front of him come clear: He needs to fix this. Not fix *her*, because it's too late, she's twitching like she's electrocuted—but fix all of this, this bad movie, this problem, this thing that's befallen him.

He drags her small, wet body out of the locker room and back to the pool, gets her clothes off, gets her into a swimsuit he finds. He has all the time in the world, because meanwhile the other Robbie, the one in the woods, is singing along with the boom box, a falsetto rendition of "Come to My Window." That Robbie is hamming it up, spinning with his arms out, as this Robbie slides Thalia into the pool, knowing, to the extent he knows anything right now, that she's still alive, that what he did in the shower might have been an accident but this is intentional, this is murder, is murder, is murder. He has time to find the bleach, to use it on the pool deck and in the hall—Omar is gone by now, his office light off—and in the locker room. He has time to vomit in the sink, to wash it down the drain, to wash his hands and face.

There are extra clothes in Thalia's backpack—a green sweater, jeans, some underwear—and he folds these neatly on the bench as if this were what she'd worn. He'll take the wet, bloodstained clothes and find a way to burn them.

He slips back out through the emergency exit. In the morning, it occurs to him that he should have left the key with Thalia, given her a plausible way to have entered the pool alone.

But then, this version of Robbie is not the one who'll wake up in the morning, because this Robbie vanishes. He becomes molecular, floats away in the damp March air.

The real Robbie is hurrying back to his dorm now with his friends, crossing North Bridge, happy and only a little drunk and only a little late for check-in.

He'll get married and have kids and live in Connecticut, and he'll never know what he's done.

The Granby Supper Club was exactly as I remembered it, except that in adulthood the excellent wine list was an option, which immensely helped the mediocre food. There's a particular charm to the glass of breadsticks on the table, the man who comes around with the basket of rolls and little tongs. We don't get many bread basket men in LA.

When the carb man left—I managed to pass, to Fran's eye-rolling—I said, "So you called Mr. Bloch a creeper."

"Why, what."

"You remember how we used to think Thalia was involved with him?"

Fran laughed, said, "Wait, do *not* let Britt say that on the podcast. Did I tell you she asked me for an interview? We're doing it Monday."

"But were they sleeping together, you think?"

"No. No! And don't let her say that. Good God. I meant he was too close to the students. I didn't mean he was fucking them."

"But you were right," I said. "Teenagers have a sixth sense for that stuff. I just keep thinking, if we thought it was happening, it was happening—or something was. Maybe not actual sex, but impropriety." I told her about Bethesda Fountain, but it didn't sound convincing.

"I mean," she said, "teenagers also believe wild rumors. Remember how we thought Marco Washington was Denzel's cousin?"

I was frustrated at her backtracking. It wasn't fair for her to plant the seed in my mind, disrupt my sleep all week, then disavow it.

I said, "They spent too much time together. I'd show up for convocation practice and they'd be in there forever with the door closed. Something was off."

Fran nodded. "You're a kid, and you think, That teacher is amazing because he hangs out with us. Like, who *wouldn't* want to hang out with sixteen-year-olds? Then you get older and you think, Huh, that person must not have had a real social life."

"That's not what I'm saying, though."

"Right. But don't say it to Britt. Do *not* let her get into that shit."

She waved at a group entering the room. I spotted Dana Ramos, my old biology teacher, with whom I'd had a pleasant breakfast the day before, asking her over coffee and oatmeal if the kids still did the hula hoop observation in the woods (they did) and if she still made kids sketch (yes) and if they still dissected fetal pigs (it was an option, but a lot of kids opted for a virtual substitute). I was never much for science, but I'd loved her, the way she gave the Greek or Latin roots of every term, the way she insisted we say zo-ology instead of zoo-ology. "It's the study of *life*," she'd say. "Not zoos." The way she articulated *photosynthesis*, as if speaking the private name of God. I loved the poetry of leaves converting sunlight to glucose and oxygen. And I loved the idea of adaptations, the ways plants battled for access to the sun: sprouting early or unfurling enormous leaves to catch more light or bearing tiny needles that hardly wanted any. "They're specializing," Dana said, "in much the same way you'll all specialize on your college applications."

Dana and the four other women in her party sat, already in animated conversation. They'd brought gift bags; it was someone's birthday.

Fran said, "So what's the gist of Britt's podcast, exactly?"

I grimaced, unsure how she'd take it. "That Omar was wrongfully convicted."

Fran nodded slowly. Our wine showed up, and when we both had a full glass and the waiter had scuttled off, she said, "But they're not actually, like, broadcasting these, are they?"

"They'll be available online."

"I mean—you're not going to amplify this anywhere. It won't get out and cause a shitstorm?"

"God," I said. "I don't know. She could throw some video up tomorrow that goes viral."

Fran looked irritated enough that I wondered if she'd brought me here just to grill me. She said, "So you think that's true? He's the wrong guy?"

I had been, until now, in a safe, neutral, academic space—or so I'd told myself. I could ask Britt helpful questions, prodding questions, devil's advocate questions. I didn't need answers.

I said, "That's not up to me."

Fran bit straight into her roll rather than tearing a piece off. She said, through her mouthful, "Maybe it is."

"Whether he *did* it?"

"I mean—what Britt does, what you do with it, where you take it." She reached for the chilled bowl of gold-foiled butter packets. She said, "Because just now, it sounded like you think Bloch had something to do with it."

I made high-pitched noises of protest. I said, "He was home with his wife and kids! I'm not suggesting that!"

"I think you're implying that."

"No! He was in the theater with me after the show. Putting everything away."

"I thought you said he was with his wife."

"That was later, it—Jesus. *Fran.* I don't think that at all. You remember how dweeby he was." I heard myself, heard how ridiculous that sounded. But it was true that I couldn't wrap my head around the possibility. The idea of you sleeping with Thalia was already more than I'd wanted to consider.

Fran said, "I know you were attached to him. I don't mean in an inappropriate way. But he showed you a lot of attention. That's what he was good at, right? He recognized people's talents. And not big, obvious things like skiing."

My feet were too hot now in their double socks and snow boots. My

Sangiovese, which the waiter had poured into a glass as big as my head, was already rendering my limbs both leaden and weightless.

I said, "I don't see what that has—"

"Look, I didn't want to put you through stuff, bringing you back. You've seemed so solid, and like—I'm sorry, I don't want you to spiral."

"Who said I was spiraling?"

"Bodie, you look like you haven't slept since you got here. You're still gorgeous, but you look like hell."

I was saved by our food arriving—steak for Fran, an oily vegetable terrine for me. I had a moment to collect myself, to remember that while I'd led twenty-three years of competent adult life since Granby, Fran had seen only a few weeks of me, total, in that time. She didn't understand how far I was from the disaster I'd been senior year.

I said, "I've had several things on my mind. I'm in an emotional swamp." I wasn't ready to talk about Jasmine Wilde's video, so I opted to tell her instead about Yahav, at length.

One of Fran's best traits is that she genuinely wants to hear the whole mess of things. Her eyes light up like she's rewatching her favorite movie.

"The problem is," I said, "it's like I have no sexuality anymore except for Yahav, like other men might as well be old women. Look at me, excelling at monogamy when it's least appropriate."

She asked if she could meet him on Saturday, at least arrange to cross paths with us on campus.

Dana Ramos had left her table and her increasingly raucous group and was swaying toward us, a glass of yellow wine glowing in her hand. She said, too loudly, "You two catching up? What's the latest?" Dana's hair had become frizzier since she'd entered the restaurant.

I could see Fran mentally rewinding to the last nonprivate thing we'd mentioned. She said, "We were talking about Denny Bloch. You remember him? He taught music?"

"Sure, he was only here a year or two."

"Three years," Fran said. "I remember because he came when we were sophomores, and he got some going-away prize at Senior Day."

I said, "They gave him a prize for leaving?"

"Oh," Dana said, "he was off to teach in Russia. No, Bulgaria. I'm sure they gave him a Granby scarf or something. That poor wife."

"Why?"

"Oh, just—well, who wants to move to Bulgaria?"

I'd somehow forgotten that you'd moved to Bulgaria. Bulgaria! At the time it hadn't seemed any stranger than seniors heading to college in California or Colorado or even Scotland, all of which sounded exotic to me.

Dana steadied herself on our table with one tented hand. She said, "I remember he left us in the lurch. Have the good grace to announce your departure in January, for the love of Pete, so we can get a decent replacement. The woman they found was just awful. But that's who's looking for a job in May."

"In May," I said dumbly, and I did remember you telling me right before graduation that you were "graduating too," surprise, surprise.

Dana said, "Then he came back and was teaching in Providence, and I don't know after that. Gordon Dar was in touch with him, but then Gordon retired. Those young teachers come and go so *fast*. Faster than the students, sometimes!"

"His kids must be grown," Fran said.

Dana said, "He was a funny one. I remember he taught that opera course. I couldn't believe kids signed up."

Fran said, "Did you ever find him a bit sketchy? Regarding the students?"

Dana took her hand off the table, stepped back and likely regretted it, pitching forward again to support her weight on the back of Fran's chair. "*Nooooo!* Denny Bloch? No, not at all! Oh, he was a sweetheart. I think," she said, "I think it's become so *trendy*, don't you? To accuse people of things."

Fran locked wide eyes with me, a look I'd known since 1991: trying not to laugh and trying not to scream. And a small part of me said, silently, "Yes, Dana, I agree, because since when is a thirty-six-year-old consensually dating a twenty-one-year-old grooming or assault?" and a larger part of me said, also silently, "You don't know what you're talking about and I'm increasingly concerned that Mr. Bloch was having sex with Thalia Keith from 1994 to 1995." What I said aloud was, "Tell me about the desserts here. Do you have a favorite?"

Dana eventually tilted back to her own table, and we ordered baklava and an ill-advised second bottle of Sangiovese.

Fran said, "Just promise me you aren't bringing him into this."

"Who?"

"Denny Bloch. Into the podcast. That would be really dumb."

"I told you, I'm not accusing him of anything."

"You just think Thalia was sleeping with Robbie *and* Omar *and* Mr. Bloch. That's a lot of people for someone kind of straightlaced."

"She was never sleeping with Omar," I said.

"Interesting. So you don't think he did it."

I said, "He could have done it without sleeping with her! And there are other possibilities, anyway. There's the guy who killed Barbara Crocker in the '70s, for instance."

I was a little drunk. Maybe a lot drunk.

I was also starting to wake up to the fact that, in my mind, for the past twenty-three years, Thalia Keith had been stalled out at seventeen as someone more sophisticated than me. But I was a mother now, for Christ's sake, and in ten years Leo would be as old as Thalia had been when she died. I was working with these sweet students, and they were brilliant, but they were also babies. And Omar—Omar had been a baby himself. I needed to stop seeing him as the worldly guy I'd perceived at the time, someone who surely could have handled himself in the face of police interrogation.

I said, "There was so much evidence against Omar. It's just that there have always been unanswered questions, too. Don't you think?"

What if, for instance, none of her friends had known about you and her? What if they'd been so invested in the romance of Thalia-and-Robbie that they couldn't see what her life was? It was possible—it was possible!—that I knew things they hadn't.

Fran said, "Right, but it's not *Perry Mason*. We're never gonna have some flashback scene."

"Do you ever think about Omar in prison? Like, as you're living your life, do you—"

"I think about Thalia in the ground," she said. "My first year at Reed, that whole year I kept wondering how long it takes a body to decompose. I kept wondering if her skin was gone yet."

"Jesus."

"That's what I think about. Forgive me if I don't have a ton of sympathy for the guy whose DNA was all over her."

I tried my hardest to change the subject.

"I wonder what happened to the Dick List" was what I came up with. "We should donate it to the archives."

"They should put it in that display case in the admissions office!"

"They should at least publish it in the alumni magazine."

Fran said, "I bet Carlotta still has it. We should put it up on one of those creepy-ass websites about Thalia. *Hey, here's some relevant info about dick size!*"

"I wonder," I said, maybe too seriously, "if someone still has the Thalia Bingo sheet."

Fran stopped laughing. "You're obsessed. You're getting obsessed."

"I was trying not to. But is it such a bad thing? You know when the time was to pretend not to care? Adolescence. That's when I had the energy to pretend I didn't care."

"Do you think—"

"What."

"Nothing. Just, do you think—I know you had some crazy trauma in your childhood. And then you got here, and senior year was such a nightmare. I feel bad that I wasn't sensitive to how hard it must have hit you. I just thought, since you weren't friends . . . Like, I assumed you going off the deep end senior year was about your family. But Thalia's death must've felt personal."

I wanted to shout that she was wrong, and I also wanted to melt to a puddle and tell her she was right.

I said, more calmly, "I appreciate that. But honestly? I think that's the reason I didn't let myself care. I'd already had personal tragedies, and this was not a personal tragedy. It belonged to other people. When, Fran—what if I should have cared more? What if it would have made a *difference* if I cared more?"

"You mean if you told the police they should look at Denny Bloch?"

"No, just—I could have mentioned Thalia Bingo, which—not that it was illegal, but wouldn't the police want to know something like that? I could've—"

And then I remembered what I'd realized the night before, that perhaps I'd already done too much, that sharing that detail about Thalia circling the dumpsters might have been an overstep.

Here was the waiter, finally, having realized things weren't going to calm down at our table. I shooed Fran's hand from the bill and gave him my Sapphire card, a weird power play. I needed water.

Fran said, "I don't think Thalia Bingo would have helped. It would've been a huge distraction. Can you imagine? *I'm . . . Lester Holt.*" It was a good impersonation, both serious and Kermit-y. *"And this . . . is a sexual bingo card."*

I laughed, my steam gone.

Fran and I realized neither of us should drive back, even that short distance, so she texted her friend Amber, a Latin teacher. We waited for her in the Supper Club's vestibule.

Fran had wrapped herself already in her scarf, parka, mittens, hat. Through her scarf she said, "Here's my concern about Britt. I know the better narrative is that Omar was the victim of racist cops, but sometimes—it's Occam's razor, right? The guy who was stalking her is the one who killed her."

"How do we know he was stalking her?" I had a mint disc in my mouth from the hostess stand.

"People had those stories," she said. "Like, he called the dorm phone a million times. He'd wait for her outside the dining hall. He'd come to tennis matches."

"Did you ever see it?"

"What, I was besties with Thalia? Her friends saw it."

I said—and it's not as if I'd thought about this much, I was doing the math for the first time—"Did you hear these stories before she died, or after?"

"After? I guess? But—"

"Right. Because everyone wants to be part of the action. Something like this happens, and everyone has a story, one time they saw something important." Like me, with the dumpsters.

Fran said, "Or maybe it was one of those things it turned out everyone knew all along. And Bodie, remember: There was DNA."

"Right," I said. I'd actually forgotten, for a moment. "There was DNA."

A Honda Civic pulled up, flashed its lights.

Fran said, "That's Amber. And listen: I love you even when you're a mess."

29

Here's a joke for you.

Two girls and a boy walk into a bar. They're not supposed to be there.

One of the girls is a round-faced quasi goth; one is loud and laughing, frumpy in overalls, Sharpied mandalas on the backs of her hands. The boy is wiry and alert, always tilted forward, looking for his next wisecrack like an animal watching for prey.

The bar is in Kern, and while it's indeed a bar, they also serve fried cheese in baskets, mountains of nachos—so at least until the drinks are in front of them, the kids have plausible deniability.

The punch line is coming. Wait for it.

The boy bellies up and orders, because although he's short he has a full chin of stubble, a decent fake ID, a voice like a rolling barrel of rocks. He orders three gin and tonics and the nachos, returns triumphant with his fingers around three glasses full of what might, passably, be Sprite and lime.

He says, "Give me your swizzle sticks," and tosses them under the table.

The loud girl says, "Is it supposed to be this sweet?"

The teacher who drove the Dragon Wagon into Kern has told them she'll be at the Chinese restaurant, that if they're not back at the van in the Hannaford lot at eight sharp she's leaving without them, although they can't imagine this is true.

The boy is worried the teacher will stop by the bar.

"She has to stay put," the goth girl assures him, "because if she, like, roves around town, no one can find her in an emergency."

Other kids have taken off in other directions. A group of girls went into the grocery store; two boys went Lord knew where to smoke; some kids went for pizza; the star skier and his girlfriend headed in the direction of the diner that's only good for pancakes.

But: Here they are now. A skier and a dead girl walk into the bar. The dead girl doesn't know she's dead.

"Oh, shit," the loud girl whispers, and the three of them angle into their booth and away from the bar, where the dead girl and the skier stand to order, but they still watch what happens.

The skier's hand is on the small of her back, as it so often is. ("It's great that he offers her such lumbar support," the boy whispers.)

The skier speaks to the bartender, and the bartender leans forward, both hands on the bar, asking something, eyebrows raised. The skier is arguing now, the bartender laughing, shaking his head. He's not going to serve them, no way. The skier pats his empty back pocket; the dead girl makes a show of looking in her little blue purse. Nope.

The boy in the booth says, "How does Serenho not have an ID?"

The dead girl pulls the skier's arm; she wants to go. He pushes her hand away, says "Get the fuck off me!" loud enough that these kids hear it.

The dead girl storms past the booth to the bathrooms. The skier turns on his heel and leaves.

The kids in the booth whisper about what happened, but they're on other topics by the time the dead girl emerges, glassy eyes scanning the bar. Then she sees them and composes herself, stops at their table.

"How are *you* all?" she says. Poised, nearly passing as happy.

She picks up the boy's glass, sniffs it, takes a sip. "Naughty, naughty!" she says, and wags a finger at him. "How did you—"

The boy turns red. He says, "I can, uh—I actually make fake IDs. I have a laminator in the darkroom. If you ever—"

The dead girl laughs. Then she says, "Oh my God, wait, could you make one for Robbie?"

"Yeah." The boy shrugs. "I'd just need him to come in for a picture."

"Shoot, no," she says. "I want to surprise him. What if—what if I brought you a picture, like from an old bus pass or something?"

"It would be way less convincing," the boy says, "but I could try."

His friends know he usually charges fifty dollars a card, but he doesn't mention money.

She says, "Could you do it by next weekend? Because next Monday is his birthday."

The boy nods. "I'll be there all day Saturday. I can do one for you, too, if you want."

When the dead girl leaves, the loud girl will say, "Oh my God, you were like, *Come pose for me! Be my muse!*" and the goth girl will crack up.

But right now the dead girl is thanking him, saying a week is surely enough time to find a decent photo of the skier, or maybe she can take one herself on some pretext. She says, "Did you see where Dorian went?" and the goth girl feels a fist in her stomach at the name, at the suggestion that she would track Dorian Culler's movements. She knows he went to smoke, but doesn't say it. "I'm gonna go find Dorian," the dead girl says, as if making up her mind to do something wild and brave. "If Robbie comes back, tell him that." She says, "Okay, Geoff, next Saturday." Then she walks out the door, and as soon as she's gone, the boy's friends launch into imitations of her and him both.

Oh, wait, the punch line:

The dead girl will never get her ID, because by Saturday she'll be dead.

30

If you're going to drink too much and feel like crap the next day, the least your body can do is pass out early so you can sleep it off. But mine refused. I ran a bath and sank into it with a sheet mask on, the room dark except for my phone. My head was a mess.

Twitter had been busy—a new post had dozens of retweets, some tagging me:

> *Jerome Wager paid for my drink, when I had NOT asked him to, at an offsite event @ArtBasel Miami, then informed me 2x he'd paid for said drink. Implications were clear.*

This sounded plausible in all but the interpretation—the kind of thing Jerome might have done when buzzed. He'd have seen himself as a humble underdog begging the attention of a beautiful woman. She might have seen him as an established artist asking for an exchange.

Another woman had written:

> *After a friend of mine had her baby, #JeromeWager complimented her figure "snapping back" and looked at her stomach in a way that made her feel sexualized and belittled. I won't name her unless she wants to be named.*

Oh, Jerome. I would have stopped him if I'd seen that, would have explained on the way home why that was inappropriate.

I did have some follow-up questions that would never be answered.

Did he stare? Did he glance? Did he ogle? Did he corner her alone at one a.m. in a bar? Or did he say this in front of other people, other women who might have joined in the chorus? That last was the likeliest. Jerome had a habit of talking like he was one of the girls, something fairly normalized for men in the art world.

Were these tweeters any different from the people who wrote about Thalia? Inserting themselves into someone else's story any way possible?

I understand: It's human instinct to put yourself at the heart of a disaster. Not even for attention, but because it *feels* true. Someone who was supposed to fly the day after 9/11 was, in the retelling, supposed to fly that very day. He was on his way to the airport, in fact. He was *in* the airport. He's not claiming he was booked on one of those flights, nothing like that, he just moves himself a few steps closer to the departure gate.

For some reason, though, with Thalia, I'd had the opposite instinct at the time.

Fran was right: I'd been spiraling all of senior year, but Thalia's death affected me more than I'd ever admitted. That spring was when the water really got down to the drain.

My depression, my insomnia, my self-destructive behavior continued into freshman year of college, and it took ten visits to the free school therapist for Thalia to even come up. (In my defense: There were the dead dad, dead brother, mom in the desert, Mormon foster family to get through first.) I raised it in passing—*my junior year roommate was murdered my senior year of high school*—and the shrink latched onto it like a bone. He wanted to know what it had brought up from my past, how it had contributed to my distrust of men, why I wasn't letting myself grieve.

I said, "We weren't even friends," and he asked me if that mattered. Yes, yes, I told him, it did.

I tossed my sheet mask in the vague direction of the trash and rubbed the remainder of the goo into my skin.

I kept scrolling:

Let's not forget that Jerome Wager's work is terrible + derivative. His Obama mural was racist AF. He's just one of the many scum men who run the planet.

What @wilde_jazz has done is ferocious and brave. If you've been harmed by Jerome Wager, DM me. I will protect your anonymity.

Can someone explain to me how Jerome Wager still has a platform? He's still on Twitter, and @CGRgallery has made NO statement denouncing his actions.

This doesn't seem like abuse to me. It seems like a shitty relationship. Are we canceling people now for being bad at dating?

How on earth was his Obama mural racist?

It's sad this has to be explained to you. Lording power over someone, even "soft power," is structural imbalance. Abuse does not have to equal rape.

Still no statement from @msbodiekane. Hello, @starletpod?

Even if #JeromeWager faces repercussions, the damage is done. How many gallery shows should have gone to other people? How much money has he made wielding his power and keeping others down?

if you need to ask how that mural was racist you're the problem.

We have ONE law in this country about the age of consent, and it's the age of 18. Someone 18 can screw someone 100, and I'm sorry but it's PERFECTLY LEGAL.

Actually some places it's younger but this is not about the age of consent, you absolute dingbat.

I was angry—I was shaking—and I was certain now that my anger had less to do with loyalty to Jerome or concern over his reputation than with the stunning contrast between this easy online outrage and the outrage any one of us should have felt for years over people like you, people like Dorian.

It was like seeing someone hanged for stealing gum when down the street someone else was robbing a bank.

I shouldn't have done anything. Sober, I wouldn't have done anything. But I was not sober. I typed out a thread of messages with my pruning thumbs, posting each after a quick scan for drunken typos:

Has Jasmine Wilde even asked for repercussions? This is a work of art, not, as far as I know, a call to action. 1/

I'm no longer with Jerome Wager, but as a survivor of ACTUAL sexual assault, this all sits wrong with me. Age is not the only form of power. You could argue that working for the gallery, Jasmine had as much career power over him as he had over her. 2/

Are we talking here about the feminism of empowerment, or the feminism of victimhood? Either a 21-year-old woman is an adult who can make her own decisions or a helpless waif who needs our protection against big scary men. Which is it? It can't be both. 3/

Are we saying a 21-year-old woman lacks sexual agency? Lacks the ability to make decisions about her own body? Whose permission does she need to date someone older? Her father's? This is infantilizing. 4/

What age range WOULD be acceptable to all of you? Is five years older okay? Is one year older okay? One month? 5/

That said, Jasmine has created an evocative piece of art. Let's leave it at that: art, not a call for a Twitter mob. 6/6

I stopped myself, because my blood pressure was only going up, and I hadn't run any of this by Jerome and there were already replies coming in that I didn't want to read. I managed not to slip on the floor, managed to make it to the bed.

31

I didn't really sleep, just rested my body and fitfully sobered up.

Across the state, Omar was awake this whole night too; this is when he removed his own gauze and made his pillowcase into a kind of bandage, lying on his stomach so it would stay pressed to the wound. But soon the blood had soaked that through as well. His heart rate was elevating, and he thought he recognized the symptoms of shock, which was odd when he hadn't been in shock that morning.

From this vantage point, I'd love to believe it was some psychic sympathy for Omar's pain that kept me up—but in fact it was largely the stupid fact that my thighs still itched, which made me think of bedbugs, which made me think of the time Thalia and I both got bedbugs and dealt with it on our own, which made me think about how smack between childhood and adulthood we'd been.

Lance, my cohost, asked once if boarding school kids were more mature, living away from home. I said, "I doubt it," and didn't remind him that I'd essentially been on my own, at least emotionally, from age eleven.

Oddly, I remember the bedbug incident with relative fondness. I was grateful, for one, that Thalia didn't blame me, didn't assume the infestation couldn't have started in her Ralph Lauren sheets and down pillows.

She sat up in bed one morning that winter and said, "What the fuck is *this*?" It occurred to me that it was the first time I'd heard her swear. She stuck a leg out toward me, long and tan in Robbie Serenho's boxers; it was covered in red dots, streaked with blood.

I said, "Oh, I have that, too." I'd been scratching at welts all week, unaware that they were in a different category than the other woes sabotaging my body—the acne, the cramps, the disobedient hair, the split-ting fingernails.

She yelped and jumped out of bed, shook her comforter. She knew right away that it was bedbugs—Thalia seemed to possess boundless adult knowledge, things like how to steam clothes and how to fix our stubborn radiator—and we grabbed the bedding off both beds and ran to the laundry room at the end of the hall. She stuffed everything in the dryer and turned it on full blast, then looked down at her own tank top and boxers, at my flannel pajama bottoms and Lemonheads T-shirt, and said, "Clothes, too."

I realize how like the start of a porno it sounds, two teenagers about to disrobe, but in reality it was embarrassing and hilarious and awful and utterly nonsexual. Plus—and I should not have to point this out—we were kids. Even Thalia, the supposed beauty of the year: She was gawky and boyish under her clothes, and I was thrilled, in that moment, to see her imperfections, or what I knew the world would perceive as imperfections—the streak of hair, for instance, above her navel, dark against her skin.

But also: She was too thin. I registered this even through my envy at her thinness; it was too much. Her ribs were more evident than her breasts. Undressing in our room, we'd always been modest. She went behind the open door of her closet, and I usually changed in a bathroom stall. But I understood in that moment that the rumors about the eating disorder were well-founded. She hadn't been this skinny during tennis season. Her winter jeans and sweaters had hidden the slow emergence of bone.

I understood that someone should talk to her about how her ribs were visible not only from the front but the back, how you could count her vertebrae. But that person couldn't be me. A chubby girl couldn't tell a skinny girl she was too thin.

I wouldn't tell anyone else, I decided. I wouldn't tell Fran or Geoff or

Carlotta for gossip, nor (it almost went without thinking) would I tell anyone in authority. This would just be another thing I knew about someone, another piece of information to hoard.

Thalia opened the dryer to hurl her clothes in. She said, "Come on," but she was already turning away, thank God, to look for something to cover herself with. She grabbed a pink towel, not hers, out of a laundry basket, and wrapped herself up. She kept digging and pulled out someone's jeans and sweatshirt, handed them over her shoulder. I'd taken the opportunity of her turned back to undress as quickly as I could, and now I held the pilfered clothes in front of my breasts, in front of the stomach I thought looked like pocked bread dough. There were muscles under there from crew, but you'd never know it. It occurred to me at the same moment it must have occurred to Thalia that the clothes might not fit me. But before I had time to register this new embarrassment, she'd swept them back from me, whipped off the towel and handed it over. The towel, mercifully, wrapped all the way around. Thalia threw on the jeans and sweatshirt, added my pajamas to the dryer.

She couldn't get the dryer door closed, and this is when we started laughing. Her dressed in baggy jeans she had to hold up with one hand, stepping back and kicking the contents with a bare foot, kneeing the door until it finally latched. We ran back down the hall shushing each other lest someone come out and see us in their clothes, their towel.

"You know what would be perfect," I said when we'd reached the safety of our own room, "is if it turns out we stole Khristina's stuff." And we laughed harder. It was a wonderful thing, to make her laugh.

We both showered and hurried to get dressed for class, until Thalia looked at her watch and said, "Oh my God, Bodie, it's only 6:50."

I said, "Fanfuckingtastic," and flopped down on my bare mattress.

"What are you *doing*?" Thalia shrieked, and I was back to my clueless, fumbling self, jumping up, brushing my clothes off, while Thalia stood as far from me in the room as she could. We were no longer in it together; she was clean and I was not.

32

My second hangover at Granby in five days: my head all cotton balls and hammers.

I filled a whole thermos with faculty lounge coffee, and grabbed a paper cup of it, too.

I stopped myself from checking Twitter by deleting it from my phone. How satisfying, to watch the little icon vanish along with any replies to my drunken thread.

I walked slowly to class, grateful for the winter air like a giant ice pack around my head.

The kids, too, were subdued at the end of a long week, and Britt in particular seemed down. Omar's attorney had emailed back, saying Omar was not available to comment on his case.

Jamila said, "I could've told you he wouldn't be up for talking to random kids from Granby."

"Sorry," Lola said, "but yeah, another white girl coming in to fuck up his life? I'm sure he's like, no thank you."

Britt sighed, put her head on the table. She said, "I'm not doing this without his voice. That would be so wrong."

Alyssa bustled in late, with donuts from the Granby Bakery. We ate until the table was coated in cinnamon sugar, listening as they all played their first episodes for each other. Britt's featured, in addition to my voice, an interview with Priscilla Mancio, one she'd need to trim.

A few minutes in, Britt asked what she remembered about Omar.

Priscilla said: *Honestly, hardly a thing, before the arrest and trial. The athletic department, they're not in faculty meetings.*

Britt: *What about Robbie Serenho?*

Priscilla: *Oh, the boyfriend. Well, yes, what they saw right away was he wasn't involved. He was in the woods drinking. You've seen those photos.*

Britt: *Sure, but I just mean, what was he like?*

Priscilla: *[pause] A talented skier. He didn't take French, so I didn't know him well, but I'll say this: Some students haven't found their best selves yet, when they come to us. And Robbie was immature. Loud in the hallways, a little full of himself. I remember his parents, very sweet. The father was a Portuguese immigrant, and the—or no, maybe they were both just New England Portuguese. Vermont, working class. The father was a—maybe an electrician, you can correct me if I'm wrong. Robbie was a scholarship case. My first husband was Portuguese, so when I met the Serenhos at some Parents' Weekend or other I struck up a conversation. You connect about one little thing and then that's someone you know.*

This threw me for a loop, and I barely listened as the other four students gave Britt editing suggestions. I'd always imagined Robbie to be from the part of Vermont with the A-frame ski houses my classmates fled to for long weekends.

Plenty of kids earned their popularity from assets other than class and wealth. Some were charismatic, or great athletes, or extremely attractive, or all three. There were plenty of reasons Robbie was a king of the school, someone with enough cultural capital for Thalia to date, no matter where he came from. Still, Robbie Serenho not being rich was a confounding development. The version of Fran that lived in my head said, *See? Just because we thought something doesn't make it true.*

Alyssa went next with her Arsareth Gage Granby project, and I stretched my arms, tried to refocus.

As a student, I'd been angry that there was no statue of Arsareth, when she'd had more to do with the founding of the school than her husband, Samuel. And yet he, alone, cast in bronze, stood there collecting snow and pollen.

But as I'd only learned years after graduation, and as Alyssa explored in her project, Arsareth, who had grown up in Virginia, did nothing to free the man, woman, and child she'd been left in her uncle's will, selling them into further slavery before she set out for the New Hampshire woods. Thank God we hadn't built her any shrines.

The story Dr. Calahan told at every fall matriculation in the '90s was that the governor granted a school charter in 1814 for the young men of the town still called Midpoint, to turn them into farmer-scholars. Arsareth Gage, a spinster schoolteacher of twenty-four, moved into a tiny cottage next to the schoolhouse and began teaching twelve boys of various ages. Dr. Calahan would ask us to imagine Arsareth leaving home for a landscape so unlike the one she knew. She'd ask us to imagine the dark of these woods in 1814, the brilliance of the stars.

The official story continued: By the time Samuel Granby came through six years later, retired young from law and seeking a place to make his mark, the school was flourishing. He met the young woman from Virginia who'd whipped up a notable school from scratch, and offered to fund a real Presbyterian college preparatory school, to build a library and a chapel and put her at the helm. While he was at it, he rebuilt the local Presbyterian church and fixed the road; thanks to his money, both school and town took his name. Somewhere along the way, he and Arsareth fell in love and married, and while he became headmaster at the quickly growing school, she maintained the redundant role of head teacher. They never had children, the boys—and, as of 1972, the girls—of Granby being their legacy.

I always wondered if her marrying him was a survival tactic. Or if she'd coldly seduced him into staying, imagining good uses for his money.

Alyssa confirmed that the version they tell now at matriculation is more comprehensive, acknowledging both the displaced Abenaki and Arsareth's onetime slaver status. Even on the school website, under the History tab, they now own the fact that although the first Black student graduated in 1860, the second wasn't admitted till 1923. Right below this is the detail that the school held a quota on Jewish students from 1930 to 1950.

Arriving in '91, I'd considered Granby tremendously diverse if only because Broad Run, Indiana, was even less so. At home I'd known two Asian kids, both adopted by white families. I knew one family from Mexico. I watched *The Cosby Show*. And that was it. Suddenly at Granby I had classmates from India, Pakistan, South Africa, Saudi Arabia, Brazil, Singapore. I was rooming with Diamond Bailey, from Kingston, Jamaica. But in retrospect, this was a small percentage of the student body. The two dozen or so Black students tended to sit together in the dining hall, at those long tables by the cereal station. I saw it only as cliquish; I failed to consider to what extent it might have been an act of self-preservation.

By 2018, there were far more students of color, and the kids mixed together on campus as if they'd been posed that way for the catalogue.

Which isn't to say things were perfect. Jamila had statistics for her project on the ways financial aid applications were prohibitive for the students most in need of assistance. The retention rate for non-Asian students of color was still lower than for white kids. She had sharp things to say about the difference between equity and equality.

But I was talking about Arsareth Gage Granby, and what I was going to say was that I made the mistake in class that Friday of mentioning the séances we used to have for her—and then everyone, particularly Alder, wanted Alyssa to hold one for her podcast, and I agreed that if they could get permission to use Gage House some night, I'd supervise and we could record. I told them this would be an exercise in making content out of nothing—a useful skill.

"So it never worked?" Jamila asked.

"We *made* stuff happen, like someone would get their friend to throw a pebble at the window. I don't think that counts."

What I didn't say was that we held these séances without permission. We'd sneak out of the dorms, confident that the building housing Alumni and External Relations would be empty in the middle of the night. It was not the tiny cottage Arsareth had first lived in, but the nice stone edifice Samuel Granby had built her, parlors and bedrooms now converted to offices.

How alarming, in retrospect, that the various keys Fran was able to filch from her parents' key chains opened nearly every door on campus. One of those keys opened every dorm room. Fran would never take the dorm door one, except a couple of times to let me back into my room when I'd locked myself out—but she'd often borrow the one that opened the academic buildings, and eventually she managed to get it copied at the Aubuchon Hardware in Kern, despite the key saying *do not duplicate* right across the top.

I'd always assumed that various students, in their interviews with investigators in the spring of '95, must have mentioned the master keys floating around, the ones passed from graduates to younger friends, sibling to sibling. I didn't mention it myself, because they didn't ask and because what was I going to do, point a finger at Fran, of all people? Now I wondered: What if no one said anything? But surely the police understood that kids had ways of getting around locked doors.

The students of 2018 were ready to go through more legitimate channels: Alyssa used our midmorning break to email the dean's office, and by the end of class we had permission and a plan. I'd be at the faculty Midi-Mini party that evening, so we'd do this all late Saturday night. Either Yahav would be gone by then, or he'd have agreed to stay over, would wait for me in my bed. The kids and I arranged to meet outside Gage House, and I gave them my number to text if anything came up.

(I knew I'd regret that, but not how quickly: I was still on my way out of Quincy when Alder sent a GIF of a woman passing her hand over a crystal ball, and the message *It's Alder P! Okay if I bring my tarot?*)

33

Walking to the dining hall for lunch, I googled *Serenho + Portuguese*. It was indeed a Portuguese name. Most of my knowledge of Portuguese New Englanders came from the working-class kids in *Mystic Pizza*—but surely some New England Portuguese families were well-off. Still, Priscilla had sounded so certain. Working class, she'd said. Every article about Thalia's death had fixated on how Thalia and Robbie were the perfect prep school couple, moneyed and talented and privileged, and Omar Evans—no mention of his mother working at Dartmouth—was this outsider. That made the best narrative.

It was unlikely that there was a middle ground, that Robbie was neither rich nor poor. Even in 2018, families either paid full tuition or were on nearly complete financial aid. The only middle-class kids were still faculty brats like Fran.

In the salad bar line, I googled *Serenho + electrician + Vermont* and found an obituary for a Roberto Ademar Serenho who'd died in 2009, survived by a son of the same name who was clearly Robbie. Roberto Sr. had worked enough places—a motor rewind shop, whatever that was, an electric supply store, a farm machinery company—that he couldn't have risen far in the ranks anywhere. He was a member of the Lions and the Elks, a volunteer firefighter. He was beloved for his pancakes and for plowing neighbors' driveways with his tractor.

I sat at an empty table and kept googling, now on my laptop, telling myself I'd stop when someone joined me. But no one showed up.

According to Facebook, Robbie Serenho was a financial planner in Connecticut. A profile picture last updated three years back showed him with his wife, two young sons, a toddler daughter—the whole family dressed in light blue, posed on a beach. It looked like he'd done well for himself. A bit of a paunch, balding, gray at the temples. His wife wasn't beautiful, at least not compared to Thalia, but she had the superficial markers of attractiveness: toned arms, long, bleached hair, unrealistic eyelashes.

Robbie didn't have many public posts. Old fundraising pages for a condition a friend's child died of, some YouTube links. A wedding picture posted on his anniversary. There was his daughter, older than in the profile photo, running toward the Christmas tree, pure joy, her nightgown blurring. There he was doing yoga with his wife. On the anniversary of Thalia's death last year, a link to Jeff Buckley's cover of "Hallelujah"— but that could have been coincidence. There he was sitting by a river; he wore an *I'm With Her* T-shirt and so did his son. Here was an article about Universal Basic Income. Three years ago, he'd attended a fundraiser for a literacy center in Hartford. I was taken aback by how much like my kind of person he seemed.

I'd already seen most of this in that first long Google dive. I'd started by looking up *Camelot* cast members, then found only a few adjacent folks before Jerome stopped me. Robin Facer, who played Lady Catherine, and who'd rowed five seat, was competing in Ironman races. Mrs. Ross, who lived in Wyoming now, was active on Facebook and friends with a lot of Granby alumni. Max Krammen, who'd played both Merlin and King Pellinore and was always stoned, was now an employment attorney in LA with a respectable haircut and everything. Beth Docherty seemed wealthy and bored, a stay-at-home mom using social media to sell essential oils for money that, from the look of her house, she didn't need.

I hadn't gotten in touch with any of these people. (I was only on Facebook incognito anyway, as Elizabeth Wager—Jerome's last name enough to confuse lazy stalkers but not my real friends.) Keeping contact with only a few Granbyites, I'd always reasoned, was a healthy limit, a way to keep the messy Bodie who'd fallen apart from showing up like a specter at my window. It helped that while the alumni magazine arrived at my house four times a year, no one my age wrote in with biographical updates.

But now, since I'd opened Pandora's box, I might as well keep searching. It was alarmingly easy to find people, to skim at least the basics of their lives.

Khristina Gura, Thalia's original roommate, was living in Florida. I found Bendt Jensen, whose Danish posts Facebook translated into semi-comprehensible political spiels. I found Asad Mirza, who was working as a comedy writer and whose work I'd seen without knowing it. Rachel Popa taught math at a private day school in Boston. That one shocked me; I'd imagined her married to a senator, maybe working in fashion. Benjamin Scott, our valedictorian (the one whose grades I'd requested upon his death), covered LGBTQ issues for *The Washington Post*. Dorian Culler wasn't on Facebook, but he was easy to find via Google: a labor lawyer who seemed to represent not corporations but unions. The sight of his face gave me chills, but his work looked legitimately important.

The ruling class of Granby ought to have grown into the entitled ignoramuses who ruled the country, the ones whose influence outstripped their intelligence. Instead they almost all seemed lovely.

Well, sure: We'd all had Dr. Meyer for English, slamming *1984* on the table as he talked about power. Dana Ramos made all of us sit still and look at plants. Mr. Levin told us all the same stories about the Greek geometers and about paying his way through college as a busboy. It was entirely possible (it slowly occurred to me) that my empathy and tenacity were not what had gotten me through Granby, but were things Granby had given me. Things it had meted out to anyone willing.

How many times did I have to learn the same lesson? *You're not special. And that's okay.*

I ended up back on Robbie's Facebook, staring my way into the profile picture where his arm circled his wife, his fingers digging into her hip as if he feared she'd be washed away by the waves behind them. I remembered Robbie waiting for Thalia after Follies practice, waiting for her after *Camelot* rehearsal. He'd be there on the steps of the theater, alone or with a friend, studying or not, ready to walk her back to her dorm.

But—and I'd forgotten this—sometimes, on the spur of the moment, you would move Follies rehearsal down to Lower Campus, have them practice under the arch outside Old Chapel. It would get dark around us as I took notes for you about blocking. I don't think Robbie ever showed up there.

I hadn't understood till then how sound travels differently at night, but I'd sit on the Old Chapel steps with my clipboard, and when you arranged the singers in a ring, their voices were rounder: lofty and silver. Like singing in the shower, if the shower were limitless.

"Who are you singing *to?*" you asked once. Sakina answered, "The last row." No, no, they'd misunderstood. You meant who is your *character* singing to, even when the word *you* never appeared in the song, because although Follies was essentially a talent show, it had been conceived as a revue, and whether they were singing show tunes or madrigals or Mariah Carey, they were supposed to be in character.

You said, "I want you picturing the listener so hard I can see them."

Someone asked, "What if you're singing to yourself?"

"No one ever sings to themself," you said, and this prompted a barrage of protests. What about Maria in *The Sound of Music*, twirling through the hills?

Finally you said, "If you don't get it, just sing to Bodie. She'll be in the booth anyway. Confess your love to Bodie, tell Bodie you dreamed a dream, tell her you're the model of a modern major general." And you grabbed my shoulders, made me sit in front of the arch as sole audience. As if all the reasons I wore black and hid backstage were utterly lost on you.

Kwan Li, up next, actually did it, locked eyes with me as he sang "All I Ask of You," his voice already remarkable. Then Graham Waite stood with his guitar and, instead of singing "Blackbird," started in on the Tom Petty song about growing up in an Indiana town. I thought that was the whole gag until he got to the chorus. "Last dance with Bodie Kane!" he sang; it rhymed and everything.

Do you remember this? Laughing till tears escaped, applauding Graham, asking if anyone had ever sung that to me before. No, I admitted. It was a good joke, and I laughed with everyone, flattered that Graham remembered I was from Indiana. But I knew already exactly what would happen: For the rest of the year, people would sing it to me in the hallways, in the dining hall, and I'd have to find some way to react.

"Okay," you said finally, wiping your face, "less literal, next time, but that's the idea."

An hour had passed, and I was still staring at my laptop. I must have looked like someone doing intense and stressful work; no wonder everyone had steered clear of my table.

We'd believed there were ghosts in Quincy Hall and Gage House. We'd believed Mr. Wysockis and Ms. Arena were dating, until he announced his engagement to a woman we'd never heard of, a grad student at UVM. We'd believed we were practically grown.

I walked to film class weighed down with the cold, and the laptop in my backpack, and the winter coat I was growing to hate. This was how I'd trudged through four years at Granby: uncomfortable and ungrounded.

It's hard to describe the dizzy headspace I was in, except to say I no longer had any sense of what was true—about Jerome, about Robbie, about Omar, about you. I didn't know if Yahav still loved me. I couldn't figure out who knew more about what happened to Thalia: me now, or me at barely eighteen. My adult self, looking back with experience and perspective, or my raw teenage self, both jaded and naïve, taking everything in fresh.

This wasn't even a question of believing a survivor, as Thalia had never said anything about you. Well, and she hadn't survived.

34

Junior year Feb Week, I stayed on campus.

Halfway through college, I mentioned "Feb Week" to someone at IU and then explained I just meant February break, and still she looked at me like I was nuts. There was some origin story about the school saving money on heat, but in reality it was a vacation about second homes and special invitations and pressure from the oldest Granby families to keep it on the schedule.

This was when I learned that it wasn't just the ski team who skied, that everyone around me had grown up casually gliding downhill. Skiing wasn't entirely a class signifier, though; for some it meant childhood trips to Aspen, but for the New England kids it might have meant a local mountain with gravelly snow, used gear, a few PE credits.

I'd never been invited to anyone's ski house, and I had no interest in, or funding for, school-sponsored educational trips to the Galapagos or the Everglades. Freshman year I'd flown back to Indiana and spent a cold week watching daytime TV and avoiding the Robesons. Sophomore year I'd stayed in the dorms and hung out with Fran, and that was our plan again junior year. Just us and a handful of international kids. Even the financial aid students, even the ones who'd never skied, would, if popular enough, tag along to someone's place in Vermont just for the hot tubs and drinking and sex. (At least, this was the picture painted by stories I heard; in retrospect I imagine it was mostly hungover cartoon watching, juvenile conversation and heartbreak, logistics around the ordering of pizza.)

That week in 1994, Fran and I were thrilled to have the dorm VCR essentially to ourselves. We watched *The Shining* and *Wait Until Dark* and part of the box set of *Twin Peaks*—anything to help us channel the vibe of the nearly empty campus. I'd just started to appreciate film, and the Hoffnungs' movie collection was a treasure trove.

One night, we broke the horror-and-suspense streak to watch the Disney *Robin Hood*, and decided, halfway through, to paint our nails. I went back to my room for polish and when I opened the door, Thalia was on her bed, arm flung over her eyes, Granby duffel on the floor spilling clothes.

She sat up quickly and said, "*That's* why the door was unlocked. I forgot you were here."

Her eyes were ringed with pink; her nose was red.

I said, "Are you sick?" It was only Thursday, an illogical time to return. School didn't start till Tuesday.

She stood, started tossing clothes from her bag into her dresser. "Let's just say that Robbie Serenho is a little bitch." She and Robbie had been dating since November—happily, I thought. She pointed at me and squinted. "Don't ever date Robbie Serenho. He's an angry little sexist bitch." She chucked *Hamlet* from the bag to her desk.

As I said, I'd rarely heard Thalia swear, which is why I remember her words so clearly. That and the absurdity of the idea that I'd ever date Robbie, or he'd ever date me.

I knew better than to ask what he'd done. I wasn't a confidante, wasn't privy to this group's drama. But my silence kept her talking.

She said, "He can flirt with whoever he wants, *apparently*. I go on a walk with one person and it's, like, nuclear war. He's an alcoholic, I swear to God. He passes out at nine p.m., and I'm not allowed to talk to anyone else? I'm supposed to, what, hang out with his sleeping body? Clean up his barf?"

"Wow," I said. I was still near the doorway. "That sucks."

She stopped unpacking, stared as if she'd just noticed me. "What do you mean, that sucks?"

"I mean—it sounds bad."

She said, "Oh, thanks a *lot*. Thanks for your vote of confidence."

I told her I'd see her later—maybe I apologized, too—grabbed a handful of nail polishes from my dresser, ran back to the common room. I told Fran what had happened and asked if I'd done something wrong. She agreed I hadn't.

When I returned late that night, my nails painted purple and black, Thalia was asleep.

Sunday, as people started straggling back to campus, Thalia became agitated again, kept asking if I'd seen Beth or Rachel. I didn't imagine anyone who'd been skiing would return before Monday, hungover and complaining that their quads were sore and they hadn't done any of the reading. Thalia came back from the showers Sunday night in her knee-length pink robe, a striped towel wrapped elaborate and high around her hair. She was changing behind her closet door when she said, "Bodie, you don't have, like, a pregnancy test, do you?"

For a second I thought this was something about me, about my stomach looking fat. Then I understood. I said, "Oh. No, I—I mean, I've never dated anyone here, so no. Only back home. Maybe the infirmary?"

"Never mind."

Later that night, she came back from the bathroom doing a little dance, singing, "I got my pe-ri-od, I got my pe-ri-od!"

I knew she was sharing all this with me just because I was the only one around, but I went with it. I said, "How late were you?"

To be honest, the only sex I'd had, back home that summer, was so brief and inept that I wasn't even sure full penetration had occurred. But half my few remaining friends from middle school were heading straight toward teenage motherhood. Home on break once, I'd helped shoplift a First Response test and another time stood outside a McDonald's bathroom stall while my friend Renee waited and then showed me the negative stick for a second opinion. I knew, at least, the right questions to ask.

Thalia said, "I just—I thought it had been about a month, and I got freaked."

"You don't keep track? In your planner or something?"

"What, I'm gonna write I HAVE MY MENSES on my calendar?"

I had not yet met Mrs. Keith, but when I did, her brittle southern formality made sense for a woman who'd apparently never taught Thalia to code her cycle. Thalia was from Duxbury, Massachusetts, but Mrs. Keith was straight out of a South Carolina cotillion.

I pulled my own Granby planner off my desk and showed her the subtle red dot I'd make in the corner of a calendar square. (My own mother hadn't had the wherewithal to teach me herself, but she'd done this on our kitchen wall calendar my whole childhood.) I flipped back to mid-August, when Brian Wynn and I had fumbled around in his basement. I showed her the purple X I'd made there after I got the planner the first week of school, counting back the days. I said, "You do this whenever you have sex. Then you can keep track of when you can take a test, too. Because they don't work for sure till two weeks in." I was really pleased with myself, let me tell you, that I had this to display. If Thalia had seen Brian Wynn, his scrawny legs, his peach fuzz mustache, she never would have taken worldly advice from me. But all she saw was the purple X.

"Nice," she said. "Who's the guy?"

"A total loser." I loved how it sounded more like dismissive exaggeration than the truth.

"Anyway," she said, "I'm never sleeping with Robbie Fucking Serenho again, so it's beside the point."

But by Tuesday afternoon, they were entwined on the bench outside Mr. Dar's classroom, Robbie sucking on her neck.

35

Dane Rubra lived in Milwaukee, but had traveled to Granby five times—first on his own dime, then thanks to crowdfunding from his tens of thousands of YouTube subscribers.

In one video, he's out back of the gym by the pool's emergency exit, talking about the faint smears of blood found on the doorframe and on the wall just outside. Those smears were terribly popular on Reddit.

"*Maybe* it's from Security holding the door open for the paramedics and the stretcher," he says, "and maybe not. The State Police come in later and find this stuff, but you know where they don't find any blood is in Omar Evans's office. They luminoled that whole place, and nothing. Which is why they come up with this story about some imaginary poster on his wall that apparently absorbed all the blood. Well, listen: The only way that works is if he hit her head once, just once, and there was very little blood. Because he does that a second time? There's blood everywhere. They need to believe Omar killed Thalia inside the building, so they need to believe the blood *outside* the building is unimportant."

We'd all known about the luminol, because it was a whole production. It doesn't work like on TV, where CSI teams squirt the stuff as casually as Windex. It has to be mixed with hydrogen peroxide and sodium hydroxide, which means protective gear, fumigation. It requires the complete absence of light, too; they taped over all the gym's and pool's high windows with black garbage bags. They set up cameras on tripods. We'd previously been allowed back in the building, if not the pool—but then for a few days it was off-limits again. Fran, who'd left her best fleece in a gym locker, was livid.

According to *Dateline*, all they found around the pool was a confusing mess. Luminol gives a bright, flashing reaction to bleach—different from its dim, glowing reaction to the iron in blood—and areas of the pool deck had recently been bleached. Or was that just chlorine from the pool? I never fully understood. There was evidence of blood, too, on the cement, but whether it came before or after the bleach, whether it came from moving Thalia's body, was unclear.

It wasn't long, though, before the police were out of the building. Spring sports needed to start up, the alumni were descending, and I'm sure Dr. Calahan was under a world of pressure to get all yellow tape and swarming investigators off campus, to get the garbage bags off the windows, lest the volleyball games look like they were happening in a fallout shelter. I remember the police spending time in Thalia's room in Singer-Baird; we were told to steer clear.

"The police have kept so much to themselves," Dane Rubra says. "This makes sense when an investigation is *ongoing*. They hold something back so when the murderer slips up and gives a detail the public doesn't know, BAM!"—he pounds his fist into his hand—"they got him. Right? But they've *allegedly* already got their guy. So okay, why no photos from the pool scene? Why no video surveillance from the campus entrance? Why no photos of the back door?" It's hard to tell if his eyes are watering from the wind howling around him or if they're always like this. "This school has the New Hampshire DA around their little finger. You know how many lawsuits they get dropped? You know how many sexual abuse cases they've covered up?"

Dane believes the door wasn't alarmed in 1995, that there was an exterior handle and lock, and anyone with the right key could have gotten in. "Someone like Robbie Serenho," he says. "Someone like Puja Sharma."

He says, "Campus Security opened that door for the EMTs. No one, in their police interviews about that day, recollects a door alarm sounding. Did they disarm it before opening the door? That would be a poor use of their time. Or was it never alarmed to begin with?"

He looks straight at the camera. "We've scoured every yearbook, but we aren't done trying. If you have photos of the back of Mardis Gymnasium on the Granby campus from *any year in the 1990s*, contact me. Don't comment below, contact me directly." His email crosses the screen. "We can arrange for compensation, we can arrange for anonymity." His nostrils flare.

He seems exhilarated being this close to everything. He's blinking too fast. He keeps wetting his thin lips.

36

Fran and I talked my housemate, Oliver, into coming to the party that night, where he was instantly surrounded by young female faculty desperate for fresh meat.

The party, to my delight, was in the Singer-Baird apartment where Fran had grown up—the floor plan the same, but the kitchen new and the vibe so much cleaner than the colorful Hoffnung chaos. I couldn't even make out whose place it was now; everyone navigated the kitchen like they owned it, and Fran casually adjusted the thermostat herself. Several small children ran through in dress-up-box splendor, but there was no telling who belonged to what adult or what children belonged to the apartment.

I grabbed a single beer, which I planned to nurse all night. I didn't want to drink too much two nights in a row—plus I was seeing Yahav the next day, assuming he didn't chicken out, and I wanted not to look like death.

(In Concord, as we began the party, Omar was starting to feel a little better, and the external bleeding had mostly stopped—although he was still cold, dizzy. He couldn't eat and his abdomen felt swollen. The nurse who'd checked his wound that afternoon had slipped him two extra ibuprofen, told him to save them for when it was important. He swallowed them that evening, and they suppressed what would still have been a low-grade fever.)

Around the kitchen island, people discussed the news story. ("It's a second violation, what they're putting her through." "I literally wanted to barf. No really, I went to the bathroom and tried to barf.")

There was a staggering amount of drinking, by any measure. No one had to drive home, no one had work in the morning, and anyone whose kids were home had a student babysitter who could stay late. A room is never drunker than when you're the sober person.

A woman who'd dropped a wine bottle earlier kept checking that we were wearing shoes.

Mr. Levin was there, and I told him the story of the time I won trivia for my team by knowing Pythagoras was a vegetarian, thanks to him. I said, "I'd buy you a drink, but I wouldn't know who to pay."

A sweet and flamboyant young English teacher named Ian convinced me to read more Shirley Jackson, but even after I was thoroughly convinced, he kept right on convincing me, splashing gin and tonic on my sweater. I typed my email into his phone so he could check in a month that I'd done my homework.

A basketball game was ending—some purple blurs versus some yellow blurs—and the party crowd seemed split in their fandom. More people gathered, more drunkenly, around the TV as the clock ticked down.

Two women whose names I'd missed—one was a lawyer, so I assumed they were faculty spouses—were onto the news story again. Mr. Levin joined them, and so did a man with a baby in his arms. The man said, "Did you see they have him on suicide watch?"

Mr. Levin said, "Well, sure. They'd better make sure no one murders him, either. Before they can get his testimony."

The lawyer said, "I wouldn't mind seeing him murdered. Sorry, but we're talking about *decades* of—did you see how he controlled her credit cards?"

The second woman said, "You know when they cover the body like that it's personal; they're showing shame."

Priscilla Mancio sidled into the conversation. She said, "It's a miracle she survived."

Ian, the English teacher, said, "That thing with the sign language? On the security camera? Like, she's sitting there spelling out the letters of the dude's name. That's—she knows she's gonna die, and she has the wits to do that?"

The lawyer said, "It's *always* the husband."

"DC is like that," Mr. Levin said. "They go through interns like tissues."

"And the *children*! I wonder what will happen to the children."

"I just can't stop thinking about the mother. She locks the daughter out of the house, and how on earth would she know there was a predator? The world is usually safe. We can't forget that."

"Those VHS tapes were in the floorboards for what, twenty years?"

Priscilla Mancio said, "I just don't understand how the girlfriend went along with it. She's as bad as him, if you ask me."

"The thing about Hollywood," Mr. Levin said, "is they'll cover up anything in the name of money. Well, Bodie, you would know. Have you been following the case?"

I didn't manage an answer. The basketball fans were getting loud; and here came someone with, improbably, a tray of pudding shots, and we needed to help clear the counter.

The second woman turned out not to be a faculty spouse but an art history teacher. On impulse, I asked, "Did you see that thing about Jerome Wager?"

She said, "Who?"

"The guy who did the Obama mural in West Hollywood, the one—"

"Oh!" she said. "Yeah! I love him. Wait, what's the thing?"

"Nothing."

Utter relief. There was Twitter, and then there was the real world.

Mr. Levin said, "Who made the pimiento cheese dip? This is *delicious*." I agreed. I needed to step away from it so I wouldn't eat more.

The television crowd erupted in shouts. Some game-winning shot they were now going to replay over and over.

Dana Ramos asked who was watching my kids while I was away.

Priscilla kept infiltrating whatever conversation I was part of, and eventually she cornered me by the sink. She put her hand on my shoulder and said, "I have to ask you something." I wished I had her bulldog to talk to again. She said, "Did you come back here just for this?"

"For this party?"

"For the—your student's thing, the Thalia Keith thing."

I went hot and then cold and then hot. This was exactly what I'd been afraid of all along. "God, no. I came because I was asked. The students picked their own ideas."

She said, "I've stayed close with the Keiths." She told me some rambling story about the Keiths' "winter place" in Florida, something about baking cranberry bread with Caroline Keith. "Anyway," she said, "they would be devastated"—she paused and, in a moment of literal condescension, stooped to level her eyes with mine—"I mean *devastated*, if there were more bullshit about this case."

I tried to laugh lightly. "Britt's podcast is just for class. We're not exactly looking at national distribution."

Fran shot me a look from across the kitchen, and I attempted to signal with my eyebrows that yes, I needed rescuing.

"But *you* have a voice," Priscilla said. "You have a big audience. I hope you own that and enjoy your fame. But, Bodie, you have to *think*. You have to consider who could be hurt."

"I don't see how this could hurt anyone," I said. Although, yes, victims' families generally did not appreciate someone poking at an already closed case. I got that. Fran was trying to make her way to me, but she'd gotten stuck behind someone dealing with a slow cooker full of meatballs.

"I got the sense, when she interviewed me, that Britt is trying to say the wrong person is in prison. You know, those stories about some man living in the woods, or it was some satanic thing. These flights of fancy."

"I don't know," I lied.

"And I think of the damage. The pain for Myron and Caroline. Sometimes they reopen these cases, and they redo the whole trial. Or they let the guy out, and then what?"

"It's extraordinarily hard to get convictions overturned," I said. "If Omar Evans were freed, it would be for *very* good reason. And that's not likely to come from a class project."

I wished I were drunk, wished time could roll over me, wished I wouldn't remember this all in the morning and worry everyone was talking about me.

"Well, and the right man is in prison. He was a monster. To take—to rip away the life of someone so young, so promising. You have to ask yourself why he sought out a job like this to begin with. You know," she said, her hand back on my shoulder, "it was all so long ago. It seems like yesterday and then I remember how young I was. It was another millennium. To these kids, it's history."

This last part I could agree with. I nodded, and Fran finally showed up at my side. Priscilla said, "I was just saying to Bodie that we should let history be history."

Fran, God bless her, told us there were cupcakes on the coffee table. She pointed at the couch in the corner, where Oliver was talking with Amber, the young Latin teacher who'd driven us home last night. They looked like a casting director's dream couple—both of them nerdy-chic and adorable. She said, "They've been leaning closer and closer all night. They haven't moved in an hour."

#4: PUJA SHARMA

How would it even work?

Puja waits for Thalia backstage during curtain call, asks if they can talk. She hates the whine in her voice. She hates that when she came backstage in the first act, Thalia spotted her, looked irritated, mouthed something. Thalia says she has a second, but there's a cast party at the mattresses. *Just for the cast.* But Puja knows it's not only the cast. Robbie and Rachel were talking about it at intermission. Thalia should have invited her. Hadn't she befriended Thalia before anyone else? Thalia treats her now like an embarrassing relation.

They walk in the dark, Puja asking what she's done to offend her, Thalia saying, "I've just been busy!" Puja tries to warn Thalia that those other girls aren't her friends, that they talk behind her back. Thalia laughs it off. They wind up behind the gym, and Puja knows how to open the back door to the pool. She shows Thalia the trick and they stand there in the dark, in the warm, humid air. Puja says, "We should night-swim. It's a senior tradition."

"Not in my clothes," Thalia says, and she drops her backpack, disrobes, pulls a stray bathing suit over her too-thin body. She dives off a starting block, long and graceful, and the water splashes Puja's jeans. She emerges, pulls her wet hair from her eyes.

Puja doesn't have a suit, but she strips to her underwear and jumps straight in, feet first. The chlorine fills her nose, hurts her face.

Thalia says, "Just ride it out, and in college you can make some real friends. Like, people you have more in common with."

Puja feels hot, her hands prickly, and suddenly she's slapped Thalia, hard.

"Jesus!" Thalia says, and touches her cheek. "This is why people have issues with you! Do you get it? Do you get it now?"

Puja needs to delete what just happened, but for some reason her instinct is to grab Thalia's swimsuit at the shoulder strap, to yank her sharply forward and then shove her back, where her head makes a sickening sound against—what was it? the edge of the pool?—like a hard piece of fruit. She expects Thalia to lunge at her, to scream, but in the dim light Thalia looks dazed, nauseated.

Puja says, "Oh God—I didn't—"

Thalia makes a noise that's not quite a scream, scratches Puja's chest. Puja goes under, swallows water. She has to get up, and she grabs what she can, which turns out to be Thalia's hair. They scramble at the lane line, and Puja, pushing her way up, pushes Thalia down, pushes her neck onto the plastic rings. She just needs to get her breath, needs time to think.

Everything sparkles with panic, everything buzzes and flickers and roars. Someone might find them. They need to get out of the pool—but Thalia is retching, shaking, slipping under.

Puja climbs out, pulls clothes back over wet underwear, thinks.

But Thalia has slipped under. Her mouth and nose are beneath the surface. If she pulls Thalia out, there's no good ending. If she leaves her there—

She watches the race clock on the wall, not trusting her own sense of time. One minute, two minutes, five. Then she runs.

She returns to the dorm a minute late for check-in, but other girls are later, rolling in from the woods smelling of beer and mud. Thalia will be missed, and at first it won't be a huge deal, but as the night goes on they'll worry, they'll look for her, they'll find her, and Puja's fingerprints might still be on Thalia's body. Can fingerprints do that? The longer Thalia stays in the water, the better. Puja sticks popcorn in the microwave, sets the timer for fifteen minutes. She's bought herself a half hour of chaos, at least.

When Puja stops sleeping entirely, when she finally wanders off two weeks later, it's not only because of what she's done. It's because they're whispering. Beth and Rachel and Donna Goldbeck. They've guessed too easily. (If she only had a bike or a car, she could get to Hanover, and then New York. She could vanish. But no one has a bike. No one has a car.)

It's also this: Her father sent a tissue-thin airmail from London, asking if she knew the girl killed, if she'll buy Mace in town. He writes, *I thought University would be the more dangerous place, but I see you need protection even there in paradise.*

For some reason, it's the word *paradise*—the suggestion that this is as good as things will ever get—that does her in.

I woke up Saturday to a flurry of concerned and cryptic texts from Lance, from Jerome, from LA friends.

My hands were shaking too badly to download Twitter on my phone again, so instead I opened it on my computer. Late last night, Jasmine Wilde had quote-tweeted my thread and responded.

As a Person of Color, she wrote, *I'm devastated that Bodie Kane feels she can define what she experienced as "ACTUAL assault" while dismissing the very real experience of someone like me.*

It went on from there, but I was back at the video, staring at her sandy hair, feeling as dumb as when I'd thought Omar was Middle Eastern. I texted Jerome: *Person of color??? You didn't feel this was worth alerting me to?*

He answered: *IDK what the hell she's talking about. I swear, that was never something she mentioned. She has blue eyes! I have no fucking idea, Bodie.*

I dug around Twitter. Someone asking in another thread what Jasmine's ethnic background was, someone else saying this question was an aggression, someone bringing up Rachel Dolezal, someone writing *She's a quarter Bolivian* and linking to an interview where she mentioned her Bolivian abuela who herself had a German father, which meant, someone else noted, she was actually one-*eighth* Bolivian. Below that, someone dropped a racist Elizabeth-Warren-as-Pocahontas GIF, someone else wrote *She doesn't even speak Spanish,* someone answered with an eight-tweet tirade about how racist it was to gatekeep ethnicity.

My first instinct was to explain myself, but there was no way that didn't make everything worse. Apology would make it worse, too, for everyone involved; I knew how the internet worked.

A text from Lance: *Please call? We just lost Flower People and Fresh Feast.*

Instead I closed Twitter and hoped it would somehow make everything go away. And it *would* go away, I reminded myself. I wouldn't say anything else. People would move on. Trump would say something dangerously idiotic any moment now, and everyone's attention would turn.

I texted Lance and said as much. I added, *I'm not going near it anymore. I will never type again.*

I managed not to defenestrate my computer, and instead took it and my headphones to the dining hall to make editing notes on the students' first episodes and wait for Yahav. This way, if he didn't show, I'd have something to do besides stew.

Sitting by the fruit salad bar (a fruit salad bar!), I watched kids roll in to brunch—sleepy and alone, or in chatty pairs, or in loud, sweaty, post-sports-practice hordes—and did my best to compartmentalize, to ignore the dull fire alarm in the back of my head.

My students would have another chance to edit, and they had a second edited episode due the following Friday. I'd told them if they produced a third, they could send it to me after mini-mester and I'd still give them feedback. The idea was for them to launch their group portal on the school website before Feb Week. I had a whole fresh wave of concerns about my voice being in Britt's first episode: If her podcast got out there now and someone angry latched on to it, Britt could get dragged into the vortex with me and Jerome.

Alder hadn't been ready to play his podcast in class, had only emailed it to me late Friday night. The episode proved a good distraction, though it was confused, too ambitious. Halfway through he came on saying, "Okay, so, Ms. Kane? I think at this point in my final version I'll do something with, like, current students? Like, asking them to read the last text on their phone?" I couldn't imagine what this had to do with the 1930s—but give me a kid with too many ideas any day.

And then, a miracle: Yahav walking in the door, five minutes early—cheeks blazing red, eyes and nose watering. He'd parked off campus, he told me, even though I'd told him exactly where to go. He might have been out of breath from the walk, but more likely it was from the stress of seeing me.

He said, "This place really is in the woods."

I hugged the cold off him and took in his smell: clean but sweaty. He was an unreasonably beautiful man. His accent was clear but rich, and everything he said sounded like a line from a sad art film. For reasons I can't articulate, he was, to me, an incarnation of some Platonic ideal of both maleness and sex, like something conjured from my own imagination. I could never quite believe he was real.

I got us both borrowable Granby travel mugs full of coffee.

My phone kept vibrating in my pocket—more people mad at me, more things I'd done wrong—and I kept ignoring it.

We walked uphill and I gave him a personal tour: *That fire escape is where I used to study. That's where I twisted my ankle, freshman year.*

Yahav had two modes—all over me, or evasive—and he'd chosen the second that day. Ten minutes in, he hadn't yet kissed me, hadn't squeezed my shoulder, wasn't making good eye contact. I wasn't about to ask for any of that, but I found myself trying hard to reel him in, to put shiny things in front of him.

I showed him Quincy, showed him the door to the former darkroom, although it was, advisably, locked to keep the 3D printers safe.

He said, "This is where you made out with boys?" He was finally teasing, flirting, relaxing a little. He raised one thick, lovely eyebrow.

"I never made out with a single Granby boy," I said. "I only dated guys at home."

"In Indiana." His accent made the word gentler, more romantic, than should have been possible.

"Just summer flings, so I couldn't get hurt. And no one at Granby could know my business or feel bad for me when I got dumped."

"*Dumped* is a harsh word," he said. "We have the same idiom in Hebrew, but at least it doesn't sound so ugly. You never went to dances?"

"Sure, in a pack."

"You must have been pretty."

I said, "I was a disaster. Did I never show you pictures?"

"Now you have to."

So we went to the library, that wall of yearbooks in the back. I showed him the 1995 *Dragon Tales*, my unsmiling senior photo, my half page of shout-outs and quotes—private jokes for Fran and Carlotta, a bunch of Nirvana lyrics, a Monty Python reference for Geoff: "You're not the Messiah—you're a very naughty boy!"

Yahav said, "Your makeup. You were—in a raccoon phase?"

My eyes were ringed in black; my face had thinned considerably, so we must have taken those photos in the spring. But not too late in spring, because Thalia's photo was on the next page, once again only Hani Kayyali separating us. Thalia in a chair outside, looking over her shoulder, a position no one would find herself in if a photographer hadn't contorted her that way.

Of course I read her entry:

These two years have been the longest four years of my life!
"What is done in love is done well"—Van Gogh
Rach-a-Beth: Can we all fit in one limo? Schmove you both!!
S-B krewww: puja, donna, jenny, michelle—remember to clean my messssssssss
Dorian: Don't EVEN
Sakina, Booboo, Fizzy, Stiles: We made it! Remember, senioritis is inflammation of the senior . . .
Mrs. Ross, Mr. Dar, Mr. W., Ms. Arena: Thanks for seeing me through.

Mom, Dad, Vanessa, Brad: You're the best people to call home.

Deeb: When you know, you know. (I know you know.) Don't start
collecting things.

Robbie: My luuuuuv. You're my 100% and my CHEEP! I won't be far!

Varsity tennis, 11, 12

October Follies, 11, 12

Granby Chorus, 11

Choristers, 11, 12

Spring Musical, 11, 12

Theta Society, 11, 12

"Rach-a-Beth" would be Rachel and Beth. "S-B krewww" meant her friends in Singer-Baird.

"Deeb." Was that you?

I said, "Hold on, I'm gonna take a photo." I laid the book on a round wooden table that had probably been there a hundred years, held my phone still long enough for the flash to overexpose the whole thing. I thought I'd show it to Britt at the séance, but then she'd surely already found it.

Yahav knew the basic story of Thalia, and I explained that this was her, the roommate who died.

He said, "She looks wise."

I led him outside and we walked toward Upper Campus, where I could offer him one of the beers Oliver had stashed in the fridge. That was usually all he needed to melt back into me.

Deeb. I'd never heard anyone call you that, but it had to be you, in this place of honor between her family and Robbie. It must have been, because she hadn't listed you with the other teachers, and she'd never leave you out. I tried to think if there'd been a Debbie, a Deepak. But Denny Bloch—that worked.

What the hell did *Don't start collecting things* mean?

I walked Yahav toward South Bridge—not the most direct route to my guesthouse, but still *a* way there.

Every time we made eye contact, he'd smile apologetically and then find something over my shoulder to look at. I could drag him around a corner, I could grab him by the belt loops and kiss him, but there was a nonzero chance this would ruin everything. Even if I just took his hand— I didn't know if he'd grip it for dear life or pull away like it burned.

Don't start collecting things might be from a song, something they'd done in choir. Half a tune buzzed at the back of my brain.

I told Yahav that right below this bridge was where we'd placed hula hoops for junior year biology, recording every change within that space from February to May. We'd been split into groups of four; mine included Carlotta, Mike Stiles, and Rachel Popa—Rachel flirting constantly with Mike, bending all the way over to regather her ponytail, asking him to pull her up the ravine slope. They never did end up dating, so perhaps he'd been immune to her charms.

"One day," I told Yahav, "we find a Snickers wrapper inside our circle. The debate is: Do we throw it away, or leave it there and write about the ants that come to explore?"

"And what was your position?"

"I said that humans, and human pollution, were worth observing. My friend Carlotta started naming the ants. She called one of them Chunko."

I was about to give the end of the story, but Yahav had stopped halfway across South Bridge. He said, "It feels like you're leading me farther from my car."

"Did you need to leave already?" It had only been an hour. I'd been hoping he'd spend the day, hoping for sex on my small guesthouse bed. I wanted to massage his temples till he relaxed, make him close his eyes and lean back and sigh. I wanted to bury my face in his hair, which always smelled, inexplicably, like tea.

He put his hands on the rail, and I knew this would be bad. He said,

"I need to make sure I tell you something. I was out here on a sort of audition. They're offering me a very attractive post, and I'm going to stay permanently."

I said, "Oh, that's great!" and I meant it, although it didn't seem like this was all he was telling me. He was quiet, and I thought I should make a joke about an attractive post, ask what material it was made of.

But he said, "I need a fresh start in general." And then he kept talking.

I could not handle that I was getting dumped on South Bridge. I had just told him how hard I'd worked to avoid letting my heart break on campus. I'd held Granby in my palm like the most fragile egg, avoided risk, kept my crushes theoretical, tried my best to hide in plain sight. I'd worked for four years to keep the same Granby I'd first glimpsed from the Robesons' car window: mythic, a place I was visiting rather than a place that could ever hurt me.

I hadn't been feeling the weather, but the air was suddenly both bone-cold and wet.

I went into self-protective mode—not a mode I'm interested in un-learning in therapy. I said I should let him get going. I didn't respond to his monologue. I started walking him back to his car as if I'd always planned to. I said, "But I never finished my story. This girl Rachel, she just brought her boot down on the wrapper and all the ants. She said, *There. You can write that my human boot smashed it all.*"

Yahav said, "Children are psychopaths."

I wanted to protest that we hadn't been children, we'd been juniors, but that made no sense.

My whole face stung as we said goodbye. I made sure to walk away without glancing back.

At the end of freshman year, I'd drawn an "A" for Ace with purple Sharpie on a smooth rock the size of my fist and dropped it into the ra-vine from South Bridge, and it landed with the letter up. A good sign, I felt, for my last days of school. I was astonished the next fall to find that the creek hadn't washed it away, the sun hadn't bleached it out. It stayed all year. It stayed the next fall, too, but after the snows melted my junior spring, it was either gone or the marker had faded completely. Still, I looked for it every time; the place where it had landed was an anchor for me, a sacred point keeping me safe at Granby. I looked for it now, as I crossed back. I only felt worse, of course, to find the spot empty.

Don't start collecting things, don't start collecting things, and then I had the next line: *People will say we're in love.* It was from *Oklahoma!*, from a song about people who were, of course, actually in love.

Fuck.

Well, there it was. I didn't need agreement from Fran or Carlotta: Thalia was telling me herself.

38

I was still in the middle of the bridge when Lance called. I only answered to stop myself from deciding to chase after Yahav. Lance sounded like he was breathing through sand. He said, "I thought you said you weren't touching Twitter again."

"I didn't!"

"Okay. Okay. Did you know that when you 'like' a response on Twitter, people can see?"

"Of course. Why? What?"

"Someone has receipts on you hearting this Elizabeth Warren GIF? It's—she's in, like, a feather headdress and she's—"

"I saw that," I said, "but I did NOT heart it. Are you out of your mind? Have we *met*?"

I sat down. The bridge was wet, and the wet soaked through my jeans.

"It's not just you liking a racist GIF but it's that you liked it as a response to that thread, like you were agreeing that this woman was only posing."

"Yes, I can see that, but I did NOT like that post."

"Go on your Twitter. Go find it."

I put him on speaker and looked at my recent activity and for fuck's sake there it was, a red heart. And I saw, to the side, "20+" notifications, which likely meant I had hundreds. I felt a hot panic, a stuck-inside-a-sweater-in-a-dressing-room wave of nausea. I hated everyone and I hated myself and I even hated Lance for calling and most of all I hated being hated.

"Jesus, I was on my phone. You know my thumbs are stupid."

"Right, sure. I believe you, but the woman who found this, she screen-shotted it and posted this thing and she's got 130 retweets."

"Literally? On a Saturday? I just unliked it."

"That might make it worse. Listen, there's a lot of other stuff, too, people still just flipping out about what you wrote."

I knew, without looking, what they were saying: I was a hypocrite. I'd spent dozens of episodes digging into the abuse of women in Hollywood, and as soon as my own husband was accused I'd scampered to his defense. It would be one thing if I hosted a knitting podcast, but now I had betrayed the cause, and I was racist, too. Maybe I only believed white women, maybe that was my problem, and also my face looked like a cabbage. Mostly valid points, except that I'd thought Jasmine Wilde was white.

"Should I close my account?"

"Maybe."

"If I light my computer on fire it deletes Twitter, right?"

He wasn't in the mood. He told me that we'd lost one of the two podcasts that cross-promoted with ours. We'd lost the hair dye ads. "There's an email sitting there from Mattress Eden that I don't want to open."

I said, "Tell me what to do." My chest was tightening.

He said, "I haven't heard from Podtopia. But it's the weekend." Lance was the one who handled everything with our production company. Because he was better at it, and because he'd actually started the podcast before I came on board, made ten episodes with a different original cohost.

I said, and heard myself say, "Maybe I should quit the show." Lance had kids and no other job; Lance's wife was a first grade teacher.

"Don't say that."

"I'm saying it. I'm offering." It was the only thing that would make this all better, in part because maybe it *was* an overreaction, and what could people want beyond an overreaction? "If things get worse, I mean. Or if they don't get better."

"It'll die down," he said. The air was so wet and so cold, and I still wanted to run after Yahav. I wanted to cry on someone, albeit tearlessly, and he was the only one I wanted to cry on.

I said, "But what happens next is they go through everything I ever said on the show. Then they pick apart everything I say next time, and the next time."

A chipmunk scuttled past me on the bridge rail, darted straight down the post and out of sight. A manifestation of my own racing, fleeing heart.

"Let me see how bad the rest of my inbox is first," he said. "Let's get a sense of the damage."

39

I was down in the ravine, its slopes all mud and ice. I had been there a long time—hours?—trying to cry but letting myself laugh, every few minutes, at how bad it all was.

My pants were soaked, my boots were soaked, my socks were freezing to my ankles. I was sitting on the bank of the creek, on a patch of ice-mud.

If I could freeze myself to the core, I could find some equilibrium between my inner and outer states. Like homeopathy, like hair of the dog, like poison as the antidote to poison.

It was not any one thing stealing my breath; it was everything at once. The sudden atomization of Yahav *and* Jerome *and* Lance. Maybe the podcast, too, gone in a puff of smoke. The slow melting of any certainty I'd had about Thalia's death, a melting I'd been terrified to acknowledge but could no longer ignore. The realization that you, one of the best things about Granby, might have been not only a fraud, not only a predator, but—it was possible, I was finally letting it creep into view—a more violent kind of monster.

I sucked in air, but it was just empty space, no oxygen.

The news story had been getting to me, too, clawing at the edges of my dreams. The way no one would listen to her testimony. The way they mocked her victim impact statement. The way they read her diary aloud.

Somewhere down here lay the rock I'd once thrown. Somewhere down here was the hula hoop circle we'd observed, a quarter century of changes within its circumference.

It was in the other woods, the ones at the bottom of campus—connected to these but drier, flatter, denser—that we'd built the Kurt shrine. Those were the same woods where Barbara Crocker's body was found in 1975, just outside the Granby property line. Those were the woods where, in the middle of the night, late senior year, I brought my backpack with the half bottle of Absolut Kurant I'd stolen from the Hoffnungs' liquor cabinet, and I sat under the tree where the magazine photos and notes and flowers had faded to scraps, and I drank straight from the bottle, daring myself to swallow more before the first wave hit me, and then more. And when it did all hit me, it was with the force of a ferocious undertow pulling me far, far out to black waters.

That next morning, I woke up vomiting—my back and neck and head throbbing, my fingers numb. I foggily remembered having fished Tylenol out of my backpack's side pocket and swallowing the seven that were in the bottle. If there had been more in the bottle, I would have swallowed those, too. I would have. I remembered having drunkenly whispered into the night air, "I went to the woods because I wished to live deliberately." It was a kind of rebuke—to the woods, the school, myself. I'd come here to live deliberately, and I'd failed. I didn't know what was wrong with me, but every day was worse. Each morning I woke to heavier air, heavier bones, heavier eyelids, even as my body grew so thin that I was always cold. I had fought with my mother the day before, but that was only one little thing. I'd been coming unraveled for weeks. But what was I going to do, run to the counselor and take a spot away from one of Thalia's grieving friends?

Now, in the ravine, I felt that time was porous, that the girl from 1995 could somehow reach through, exchange her breath for mine. She had woken up back then by stealing my breath, my heartbeat, from this present moment. In exchange, she'd handed me her asphyxiation, her organ failure, her descending oblivion. Here they came.

The Tigerwhip would be about three feet deep here, plus the ice on top, plus the sludge on top of the ice that made it impossible to tell how solid the ice was. Rabbit tracks crossed it. The rabbits hadn't fallen through.

I stepped onto it to see if it would hold me, certain it wouldn't. I waited for everything to crack, waited to fall in, waist-deep. Everything shifted under my feet, the edges of the creek groaned metallically, but I didn't fall. Maybe there was a lesson in that. I knew I should take my good fortune and leap to safety, but I didn't move.

Here is what I want to say to you:

When I was still raw and unformed, everyone failed me. No one was permanent. Back home there were people with good parts to them, but on the whole, they couldn't be relied on. By fourteen, my bitter understanding was that I could rely on myself and only myself. So here I was in a place that looked nothing like home, and I was an island. You were one of the only people who saw me as that—as an island—and made me feel good about it.

We're meant to reject the selves we were at fourteen, meant to grow and learn. That college therapist worked so hard to convince me to trust, to find people I could rely on, to believe they wouldn't vanish on me.

So every year after Granby I tried harder and harder to lean on other people, and to defend them in turn. Partners and Jerome and my friends and my colleagues. And the problem was, I *had*. I'd leaned on them with all my weight. I'd sworn my loyalty. I'd always known, deep down, that it was a mistake.

I had been in the ravine so long that the sun was setting.

What I know now is that while I was in the ravine, Omar was found unconscious in his bed with a temperature of 105 degrees. They transported him to Concord Hospital for the scans he should have received from the start, and found a seven-centimeter sickle-shaped sliver of glass lodged in his liver, where it had caused ongoing internal bleeding. The fact that the external wound was infected—and the resultant fever—had likely saved his life by getting him there: The glass had lacerated a major blood vessel in his liver, and he required immediate surgery.

While Omar's body burned, I was made of ice. I could freeze myself to the creek, I could become part of it, a snow child who'd haunt these woods forever. As my eyes stopped watering, as my face went numb, I settled, with a singular fury, on you.

You were the older man giving her trouble. You had keys to everything. You had the protection of being preppy and white and respected.

Who the fuck moves to Bulgaria?

I didn't know how it was possible, when Omar's was the DNA on her, when Omar was the one who'd confessed; but I knew you'd hidden things. I knew you did something or knew something or made something happen. I knew it was you.

Fran was right: My loyalty was a fierce thing. It was a dangerous thing. But you no longer had it. I owed more to Thalia than to you.

This was what pulled me off the ice, what sent me scrambling for tree roots to pull myself up the slope.

I took a huge gulp of air, and it hit my lungs, cold and full.

It was dark. I needed to shower, I needed to change, I needed dry clothes. I had to get ready for, of all things, a séance.

40

What if I said that when I took the kids to Gage House, Thalia's ghost told us all about you? What if she spelled your name on the Ouija board?

Don't worry, she didn't. She made herself scarce.

The living room of Gage House is still set up that way, as a parlor for schmoozing donors and alumni. Photos of historic Granby on the walls. Starting at 10:30, we perched on uncomfortable chairs and settees angled toward the empty stone fireplace, the room lit with dim lamps. Alder had lugged an urn of coffee from the dining hall and appointed himself "séance barista," with the unfortunate side effect that the kids were wired. Britt seemed quiet and moody, but her silence was overridden by the other four, giddy as middle schoolers.

Being here was good for me, a reason to stay away from alcohol tonight, a reason to stay offline. And their teenage ebullience was a salve for my angry heart.

The feeling had returned to my fingers and toes.

The kids' energy, their improbably fresh faces glowing in the low-watt bulbs, reminded me again that they were *kids*. Yahav was right. We get so used to twenty-four-year-old actors playing high school students, and we seem so mature in our own memories, that we forget actual teenagers have limited vocabularies, have bad posture and questionable hygiene, laugh too loud, don't know how to dress for their body types, want chicken nuggets and macaroni for lunch. It's easier to see the twelve-year-olds they just were than the twenty-year-olds they'll soon be.

The cheerleader trope in most grown men's heads is about adults (God, let's hope they're adults) putting on pigtails and squeaky voices for porn. It's about what we think we remember. It's not about actual adolescents unless there's something wrong.

Which is all to say: I imagine you told yourself you loved Thalia. I imagine you promised her the same. And you might still believe it. But I'm telling you, from a furious place in the bottom of my gut: It might have been about power, it might have been about sex, it might have been about control, it might even—in some broken part of you—have been something warped but paternal, something tender and blind. But it was not about love.

After the first few Ouija attempts (our ghost was named XGHERERE, and YES, it was at peace, and NO, it didn't know anything about the ghost of Arsareth Gage Granby), Alder asked if we could try to summon Thalia's ghost, or if that would be too weird for me. I said they were welcome to try. Britt didn't make a move toward her phone to capture it for her podcast, so Alder recorded with his.

This time the kids were smarter. They didn't ask the ghost's name, just asked if it was Thalia and, consciously or subconsciously, nudged the pointer to YES.

"How can we prove it's her?" Jamila asked me, and I said, "Ask if Khristina stole her running shoes."

The pointer went to YES, and I shook my head. "Fake ghost," I said, and filled them in on the bra.

Something cracked, one wall of the house settling in the cold, and they all jumped. Alder squealed and scooted up next to Britt, hugged his knees to his chest in a way everyone seemed to find funny and endearing. I tried to imagine a boy doing that in the '90s, and all I could think of was the freshman everyone called "the Oklahomo," whose dormmates duct-taped him naked to a Couchman pillar in the middle of a lightning storm. I was only mildly horrified at the time; it just seemed like standard hijinks, and the other boys barely got in trouble. He didn't return the next year. I hadn't thought of that in years, and I felt a guilty stab, an actual cramp, even though I'd barely known the boy and hadn't been there. I doubt the episode, or our indifference to it, were things my students could even have computed, these sweet souls who'd been trained in antibullying since kindergarten.

I didn't tell them that story, but I did tell them they were more conscientious and kind and artistic than my own classmates. Jamila let out a snort-laugh. She said, "That's because of what you're teaching. You should see who's taking the stock market class and the, like, Get Your Dad to Fund Your Startup class."

"There's a lot of douchebags," Lola said. "And we've still got those secret societies. Like, only white boys whose grandfathers went here."

Alder said, "What do they even do?"

"Nothing. My uncle said they just told each other enough secrets that they could blackmail each other—to make them stick together. And I guess they give each other jobs after college?"

"Wait, was he in one?" I asked. We used to speculate who was in the Peregrine Society, the alumni of which had built the ice rink, and Omega, whose main activity was blanketing campus with Xerox copies of their logo in the middle of the night.

"He wouldn't tell me!" Lola said.

Alder said, "That means he was." Then, "Oh my God, Britt, you have to look into all that! What if Thalia found out their secrets or something? That's one of my theories. I have eight theories."

Britt closed her eyes and smiled with only her mouth. She looked as numb as I felt.

"Ms. Kane," Alder said, although most of them had taken me up on the invitation to call me Bodie, "what do you think happened? Hand to God?"

I took a long time to answer, navigating my still-spinning mind. I said, "You'll have to stop recording first." He obliged. I was careful, the way I spoke. Partly because I hadn't articulated much of it to myself yet.

"There's a bunch of evidence against Omar that I can't explain. But really they didn't cast a very wide net. Personally, I think Britt is right that they missed important details, and they missed important people."

"Wait!" Alder said. "Wait, you didn't say that before! Like who?"

"There were close friends who weren't in the woods. There was a girl named Puja Sharma who had a really strange mental health episode a few weeks later, and then she left school. There was this kid Max Krammen in *Camelot*, just a sketchball. I do *not* think either of them did anything; I just think those were people to look at." There had been rumors that Max was the one who started the bingo card, although that seemed awfully ambitious for him. I said, as if this name weren't any more important than the others, "There was a teacher named Denny Bloch."

I wonder if you felt some twinge just then, of betrayal or guilt. Maybe I crossed your mind for no reason. Maybe a rooster crowed three times.

"He did Choristers and orchestra and Follies and spring musical and taught a few classes."

Jamila said, "They had *one* person doing all that?"

"It was a different place. But he—Britt, you should look into him. He was married with kids, but I'm pretty sure they were having an affair, him and Thalia." The kids' jaws dropped, all but Britt's. "Or—I mean he was preying on her. That's not an affair."

I hated how part of me—still!—held on to the notion that Thalia was, with full volition, choosing to sleep with you because you were young and everyone thought you were cute and it was a matter of status among her friends. But no. There was a line, a solid line, between Thalia and someone like Jasmine Wilde. A line of age, a line of agency. And there was a world of difference between you and Jerome.

I remembered Puja asking, right after I'd started rooming with Thalia, "Don't you think she's a little hoey?" I hadn't understood the word, especially with her London accent, and I'd asked what she meant. *"Hoey,"* she said. "Like a ho." I assumed this was a common word I'd missed. It remained part of my conception of Thalia. An adjective I would never hear used for anyone else.

Alder said, "Wait, I know who this is! It's the guy onstage at the end of the *Camelot* video?" I nodded, although I wanted to know why Alder was asking the questions, rather than Britt, miserable next to him on the lavender settee.

Britt spoke, finally, in a monotone. "I know they interviewed him, but I don't have any of the interview transcripts. Not that it matters now."

Jamila let out a dramatic sigh from where she'd sprawled on the floor. She said, "Britt, I said what I said but you don't have to pitch a tantrum."

The other three grimaced but didn't seem confused; whatever had happened, they'd been party to.

"I'd love to know why we're doing Greek theater tonight," I said.

A long silence that Lola finally filled: "Jamila made a joke," they said, "about Harriet Beecher Stowe."

It took me a second. "The author?"

"Like, that Britt was doing some white savior thing."

"I was seriously just messing!" Jamila said. "Knock yourself out. Do what you want."

Britt said, "That's obviously not how you feel. And honestly, Jamila, I was mad, but I hear you and you're right. This is not my story to tell."

"Which is not what I said."

I was in over my head, but I managed to ask Jamila if she wanted to voice her feelings.

She said, "My feelings are, I was kidding because I knew she'd freak out."

I told Jamila that if she wanted to talk to me later in private, she was welcome to. I couldn't tell if she was upset or not; I only understood half the dynamics in the room. My instinct in these situations is to sit back and listen and learn—but they were looking at me like I was supposed to solve it all. This was fragile, and these were fragile kids. And I felt derailed: I'd spilled this idea about you, and it had just vanished into a fog of adolescent angst and white guilt.

I said, "These are really important conversations to have, and maybe we could even weave them into the podcast. But we're halfway through the class. Britt, I don't know that it's practical for you to change projects."

Also: I found that I was as upset now at the thought of Britt stopping the podcast as I'd once been at her starting it. I needed her to keep prying. I couldn't do it myself, what needed to be done; I needed to stand behind her.

"I know," Britt said, and I worried we were about to have actual tears.

So I said, "Alder, can you pour me more coffee? Who wants more coffee? And you can tell us your theories."

"Wait!" Lola said. "You were telling us *your* theory. You think the music guy did it?"

I hesitated. This was where things fell apart for me. I didn't trust anything about you anymore, I believed you were involved, but I just couldn't picture you bashing her head in. Why couldn't I?

Because I knew you as a good teacher and an attentive father? Because you liked opera? Because you blushed so easily, and that made you seem sensitive? Because I'd fallen into the most obvious trap, finding it easier to imagine darker-complected Omar acting in anger?

I'd had time, of course, to get used to the idea of Omar as killer. I'd pictured him that way for the past twenty-three years, his mug shot and conviction overriding the fact that I knew *him* to be a sensitive person. Omar taught me how to tape my own ankle, the spring I twisted it. Omar taught the rowers alternate-nostril breathing for meditation. Omar was allergic to the dye in yellow Skittles, and rather than throw them away he'd leave a little bowl of just the yellow ones on his desk, for anyone to take.

My head was a mess. My throat felt raw, and I wondered if I'd made myself sick in the cold.

I said, "My point is, there were five hundred students on campus.

There were dozens of faculty. And Britt is right that Omar's the only one they really looked at."

"Plus whatever staff, right?" Alder said. "Grounds crew and dining hall?"

Britt shook her head. She said, quietly, "No one who didn't live on campus was still here. Except Omar and one security guy. The Crown Street exit had video, and the access road was closed for the night—so they knew every car coming or going. And then, I mean, I guess when the fire truck came for the smoke alarm, there were firefighters around. That seems like a stretch, though."

Alder asked, "What time *did* Omar leave campus?"

"11:18," Britt said. "Which lines up perfectly with her time of death, so that wasn't good for him. He was speeding."

"It was on *Dateline*," Alyssa said.

I'd forgotten that. Something in me sank, settled. I said, "Right. And his only alibi is that he was alone in the same building where she died, at the time she died. Which is not an alibi. That's the opposite of an alibi."

41

Now they all wanted to watch *Dateline*—which sounded like a better way to fill the time than sitting around watching Britt sulk—and so Alyssa set up her laptop and we found it streaming.

We skipped the intro and started a few minutes in. Here were Myron and Caroline Keith at their kitchen table, glass cabinets full of tasteful dinnerware behind them.

Alder said, "Wait, go back, we missed *Camelot*!"

He was vetoed.

Myron Keith said, "She was our tomboy." There was Thalia, no front teeth, kneeling in a soccer uniform. "But before we knew it, she was a young woman."

"She wasn't happy at home, sophomore year," her mother said. Caroline was lovely, thin, hair a silver pixie cut. "She'd had a bad breakup, and she'd fallen out with friends. We thought boarding school would be a good change. And the school assured us they kept the kids close, watched over them." Here, a crack in her voice.

The camera cut to Thalia's younger sister, then in her early twenties. I remembered Vanessa as a confident eleven-year-old, speaking in a fake French accent as she helped the Keiths pack up Thalia's side of the room at the end of junior year. And I remembered her, somber but fidgety, sitting beside her parents in New Chapel the next spring for Thalia's memorial. On-screen she looked tired, her foundation applied too thickly by the makeup crew.

"She was happy there," Vanessa said. "At least she seemed happy."

Thalia's older half brother, a soap-star-handsome guy I'd never met, nodded gravely. He talked about visiting her on campus, being so impressed with the place.

And here came the stock footage of Granby: Founders' Day, students with backpacks crossing Middle Bridge, a boys' eight rowing down the Connecticut. Full stands at a football game, fans singing *You can't beat the Granby Dragons! Your offense is awful and your defense is laggin'!*

"Oh," I said at the next shot. "That's Mr. Hoffnung! That's Ms. Hoffbart's dad!" He scribbled on the chalkboard as students took notes.

Dr. Calahan appeared in her office, prematurely white hair tucked impeccably behind her ears. "Thalia was an excellent student and athlete, well-liked, social," she said, careful warmth suffusing her voice. "She embodied the spirit of Granby."

After her interview, the part we'd come for: Lester Holt somberly laying out the timeline of March 3, 1995. "By nine p.m., *Camelot* was over."

"Questionable!" Alder interjected.

They showed curtain call—Thalia bowing on the arm of Max Krammen's Merlin. "Students headed back across the crisp snow to their dormitories, where their books awaited them."

"Wrong," I said. "It was slush and mud."

A shot down the hallway of Singer-Baird, all the doors closed. "By the eleven p.m. curfew, however, Thalia Keith was elsewhere." No mention of Jenny Osaka, the microwave incident, the reasons Miss Vogel overlooked Thalia's absence.

"The next day was Saturday," Lester Holt continued, "a day with no scheduled activities. Even at the rigorous Granby School, students are free to enjoy their weekends. But come Saturday afternoon, Thalia Keith . . . was nowhere to be found."

"I hate the way he says 'Granby,'" Jamila said. I agreed. It was somehow both mocking and precious. "These shows, they make everything sound like someone going alone into a haunted house."

That was exactly it. As if anyone with street smarts would have stayed away from a boarding school in the woods, a place where kids were so privileged that karma was surely out to get them.

Lester Holt explained how suspicion soon settled on the twenty-five-year-old athletic trainer, the only other person known to be in the athletic complex that night.

Omar had returned at 8:15 from traveling with the girls' hockey team to an away game at St. Paul's, we were told. He unlocked the gym, caught up on paperwork in the training office, and from 8:53 to 10:02 p.m. was on the phone. As Britt had said, he sped off campus at 11:18—giving him just enough time, the State Police believed, to kill Thalia, clean up, and get out of there.

"An independent medical expert brought in by the defense," Lester Holt said, "attempted to argue that Thalia died before ten, thus giving Omar Evans a solid alibi."

"Who was he even calling?" Jamila asked. "He could've been on hold at some company and put the phone down."

Britt shook her head. "It was a parent and a doctor, talking about an injured kid, and then right afterward it was the athletic director. They gave affidavits."

Now here was Omar's lawyer, explaining that New Hampshire is not one of the states that requires recording of custodial interrogation—meaning there was no record of what happened when Omar was questioned for over fifteen hours without a lawyer present. There was no record of what was said and done before he signed a statement that he'd been sleeping with Thalia Keith, bribing her with not just pot but hard drugs, that he'd been angry when she tried to end things, that they fought in his office and he hit her head on a poster on his wall, that he choked her and threw her in the water and left her for dead.

He recanted his confession less than twenty-four hours later, saying it was coerced.

Omar appeared on-screen in a forest green jumpsuit, head shaved, his last name written on a piece of medical tape on his chest. His face had thickened along with the rest of his body, but he had the same broad chin and sharp eyes. He said, "They came up with a story, they wrote the story in their own words, and they made it sound like if I just said this stuff, they'd put it down to an accident, like that was my best shot."

When I first saw this, I'd firmly believed he was lying here. I'd stared hard at my TV, trying to see his tells. This time, all I saw was resignation, exhaustion, a lingering bewilderment.

"Jesus," Alder said. "This is why you always wait for a lawyer. You think it'll make you look guilty, but dude. You have to."

The kids' talking drowned out the rest of the show: Omar's conviction and appeal, Thalia's family fighting to keep him in prison, Lester Holt straining hard at the end for *Camelot* parallels, something about "no happy-ever-afters."

The slow, slow wheel of my brain finally turned.

There was alcohol in Thalia's stomach, but it wasn't in her bloodstream yet.

If I was right that she'd drunk from that flask backstage, she died very soon after *Camelot* ended.

If she died soon after the show ended, she died while Omar was on the phone.

Oh.

I did the math again.

Jesus.

But who would remember, after all this time, if she sipped something backstage that particular night? Who could ever testify to that?

"Can we listen to music?" Jamila asked, so we did.

It seemed we were waiting for midnight. These kids were young enough that the stroke of twelve still connoted mischief, parties, ghosts, rather than work deadlines and colicky babies and red-eye flights.

I had not yet mentioned the flask, the timing. I wanted to think about it, clearheaded, in the morning. I wanted to triple-check my math.

"We should turn the lamps off," Alder said at 11:58. "We should sit totally silent and send out welcoming vibes. And we should record again!"

Jamila said she'd fall asleep—she was already lounging on the floor—but Alder's motion passed.

Let's say that instead of Britt and Alder giggling uncontrollably, shushing each other, instead of Lola shrieking when Alyssa tickled their neck, instead of the hush that finally settled over us, let's say that Thalia showed up, that her face glowed in the window. Say she had a flask in her hand.

I'd been thrown back, that week, to a mental state in which I could remember the sound of her voice. The way, for instance, she said "How *random!*" The way she'd get hiccups when she laughed. The way she'd sing choir music as she got dressed, the soprano part of "Wade in the Water" rising over her open closet door.

So let's say that this night in Gage House, her face appeared and she said what she'd say if she could: *Bodie. The drug theory came from you. You made it up, and they listened. Omar was on the phone. What did they know about DNA in 1995?*

Let's say she said: *Who has more reason to kill a girl? The guy who tapes her elbow, or the guy she's sleeping with?*

Let's say she said: *How often have you thought of my body in the ground? How often have you thought of Omar's body in prison? Whose body gets to be free?*

Maybe she said: *It was all of them. Denny Bloch and Omar Evans and Robbie Serenho and the teachers who didn't intervene and the boys who thought it was all so funny. Dorian Culler and the cast of the play and Mrs. Ross and Rachel and Beth and my parents, who sent me away, and Khristina, who made my bras and my body a topic of conversation, and you and you and you and you and you.*

But no—my eyes were closed and I was drifting off. At 12:05, Alder turned one lamp back on, and we sat there with the calm of people who'd just finished yoga class. "I *felt* something," he said.

Lola said, "That's what *she* said," and they were gone again in chatter and giggles.

#5: ME

I did it myself. I don't remember it, I don't know how it's possible, but I did it in a fit of jealousy and I blocked it from my mind completely, and all the subconscious tugs bringing me back to Granby, leading me to this moment, came from the molten core of guilt in my soul.

A ridiculous thought, but as I spiked a fever Sunday morning, as my body paid for those hours in the ravine, I half slept and rechewed the same dreams and occasionally became convinced that I'd followed Thalia to the pool. No, I'd led her to the pool. Or I found her in the pool, and we swam together until she looked at me and held a hand to her bleeding head.

What alibi did I have? That I shut down the lights and the sound-board, that I reset the props and locked up the theater, went back to the dorm, studied alone until the fire alarm went off.

What if my memories were as false as dreams? What if my dreams were really memories? What if we swam together in borrowed suits until the water became heavy and thick, until Omar tried to throw us the life preserver, but it only sank? There you were, throwing rocks from the observation deck, and they kept missing us, so I grabbed one and helped you, I lifted it over Thalia's head and brought it down. Then I sank to the bottom, a rock myself; I sank there and lived there for years.

44

That afternoon, with most of my fever slept away and the rest medicated down, I FaceTimed Jerome. The kids tore around the house with the iPad, showing me the gerbil, the fish, the cat's butt. Leo wanted to know if there was snow in New Hampshire, so I took my phone outside and showed him the unimpressive crust. He requested that I make a snowball, and I did my best.

"Mommy," Silvie said, "I'm eating my hay." Pieces of yellow yarn hung from her mouth.

Jerome sent them to the basement and I asked how he was holding up.

He said, "I don't think this is going away." He meant for himself.

I said, "So I got in some hot water defending you."

He rolled his head back. He said, "I know. You shouldn't have done that. I mean, you didn't need to. You go into mama bear mode."

He didn't seem to know about the fallout for the podcast, and I didn't need to lay that on him just now, nor did I want to speak it aloud.

He said, "Aren't these the same people who believe in rehabilitation? Honestly, if I'd shot someone in a robbery fifteen years ago, they'd be fighting for everyone to forgive me. They'd say I learned from my mistakes."

"That—Jerome. Come on."

"Who's that singer from Boston, no one even remembers he tried to kill someone."

"I'm glad you didn't shoot anyone. You wouldn't trade this life for that."

"But being bad at relationships, that's worse than murder. I don't get it. I want to stay home and never talk to people ever again."

"Why don't you cook with the kids? That always helps."

He said, "You're okay in all this, right? You'll be okay?"

Silvie was back, crying. She said, "Mommy, Leo stepped on my tail. He won't apologize, and my tail hurts and my mane hurts."

45

Monday morning, an inch of fresh snow had settled on every tree branch, every railing. On the ground, it covered the old, hardened patches so your boot drifted down through soft new clouds only to hit solid ice.

I hadn't seen snow like this since I'd left. Not in New York, where the piles turned grainy and black within hours. Not in my time in London. Obviously not in LA.

I imagined that if New Hampshire suddenly thawed, I'd find my own lost things in the melt. I'd find the calculator I lost junior year and had to use all my babysitting money to replace. I'd find the glass bead bracelet Carlotta gave me for Christmas, the one that fell off my wrist on North Bridge. I'd find, in twenty-three-year permafrost, some small, perfect object Thalia had dropped, something hugely important. Her diary, a pen with important fingerprints, a handkerchief embroidered with the initials of her killer. I'd find Yahav, I'd find my podcast, I'd find the unshattered, adult self I was just a week ago.

I crossed campus breathing the cold in deep. The sun emerged, only to glare down hard, bounce back up, blind me from beneath.

(Across the state right then, thirty-six hours after his surgery, Omar was finally getting up to walk the hospital halls—flanked by both nurses and guards. This was possible only when they'd had a chance to clear the halls of all other patients and hospital staff, which meant his walks wouldn't be nearly frequent enough. And he'd be returned far too soon to the prison infirmary, since it was deemed too expensive for the state to keep staffing his hospital room for the full week he ought to have stayed. Still: He was healing. He was moving. He would, by sheer luck, make it through this particular injury. When he finished his stroll and returned to his room, they handcuffed his right wrist and left ankle back to the bed frame.)

In Quincy, the kids were already in their seats, stewing in tense silence. Foolishly, I thought maybe it was about me; maybe they'd gotten word that I was sexist and racist, an enabler of predators. Maybe they wanted out of the course. Maybe they wanted me off campus.

Britt said, "Can I talk to you in the hallway a minute?" But it was time to start class, and in any case she kept talking. "I'm thinking I could switch to the murder of Barbara Crocker."

"We're more than halfway through," I said. "Your second episode could pivot to that, but—"

"No," she said. "I want to scrap what I already did."

Jamila sighed loudly. She said, "Britt, just get over yourself and finish what you started. It's like you're trying to punish me for my criticism."

"I am *not*!" Britt shrieked. She seemed close to sobbing.

Alder said, "Hey. Hey. Okay." He patted his thighs. "Hold up. Hear me out. I've been wrestling with my own project because honestly I don't even know what it is anymore." I wasn't going to disagree. "What if—"

"I don't want to trade with you," Britt said. "I just want to stop."

"No! What if we did yours together? I'm not gonna take over, but you know I'm obsessed with this case now."

Jamila rolled her eyes, as if rescuing white girls from awkwardness was something Alder did all the time.

Alder said, "Would that work, Ms. Kane?"

"I think it would be fine." Especially if it meant no one would cry right now. "And maybe you two can owe me a couple extra episodes, just to be fair."

Britt looked hugely relieved, and Alder looked thrilled. Jamila whispered something to Alyssa, and Alyssa smirked into her notebook.

"Because honestly," Alder said, "I've stayed up basically every night googling it."

I said, "Britt? You're okay with this?"

Britt glanced at Jamila, who wasn't about to give her validation. "Yeah, I—that would be a lot better. Just having more—more points of view. And four episodes is no problem."

"I think we're in good shape then."

Lola said, "So tell her the *development*!"

"Oh." Britt managed a small smile. "I heard back from Thalia's sister."

I hadn't known she'd contacted Vanessa. I tried to calculate how old she must be now.

"The parents didn't write back, but she did. She seemed pissed, like not interested in talking. But she sent me this list of what she has, all the medical reports, and she has the on-campus interview transcripts from both the State Police and the private detectives. Which is huge, because that's not on the Free Omar site. But she didn't offer to share it. I think she might've thought we were doing, like, a more official thing."

"She *has* all that?" Alder said. "What—okay, can I talk to her? I'll Uber to wherever she is. Literally right now."

Britt shrugged. "She sounded super not into that. I'll show you what she wrote, at least."

I said, "Would you mind showing me as well?" I wanted to see every document Vanessa had, and immediately. My sore throat and earache were gone. I felt awake for the first time in days. The interview transcripts were something I could spend hours in, weeks in. It occurred to me that my own words would be in there. I said, "I won't interfere, but I knew Vanessa. I might—I could at least drop her a note and say you're my students. I don't know that she'd remember me, but it couldn't hurt."

I told them then about the flask, my theory of the timing. It seemed to cheer Britt up entirely; here was something to start her second episode. Lola said, "You can ask my uncle! If there was booze backstage, he was most definitely involved."

46

Britt and Alder asked for more classmates of mine they could talk to, and I had to think hard who'd be open to it. I hit upon Geoff Richler, who'd barely known Thalia but who had, after all, been the one to develop Jimmy Scalzitti's mattress party photos, and that was something. Besides, Geoff was funny and smart and would make a good podcast guest. He was living in New York, and occasionally over the years we'd made noise about having a drink when I was in town but had never gotten our act together. He would text me every time he listened to my podcast, things like *I'm at the part where she's hooked on amphetamines. Run for your life, Judy!* I got back at him once by watching his TED Talk online and texting him constantly. (*You're turning to the left! You just cleared your throat! Oooh, the online marketplace as an unlikely spur for local growth!*)

I texted him a heads-up about the students, and he sent back a GIF of a monkey eating popcorn.

My film class was meeting in the evening for a change, so after lunch I borrowed Anne's snowshoes and Fran and I hit the fresh snowfall on the Nordic trail; Geoff was a topic of conversation. "The last girlfriend," Fran said, "was ridiculously hot." She had seen them both at our twentieth reunion, which I'd missed.

I said, "Like—I look at him objectively now, and I guess he's attractive and successful. But this is our little Geoff."

"Wasn't there an actual model in there at one point? Or no, wait, a fitness coach."

"That boy did not have a moment of action at Granby," I said.

"Sure. He was too busy fawning over you and Carlotta."

"Umm," I said, "*not* me." I tried to give her the look she deserved, but she was ahead of me on the trail. "Just Carlotta." But Fran made a sarcastic humph.

She said, "Do you remember those shirts he wore? I think that was half his problem."

It came back to me from the ether, how freshman year he'd had three of the same shirt in different colors—these jewel-toned rugby shirts with white piping at the collar and cuffs. Something you'd put on a five-year-old.

"Poor Geoff," I said.

I was out of breath keeping up with her. One thing about living in LA is you forget how to move in clothing or gear that weighs anything.

We were up around where the mattresses must once have been, although the trees and even the trail had changed enough that I couldn't have found the exact spot.

Fran said, "We're good, right? You're not mad at me about the other night? I just don't want you falling into this whole conspiracy mindset."

I wanted to ask if she thought I was morphing into Dane Rubra, but that would mean acknowledging I knew who Dane was, which wouldn't help my case.

"Like I said, it's not my project. If I knew how to brainwash teenagers, I'd be rich."

"Okay, good. There's so much crazy stuff out there. We all killed her in a satanic ritual, right?"

"I'm still mad I wasn't invited."

"And there's all the stuff about Barbara Crocker's killer. And the dot theory thing."

I made her repeat herself twice and still had no idea what she was saying.

"Her planner? Oh my God, do *not* look this up, they'll get to you. I guess her planner was in her backpack when she was found, but it was never admitted to evidence."

"That seems . . . ungood," I said.

"Because it was just academic stuff. She didn't put her social life in there. But there's a thing about colored dots on certain days, like the Reddit crazies think it was some kind of code."

"Her period," I said, proud both to know this and to sound so reasonable.

"That seems way more logical than them being Masonic code or something."

I said, "Unless they're braille, I'm *sure* that was her period. That's what she did when we lived together."

It was true; sometime that spring, after I'd shown her my system, she asked to borrow a red pen. She said, "Look at me! I'm being so good!"

I'd said, "Oh, funny. I just mark the page with my actual period blood." Thalia looked horrified, letting out only a small, cautious laugh. I had to ruin the joke by telling her I was kidding, lest she repeat this to her friends.

We crested the highest point of the trail and stopped, looking down on campus from above. You could see the Tigerwhip, and you could see the tops of both Old Chapel and New Chapel poking through the overstory.

We discussed the gossip of the day, which was my housemate's budding relationship with Amber, the Latin teacher he'd been into at the party. Oliver lived in New Jersey, but that wasn't too far away to keep up something promising.

"The only question," Fran said, "is whether we lose Amber to the world, or keep Oliver here forever."

I'm sure Fran would have kept trekking several more miles, but she took pity on me and after a minute at the crest, we turned back.

She said, carefully, "So you know I follow *Starlet Fever* on Twitter."

"Oh, good God."

"I can't even figure out what's going on."

"It's about Jerome."

"Right, I mean I got *that*. But what the hell happened with *you*?"

What she'd seen were the irate, cryptic screeds people were posting under each of the show's old tweets. I filled her in as best I could, even managing to laugh at myself, at my drunken bathtub thread, my awkward thumbs.

I said, "I offered to quit the podcast. Maybe I do a book now. The early women screenwriters, Anita Loos and Frances Marion and everyone."

"I have no idea who those people are," Fran said, "but no, you don't quit your *job* over this."

I said, "Before 1925, almost half the films produced in Hollywood were written by women. But as soon as there was real money involved, men took the jobs."

"Twitter is just Twitter," she said.

I said, "We're finally back at something like twenty-five percent, but for a long time it was closer to zero."

"*Bodie,*" she said. "Just ignore it, and it'll go away."

I loved that Fran's advice always started with the word "just." (Just tell that boy you like him, just take an extension, just ask the Robesons if you can stay with me, just say you want a raise.)

"It might be too late," I said.

"So maybe it's a lesson learned. Stay off the internet, where everyone's nuts."

I chose not to acknowledge that she was talking about more than the Jerome situation.

She said, "Life isn't that messy if you stay away from mess."

47

The best thing I overheard on my secret pay phone was a conversation between Geoff Richler and his mother, fall of senior year. I listened for only a minute before I felt too guilty about eavesdropping on a friend and hung up. She'd been telling him how there were possums on the lawn, and the community board wouldn't do anything about it.

"I never think about possums," Geoff said. "I'd forgotten possums existed till this very minute."

"Well, they're nasty," she said.

"Tiny little devil eyes," Geoff agreed.

"And fangs!"

The next day, Geoff and I had jimmied open the athletic equipment shed because it was too rainy to get to the mattresses to smoke. The shed sat by the rear of the gym, right next to the football field and track, with an open-air press box on top. The room itself was so hazardous and gross that when people needed to access the press box, they usually climbed the ladder stuck to the building's side rather than clambering over the mess of orange cones and sprinklers and lacrosse goals to use the rickety indoor stairs. We sat on the blue high-jump landing pad, partly because it was squishy and partly because it kept my feet off the floor, where there might be mice. We joked about how many people had gotten naked on it, but I cared less about germs than mice. The place *smelled* like mice, like dust and decay and spiderwebs and mold. It was only the size of a couple combined dorm rooms, but there were infinite corners and crevices where vermin might hide. This is how I knew I was addicted: I was willing to come in here just for a cigarette.

I said, "You know what's worse than mice? Possums."

Geoff said, "Oh my God," but before he could finish I went on.

"They have those tiny little devil eyes. They just crossed my mind yesterday for some reason. I was sitting in my room at four o'clock and suddenly I was, like, *possums*. Is that weird?"

I couldn't see well—the shed was lit only by one pull-string lightbulb—but I could make out Geoff's wide eyes, and he was silent several seconds, which might have been a record for Geoff.

He said, "Bodie, you're freaking me out."

"You're scared of possums?"

"No, I—I think I'm dreaming?"

He explained his déjà vu, and I didn't let on in the slightest. Partly not to spoil the joke, and partly because I loved the idea that he might think we had some special psychic bond. Maybe I did have a crush on Geoff, maybe I always had. If so, it was profoundly different from the theoretical lust I felt toward someone like Mike Stiles. Geoff was a little short for me, which I think is what let me convince myself I didn't have feelings for him—which in turn let me get closer to him than I otherwise would have.

The door creaked open, a strip of light illuminating three freshman boys who looked terrified to find us there. "We were exploring," one said quickly. Maybe he thought we were prefects. He probably couldn't even see, in the dark, who it was.

"That's funny," Geoff said, "we were in here to investigate the alarming smell of cigarette smoke. Would you boys have any idea where that was coming from?"

The bravest said, "You guys getting it on in there or what?"

"Come in and find out," Geoff said, starting to unbutton his shirt. The boys swore, ran away laughing.

In another universe, I kissed Geoff then. In that other universe, I understood that I was not disgusting, that Geoff might have welcomed it or in any case would at least have been flattered. I'd have let down my guard, allowed myself to like a real and attainable person, rather than dead musicians and the hottest boy at Granby. But in the real world, it never crossed my mind.

48

I'd arranged to show the film students a double feature of the original and 1983 versions of *Scarface* in the theater that night. In addition to *Memento*, they had already watched *Eyes Without a Face* and *The Cabinet of Dr. Caligari* and *Fargo*, but on their own. Here was the same stage I'd illuminated as my peers sang and danced, the same stage on which we'd occasionally been allowed to yank down the overhead screen and project VHS movies. Now, there was a hookup for my laptop, and a remote control that brought a screen as large as the stage gliding soundlessly down.

The place smelled the same, sawdust and sweat and paint—but my lighting booth had been replaced when the theater was gutted and expanded. Still, as I told the students before we started, this room was where I'd discovered film. "I was one of the only students allowed to work the projector," I said, "so I was essentially forced into joining film club." I rambled about Geoff Richler introducing *Bringing Up Baby* to the handful of us assembled, how he explained that no one had dovetailed their lines like this, like Hepburn and Grant did, before Howard Hawks—who'd also directed the 1932 *Scarface* we were about to screen—whipped them into overlapping comedic frenzy. It was the first time I'd watched a movie for anything other than plot. It wasn't long before I was interested in the camera work and the history and, eventually, the theory of film.

My students were notably less zealous. They were spread all over the room, some in pairs, some solo. I said, "Just a reminder that when you look at your phone, I'll know. Your chin glows blue in the dark."

Within ten minutes I'd broken my own rule, but then I've seen each *Scarface* a dozen times. Sitting in the back row, I thumbed an email to

Vanessa Keith, who was now Vanessa Birch. I reminded her I'd been her sister's roommate, not mentioning that Thalia and I were randomly assigned. *I want to thank you for any info you're able to share with my students,* I wrote. *They're not interested in stirring up trouble, and I think their focus will be on how the school itself impeded or aided the investigation.* I wasn't sure that was true, but I hoped it would read as anodyne. I added that I'd lost a brother at around the same age, that I understood how long and complicated grief can be, and I didn't want to upset her. Then I settled back and watched the film.

We were only at the part where Poppy asks Tony about his jewelry when I got a reply.

She had sent an actual Dropbox link. No message.

I was thrilled, and I was terrified. Terrified of finding myself in the interview transcripts, and terrified to be drawn further into this vortex, and terrified that there would be nothing useful here at all.

One night years ago, when I was fairly sure Jerome was sleeping with another artist, I stole his phone and took it into the bathroom. It wasn't till I found nothing at all in his text messages that I realized I'd been *wanting* to find proof, if only to validate my instinct that something was terribly wrong between us. I felt the same way now—hoping, oddly, for the worst, the glaring evidence that would tell me I needed to be involved, needed to drop everything and devote the next years of my life to sorting this all out.

I was afraid my shaking hands would delete the link—if they'd liked that awful GIF, who knew what else they could do—but I managed to open it, to sit in the back row having my own private, horrible Christmas morning.

There were over four hundred pages of documents. First, an enormous number of both medical and legal records that looked equally incomprehensible. I'd have thought I'd be a better reader for legal papers than medical ones, but it was all motions and codes and filings.

But there were also the interview transcripts I'd been hoping for, from the weeks after Thalia's death—much more than the day or two at Miss Vogel's kitchen table that I remembered. It seemed the State Police had returned several times to interview Thalia's close friends. I wanted to print these all out and read them thoroughly, didn't want to stare at the scanned Courier type on my phone, but I couldn't help skimming a few.

Here were Bendt Jensen's account of the mattress party, Jenny Osaka's of the dorm fire alarm. The first interviews indeed seemed to be from Saturday, March 11, a full week (a full, inexcusable week) after Thalia's body was found.

Yes—oh God—my own brief interview was there, but I wasn't ready to read it. Partly because reading it first would make me feel like some desperate opportunist (See, look! I was really there!) and partly because I was mortified to see what I'd said about Thalia being on drugs.

I scanned forward for any mention of Omar.

Here was Beth Docherty saying, "There's this guy who works in the weight room who's super sketchy. He'd definitely go to girls' sports practices a lot. Maybe that was part of his job, but it was weird. Thalia said this thing to me, she kept saying, 'Don't get involved with an older guy, it's not worth it.' But Robbie's only like a month older than her. So that makes me think."

Puja Sharma saying, "As a girl you have unwanted attention, at least if you're reasonably attractive. I think most boys left Thalia alone because she was dating Robbie. I don't think this was a student, because a student, you know, would see Thalia a certain way. You want to look at the people who—you want to ask, who around here knows the students, but *isn't* a student?" The interviewer asked if she meant anyone in particular, and Puja said, with surprising directness, "What I've heard is you should be looking at Omar, from the gym."

A Detective Boudreau from the Major Crimes Unit was asking most of the questions. "Did she tell you her plans for that evening?" he asked everyone, and "Did you know Thalia to be sexually active?" and "Was Thalia hurting herself in any way?" The questions seemed irrelevant to the case, as if he'd be asking the same things no matter who died or how. There was an occasional follow-up, a "How so?" or "Could you spell that?" or "What time would that have been?" but nothing terribly incisive.

I hoped against hope that someone besides me had mentioned her being on drugs, at least smoking up once in a while. I needed that not to have come from me alone. So far, though, my skimming turned up nothing else.

I'd need to read thoroughly later, with a clear head, in an organized way. Or Britt and Alder would, rather. I forwarded them the Dropbox.

From somewhere in the dark, the voice of one of my students: "Wait, he's her *brother*? He's way too into her." Someone else shushed him.

I'd ordered pizzas, and toward the end of the 1932 version, I had to stand outside and wait for the delivery. I was shifting from foot to foot in the cold when my phone pinged with a text from Mike Stiles. That Lola had included me when they introduced their Uncle Mike to Britt via text on Friday made this only a bit less shocking. There, in my phone, *Maybe: Mike Stiles.*

The text read: *Hey, Bodie, it was so good to hear your name from Lola. I can't believe how long it's been! I have a few reservations about talking to these students. Would you be able to chat sometime tomorrow?*

I had the sudden feeling of being watched, out there in the cold. I felt the need to compose my face, to tug my coat down smooth over my stomach, pull my shoulders back. I thought of typing a response, but it was too cold to take my gloves off, and it would probably be better just to call tomorrow. Plus here was the pizza car.

My timing was perfect; I returned to the theater just as Tony died in the gutter, just as the sign behind him announced that the world was his.

By two a.m., I'd gone through every document Vanessa had sent, reading the ones I could understand. I'd looked at my own words, which took up just two pages. The dumpster story was the only thing of note that I told them. I talked about the musical, but they never asked what time it ended.

In those earliest interviews, I was indeed the only one mentioning drugs. I felt increasingly sick; who knew what I'd started by trying to be relevant? They asked Thalia's friends if she was on drugs, if she had a drinking problem, if she'd been suicidal, and they all answered no. But by the second round, as the questions centered increasingly on Omar, as they asked things like "If Thalia were looking to buy drugs on campus, who do you think she'd go to?" everyone seemed to warm to the idea. They couldn't say she *hadn't* been buying drugs, and everyone knew, they said, that Omar sold. The same guy they'd been mentioning from the start. Puja and Rachel and Beth; Robbie, Dorian, Mike, Marco Washington—they'd all brought him up.

It was still possibly true that Omar had followed Thalia around, that he'd "made her uncomfortable," as Robbie said, or "sketched her out" as Marco said, or "kind of stalked her," as Rachel said, or that he'd joked about tying Thalia to the weight bench, as Dorian and Mike and their ski friend Kirtzman all mentioned.

But it was also possible her friends had jelled their memories together, even subconsciously, in the days before their interviews, around a person who wasn't part of their group, wasn't a teacher or a student—someone who seemed enough of an outsider to have done a thing we couldn't imagine one of us doing. As humans have intuited since the dawn of time, blaming the problem on someone outside your circle takes the problem far away. And it made sense that even Marco, a Black Granby student bound for Babson, would see Omar as fundamentally different.

By three a.m., unable to close my eyes, I was looking at timelines on Reddit. Reading everything I could about the details and circumstances of Thalia's death no longer felt like a trapdoor to anxiety; it felt more like the single rope on hand as every life raft around me sank. If holding on tight meant staying up till the sky lightened, so be it.

By four a.m., I was back on Dane Rubra's YouTube channel.

"Let's talk for a minute," Dane says in one early video, "about the 1975 murder of Barbara Crocker.

"Barbara Crocker is a young, beautiful Spanish teacher at Granby. She's from Quebec, living off campus in the town of Kern. She goes missing in late April of '75, and on May thirteenth her body is found decomposing in the woods adjacent to the Granby campus. Who goes to jail? Her boyfriend. Sure, okay. Usually the boyfriend does it. I'm looking at you, Roberto A. Serenho, Jr. Usually it's the boyfriend."

Dane disappears, is replaced by the same grainy photo of Barbara Crocker that ran in the *Sentinel* my senior year, when Rachael Martin wrote a *did you know what happened here twenty years ago* piece: Barbara's long, dark hair parted down the center, glasses no one could ever have found attractive. She looks so much like 1975 that you can't imagine what life she might have lived outside it.

Dane returns to tell us the case against Barbara's boyfriend, Ari Hutson, was largely circumstantial, but then there was a mountain of circumstance: He had not only paid her end-of-month phone bill, but also signed a birthday card to her nephew, imitating her signature. Neighbors had seen him come and go from her place in the days after her death, days in which he did not report her missing. He was the only one who could have bleached her carpet, who could have washed the murder weapon and returned it to Barbara's knife rack.

Here's a fun fact Dane Rubra does not include: It's not always the boyfriend. The actual statistic, if you care, is that worldwide, 38.6 percent of murdered women are killed by intimate partners. In some countries that's much higher.

But if you're looking at a young woman who wasn't involved in illegal activities, who wasn't on the streets, who wasn't involved in sex work, had a support system, wasn't robbed outside a nightclub on vacation, who *had* a serious boyfriend, or two—yes, someone she was sleeping with did it. Which is why it's important for the police to know who she was sleeping with.

But in none of the State Police interviews did anyone suggest this might have been you. Your name comes up as one of the last two adults to see her, as a teacher she was close to. The police took little enough note that they consistently spelled your name "Block."

And then they interviewed you, for all of seven minutes. You said the blandest, vaguest things possible. They did ask where you were that night, but only in the most perfunctory way, and after all you had your alibi—you cleaned up, you talked to me (there was my name even, from your mouth), you got straight home to your wife and kids. They were more interested in whether Thalia's grades had been sliding, whether she'd seemed distressed. You said, four different times, "She was a great kid."

Dane Rubra says, "Let's grant that Crocker's boyfriend kills her in a crime of passion. But Granby doesn't want a crime scene messing up their reputation. What gets into the papers is the body being found in the New Hampshire woods. Eventually it comes out that it's near campus." Dane shows a series of maps and argues the body was found *on* campus, that the school got the DA and coroner to move the official location fifty yards.

"What I'm saying," he says, and he should wipe the sweat off his forehead, "is the pockets are deep, and the conspiracies run deeper."

#6: ARI HUTSON

We all know there's a man who lurks at the edge of the campus, who lives in a lacrosse goal in the woods. Everyone knows someone who's seen him, and we've assigned him various names—Lurch, the Hermit. Fran and I joke he's the one adding notes to the Kurt shrine. According to one story, he's a Granby student who left school one credit shy of graduation. Geoff Richler says, "He's out there trapping raccoons. Them's good eats."

The story that sticks: He's Barbara Crocker's convicted boyfriend, out of prison, returning to the scene of the crime. He has an apartment in Kern but camps out at Granby in warmer months. Ari Hutson was released in 1989; it isn't impossible.

I've found photos of him online, featuring a mop of friendly hair and a scraggly beard. In one, he wears a striped turtleneck and laughs with someone at a party. To be honest, I can see the appeal. In a 1975 way.

On March 3, he's in the dark by the gym when Thalia appears. She's there to wait for you. She took off fast after curtain call, but you have things to oversee, percussion to lock up, stage managers to talk to.

By the time you get to the meeting point, Thalia's not there. You try the front gym door and it's open, which it shouldn't be. You look around inside, not wanting to call her name, but everything in the building is dark.

You go home to your wife and your kids. The next morning you look for Thalia at brunch, but it's the weekend and kids sleep in, so you're not worried, only irritated, and you wish you could call her. You think of ringing the Singer-Baird pay phone, asking for her in a disguised voice. Maybe you even do it, but the girl who answers just tells you Thalia isn't in her room. You'll see her at dinner, and if not, certainly you'll see her that night for *Camelot*.

Of course you don't tell the police she was there to meet you. You don't tell them where she might have been standing when someone came across her. You don't tell them that you know she wasn't sleeping with Omar. You know the older guy her friends heard about was you. You don't tell the police anything at all, except to give your own alibi and tell them what a lovely girl she was, what a promising student. A great kid, a great kid, a great kid.

You've had to live with yourself for a quarter century.

50

I must have slept a few minutes at least, because I woke having dreamed about Yahav. I felt like I could turn and he'd be there—hadn't he just been spooning me?—but no, that pillow was cold, with none of the dark, soft hairs I'd always find after he'd shared my bed. There was an urgency to the dream, though, a sense that I was supposed to ask him something, tell him something.

And maybe I should. Not about me, not about him, but about the case.

Yahav wasn't a practicing criminal lawyer, but he did teach evidence law, which seemed quite relevant. Yahav and his parents had become US citizens when he was seventeen, the same year he caught Paul Newman's *The Verdict* on TV and became obsessed with the American legal system. He excelled at dismantling the legal premise of anything we watched together. I questioned my own motivations—did I simply want his attention?—but I knew my only chance of getting him back was to leave him alone. Instead, I needed to do the opposite.

I sent him a link to the Free Omar website, and I sent him the Dropbox link. I wrote, *I'd love your take on this. You remember what I told you about my roommate. Does this conviction seem solid to you?*

Alone in my classroom in Quincy half an hour before class started, I remembered I could google *Granby + Thalia + dots + planner* to confirm that I knew the answer to that particular riddle. I should have been listening to the students' revised episodes—though I'd already decided to give them all As, regardless. Who was I to come in and blow someone's GPA?

I wonder if you've seen the scanned pages yourself, if you've googled the minutiae of Thalia's case alone in your office late at night—or if you've put up a wall, never let yourself type the letters of her name.

Although the planner had never been admitted into evidence, multiple websites now showed the layout. Someone—the police? Thalia's family?—had made public the two pages for the week ending Friday, March 3, 1995, with the weekend of the fourth and fifth compressed in the margin. As I'd imagined, the dots in question occupied the bottom corner of each day's box. It looked legitimate; I recognized Thalia's careful handwriting.

Something Fran hadn't mentioned: It wasn't only dots. At the bottom of Monday, February 27, one red dot. Nothing on Tuesday. On Wednesday the first, a blue X in brackets. On Thursday the second, both a blue X and a purple one.

One Reddit theorist insisted the marks were times Omar hit her. That she was documenting them in order to report Omar, and he killed her before she could. Someone trolling that poster kept insisting it was about bowling scores, that the Xs were strikes. *You're only proving my point,* the original poster wrote. *If an X is a strike, maybe that was her association. Today I was struck.*

I understood why they hadn't used this in court, not without an explicit key in the back of the book. Still, I would have loved to see the rest of the planner. If the red dots went back a few days, that was obviously her period. If she'd followed my system (could I flatter myself to think so?) that would mean the Xs were sexual contact. Perhaps the parentheses meant a different sex act, or a truncated effort. Maybe the blue X and the purple X meant different people she was sleeping with. One for Robbie, one for you? Or maybe one was for protected sex, one for unprotected.

Vanessa hadn't written back after I'd thanked her for the Dropbox files, but I sent her another email: *I absolutely understand if you aren't interested in additional information at this point, but I can't help but mention that I think I know how to read the dot and X codes in Thalia's planner, which*

I didn't see until recently. They're based on something I used to do myself. Please disregard this if it's too much to deal with.

And then I dove back into Reddit.

The Xs were times she cut herself.

The dots were hang-up calls she'd gotten, and the Xs were threatening letters. Well, we didn't have phones in our rooms, so that one didn't work, did it.

It was about diet, several people insisted. Times she'd binged and purged. *I had the exact same system,* someone wrote. That one was possible, I had to admit.

Britt entered the classroom first, and I don't know what look was on my face, but she took a step back, said, "Oh—am—is it too early?" Britt wore a long floral dress with Docs poking out underneath, a long ratty cardigan over that. Like a sweet, ironic girl right out of 1994.

I said, "Lord help me, but I think I've fallen into this dot conspiracy. Thalia's planner."

She grinned. She said, "I knew we'd get you hooked."

Just before class started, a text from Yahav. I hadn't actually expected him to delve into details. I'd imagined that if he replied at all, it would be some kind of "Looks interesting, but these things are difficult" response.

But what he wrote was: *Been reading up all morning. Give me a call? I have a lot of thoughts.*

51

The kids played new material that day, things they'd use in their second episodes. Alyssa had distilled our séance to two fun minutes, with jaunty music.

Lola had tape of a Foxie's waitress saying, "My nephew, he applied up there because you figure, aren't they gonna educate the kids right here in town? They got scholarship money to hand out, but they can't see fit to give it local, they go look for kids in California. He's flat-out rejected. And they never did tell us why. He's got mostly Bs and As, some Cs. You're gonna reject someone whose family has worked for the school a hundred years, no explanation?"

That one gave the students pause. I could tell it bothered them, despite their default progressive stance—this assertion that a random B student from town, someone without innate genius or a story of trauma overcome, might just pop into the Granby freshman class on a scholarship that could have gone to someone extraordinary.

Alder said, "Did you, like, try to explain it to her?"

Lola shrugged. "I'm an impartial reporter."

When it was Britt and Alder's turn, Alder raised his hand tentatively, as if he were about to swat a bug that might startle. He said, "We have something we don't know what to do with."

Britt looked frustrated; clearly, he wasn't supposed to bring this up. She said, "It's not even audio."

"It's audio if we read it aloud." He opened his laptop and cleared his throat. "Okay, this is Sonya Rousseau. She was the one—she was married to Omar for about a year, before he came here. So, she gave an interview on this random website five years ago. It's her, it checks out." He angled the computer so the rest of us could look. I recognized the name of the site, remembered someone on Reddit referencing the interview, but I hadn't seen it.

I knew about Sonya before the news reports, because Omar had talked about her. He'd chat when we were on the ergs, tell us how after UNH he met and got engaged to a Dartmouth senior whose parents disapproved. They eloped, but were separated by their first anniversary in 1991. She'd left him with no warning, cleaned everything out one day while he was at work—even the TV, even the cat. Omar brought her up obsessively: *She was smart like all of you,* he'd say, or *My ex could never lift more than ten pounds. She was like, Ow, my arms!* He didn't say it in a vengeful way. He didn't call her crazy, or a bitch. But it was constant.

Alder began to read her words: *Omar's temper scared me, and it scared my parents. He locked me out of the house once. It was twenty degrees and I didn't have my boots. He'd yell, he'd grab my shoulders and get right in my face. You have to understand, he's six foot two, he lifts. Sometimes I'd agree with him just so things didn't get physical. He didn't have to use his body to be violent. Does that make sense? And when he was mad, he wouldn't give up. Once, he stormed out of the house and I locked the doors behind him. He decided to get back in, so he started banging, and he climbed up onto the porch roof and opened our bedroom window. I called the police, and they didn't understand. How do you explain that yes, this is your husband and this is his house but no, he's not supposed to be here?*

"Wait," Lola said, "so she's saying it's bad that he locked her out of the house but also *she* locked *him* out of the house and that was good?"

Alyssa said, "Yeah, but he does sound intimidating."

"Depends what she means by *grabbed her shoulders,*" Jamila said. "Like, we've all grabbed people by the shoulders. There's a normal way to do it, and a scary way."

"But she's saying it was the scary way."

"Right," Lola said, "but she's a white woman saying this about a Black man *after* he was arrested for murder. Her perception might be skewed."

They started arguing, and I couldn't follow anyone's voice.

This—I realized it, and it sank me into my chair—this was why I shouldn't be involved. Because what the hell did I know? Maybe Sonya was bitter and exaggerating and he was the same Omar I knew, outgoing and kind; maybe she was telling the truth and Omar killed Thalia, would have killed again if he weren't in prison; maybe he was indeed a terrible husband, an aggressive man, who had *not* killed Thalia but whose vibe had given Thalia's friends just enough fuel to convince each other it was him.

If it was inappropriate, in 1995, for Thalia's friends to speculate, for their opinions to weigh something—for me to offer my unhelpful memory to the police, too—maybe it was equally inappropriate for *these* students to get involved. What measures did any of us have for the truth?

But who was I kidding? I wasn't going to stop the kids, or myself.

I put on my most convincing teacher voice and I said, "The back-and-forth on this will make it a better podcast. Remember, we want questions. This raises such great questions."

52

I wanted to call Yahav after film class, but I knew he'd be getting his kids dinner—he was the family cook—plus I'd told Mike Stiles I'd call.

I hate the phone. It's one thing talking to family or the pharmacist, but a scheduled call with someone I sort of know makes me want to pull hairs from the nape of my neck. I do best when I'm moving, so after a hot shower in the guesthouse, I put in my AirPods and started my walk toward the dining hall.

He answered, mercifully, with "Bodie!" so there was no need to stammer an explanation, remind him why I was calling. He said, "How's everyone? How's everything?"

I gushed about Lola, the class, campus, told him who was still around. I said, "I hear you're at UConn." He mentioned that he had three kids, that the oldest was twelve.

I was crossing Middle Bridge, and told him so.

"I'm jealous!" he said. "Lola knows I'm coming to graduation whether I'm invited or not." And then, "So speaking of Lola, this—this project."

"Oddly," I said, inanely anxious that he know this, "I had nothing to do with the idea." I explained about Britt's interest predating the class, how the kids saw the whole thing as ancient lore.

Mike said, "It's been on my mind a lot, actually. The past couple years."

"It means something new when you have your own kids."

"Sure," he said, "sure. But I guess I just mean this moment we're in, the stuff—we were so—God, Bodie, I don't know."

One of the first things I'd taught the kids about getting someone to talk was biting your tongue. ("Literally," I said, "if necessary.") Sure enough, he filled his own silence.

"If I had to play the odds, I'd say Omar did it. But you can't arrest someone on rumors, right? I remember we had that sign-up sheet, and we went in—we said what we knew, but we'd for sure already talked to each other. You're sitting around for days trying to process, trying to figure out what happened, and people are saying stuff about Omar. It starts to make sense."

I was at New Chapel now, and snow had started to fall again, fast and thick and wet, landing on my face and scarf, blowing into my legs. I ducked inside, stood in the vestibule. There had once been a pay phone here; now there was a phone charging station.

"Then Omar confessed," he said, "and even if he recanted it was like, *okay*, well, there's your answer. It's solved, like the end of a TV show. But, Bodie, what I know now—false confessions are so common."

It was wild how familiar his voice sounded. He'd never talked in class, and I hadn't spoken to him much—but then I'd listened to him every night in *Camelot* rehearsal, heard his gravelly voice not too long ago in the YouTube version, saying, *My teacher Merlin, who always remembered things that haven't happened better than things that have.*

Mike said, "Especially—I look at this case, and they had Omar on drug charges, easily. We basically handed him over on that. They're asking who could have done this, and we all said, *Well, this guy follows Thalia around, and we heard he sells weed.* I mean, we *knew* he sold weed. I'm sure when they searched his place they found enough drugs to put him away. I was never there, but—the guys who'd been to his apartment said he had grow lamps and everything." I wondered if those guys had really been there, or had claimed this only after Omar's arrest, but I didn't ask. "And it's possible the drugs were a factor in his confession. What did they really have him on, besides that initial confession?"

"He had access to the pool," I said. "He was in the building." I didn't consider this solid evidence anymore, but Mike had asked.

"That's absolutely circumstantial. And also. Bodie. We *all* had access to the gym, if not the pool. How many master keys were circulating? If that one pool door wasn't locked, any of us could've gotten in. And some kids probably had the pool key, too. I remember I'm answering their questions, and I'm thinking, Christ, I have two different illicit keys under a sneaker insole in my closet right now. I remember thinking that if they knew, they'd arrest *me*."

"And Omar's DNA was on the swimsuit," I said. "And he drew that noose."

"Right." He sighed. "Right." He was quiet a moment.

It was a relief to talk to another adult about this. Fran didn't want to, and Carlotta didn't want to, but Mike seemed less interested in chatting about his participation in the podcast than in the details of the case. It made me feel less crazy; he'd clearly spent time thinking about this, too.

I found myself halfway down one of the two chapel aisles. A living room was set up on the stage—flowery sofa, a lamp with no cord, a coffee table with a lace throw—and I remembered the posters around campus for the one-act festival happening here. The sun was setting through the stained glass on the west wall. Everything smelled like warm, ancient wood.

I said, "Would he really trade a drug charge for a murder charge?"

There was a long pause, and a couple of times I heard him take a breath to start, but nothing came out. Finally he said, "A lot of my research touches on amnesty and human rights. And I'm seeing this case, and I feel like such a hypocrite. I contributed to this."

"Plenty of people contributed."

"Probably he did, but what do I know? It's not up to me to decide, and teenage me shouldn't have had a say either. Maybe we shouldn't have let, you know, a bunch of kids hand someone to the police. What I mean is, the stuff they had on him—it came from us. Except the DNA, I guess. But none of us thought, hey, I'm personally framing this guy. And—very much off the record—maybe we did. We might have set up a guilty guy, but we set him up."

By that point I felt physically unsettled in a way that had nothing to do with speaking to someone I'd once found attractive. He didn't mean to include me in his "we," but he had.

I walked back to the vestibule and headed into the bathroom, although I didn't need it—bathrooms simply being the place you go when you feel sick, when you need to be alone. The door was old and swung in on two familiar decrepit stalls, a familiar sink, the warped mirror above it, the crank paper towel dispenser. I couldn't have told you a thing about this bathroom five seconds earlier, and now I recognized every inch.

There was a radiator under the tiny frosted window, and I leaned back against it, grilling my butt through my jeans.

I said, "This is random, but do you remember if students were drinking backstage that night, at *Camelot*? Would Thalia have been drinking?"

He puffed out air. "I mean, in general, sure. That night? Who knows. Why?"

I explained, as best I could, my concerns about the timeline. He gave a noncommittal "Huh." He said, "I just—God, this could be such a mess. I don't trust my memory of what I ate *last night*. What do you think happens to memory over twenty years? Anyway, your students ask me to chat and this is what goes through my mind. I just feel like—it's such a can of worms."

I couldn't figure out if he was arguing against looking into the case. Surely not. But he sounded pained.

"It's only a student project," I said, feebly.

"So was Facebook."

He agreed, in the end, to talk to Britt and Alder about his memories of Thalia, at least; he'd see how he felt about whatever else came up. I'd taken off my coat, enjoying the stuffy heat of the small bathroom, scooting around on the radiator to warm different parts of my legs. I said, "Lola says you found me scary in high school."

"Oh. I mean—you were a little prickly, maybe. Or maybe you just didn't want to deal with me. I was passing as a dude-bro. I'm sure I was terrible."

"You were nice to me."

"Well, sure. That's what you do when you're afraid of someone." He was laughing, though, and there was something flattering about the idea that he'd looked at me with anything other than pity or scorn. "I could never figure you out. This goth kid who rowed crew and did musicals." That was two more things than I'd have guessed he remembered about me, even if I hadn't quite *done musicals*. I couldn't parse the nostalgia, or maybe even tenderness, in his voice.

He had to go; he'd be in touch after he talked to the students.

"You have my number," I said, and wondered if my tone was more like someone in a business meeting or in a romantic comedy. Ridiculously, I wondered if Yahav would have been jealous if he'd heard me.

I was hanging up when my phone buzzed with a text from Carlotta, and for a moment it was 1995, me debriefing with her after I talked to a cute boy. *You okay?* the message read. *Plz lmk if there's ANYTHING I can do, seriously.*

I put on my coat, toasted dry from the radiator. I'd love it if this were about my students' podcast, but I knew that even though Carlotta wasn't on Twitter, it was about Jerome and about my own downfall, information making its way through the private messages of people who knew me.

I got hotter and hotter as I stood there, and when I stepped out into the ridiculous cold, it came as a relief.

53

Things constantly on my mind:

The next time I'd hear from Lance. Whether I should check Twitter. Whether I should check my inbox. Whether it was time to switch careers or change my name.

Whether Jerome was sleeping and eating enough that he could safely drive the kids around.

Whether quitting the podcast would mean I was financially dependent on Jerome again. Whether Jerome still had an income for me to depend on.

Omar's mother, in front of her piano.

Thalia's parents, at their kitchen table.

How quickly I could get to Boston and grab Yahav and convince him to spend just one afternoon in a motel so I could drink in enough of him to last me a few months.

What you might have done after you left the theater that night, just moments after you said goodbye to me.

What I'd once seen as a pile of evidence against Omar quickly turning to sand.

(But then: His ex's words, her fear.)

The news story, which I couldn't avoid even when I wasn't online. Another woman had come forward. The president called her a dog.

Loose ends on the Rita Hayworth episodes I might never finish. The way her flamenco dancer father took her on the road at age four, abusing her physically and sexually, setting her up for a lifetime of terrible relationships. She considered herself a dancer throughout her career—more than an actress, certainly more than a sex symbol. When she was upset, Orson Welles, her second of five husbands, would put on a record of Spanish music and leave her alone to dance out her stress. What happens when your only escape is the same thing you're trying to escape? Here's the soundtrack of your tragedy: Dance to it.

54

My classy move: Rather than getting Yahav on the phone myself, I invited him to conference call with Britt and Alder after class on Wednesday. The whole group ended up staying, though, gathered around my faceup phone. Yahav's voice was ice in a whiskey glass, and I could feel it through the table, through the floor, up my legs.

He said, "I'm not so interested in guilty or innocent, strange as that might sound. I'm interested in due process. My perspective is maybe this guy did it, but the case was shit."

Britt typed frantically at her laptop, despite the fact that we were recording; Alder did a happy dance with his arms.

"I don't know New Hampshire law precisely," he said, "but I can speak to the issues in general. The only evidence that isn't horribly circumstantial is the DNA and the confession. And this was *trace* DNA. DNA is tricky. A few years ago, they find DNA on a dead girl's jeans, they spend all this money, and they end up tracking it back to a worker at the Taiwanese factory where the jeans were made. Not helpful. Plus, in 1995 the DNA science was horseshit. You have a much smaller pool of samples back then, so they end up saying, like, *This is a one in eight million match*, when now they'd say it's one in two thousand. It was a brand-new field."

My students were grinning, which I imagined was partly because he said words like "horseshit" in such an elegant accent. I hadn't heard the story about the jeans before. If all the DNA showed was that Omar had once touched that swimsuit, well—if I were on a jury, I wouldn't have found that compelling proof. I ticked off one more mental box. A big one.

"Then we have the confession. As soon as drug allegations are involved, my antennae go up. Because you know what they do: They say they're handing you to the feds on drug charges, but if you cooperate in this local investigation maybe they can protect you. They say, Did you let her into the pool that night? You must have seen her, or how else did your DNA get there? They say, This looks bad, we've got you at the scene now *plus* the drug charges, your only hope is to confess."

So he had actually dug into the case. Under other circumstances I'd have been overwhelmed with romantic hope, but my heart was pounding, instead, over Omar. The real Omar I'd known, not the guy in the mug shot. The real Omar, spending the rest of his life in prison. And while Yahav might not have been convinced yet of his innocence, Yahav didn't know about *you*.

He said, "You've heard about these cases, yes? People so sleep-deprived they'll sign anything, or people who believe lies about evidence or leniency or getting to go home. It gets worse from there. Actual violence, actual torture. Even in America."

"This is amazing," Britt said. "Can we, like—"

But Yahav was in lecture mode. "This many years later," he said, "to appeal again, Mr. Evans would ideally have two things in place. One is a reasonable case for ineffective assistance of counsel, meaning he didn't have adequate help from his legal team. They tried to claim this in his appeal in '99, along with some things about the way the evidence was submitted, but it's incredibly hard to prove IAC unless your lawyer actually fell asleep every day in court. He had a terrible lawyer, but that's not the court's problem."

Britt had been talking just that morning about how Omar's original attorney hardly did any independent investigation on the Granby campus. Omar's uncle, his deceased father's brother, had done well for himself as a commercial pilot, and insisted on hiring and paying for a friend of his, a high-profile Boston attorney.

New Hampshire's public defenders are apparently excellent, and know everyone in the legal system of what is, after all, a very small state. They know the culture, and they don't overdress for court. But the Boston attorney—I remembered him from *Dateline*—was a designer suit guy with thick black hair and a bright blue Miata that he'd park around the corner from the courthouse. He didn't stay in Kern during the five-week trial but half an hour away at a nice hotel in Brattleboro. None of this had gone over well with the jury. The juror Lester Holt interviewed, the lady with big yellow hair, called him "that slick lawyer from Boston." But more importantly: The man came in with enormous hubris, did as little work as possible, hardly raised any objections to hearsay testimony, then acted shocked at the conviction.

Yahav said, "So since that appeal failed, Mr. Evans's best bet now is the appearance of new evidence. Not just any evidence, but evidence that would upend the case. New DNA, for instance. And if he can argue this was evidence his original lawyers should have found—if he can make a new, better claim for ineffective assistance of counsel—he *might* have a shot at a new trial. That's the needle you'd have to thread."

Britt said, "So, as you know, we're high school students. But we *are* invested in this, and I plan to go to law school, and I kind of want this podcast to continue for however long, until we get some answers. Maybe we could at least stay in touch with you about it."

He took a deliberative breath. He said, "I don't have time to get too involved." Then he said, "Post-conviction litigation is a nightmare. Unless you got a video of someone else doing it, the reality is they're not letting Mr. Evans out. Even if you *did* get a video, it's a long shot, believe me." He laughed sadly. "But sure, we can talk again if you find something."

After the kids left, I texted him my thanks. He wrote back: *Most likely outcome after years of work will be more people know it was a crap conviction, but nothing gets overturned.*

Three dots danced for ages as he typed. Long enough that I wondered if he was going to say he missed me, say he regretted Saturday.

But no. He wrote: *As a matter of principle, I do think it's worth pursuing.*

I'd just advise against getting hopes up. It could be horribly unsatisfying, to halfway unsolve a murder. He stays in prison, but now no one has closure, including the victim's family. That's all you ever get from this.

As I stepped out onto the quad, as the cold air punched me in the face, I let myself acknowledge several things.

For one, it had fully settled in my gut: Omar didn't do this. Or at least: Every reason I once believed in his guilt had fallen away, and I no longer believed he was any more likely than any number of other people to have done it. (Whether or not you did it was, for the time being, irrelevant. You weren't about to confess, and we weren't about to find your fingerprints on the pool door after all these years. What mattered was the travesty of a case against Omar.)

Another thing: If I no longer had *Starlet Fever*, I had more time on my hands, not just this week but for the foreseeable future. This was still the kids' project, but I had bandwidth to help. I could try to find them distribution. I could advise or consult or even produce. I could do that alongside other projects, like the book that I really did want to write.

And another: At the end of this week, there was no way I'd be able to let go of the spring of 1995, of the questions and people I needed to revisit.

And another: Didn't I personally owe it, after all, to Omar?

55

When I returned to the guesthouse after dinner that night, Oliver was at the kitchen island with a bag of tortilla chips and a jar of salsa.

I sat on the stool next to his and resisted grilling him about Amber the Latin teacher, who I was pretty sure had slept over last night. Instead, I asked if he could believe our two weeks were almost done.

Oliver shook his head. He said, "I can't get over it even existing. The kids, and the place. I want to hate it, but I don't."

This was when a text came through from Jerome: *I quit Otis so they wouldn't have to fire me. That's better, right?*

I managed to keep talking to Oliver, somehow. I said, "I mean, it's an *incredible* school. And it's way better now than it used to be. But—my grades in middle school were terrible." I turned my phone facedown. "And they still took me. There are prep schools as selective as Harvard, you know? This was a place kids came when they couldn't get in those places, or when they failed out. I didn't know that when I got here. I thought it was full of the smartest kids in the world, and I was gonna flunk. I wasn't a great student, but I passed my classes just fine."

Oliver looked confused, and I could tell I was rambling. I was busy thinking that if I no longer had a job either, we could get by on Jerome's sales—but it occurred to me that those might dry up, too.

"All to say," I said, attempting to recover, "it was a very special school for perfectly average kids."

He said, "I can see how this school would draw you back. Like your friend who never left. It feels like a place you could settle into." He looked terrified, and a little glassy, and I understood that he was falling in love.

Presumably with Amber, but maybe with the place, too. He was picturing a life for himself at Granby, with her.

I said, "I really believed in magic when I was here. Maybe that's because of the age I was, but—I had a lot of magical thinking going on." I was glad he didn't press for details, because I couldn't explain about the marks I made for Ace, the pay phone, the earnest séances, the way I took everything as a sign.

Maybe I was falling into that thinking again, but the universe seemed to be pointing me in such an obvious direction: Bring me back to Granby, throw Britt and Alder in my path, take away Yahav, take away any stability Jerome had once provided. Give me Thalia's yearbook quote and the dots in her planner and show me Beth Docherty's flask. And what was left in front of me but one clear path?

Oliver stared into the salsa as if it might hold answers for him. I'd seen him on that couch at the party. I'd seen his eyes as he talked to Amber over giant dining hall waffles. I said, "This isn't the moment for caution." He looked up at me, either startled that I'd seen into his soul or baffled.

I stood, because I needed to go upstairs and email Lance and tell him that I really truly was done, that I released him, that he should look for a new cohost right away. I had a few in mind.

I said, "You should tell her how you feel."

56

When you're eighteen, a month is a few years. Thalia's death, Puja walking out into the night, the Oklahoma City bombing, the Tokyo subway attack, the O. J. Simpson trial, the Bosnian war, our classmates' car crash—they were all the clutter of one busy spring and didn't seem to occur in any particular psychological proximity.

What I remember: Puja, having fallen out with Rachel and Beth, taking off into the night, then getting swept away from Granby. Tim Busse and Graham Waite driving back drunk from Quebec and crashing, Graham holding on for a day in the ICU without any real hope. (Two boys I'd rather liked: Tim, whose voice was the first I'd heard on my magic pay phone, and Graham, who'd sung me Tom Petty.) Three memorial services, all a blur. You leading the Choristers in the same songs each time: "Bridge Over Troubled Water" and "Jerusalem." That reporter hanging around town, trying to intercept us on our way to the bakery or the pharmacy for her *Rolling Stone* article.

Was it any wonder Thalia's death folded into the others, both in our own imaginations and the public's? Hani Kayyali, who'd taken over as class president when Jenny Osaka stepped down, gave a graduation speech about healing and moving on—meaning from all of it, the bitterness that had seeped into every interaction, the new wave of uninspired vandalism on campus, the muck of accusations and regret and distrust.

We listened numbly on the quad, the girls in white dresses that ranged from casual bridal to Vegas cocktail, the boys in khakis and dark blazers. We froze, they roasted.

When you found me to say goodbye, I was standing between Severn Robeson and my mother, holding a plate of cake. I doubt you remember the awkwardness, me not knowing how to introduce them, you not fully understanding who they were. But it was chaos anyway: infinite aunts and uncles and godparents swarming, illicit cigars and flasks in every direction. After four years of forced intimacy, we had all just learned each other's middle names. Our rooms were already emptied.

I remember you saying to my mother, "Bodie's been my Girl Friday the past three years. I wish I could clone her."

This was the only time my mother set foot at Granby. She'd sniffed her way through my campus tour, calling every building "fancy." She wore capri pants and a floral T-shirt to the ceremony, and I avoided her as much as possible. It was only partly embarrassment; mostly, I resented her invasion of this place she didn't understand, her skeptical glances at the spots I was bereft to leave.

And then there was Severn, whom everyone took for my father. While I'd grown up thinking of the Robesons as elegant and rich, here he seemed positively Midwestern and middle-class, a hard-bellied guy in an ill-fitting sport coat.

My mother said to you, "And what do you teach?"

"Music," you answered, and she glanced at me, baffled. You thanked me for the gift I'd left outside your office door (one last RC Cola, for the road). And before someone dragged you away for a picture, you said, "I don't know my new address yet, or I'd say to write, but I suppose I'll just hear about you when you're famous."

"What did *that* mean?" my mother said as we walked toward the mostly empty tables. I sat with her and Severn as, across the lawn, my classmates who'd managed to ditch their families posed for photos. I longed to join them. "His Girl Friday? And what are you supposed to be so famous at?"

Dorian Culler walked right up to our table then, a couple of snickering skiers trailing him, and extended his hand to Severn in the most well-bred way. He said, "Mr. Kane, it's a pleasure. I've been courting your daughter with no success for years. Perhaps you can talk some sense into her. I plan to make a good living, and treat her well. She can have all the babies she wants. Six, seven babies at least. My name is Bueller," he said, and here his friends lost what was left of their composure, doubled over. "Ferris Bueller." Dorian's face never cracked. Severn said something confounded but polite, and Dorian bowed slightly before he walked away.

Severn said, "Well, it's grand that everyone's in high spirits. I'd hate to see the place get too serious."

I watched Dorian make his way back to the clump of loud, cigar-wielding families who seemed to know each other already. To my surprise, his mother had shown up in a wheelchair. Fran filled me in later, info from her parents: Mrs. Culler had been in a wheelchair since shortly after Dorian was born. We'd had no idea. We'd never seen her on campus before; maybe she'd never come. The paths around campus were too rocky even for a bike—the mailing they sent us before freshman year directly advised against bringing one—and it looked like serious work just getting her around the quad. Robbie, who'd likely been to Dorian's house in Greenwich many times, had taken it upon himself to wheel her across the rough terrain, to bring her cake and punch, to take his own boutonniere off and pin it to her dress.

I hated Dorian Culler with every organ of my body, but for the first time ever I felt the urge to talk to him. To say, "I had no idea, and you have no idea about me."

But everyone was dispersing, climbing into overloaded cars. It was time to go.

57

On Thursday, it sleeted. To be honest, I'd forgotten about sleet. You don't see it in movies; in the movies it either rains or snows. Why would Hollywood replicate this horrid, stinging slush?

I never had an umbrella at Granby. What a freak you'd have to be, to carry an actual umbrella, like some old lady, like someone who wasn't at home here in the woods. Never mind my sore throat from November to April, my hacking coughs, the low-grade fever I had for three full weeks late senior year, lurching to class, living on infirmary Motrin. I tried to remember if that fever was before or after my weeks of meltdown, my dangerous episode by the Kurt tree. It was around that time, certainly. I'd brushed off everyone's concern about my pallor, my vacant eyes, by telling them I was sick, which wasn't false.

We had a low-energy class that morning, the kids fuzzy-brained. They each had a final project due for their other class tomorrow as well; Alyssa had stayed up all night, something to do with a suspension bridge model.

They were only halfway out the door when I checked my email (a reflex, the worst habit) and called for Britt and Alder to stop. Between hate mail about Jerome and hate mail about me, an answer from Vanessa. It was curt but not angry.

I do have Thalia's planner, she wrote. *But if you're asking for scans I'm afraid I'm not comfortable with that. I live in Lowell, Mass, and could meet you somewhere between here and Granby if you'd like a look. I'm not keen on student involvement, but I can show you pages. I'd need to see some ID from you just for my own peace of mind. Perhaps this weekend?*

I was flying out Saturday morning. I could delay my flight, but it would be expensive and I didn't know what shape Jerome was in, how much longer he could watch the kids, whether they were keeping him sane or making things worse. But I couldn't miss this chance.

I wrote back saying early tomorrow morning would be significantly easier, hoping she wouldn't find me pushy. *I could come all the way to Lowell*, I wrote. I'd ask Fran to drive me, or I'd hire a Lyft. By the time I checked email again on the way into that afternoon's film class, she'd agreed, named a coffee shop where she could meet at seven a.m.

#7: YOUR WIFE

Let's say it was your wife.
Was it your wife?

58

Fran barely concealed her displeasure at my mission. She had no interest in getting up at five, but was fine with me borrowing her car. She said, "I hope this gives you closure." I kept myself from laughing, from bleating back the word *closure*, the very opposite of what I sought. Better to let Fran think we were wrapping things up.

In the still-dark of Friday morning I set off, flying over hills, watching out for moose. I hate LA driving so much that I'd forgotten I actually love regular driving.

I refilled her gas tank on the way and used, on impulse, the credit card I only use for business expenses. Because yes, wasn't this now my only job? I hadn't yet suggested to Britt and Alder that I'd help them continue the podcast—I couldn't show favoritism before the class ended—but I'd tell them that afternoon.

I found Vanessa at the corner table where she said she'd be, in yoga clothes and Uggs, her face older than I could reconcile with either the child I'd met or the young woman on *Dateline*. I pulled out my driver's license as I sat, and she looked at me like I was nuts. "You said," I started, and then she remembered, scanned it quickly, laughing at herself.

"I recognize you, believe it or not. When you're a kid, your older sister's life is fascinating."

She slid my latte across the table; she'd texted to ask my order.

I said, "I want to make sure I'm not misrepresenting myself. We weren't close friends, but we did live together, and—"

"It's fine," she said. "It's good, actually. Her close friends didn't protect her, did they? If you were one of them, it wouldn't help me trust you."

This was unexpected, a reassurance that sank deep in my bones.

She said, "I don't even know why I agreed to this, but I hate the way they talk about the planner online. That the marks are because she was bulimic or whatever." I didn't interject that I was pretty sure Thalia was at least a little bulimic. "I guess if you think you know something, I'd like to know it, too."

I nodded, worried I'd disappoint her.

She said, "So many terrible people reach out to me about the case, but after all these years, you're the first person from Granby, the first one who knew Thalia there, who's ever gotten in touch. Well." She reached into the tote bag hanging on her chair and pulled out an ancient spiral-bound Granby planner, the green cover worn to pulp. I received it gently, worried it would disintegrate. Inside, though, everything looked brand-new, as if Thalia might at any moment cross off one commitment and enter another in her neat, loopy writing.

It was an August-to-August planner, and I flipped through the pages of preseason tennis, the phone numbers jotted in corners, the project due dates and homework reminders and choir practices. Monday through Wednesday on the left pages, Thursday through the weekend on the right. On December 8, *Camelot* auditions. On December 9, the Lessons and Carols concert. The week of the twelfth, midterms. And all through it, the three kinds of marks: red dots, blue Xs, purple Xs. Sometimes the dots were roughly four weeks apart, and sometimes they were six weeks apart, or eight. But Thalia's period wasn't predictable—hadn't that been part of the problem? She had been so thin. No wonder she didn't always bleed, no wonder she had those scares. She didn't mark off all the days she bled, like I did—just what was probably the start date. That made it harder to interpret, but I was sure.

I said, "You know the red dots are her period."

Vanessa nodded. "That's one theory."

"No, seriously. I taught her how to keep track like this. You don't have the one from the previous year, do you?"

And to my surprise Vanessa pulled a second planner from the bag, the '93–'94 one, with its yellow-gold cover.

"Oh my God, perfect." I turned to the end of junior year Feb Week. There, that Thursday, the day she'd come back early, was a red dot. I said, "She had a pregnancy scare, and she was so relieved when her period came. This was it."

Vanessa nodded slowly. "Okay, so that—yeah, we know she wasn't pregnant when she died, but I guess some people thought maybe she *believed* she was. But there was a dot—" She took the senior year planner back and opened easily to the two facing pages that were viewable online. This was where the book had been pressed flat in Xerox machines and scanners at some point in the investigation. Monday, February 27, four days before she died, a red dot. She said, "I never liked that theory anyway. That she told Omar she was pregnant or something. Because they weren't together. I'm sure of that."

Perhaps this was just an inability to picture Thalia in a relationship with the killer she believed Omar was, but still her opinion was validating.

I turned forward from Feb Week in the junior planner. A blue X on Tuesday, a purple X on Thursday. Blues and purples scattered all through the spring, tucked into the bottom right-hand corners of days.

I said, carefully, as if Vanessa would be scandalized after all this time, "The Xs, I'm pretty sure, are times she slept with someone." And here, as I flipped, was Spring Dance, which she'd attended with Robbie. Two blue Xs in the corner. Spring Dance was at the Hanover Inn, and students who signed out for the weekend could take off afterward, ostensibly for home but really for party houses. There was a blue X the next day, too. I turned the planner toward her, pointed at where Thalia had written *SPRING DANCE* in orange highlighter, had outlined the letters with a black gel pen. I said, "The blue is Robbie. I think the purple is someone else."

Vanessa shook her head quickly, hair against her cheeks. "She wasn't sleeping with Omar. If they'd had a relationship he would have said so even after he recanted his confession. He would've used it to explain his DNA on her."

"I agree. It wasn't Omar. Wait."

We traded planners and on a hunch, I started scanning our senior winter. Thalia had convocation practice with you on Mondays, right before I did. There was a purple X on Monday, January 30. One on Monday, February 6. None the next week, which was Feb Week, when she was off with Robbie and there were plenty of blue ones. A purple one on Monday, February 20. Not every single Monday, but enough of them. Good God, if I was right, you were sleeping together while I was out there waiting in the hallway. On the couch, the brown corduroy couch beside your desk? And so let me get this straight: I would come into the room, I'd sit on that couch, and you'd talk to me, you'd look at me sitting right where this had happened. I could not process that in the coffee shop, and I can't process it now.

On Saturday, February 25, less than a week before she died, she'd written *DB, o/y*. You'd have to tell me what the second part meant (one year? only you?), but on the same day was a purple X. I turned the planner around for Vanessa. "Have you heard the name Denny Bloch?"

I told her everything I suspected about your relationship with Thalia, and she was disgusted but not shocked. How could any woman truly be shocked by predation?

We pored over the planners for the next twenty minutes, both of us mindful of the time—I'd have to race back for class—and there were definite patterns, like the correlations back in the fall between purple Xs and the nights we had Follies practice. And then, a gold mine: During the October opera trip to New York, three blue Xs and two purple ones. "There were only two other guys on the trip," I said. "Definitely not Omar Evans." I wrote the other names on a napkin for Vanessa: Kellan

TenEyck, who was dead, and Kwan Li, now a principal tenor with the English National Opera. I told Vanessa what I'd seen at Bethesda Fountain.

Even so, the purple and the blue could both have been Robbie—could have been, for instance, intercourse and blow jobs. Vanessa was the one who proved otherwise. I went through '94–'95 and she went through '93–'94. We were quiet until she hit her pen on the table. "Here," she said. Thalia had written *Ski Team—away at Hebron* across the whole weekend of March 4 to 6, 1994. A time when the ski team was definitively gone to Maine. But there was a purple X that Saturday. "She wouldn't have gone with the ski team, would she?"

I shook my head. "They didn't let friends travel with the team. She maybe could have signed out to someone's house and—but no, look, she had tech rehearsal that weekend." *Little Shop wet tech* was written in much smaller letters than Robbie's ski team commitment, but it was there. And if Thalia had failed to show for tech rehearsal, the one vital day when I was fully in charge, it would have been seared in my memory.

"So," she said.

I nodded. "So."

Vanessa pulled the senior planner to the middle of the table. "The week she died," she said. "The blue X here on Wednesday, in brackets. What are the brackets?"

"Maybe she still had her period," I said, "and they—maybe it was something other than sex."

"Maybe he pulled out," she said, and I reminded myself that yes, Vanessa was an adult, not someone I needed to protect from any of this.

I said, "She was with *both* of them on Thursday."

"It's so much sex," Vanessa said, and laughed drily. "Can you imagine being that young?"

I shook my head. I said, "My impression—and maybe you know more than I do—my impression is that Denny Bloch was never really investigated. For Thalia's death." I didn't know how this would go over, didn't know how upset she might be at the suggestion that the case wasn't settled, hermetically sealed.

Vanessa was focused on something other than my face, something over my shoulder. "He was how old, again?"

"Thirty-three," I said. "Married, two kids. He's still teaching."

Her fingers went to the bridge of her nose. "Christ."

I said, "I worry—I mean, the kids all talked together before anyone got interviewed. You know how the rumor mill can be. And I'm sure they were all concerned with protecting Robbie, since he'd obviously be the first person they looked at. I never thought I knew more than her friends. I assumed if they were pointing at Omar they had information I didn't. But what's occurred to me lately is that maybe I knew more. Or at least I knew this one thing, this one important thing, and no one ever asked me."

There was a crash behind the coffee counter and then a shrieking giggle. Vanessa turned, and in the light her face looked even older—resigned, hardened. Suddenly, she was every sister of every murdered girl they ever put on the news.

She looked back at me, her face unreadable aside from a general bewilderment. She said, "I'm glad you told me this. It's hard to know what to do with it."

I tried to read her face, to see if she could ever entertain doubts about Omar's guilt, or would want him to stay behind bars forever. Or if she was like I'd been only a few days ago, deeply unsettled by any step away from certainty.

I said, "It shouldn't have to fall to you. They should have done their job, the investigators, way back. I mean, the police, but also—Omar didn't have a good defense team. The defense investigators are supposed to do a lot of this work, looking at other suspects. If only to put everyone's mind at ease."

Vanessa said, "I need time to process."

I nodded. "If you happened to have—in her letters, or her yearbooks—if there were anything from Denny Bloch, or anything about him . . . I wonder if he wrote to her over the summer, for instance."

I got the sense she wasn't listening. She said, "I didn't expect anything to come of this."

"I don't know if Omar could ever get another appeal. And I don't know how you'd feel about that. But if my students keep working, if they dig stuff up, maybe things at Granby the investigators never bothered with—"

Vanessa said, "I'm in touch with him. With Omar."

I'd been about to stand up, to awkwardly hug her goodbye, but now all my weight sank into my chair.

"It was something my therapist suggested, a few years ago. To work on forgiveness and peace. I drive up to Concord once a month to see him. I mean, first I wrote, and then we talked on the phone, then I started to—like, we don't talk about it. He told me once that he didn't do it, that he barely knew Thalia, and we haven't mentioned it since. We more . . . we talk about our lives. My parents don't know. They wouldn't understand."

I said, "That's amazing. Not everyone could do something like that." And then, because I couldn't help myself, "My students would love to talk to you, and to him, too."

She lowered her voice. She said, "I'm not supposed to know this, and you're definitely not supposed to know this, but he's in the hospital right now. Or at least he was, a couple days ago."

I said, "Oh. Is it something serious?"

She looked at me like I was dumb. "They only take them to the hospital for life-and-death crises. I went to visit the prison Wednesday, and this woman I've gotten friendly with, this woman who visits her husband, she was coming out and she told me Omar was attacked and he wasn't there. I mean, she didn't really have the details. I'm so worried, and there's no way to get more info. But listen, you're *not* supposed to know. His family probably doesn't know, even, or they won't till he's back in his cell. Prisoner movements aren't—"

"I won't say anything."

It had somehow not occurred to me that our window to help Omar might be small. I'd imagined a long life for him. Hadn't he always been brimming with health? Idiotically, I hadn't considered how easy it was to die in prison.

I said, my voice thin, "Maybe—if you're willing to chat with my students sometime, if it goes well, and once he's better, assuming he's okay—maybe you'd be willing to make the introduction, vouch for them. They're not trying to make trouble. They're great kids." I chose my next words carefully, aware that Vanessa, despite her visits to Concord, still believed—unless I'd just convinced her otherwise—that Omar was guilty. "If there are unanswered questions, maybe they could put some of them to rest."

She closed her eyes and half smiled, made the slightest dip of her head. It didn't particularly mean anything, but it was an end to the conversation, or a bookmark at least.

How odd it must have been, to meet Vanessa in a regular way—as a colleague, a neighbor—and learn only later that she'd been cast in this lifelong role of surviving sister. At first you'd simply think she had a strong center of gravity, just had tired, penetrating eyes, and then you'd realize she'd been exhausted her whole life. Although, I reminded myself, she wasn't always like this, wasn't always meeting someone who was attempting, in the corner of a coffee shop, to undo any peace she'd found.

On my way back to the car, every person I passed emanated waves of grief. Every person was someone's uncle or niece or babysitter sitting on an overstuffed sofa, telling the camera what it was like to find the body, or not find the body, or hear the voicemail, or find the purse she never would have left behind. What woman leaves a purse behind? What woman has ever left her purse?

The lady taking up the whole sidewalk with her stroller looked happy, if tired, but she couldn't be. She was late for walking Lester Holt around the scene of the crime. She needed to show Lester Holt the spot where she'd looked into the snowbank and saw what she thought was a mannequin. She needed to take Lester Holt into the ravine, where he would step so carefully over the fallen logs with his Italian shoes. She needed Lester Holt to see the bed, the pillowcase, the broken curtain rod, the hairbrush.

Look, Lester Holt: This was her wallet. Who would leave a wallet?

Let's go there, at last. Let's picture it.

You make sure you're onstage at the end of the show. It's not so much about being seen but about looking calm, happy, paternal *on tape* so people will look back and think, *This is not a man who's about to kill someone.*

Thalia has said she thinks she's pregnant, although there's no way, you're too careful. Every couple of months she's sure she's late. You tell her she needs to keep better track of her periods, and she says, "You sound like Bodie Kane. She had this whole *system.*" You aren't aware that Thalia has followed that system for the past year, knows damn well she's not pregnant. As far as you know, Thalia isn't meticulous about anything: calling when she says she will, taking the pills you pay for, keeping things secret from her friends.

Your wife keeps asking her to babysit, and she keeps saying yes. At first the babysitting was a ruse so you could walk her home at the end of the night, but you've come up with better plans, and now you tell Thalia to say no when Suzanne asks, but there she is at your house on a Saturday as you and Suzanne head out to dinner with friends in Hanover. That Monday, she sits in your office and pouts and asks where you and your wife honeymooned, and it becomes clear from her follow-ups that she's looked through your photo albums. Later that week, Suzanne can't find her blue nightgown. A few weeks later Thalia babysits again, and that night as you climb into bed you find her silver teardrop earrings on your own nightstand, as if you'd bedded her right there, as if Suzanne were supposed to find them, as if Thalia had copied the moment wholesale from some movie. You scoop them deftly into the pocket of your pajama pants, where, at two in the morning when you roll over, they stab your thigh, thankfully just your thigh.

You've tried three times now to break things off—not because you want to, but because as graduation looms, you worry Thalia's planning to go out with a bang. She's told you about a girl she knows of at Andover. The girl and her math teacher were madly in love, and as soon as commencement was over he quit his job, he picked her up in his arms in front of everyone, and they left in his car, her parents aghast. She's told this story multiple times. She's said that her yearbook quote is all about you, just wait till you see, joked that she'll get up at Senior Talent Night and dedicate a song to you. She's asked how you can live with a woman you don't love, brought you brochures for UMass Amherst's graduate programs, developed a loathing for your wife that scares you. Suzanne goes to a Saturday afternoon yoga class in town, and Thalia has started attending it, too.

Three times you've tried, said she'll want freedom at college, said Amherst will be a world of possibility. On your second try, she says, "The only way I could get through this without hurting myself is if I went to a shrink. I need to talk to Dr. Gerstein." And Barry Gerstein, while he might be bound by confidentiality, is also a contractor at Granby. He knows your colleagues, your administrators, you.

The third time you tried, she began hyperventilating, heaving into her knees on your office couch, and she said, "I need to talk to my mom. I need to go home and just—I need to tell her everything." And you rubbed her back, told her she was misunderstanding, that you could work everything out.

Let's take this the rest of the way:

You've asked Thalia to meet behind the gym, but first you stop home, tell Suzanne you'll be in your basement office awhile. It's 9:45 and she's heading to bed, exhausted from the kids. You hand her a Unisom, talk about how much work you have. You go down, start a long print job (the screenplay a friend asked you to read), close your office, exit through the storm doors. You wear your Granby sweatshirt and Granby ski cap so that you could, from a distance, be anyone, teacher or student.

Thalia tries to kiss you, but you stop her; you don't want your DNA on her. You give her one more chance. You say, "Thalia, we need to end things, and I need your word that you won't say anything *ever* to a living person."

Even if she said yes, you wouldn't believe her. But she makes it easier on you by hurling her backpack to the ground, bucking back against the wall, crying so loud you have to clamp your glove over her mouth. She obviously can't handle this, and so many lives would be collateral damage. Her own, too, though she doesn't understand that. What life will she have if this gets out? What life will her parents have? There's you, and Suzanne, and the kids. There's Granby itself. Granby's good at hushing things up, but only when everyone involved is determined to stay quiet. Thalia will scream about it, just like she's screaming now, and it's not hard for the hand over her mouth to turn to a hand that's slamming her head back, two times, three times, not hard for your other hand to find her throat. As it turns out, it's not so much that you're capable of this, but that you're capable, having started, of needing it to be over as quickly as possible. Your urgency becomes physical strength, and while you didn't mean for her to bleed, just meant to knock her out and get her into the pool, your fingers find her neck slick. The blood tells you: This is final and real. The Rubicon crossed.

You loved her once. The way you've moved on from that love means you can move on from anything. You excel at compartmentalizing.

You stick to the rest of your plan, unlocking the back pool door you disarmed this morning, getting her into the extra suit you made sure was here, a large one that's easy to slide onto her too-thin body. You roll her into the water, hold her head under with your gloved hand—although the blood won't make sense, won't fit the simple narrative you wanted. You watch the blood swirl from the wound, fade to pink, dissipate. A sign that everything about this will float away, become lighter in your life until it's nothing. You arrange her backpack, her clothes, as if laying them out for your own daughter's school day.

When you get home, the print job is done. You stick your clothes in the washer, change into sweatpants and a T-shirt from the dryer, head up with your friend's screenplay in hand. Suzanne opens her eyes. "I hope the printer didn't keep you awake," you say, waving the pages. It's a particularly loud and crappy printer, and she's complained before. She asks how the screenplay is. "This thing's a mess," you say. "It's giving me a headache."

You shower, something you often do at night because you prefer to fall asleep with your hair wet like you did as a child. You return to bed, curl yourself around her body, hold her like a buoy.

59

Back at Granby, everything was still—a snow globe no one had shaken in days. No one crossed the quad, no one scuttled from Commons with an Eggo and a coffee. I was the only thing moving, because I was late; I'd texted Alder to tell the class to start without me. I left Fran's car in the lot behind Quincy and raced up the big wooden stairs to the second floor. I took them two at a time, something I'd last done senior year.

I'd sobbed on those stairs freshman year after I failed my English midterm. I fell down them once, bruising my tailbone. And one time on the landing, Dorian Culler and the postgrad senior we called Peewee cornered me and Carlotta.

I told you before that I had a story about Peewee, and this is it.

Carlotta and I sat on the landing, on the top step of the bottom half of the stairs. I wonder if you can picture the way they double back, the curve and deep patina of the banister—but maybe you didn't spend much time in Quincy. It was after classes; Carlotta was practicing "These Are Days" on her guitar, for one of the several occasions on which she'd perform it that year and make us cry. The song had been around awhile, but didn't become our emphatic anthem till we found ourselves about to graduate.

The boys had a camera, not odd since we were right by the darkroom. Dorian took a picture of us, and Carlotta stopped singing, asked what he wanted.

"I'm using up my roll," he said. And then, "Peewee, get in the picture." Parkman Walcott bounded up the stairs to plop his huge self between us, smelling like sweat and Drakkar Noir. I wasn't falling for Dorian's bullshit, wasn't about to grin for the camera, and neither was

Carlotta. In the instant after the flash went off, Peewee reached around both of us and grabbed my right breast and Carlotta's left, hard enough to leave fingertip bruises. Carlotta bucked like a horse, getting Peewee off her, off us, and—unintentionally, but conveniently—ramming her guitar head into his Adam's apple. There was some aftermath with him swearing, her screaming that she'd get his nuts next, me not knowing what to do, Dorian doubled over laughing—but I don't recall how we got out of there.

I hadn't thought of it more than once or twice between 1995 and that moment. It wasn't something I'd suppressed, just something I hadn't revisited. But in 2018, halfway up those same stairs, I did the math. Dorian Culler had shoved his dick in my face three times, had photographed his friend grabbing my breast, had humiliated me in front of my peers for four years. Things had amplified, had gone incrementally from something he could have laughed off as a joke to now, for the first time, physical force. This was fall of senior year, because yes, what Carlotta had been practicing for was the Parents' Weekend bonfire; I remembered now for sure, because she was cold to me for a few days after the stairwell incident, and we finally had it out the night of the bonfire. She blamed me for what happened and said she was tired of me being such a wimp. She called me a noodle. I started to say something about my childhood, my dad, my brother, and she stopped me and said she didn't want to hear it. Then she apologized, and we cried. So this was October.

And October was when I stopped eating, my veganism a convenient cover. It was when I started smoking like cigarettes were my only oxygen. It was when I began starving my body to the point that, by spring, I couldn't row a Girl Scout canoe, let alone compete in sprint season. From this distance, it was clear: I had been in the process of erasing my body.

It wasn't that a boob grab was the worst that could happen to me. I had survived far worse. It was just one thing too much.

And then when Thalia died—the way her body had been mangled—

the way she'd been tossed in the water—the way every girl was just a body to be used, to be discarded—the way that if you had a body, they could grab you—if you had a body, they could destroy you—

And I ended up by that tree in the woods.

And I ended up hurting myself in slower ways, too.

Loretta Young didn't understand that Clark Gable had raped her. She considered their daughter a "walking mortal sin" until, in her eighties, she learned about date rape by watching *Larry King Live* and realized her inability to fend him off hadn't been her fault.

I decided to tell the Loretta Young story to my film class that afternoon. It was something to send them off into the world with.

For now, I was at the door of Quincy 212, my podcasters waiting inside for our last meeting. I had a lot of news for them. I took my coat off, fixed my hair.

When I opened the door, the sun shone behind them and they were made of light.

60

Saturday morning, Anne drove me to the airport while Fran took the boys to tumbling class.

On NPR, they were talking about the news story—the one where the small-town mayor killed himself the day after his former secretary reported him for sexual harassment.

Or rather, the one where the chef hanged himself in his empty restaurant because the rape charges were about to be filed.

The one where the ex-husband showed up at her door and said he'd already swallowed pills, and unless she took him back he wouldn't let her drive him to the hospital.

I'd brainstormed conversation topics ahead of time, lest the hour and a half in the car grow awkward, but it turned out Anne had an agenda. We were only turning out of the campus drive when she said, "The thing with Fran is she's just so protective of the *school*."

I had picked up a piece of purple onion skin from the passenger seat, a stowaway from some grocery trip, and now I folded it into smaller and smaller pieces, felt its fibers crack cleanly each time.

I said, "She wants me to drop it. I'm aware."

"I know it comes out as her disagreeing with you, telling you you're making things up. She doesn't want to rock the boat."

I couldn't control the noise I made, an outraged puff of air. "Christ," I said. "This is not about anyone's discomfort. If Omar—"

"No, I know."

"It's funny," I said, "because Fran is the person who taught me how to rock boats."

"Well. But this is her home. You get that."

And yes, although I fundamentally disagreed, I did understand that her instinct was to protect Granby, in the reflexive way a drone will protect a beehive. I couldn't imagine having that level of attachment to a place. By the time we met, I was someone without a home; Fran was someone who would never leave hers.

While other freshmen were still figuring out where various classrooms were, Fran was showing me the storage closet off the wrestling room where they kept the extra Frisbees. She was showing me where they kept the liquor for reunions, although we never dared. She showed me the three small gravestones in the woods—farmers who'd died two hundred years back.

To know those secret places was to know the school, to take ownership. There were plenty more of them, places you could go to be alone, or alone with one other person.

There were the theater spaces, the ones that were mine by senior year: the lighting booth, the gel room, the prop storage, the catwalk. I never invited friends; I'd have been no fun, yelling every time someone set a soda can down.

There was the darkroom, so thoroughly Geoff's that it became mine and Fran's and Carlotta's by default.

There was the athletic shed, but I rarely went there—I couldn't get over my mouse issue.

There was a nonfunctional fireplace in Jacoby Hall with an upright piano in front of it, and a few couples were in the habit of claiming the space, pulling the piano tight against the opening, making out in there.

There were the woods (the mattresses, yes, but a dozen other meeting spots: notable stumps, part of what used to be a brick wall), although so much of the school year was dark and cold, the ground either unforgivingly hard or boot-suckingly soft and wet.

There were the places accessible by contraband keys, for the brave. A classroom belonging to a teacher who lived off campus was often a safe bet—but then, this was how Jorge Cardenas and Laren Willebrand got caught by Ms. Arena junior year, mostly clothed but still humiliated.

There were ways to get around curfews and door alarms and on-duty teachers. Fran was in a strange category as, technically, a day student—but unlike the twenty or so students who commuted, she was not exiled from campus after the start of evening study hall. Mr. Peloni once caught her crossing the quad at ten p.m. on a school night and tried to make a deal of it, but Fran successfully argued that other day students were not confined to home once they left campus. What if she needed to walk the dog? What if her family grilled on their patio? After that, she was only bolder in her wandering. She'd pull up a chair outside my ground floor window senior year and we'd talk.

I can't imagine that you saw campus this way—overlaid maps of public and private spaces, the private ones so rare and precious we'd risk everything for them. You had your apartment, you had your classroom. You had a car, and the places a car could take you.

All we had were our feet. For all our freedom—teenagers with few real responsibilities, dozens or thousands of miles from home—we felt trapped. Lab rats whose only option was to retrace the same paths. The stone steps leading into Quincy bore soft grooves in the middle: two centuries of shoes and boots hitting the same spots.

In Anne's car, NPR was still going.

It was the one where they found green synthetic fibers between her teeth.

It was the one where her shoes were gone.

The one where her bike was gone.

The one where her fingernails were gone, broken in the fight.

Anne was saying, "Even just when someone googles the school, I have to think about that from an admissions perspective. The deep past is one thing, but ongoing drama is a nightmare."

The tree arms had turned to chaotic blurs, the scratchy handwriting of someone in a hurry, a doctor's prescription only the pharmacist could read.

I was answering Anne, saying I understood, but I was thinking about the equipment shed. It was beside the rear of the gym, maybe ten yards from the pool's emergency exit. No floodlights back there. I was thinking about the shed door that half the school knew how to open. I was thinking about the press box above it, where anyone could climb up, where kids often did.

Had they ever luminoled the walls of that dank shed? Had they climbed up to the press box? What about the bleachers? The yards of clanking metal, all the space beneath. What about the places two people might actually go, late at night, to talk? The places close enough to the back pool door that, disaster having occurred, made the pool the most logical place to drag someone? I only remembered that yellow caution tape around the gym itself.

Of course—because if Omar did it, it happened in the gym. Why look elsewhere?

On a whim I texted Alder, whose messages were still high in my queue. I'd talked to him and Britt after that last class about my supporting their podcast if they continued. I told them that if they got too busy I'd maybe do something myself. *Here's a goose chase for you*, I wrote. The shed and press box still stood, despite there being no more need, post-football, for announcers. I wrote, *I'm sure things have been painted over, but if anything, that . . . might preserve blood?* I wasn't asking them to play CSI themselves, just suggesting they look into whether those places had been searched, access facilities records to see when things had last been painted over, when the bleachers had last been replaced.

Then I checked my United app to see if I'd been bumped up to business class.

I had no idea what I'd done.

Part II

And then, on a frigid Wednesday in March of 2022, I was back.

Not to campus, exactly, but to Kern, where I'd be staying at the Calvin Inn. Kern had changed maybe twenty-five percent from the days of our weekend Wagon runs. There was no more movie theater, and the Blockbuster was now a credit union. But Taste of Asia had the same neon sign. The bar where Geoff had ordered us gin and tonics was still there, under a different name. The tiny shops on Main Street had mostly survived the pandemic.

Aside from a few small motels and campgrounds, the Calvin is the only hotel in town. There's an Embassy Suites and a couple of bed-and-breakfasts in Granby itself, but the Calvin—rambling and run-down, built for days when Kern was more of a county hub— is closer to the courthouse and counterintuitively cheaper, maybe due to its spotty heat and its inexplicable plethora of rooms. It's also more willing to accommodate multiple open-ended reservations, especially outside foliage and wedding seasons. I knew the inn's façade well, its wraparound screen porch topped by two stories of brick, topped in turn by a wood-sided fourth floor with dormer windows. But I'd never been inside.

The defense team had budgeted to fly me in from California and put me up, but I paid my own way. Every penny saved for the defense was a good thing—plus this way, I could stay a few extra days, could get there with a nice buffer and stick around afterward just to be nearby, even if I couldn't do much. When you're a witness, you can't sit in the courtroom, and you can't talk to other witnesses, at least not about the case—but you can still *be around*.

Some trivia for you, Mr. Bloch: In a hearing on a motion for retrial, that longest of long shots, innocence is no longer presumed. The onus is on the defense to prove the new evidence strong enough to cast serious doubt on the validity of the original verdict—in other words, to prove that no reasonable jury would now convict. For this reason, the defense goes first. The best result would be the judge vacating the conviction, which would not mean Omar went free; it would mean back to square one, as if he'd just recently been arrested for Thalia's death. Unless the state then dropped the case, it would mean a new trial—one in which he was again innocent until proven guilty. This happens almost never.

I paused on the porch, looking back out to the town square. There was the courthouse, with two separate clusters of colorful coats mounting the broad steps. Just one news van, plus the giant Court TV truck, nothing happening around them. I feigned interest in the plaque by the door (apparently the inn was founded in 1762 and rebuilt after a fire) so I could scan the lobby. Aside from one elderly couple, it was empty. I stepped in onto carpet that might once have been red. It covered dramatically uneven flooring; if I'd taken my hand off my suitcase handle as I waited at the desk, it might have rolled away.

On my phone, a zillion texts.

Fran had written *Welcome*, followed it with an upside-down smile emoji. I sent back a photo of my own face: airplane hair, glasses instead of contacts, a cloth face mask with little ferns—voluntary here as of a couple weeks back, but providing me some nice anonymity in addition to protecting my health. I wrote, *My cunning disguise.* As much as I'd planned to stay behind the scenes of the podcast, it hadn't necessarily worked out that way.

Leo, now eleven, had texted to ask if I remembered to get batteries for his drone, and if so where they were.

Alder wrote: *Your plane land? Welcome to Kern Vegas!* (I wrote back: *Yup, but remember we're not really supposed to text!*) Alder was technically a member of the press, and it didn't look good if I talked to him. Britt, meanwhile, was also a witness for the defense and couldn't talk to either of us about the case.

Geoff Richler, who hadn't been subpoenaed, was thinking of flying in: *Are you there? Are other people there? Is it more like THE BIG CHILL, or the second half of IT?* I sent back a clown emoji and a balloon emoji. He wrote, *I'm gonna do it. I can swing an extra-long weekend.* I didn't fully understand his impulse, but I was eager for the company of someone I was allowed to talk to. He wrote, *I can be your personal court reporter.* I wrote, *Nope, but it'll be fun to see you!*

I had calls to make, but not till I was alone in my room. I had to tell the defense team I was here, to report myself landed and officially sequestered.

The pockmarked teenager at the desk asked my name, and when I told him, he grinned. "I'm a fan," he whispered. Then he spent too long squinting at the computer. I angled myself so I could see the whole expanse of lobby.

The elevator dinged behind me, an icicle to my neck, and I turned to see a woman too young to be anyone I knew from Granby. She stepped off, adjusted a baby in a sling.

"The fitness room is back there behind the elevators," the desk boy said. "Our indoor pool is open, but it's a little cold." He said this with no awkwardness, as if the people congregating for this particular hearing would love a good swim. He offered no explanation for an indoor pool at a hotel older than the country, but this seemed like the kind of place onto which they'd patched many hopeful additions over the decades.

He gave me the wi-fi code, handed me an actual metal *key*, told me the elevator button could be tricky. I started to turn away, but I figured I had a chance here, so I leaned in and whispered, "Can you tell me how many reservations there are?"

"Oh, for the, um . . . Right now? Yeah, twelve."

"Are some of those lawyers, though?"

He shook his head. "I think the—the, like, legal teams are mostly at Embassy Suites. My friend there says they're packed."

"Twelve. You can't tell me who, can you?"

I had hoped his conspiratorial tone meant he'd break the rules, but no.

"I'll—what I *can* say, though?" He was whispering now, too. "I definitely recognize some of the names."

2

That all of our names had become well-known—not just Thalia's and Omar's, but Robbie's and Mike's and Beth's and Puja's and mine and, yes, yours to a certain extent—still feels like the strangest part of all this. The corners of the internet were one thing; the public consciousness was quite another.

I do hope you know they never named you on the podcast. I talked about you in one of my guest appearances, but only as "a male teacher" to whom Thalia was perhaps problematically close. I didn't even say what you taught. I didn't fixate on you any more than on other viable suspects, ones the state never looked into in their blinkered focus on Omar. It wasn't because I wanted to spare you; my hands were tied. We were getting legal advice by that point, and one of the first things we were told was not to name publicly as a suspect anyone who hadn't been a person of interest in the case. So I was treading lightly, keeping you in my back pocket. But it took only a few hours for the armchair detectives of Reddit to figure out who you were, after a Granby alum—I'll never know who—eagerly spilled what "everyone knew" about you and Thalia.

I'd been hoping it would be your moment of reckoning. I'd hoped to start hearing from other students of yours, young women from Providence or Bulgaria or Granby who knew things, who could speak to your predation, provide the details that would prove your earnest demeanor masked a capacity for manipulation, obsession, violence. I was waiting for the same flood of recriminations Jerome had faced—everyone he'd ever wronged coming out of the woodwork. I was waiting, at least, for people to dig into your life and prove I wasn't nuts. Maybe you'd never be arrested in place of Omar, but the attention could protect your current students and ensure that you lost your job. The storm didn't come, though. Just a few drops—threads on message boards, ones you might not even have seen.

Your enormous luck: Two other big things happened in the case that week. A man who lived in Vermont confessed, but then turned out to have been on a navy ship in the Persian Gulf at the time; and Thalia's half brother published that Medium article asking everyone to leave the case and his family alone. The chatter about you got buried so quickly. And there were dozens of other conversations: someone saying it was sweet Mr. Levin, of all people, that Thalia had been seeing; someone with dirt on a man who worked at the Hannaford in Kern; people saying it was clearly her half brother himself, or why else would he want to shut the conversation down.

For you to stand out as a suspect, it would have taken someone like Dane Rubra adopting the theory. Lucky for you, he was on to other scents just then, trying to track down Robbie Serenho's college girlfriend. Plus, he resented the podcast for taking the reins of what he so clearly believed to be his story. He wasn't about to run with anything we'd brought up.

The important thing, the thing that would help the case, was your name arising at the hearing itself—as a viable suspect, as someone important who was never investigated. Whatever emerged about you before then was up to fate.

I couldn't be the one to drag your name into it, with no actual evidence, or I might lose credibility as a witness in Omar's case. I couldn't even post anonymous things online, in case someone traced them back to me.

Don't get me wrong: I wanted your head on a pike. I was just willing to wait.

In the elevator, a poster advertised the hotel's "quilt-in" that April. In my room: a stippled white bedspread, a framed old map of New Hampshire.

My room had a balcony with a view of the Connecticut River. We had rowed past this very spot hundreds of times; I had looked up at the rambling old hotel and imagined it was far fancier than this. It was too cold to make good use of the balcony, though, without the excuse of a cigarette to smoke—and I hadn't smoked a cigarette since 2005.

Another message from Alder: *Okay, won't text anymore but Lola says their Uncle Mike is getting there tonight, if that's useful intel.*

Then another: *What if we used Snapchat or something? Messages will self-delete? Britt says hi.*

Another: *I think things going well but not sure. Judge has world's best poker face.*

Another: *Do you have a Snap account?? I can set one up for you.*

I wrote: *Tell Britt I said hi and STOP TEXTING ME!*

I'll never know if you listened to the podcast—not *She Is Drowned*, which Britt and Alder shelved after those four rookie episodes, but the actual, public one they did with me and my producer, the year after I'd taught them at Granby—although I do imagine you know that the message I'd sent Alder, that afterthought about whether they'd searched the equipment shed, was the start of everything. We framed it that way at the end of the first episode. Alder's musical, gossipy voice: "She was halfway to the airport when she sent us a text." Britt's voice, lower than Alder's, going for drama: "It was a text that would, eventually, upend everything we knew about the case, everything the world had known about this crime scene for the past twenty-three years."

They didn't say yet what my text *was*, didn't talk until the second episode about how Britt got her AP chemistry class involved in making their own luminol, which was surprisingly easy to do—and how there had been enough blood on the bottom of the inside of the equipment room door, and especially in the cracks of the cement floor, that it showed up even twenty-three years later. Blood sticks.

It was only because construction on the new seven-million-dollar field house had been delayed that the structure was still standing. The door was metal, a rusted brown—and while the handle and lock had been replaced, my God, it was the same door we used to jimmy open. It was far from the oldest thing at Granby, but it was the oldest ugly thing.

It would have made a better story to say, as the press sometimes implied, that the chemistry class waltzed in there and discovered everything at once, but in fact once they saw the spatter glowing dim blue, the chemistry teacher had the sense to get the kids out of there as fast as possible, reminding them that other things besides blood could make luminol glow. Certain paints, for example. The flesh of turnips, unlikely as that might be. She had the further good sense to turn things over to the headmaster, who in turn contacted the police, who in turn spent the time and money they should have spent in 1995 to seal the place off, to go in with higher-quality luminol and lights and cameras and—because the cinder-block walls had been repainted in 1996 and again in 2004, and because there was graffiti beneath both those layers—with chemical paint strippers and fine-grit sandpaper and razor blades. Not all the samples were testable, but enough were: This was Thalia Keith's blood.

The inside of the door offered up not only blood spatter but also the long-invisible print, low down, of a bloody sneaker toe, one that perhaps kicked the door open. But even more than on the door itself, there was blood on the wall to the left of the door. Something I hadn't known: The first impact of a head on a wall would cause no radiating spatter. The second one would—a bleeding wound, a pooled blood source, hitting something hard. So what the pros could figure out was where Thalia's head hit the wall a second or third time. She was still standing, or more likely being held up. Maybe by the neck. Facing her attacker.

Much of that blood had been scrubbed, not long afterward—obliterated into circles the naked eye couldn't see, especially not in a dark equipment room with only one lightbulb. Maybe fresh graffiti had been added right away, a quick perfunctory round of spray paint meant to blend in with the other spray paint and Sharpie and chalk. And even if someone did spot a faint brownish circle on the wall, at about head height, in the middle of a room filled with infinite stains and cobwebs and rodent droppings—why would they assume it had anything to do with the girl who'd drowned in the pool?

The discovery was significant for several reasons. "A-number-1," as Fran would say, it made a strong case that Omar's original defense team had not done their own proper investigation. This might not have been grounds to argue ineffective assistance of counsel again if the new evidence didn't suggest that the verdict might well have been different. And indeed the verdict *might* have been different, had (number 2) the prosecution not relied on the argument that it was impossible for someone to be murdered in the pool without Omar hearing or seeing something. But it was clear now that Thalia hadn't been attacked inside the athletic complex at all. And the proximity of the shed to the pool's emergency exit (plus the trace blood on that doorframe, earlier dismissed as the messiness of Campus Security) strongly implied that this was the way Thalia had been brought into the pool—not via the hallway outside Omar's office. Add to all that (number 3) the fact that the methodology that had matched Omar's DNA to Thalia's swimsuit and the hair in her mouth was now laughably outdated. And number 4: Several classmates were now willing to testify that Thalia had been drinking backstage at the end of the show, suggesting an earlier time of death. And number 5, a further demerit to the original defense: They had failed to follow up with those same witnesses—and they'd never talked to me, a person who could have decoded Thalia's planner.

In any case, that's how the public podcast began, in 2019—with my text and its fallout. This was why people were willing to listen to a show hosted by two teenagers: They were teenagers who, in the aftermath of the equipment shed discovery, had been featured in *People* magazine, teenagers who'd already been invited onto other podcasts, teenagers who'd been interviewed by Savannah Guthrie under flattering television lights. I coproduced and appeared as an occasional guest, but it was important to keep the show theirs. Partly to preserve my integrity as a potential witness; partly because I was worried that the squickiness that still followed me and Jerome around could taint the project; and partly, yes, because of my lingering, irrational, adolescent fear that classmates would wonder why I, of all people, was getting involved.

Still, I was the one drawing the most heat online. There were notes of accusation (I was a fame whore, I was tampering, I knew more than I was saying) and there were personal notes (a message asking who the hell I was—from someone with only ten Facebook friends, one of whom was Beth Docherty; make of that what you will). Some people pointed out that I hadn't believed and supported Jasmine Wilde, and here I was believing Omar, who was a man, and *wasn't that interesting*. But I could handle it. I was a human shield between the kids and the public, absorbing some of what came their way. I ignored almost everything. I plugged away at my book about female screenwriters and, when the Jerome mess mostly abated, found an agent based on the proposal and two sample chapters.

My friend Elise, who loves astrology, told me I'd probably experienced my Uranus opposition. It happens to everyone in their early forties, she said—a huge shake-up, a burn-it-all-down time, voluntary or involuntary, that rearranges your life. "Some people have an affair and buy a sports car," she said. "But you, you go vigilante. I love it. And you've never been so . . . *energetic*. It's like you're turbocharged now."

It was true that my life, which had lost all shape in those two weeks back at Granby, had reconfigured around these two projects. And of course there were my kids; they'd never gone anywhere. Jerome and I had officially divorced. Not because of what happened online, but because we'd been heading in that direction all along. He still lived next door.

So my life had purpose, but here's one thing that churned my gut at night: Thalia's family, aside from Vanessa, didn't want any of this. Her half brother was speaking on behalf of her parents, her cousins, all of them, against what we'd done to the family, to their grieving process. They needed to believe the case was settled in 1997. They already had their closure, and even entertaining the idea that the wrong man was behind bars would shatter that. The fact that we were right, the fact that on the balance scale of misery their strife was utterly outweighed by Omar's past twenty-five years, rendered this concern irrelevant—but they didn't see it that way. "It's like we're losing her again," Thalia's brother had told the *Union Leader*, in an interview that seemed aimed right at me. I was the one reinflicting this pain. Plus Vanessa was estranged now from the rest of the family. I couldn't help but feel the weight of it all.

By the time their podcast wrapped up a year later—Britt then a sophomore at Smith, Alder a freshman at Columbia, both finishing their school years online in lockdown—the New England Innocence Project was involved, and cash was pouring into Omar's legal defense fund. The *Spider-Man* actress was suddenly interested again, contributing less money than you'd think but talking about it a great deal.

The podcast ended with the announcement that Omar had been granted a post-conviction relief hearing—one we didn't yet know would be hugely delayed thanks to the pandemic and the backlog of cases.

They promised to release bonus episodes as things unfolded. By that point, there were at least five other legitimate podcasts dedicated to the case. One with lawyers close-reading the evidence, one looking at forensics, one hosted by a retired cop and a victims' rights activist, and a couple that just synthesized everyone else's work and gossiped about it. Figures from Granby and people involved in the case appeared on various shows. Vanessa went on many of them, against her family's wishes. And Yahav appeared regularly on Britt and Alder's show, speaking to the legal side of things. He was still married to his wife. He was still beautiful.

Omar himself only talked to Britt and Alder—and only once, having been subsequently advised by his lawyers not to speak publicly lest it affect his case. Did you listen? After all this, I'd still never spoken with him myself.

Here's something for you to chew on, Mr. Bloch, something I've dwelt on a lot over the past few years. The hell of imprisonment isn't the terrible food, it's the lack of choice of food. It isn't the cold, wet floor, it's that you can't choose another place to stand. It isn't the confinement so much as the fact of never running, never getting in your car and speeding off, as Omar loved to do. The New Hampshire State Prison for Men is almost two hundred years old, a stone building that, according to Vanessa, is always either freezing or sweltering. For more than half his life,

Omar has not been able to choose when to wake up, when to eat, when to sleep. He has had to ask for every square of toilet paper. That incident in 2018 was not the only time he was attacked; it was simply the worst, so far. He has seen the murder or suicide of countless men. He was not with his mother when she died of COVID. I can't imagine that's the worst of it. I'd love to know how much time you've spent considering this.

The official run of the show went out on the voice of Dr. Meyer, who, on the verge of retirement, had taught both Thalia and me in senior English. "We'll never feel we have justice," he said, "unless someone confesses." His voice was impossibly old. "You get one man out of jail, you put another man in. Is that justice? We'll never know. It'll never feel right. If you believe in God, maybe that changes your view. But unless we could go back in time and know for sure—I mean. We're never getting that. We're never getting that."

You have to understand that with the music underneath, this was quite powerful.

5

Leo and Silvie FaceTimed me from the back of the car on their way to Silvie's gymnastics class. Leo was bitter about being dragged along. Silvie wanted me to tell Leo that her eyes were darker than his.

"*Without* shoving the phone in your father's face while he's driving," I said, "could you let me talk to him?"

The picture was suddenly of the car ceiling; I figured the kids had launched the phone into the passenger seat.

Jerome's voice: "We're stuck on the 10. Why do all their activities start at five p.m.?"

I said, "We could always go back to Zoom gymnastics."

A howl of protest from the back seat.

"How goes the trial?"

"It's a hearing. And I wouldn't know yet. You remember what I said, though; there's a chance of winning, but it's slim. These things like to stay solved."

"There's been lots of coverage."

"I know, and please don't tell me about it. I'm sequestered now." It didn't seem they were going to be terribly strict, but I didn't want to risk it.

"How do I get myself sequestered?" he said. "That sounds delightful."

I mentioned that Jerome's mess had died down, and it did, but only temporarily. That previous fall had brought a second wave of disaster—for him, if not for me. After the initial hurricane, after he quit his job and his gallery dropped him, there was a long stretch of quiet. People forgot, and his art itself never lost value. The commissions came back, and he found new representation. There wasn't even much online chat-

ter. But then in October of '21, Jasmine put on a month-long performance piece in Washington Square Park, during which she ate only the
food people brought her and wore only the clothes people brought her.
How this wasn't just vagrancy and an insult to the homeless, I was unsure. It garnered enough attention that in January she was the subject of
a lengthy feature in *New York* magazine. The article revisited her piece
about Jerome, included new quotes from her about him, and featured a
black-and-white photo of the two of them at a costume party in 2003 as
Artemis and Zeus. There was no new revelation, just a bigger platform.

Twitter was once again where the fallout happened. People tagged
Jerome's new gallery, telling them to drop him. They asked Jerome for a
long-overdue public apology. (This, he'd been advised, was a trap: There
was no apology they'd accept. And defending himself would be worse.)
They tried to drag me into it again, asking how I could stand by him.
Fortunately, they caught on soon enough to the divorce going through,
and assumed Jasmine was the reason. I didn't correct them.

You might guess that I had come around on Jasmine Wilde. That I'd
realized how wronged she was, how much a victim. Or maybe you're
hoping that I realized: If Jasmine had voluntarily dated Jerome, maybe
the love between you and Thalia was just as simple. Absolutely not.

I'd thought about it, how Thalia, at seventeen, had only been four
years younger than Jasmine was when she dated Jerome. It seemed so
little, but then four years is the difference between eleven and fifteen—
ages no one could argue are the same. Four years was the length of my
entire time at Granby: an entire education. It had been four years now
since I'd returned there to teach and my life had changed.

The good news was, I was not the arbiter of Jerome's goodness. And
the divorce made that official.

I'd seen someone for a few months before the pandemic hit, and then,
during that brief wave of postvaccine optimism in the summer of '21,
Yahav flew out to LA for a conference and we spent the weekend
sleeping together, which threw me back into full-tilt longing and then

into a pained equilibrium, an acceptance that Yahav's place in my life would be two to forty-eight hours here and there for an unspecified number of years. Like a stomach bug that overtook me entirely for a weekend and then vanished.

"By the way, funny thing," Jerome said. "Somebody rang *my* cell yesterday looking for you. They were trying to figure out your address. I hung up."

"Yeesh," I said. "Man? Woman?"

"Sounded like a young woman, pretty nervous. I think, you know, an amateur sleuth."

I'd been so flooded with emails in the past three years that I'd put an autoreply on my account asking people with information about the case to contact the defense team. The thing was, no one ever had information about the case. They had *theories*. There was that one serial killer active in Maryland in the early '90s who resurfaced in Quebec in 2001. They wondered if the nearest Planned Parenthood would tell us if Thalia had been there. They wanted me to know that their brother had been wrongfully convicted of a gas station shooting in Texas and wondered if I could help. Once in a hundred emails, someone still wanted to tell me something about Greta Garbo.

Leo's voice: "Mom, they're not gonna stalk us, are they? Are people gonna find our house?"

"No," I said, "of course not," although that had already happened twice. One woman filming on a phone, two young men who wanted me to come on their video podcast and figured since I hadn't answered their emails they should try me at home.

Silvie said, "What if the killer—"

"Nope," Jerome said. "Silvie, we've covered this. No one dangerous is interested in us."

"Okay, but what if the killer wants to kill everyone who knows who he is? He could ship poison in the mail."

"Well," I said, "no one knows who he is. So we'd be safe." It probably wasn't the most reassuring thought.

Poison, I thought, did seem like your style. More than strangulation, more than head injuries. Poison fit into the sly, ironic, aesthetically pleasant bubble you walked around in. You'd have made a good *Masterpiece Theatre* villain.

Jasmine Wilde had used that word in her interview. "What he did," she said of Jerome, "was he poisoned the well."

6

Omar's voice on the podcast is scratchy and deep—not a voice I would have recognized. The phone line isn't great and there's background noise.

Granby was a good job, he says. I look back and it was a job I might've kept five, six years. Then I move on, right? It'd just be this job I had once.

One thing that happens in here: The last people and places you knew outside, they're the clearest things you have to look back on. I remember Granby so well because it's not like I've been anywhere since then, except here. Court and here. Your brain doesn't cover it with other info.

I could tell you where every piece of equipment in that weight room was, for example.

But then, it's a million years away.

Alder asks what he remembers about the night Thalia died.

Nothing, really. The cops asked so many times, and I know what I told them when it was fresh in my mind. That night I was in my office. I'd been on the road with girls' hockey, their last game of the season, and I had these phone calls and order forms and I was doing time sheets for my student trainers. I listened to the radio a little. Then I went home, I called this girl Marissa I'd been seeing, we talked from about one a.m. to two a.m. She testified to that.

Later in court it becomes this whole thing, my calling her at one. They say I called her because I couldn't sleep, because I felt guilty.

The next day was Saturday and I didn't have to work. We were be-

tween sports seasons, no games or meets. This is one of my only weekends off all school year, so I basically slept all day. The next day, Sunday,
I see this girl Marissa, then I go to my mom's for dinner, and when I get
back to my place there's a squad car out front.

I honestly—I grew a little weed, and it's the only law I'd ever broken
besides running a few lights. So that's where your mind goes. That's
what I assumed was up.

They want me to come back to the station in Granby, and they won't
say why. What I know now is, you get a lawyer, always. But at the time,
I figure that looks weird. Especially once they tell me what it's about,
and I realize it's not the weed. I'm spooked hearing about it, this girl I
kind of knew. I thought she was great, and she's dead so young. She's
dead at my place of work. That's a mindfuck.

This first round of questioning, they're chill about it, they're like, *We
just want to see if you heard anything.* So why would I go, *Hold it, I gotta
lawyer up*? It's like you're announcing you've done something wrong.
And I hadn't.

It's the local police. The State Police weren't involved yet. I'm not
even sure when they finished the autopsy.

They aren't faking being casual because at this point, they still think
it's a drunk accident. They're just trying to figure out how she got in the
gym, just writing up this little police report. And it makes sense that it's
an accident. I'm sure some people thought those kids were angels, but I
got to hear a lot of shit. I wasn't a teacher, so they'd talk right in front of
me. Just drinking, sneaking around, nothing you wouldn't expect, but
these kids are bored in the woods, they've got money, they get up to shit.

So I go back to work Monday, and things are almost normal except
the pool and back hallway are taped off. But other than that, like, there's
kids all over that gym until they kick them out again a couple days later.

Early the next week, they call me in again. This time it's the State
Police, and by now we all know something looks wrong about the way
she died. They've been questioning students and teachers, I know. So

okay, I didn't need a lawyer the first time, why would I need a lawyer the second time? They tell me this is about loose ends. Then they do this shit where whatever I say, they just shake their heads and look disappointed. That starts messing with me. They leave me alone for an hour, come back, ask the same stuff again. Then they lay out two things. They say, these kids are telling us you grow weed and you sell weed. And they're saying you were obsessed with Thalia Keith.

At this point, why would I admit to the weed? They make it sound like it's all tied in, like if I admit to having a couple grow lights I'm confessing to murder. And I wasn't into Thalia. I liked to tease her, but that's how I was. I was immature. I knew Thalia because she played tennis, and she messed up her elbow a few times. I'm out there at matches, but that was back in the fall. I haven't seen her all winter. It's not like she's coming in to lift, right?

They ask for a hair sample, a saliva sample. I do that, and they let me go.

Actually—wait—I should explain this. You know what they do? They have to get something like a hundred hairs. This lady stands over me with rubber gloves pulling hairs out by the root from every part of my head, and then from my arm and leg. It's torture.

Then that Friday, I'm in my office at school and they come arrest me. I don't even think anything's up when they come in. I got used to them poking around the building.

But they have me stand up, they do the cuffs and my Miranda, and all I can do is laugh. It's a weird response, I know. Not laughing hysterically, I mean I'm just sort of laughing in disbelief. It felt like a movie. But then yeah, two years later in court, the one officer testifies that when they came and got me I was laughing. I sound like a maniac.

What they had on me, what they thought they had, was a very small piece of my hair in Thalia's mouth and my DNA on the bathing suit. I don't know what to say here because either it was shit luck or, I gotta suggest, maybe they gave themselves a little help. They do what they can to strengthen their case because they're under a metric shit ton of pressure to solve this thing. And I'm a solution that makes the school happy. I'm not a student, I'm not a teacher. I'm not some huge part of the community. They probably think they've figured it out, and they just need that little bit of extra help.

Or maybe it's legit. I swam in that pool a lot of mornings. I'd lift, rinse off, go for a swim, shower, get to work. So sure, maybe some of my hair is in the pool. The bathing suit, I have no idea. I touched a lot of shit in that gym.

They say "DNA" and it sounds so definite, like it must be my blood or semen. And DNA evidence was this new, exciting thing back then— like this was something juries had maybe heard about on TV but just barely. They hear *DNA* and, *wow*, that's official.

But what you've got is a quarter-million gallons of water in a pool with fuck knows what floating in it, and one of those things is a piece of my hair.

The thing is, the cops don't tell me it's a hair and some trace stuff on a bathing suit. They tell me my DNA was all over this girl, and they say the only explanation is either I killed her or I was sleeping with her. They say this at about three in the morning. Not that I know what time it is. They took my watch away. All I know is I was there for fifteen hours. They say, "Just help us understand why your DNA was on her, and we can eliminate you as a suspect. If there's a logical reason, you're okay. And the logical reason is, you were involved." They tell me the age of consent in New Hampshire is sixteen, that if I slept with her maybe I'd get fired but if this was all recent it wasn't even against the law.

I can't understand what went on in my brain, but it seemed like a way out. I'm not even fully awake, like I keep looking at this cold-ass table in front of me, hoping it'll turn into a pillow. So I say yes. But that's not the end at all. Now it's "You were sleeping with her, you were the only one in the building, you would have heard whatever went on, we have your DNA. You did this." They say, either they nail me on murder *and* drug charges, or I confess to murder and they forget the drug part. And they say the drug charge would go to the feds if they found out I'd crossed state lines, which technically I did, because I had this friend in Vermont. They go, "Maybe it was an accident. Involuntary manslaughter. She slipped, she fell in the pool, right? This isn't so bad for you, but if we get you on both murder and drugs, you look like a career criminal."

You have to understand—this is what's sad and funny to me now—the amount of weed I had in my house, it was nothing. The laws were harsh back then, but—I don't know. Jesus.

Then they put the Granby face book in front of me like some trump card. It was something I did every year, wrote nicknames in there to help me remember names and faces, but then the boys' hockey team found out and they'd sit around giving me names to write. Like I said, I was immature. The reason I wrote that under Thalia's picture, I wrote *jail-bait*, was some rumor one of those guys told me about Thalia and a teacher at her old school. The cops show me this noose around her neck, and I have no memory of drawing it. Maybe I did, just doodling when I was on the phone. But the hockey kids were all over that book, marking it up. My guess is, some fifteen-year-old did that. I mean, they found swastikas on some other kid's picture, and I *know* I didn't do those.

Anyway, they eventually get me saying I attacked her in my office, they get me to say I hit her head on the wall. Then they remember there's no blood in my office and they say, "Okay, so you had some kind of poster. What kind of poster would that be?" I look back on this, and it's like a dream, like I was hypnotized.

A couple hours later I finally remember I can ask for a lawyer. They go, "Sure, sure, but if you only make your statement after the lawyer comes, it looks like maybe the lawyer told you what to say, like maybe you're holding back. You get this done now, we get the lawyer later, and everyone knows you're coming clean." They actually say this to me. But none of it's on tape.

So they get me to write this thing, the statement, which I'm sure you've seen. They're telling me what to write, I'm writing it. And they get me to sign it and read it out loud, which is the only thing they record, out of that whole night.

Britt asks if he blames Granby for what happened. There's a long pause.

He says, I don't think they set out to use me. But I think Granby leaned hard on the police to solve this, and they leaned hard on them not to look too close at the teachers and students. That school has lawyers you wouldn't believe. They got money you wouldn't believe.

I'll give them the benefit of the doubt, I don't think any one person said, "Hey, let's pin it on Omar." But you lean that hard on people, they'll hand you what you want. What they wanted was someone like me.

The adrenaline I felt walking to dinner that night was anticipatory: I knew I'd run into people, whether old classmates or folks connected to the hearing or opportunists. I knew I'd need to avoid most of them. I just didn't know when they'd pop out at me.

The teenager at the counter had recommended an Italian restaurant a few blocks away. It turned out to be one of those places with a ridiculous amount of seating—useful for weddings and presidential primary dinners, but largely empty on a Wednesday night. Perfect for social distancing. I asked for a booth (a carapace, really), ordered a glass of Shiraz, and immediately opened my laptop. How any woman ever ate alone in a restaurant before she could use a laptop as a shield, I have no idea.

I recognized, several tables away, Amy March, the lead defense attorney. My joy at learning her name was Amy March had been surpassed only by my delight at learning, via Zoom, that she raised her own chickens and dressed exactly like someone who raised her own chickens. She'd been a public defender for years, and was now in private practice. I hadn't yet met her in person—our practice testimony was scheduled for the next day—but here she was, wearing a sweater dress and leggings and clogs. Her hair featured an impressive reverse-skunk effect: One streak of original black remained in a cloud of gray. She sat with two other women and a man, in serious discussion—their food long finished and their wine half-drunk. The man kept texting someone, then reading aloud from his phone. The defense had opened two days ago, and I assumed had gotten through several witnesses today.

My intention was to walk by the table, catch Amy March's eye, wave, and continue to the restroom, which I did need. But before I reached her group, I heard my name, called from the adjoining bar area. It was Sakina John.

She said, "Holy hell, Bodie Kane, get *in* here!" When I did, she dropped from her stool, squeezed my face between her hands. "Are they making you testify? I had to go this morning. I, holy shit, Bodie, I was shaking the whole time. I don't shake when I'm doing actual *surgery*, but I'm up there and they ask my name and I'm shaking. At least it's just a judge and not a jury, but then I'm like, Do I look at the judge? Do I make eye contact? And I'm facing the judge, which, I don't know if that's a pandemic thing, but I'm all the way across the room and I'm facing him. And just a heads-up, if you want to wear a mask in there, it's this creepy plastic thing, this clear thing so they can see your mouth. I was like, *No, I'm good.*"

Okay, she was a little drunk. When I told her I'd been sitting in the other room, she went, grabbed my wineglass and bread basket, brought them to the bar. So apparently I was seated here now, on an unbalanced barstool, listening as Sakina told me how the defense had asked her the same things they'd practiced—mostly about Thalia drinking backstage at the end of the second act, but also about how Omar's original defense team had never contacted her or any of the other kids who'd been with Thalia earlier that evening. They'd read over those cookie-cutter State Police interviews and never thought to ask more. And the State Police never even asked if Thalia had been drinking that night, which seemed basic. They'd asked instead if she'd seemed inebriated. No, her friends all answered honestly, she hadn't.

The state, Sakina told me, had cross-examined her about what she remembered—Thalia sipping from Beth's flask and tucking it into the bodice of her dress, a joke—and then turned to asking about the rest of the night. "They go, 'If your memory of backstage is so great, then your memory of the rest of the night must be impeccable, so walk us back through that.'"

"You're not supposed to tell me this," I said, but Sakina just looked around the bar at all the people who weren't listening, large local men with microbrew T-shirts, and shrugged. I angled myself so I could monitor the door to the main dining room. I couldn't see Amy March's table from here.

She said, "But they wanted every detail of the timeline, and it's like, I don't even remember what happened. I remember what I *told* you. I remember what I remember remembering."

I'd been involved in enough debriefings before my sequestration that I wasn't surprised; the state was trying to shore up the original timeline of the night, the one that had suggested it wasn't worth looking into people like you or Robbie. And Sakina, while she'd been the first to contact me and volunteer that she remembered Thalia drinking, while she'd appeared on the podcast and said she'd harbored private doubts for years about Omar's conviction, had never changed any details of the night.

She put a hand on my arm, suddenly serious, leaning close. "They told me I could get recalled, and I'm thinking, I'm not flying all the way home to Seattle just to turn around. I'll take a few days out here. But now I'm learning, okay, they could recall me *weeks* from now. So I'll go home, but first I'm driving down to Philly to see my cousin. Also"—she raised her wineglass—"vacation, am I right? Let Darius deal with sixth grade math homework."

I wanted to grill her about what else had come up on the stand—but my asking questions, rather than listening as she rambled drunk, would be a step further down the road of verboten witness behavior. Luckily, she pivoted to asking about my kids. She pulled out her phone to show me new pictures of her daughter, Ava, who'd been born the same day as Leo, saying we were going to set them up, we'd send them both to Granby and they could be Homecoming dates. I would never in a million years send my kids to Granby. Among other things, while fourteen had seemed a reasonable age for me to leave home, it seemed unfathomably young for Leo, who was only three years from fourteen and still slept with his bed full of LEGOs.

She started saying something about Ava's dance teacher, and then she was waving over my shoulder and the film skipped and Mike Stiles loomed above us, grinning down. He'd apparently been here and gone outside and come back. This was his half-drunk beer in front of me. I was too shocked to be self-conscious. We hugged like old friends, because we were. You don't have to have been friends with someone to be old friends with them later.

"He's not even testifying!" Sakina announced, which I already knew. Mike didn't remember seeing Thalia drink backstage. If we were lucky enough to get a retrial, he'd be a great witness, though. He had come around fully, and publicly, to the idea of Omar's investigation and original trial being botched; he'd written about the case on his academic blog.

Mike sat on the other side of me. I pulled my stool back from the bar, putting us into a triangle. He had the wild eyebrows of an aging man, long gray strands emerging from the dark ones in a way that oddly suited him. His brow ridge, the one Fran used to call Neanderthal, was now marked by a deep skin crease. But he looked somehow cheesy overall, too handsome to take seriously. At some point in my twenties, I'd outgrown my attraction to symmetry. I decided that Mike was more attractive for being older, but less attractive for being, still, someone out of a tooth-whitening ad.

He said, "My nephew's a freshman now. Lola's little brother. So I'm partly up visiting him, but also Serenho's getting in tomorrow, and he'll need distracting."

Sakina said, "He's testifying? For the defense?" I wanted to shush her. I glanced back toward the dining room.

"I guess he's on the list." Mike looked somber, as if he were speaking at his friend's funeral. "They're gonna get him up there and make him look like a suspect. What it is, he did that interview where he said Thalia wasn't on drugs, and they mostly want him to repeat that, because the drug thing was part of the state's whole theory. But you know what'll happen once he's on the stand."

The interview hadn't happened on Britt and Alder's podcast but an episode of a much sleeker, more long-standing one, one that was able to pay him substantially for his appearance. He talked for only five minutes, and mostly said bland, predictable things, but he stated emphatically that Thalia had never done drugs, not even pot. "I don't know where that idea came from," he said, and my stomach went on a short roller-coaster ride. If he'd paid attention to our podcast, he'd have heard me blaming myself for the detail. "Listen, I can say this now, in 2020. I tried! I tried to get her to smoke a little pot. She was not interested. So I don't think that was her relationship with Omar. I don't think she had a relationship with Omar at all. I think that was all a fantasy in his mind. And when she wouldn't play along, he snapped."

I kept waiting for my memory of Thalia circling the dumpsters to lock into place, to fit with some adult knowledge I'd gained, but it remained a mystery. She might have been sleepwalking. She might have accidentally thrown something out—her retainer, a term paper—and been working up the courage to jump in and dig it out. She might have been waiting for you. Regardless: I'd misread the scene as dramatically as Bendt Jensen had misunderstood the fireflies.

I said, "That's the main reason he's up there, the drug thing. They're not putting him on trial. Plus to show no one else was investigated."

"Sure," Mike said. "Sure." He noticed the bread basket we'd brought from my table and folded a large slice of baguette impressively into his mouth.

Mike was an interesting case study: someone with a career's worth of experience in human rights, who still couldn't quite handle justice if it would affect his buddy.

Not that I was callous about the fallout for Robbie. It was a source of nagging guilt for me that in reopening the case, we'd brought him the attention he never got the first time around, pre-internet. Colleagues and friends would now be looking at him at least with pity, if not unfair suspicion. I didn't want to imagine what people might say to his kids. There was a website, not terribly active, called RobbieSerenhoIsGuilty.com. Dane Rubra had fixated most recently on the theory of both Robbie and Thalia leaving their dorms in the middle of the night to drink, Thalia's time of death being incorrect, Robbie having a 'roid rage issue. Which was ridiculous, because coke and pot maybe, but Robbie Serenho was not on steroids. He'd been all wiry muscle, designed for flying downhill.

"Is he doing okay?" I asked.

Mike just shrugged.

"Show me a picture of your nephew," I said, and he spent a minute on his phone, then showed me a boy who looked exactly like himself at fourteen, only a bit like Lola, too, foggy-eyed, thin-lipped.

I said, "He's gonna break some hearts."

I once told a male friend that an army photo of his grandfather, back when he'd looked just like my friend, was the hottest thing I'd ever seen. I once told a writer that I had a crush on his (clearly autobiographical) main character. I think of this as oblique flirting, and it works surprisingly well. To be clear, I wasn't coming on to Mike Stiles, exactly. I was more demonstrating—on animal instinct—the fact that I *could*. It was a display of dominance. I was now a person who could amuse myself by flirting with him, or not, as I saw fit.

It was also part of my broader attempt to steer the conversation away from the hearing, but we were back on it just moments later, Sakina saying that if things took as long in medicine as they did in law, all her patients would die.

"I know they have to do things right," she said, "but I have to do things right at three in the morning sometimes. We don't just wait for the perfect moment. Like, sorry, lady, I can't give you a C-section for two more months because we need this paperwork first."

"The wheels of justice—" Mike started, far too sincerely.

"The wheels of justice came off the wagon a long time ago," I said.

He laughed, sort of. He said, "Were you always funny?"

I hadn't meant to be.

Sakina said, "It's turning into a class reunion up in here. You ever think the three of us would be drinking together? You ask me in 1995 who I'm having drinks with from Granby in 2022, and what are the chances my answer is Bodie Kane and Mike Stiles? And, Mike, look at Bodie! Didn't she turn out hot? Who could have predicted?"

Mike looked mortified, but I couldn't tell if it was because he was a married man being asked to appraise a woman's looks, or because he was offended on my teenage behalf. He reached for his beer like it would save him, and raised it. "To the present," he said.

8

In late 2020, just as we got the news that Omar's hearing would be further delayed, I got a call from Fran and assumed it was related. She had mostly forgiven my meddling once the blood was discovered. Or rather, she was still upset, on behalf of Granby, but more at the world than at me personally.

But she wasn't calling about the case; she was calling to tell me Carlotta had stage 3C breast cancer. "Inoperable is apparently not the same as untreatable, though," Fran said.

I understood that Carlotta only had energy for one Granby phone call, but it still stung that she would call Fran and not me. I swallowed my selfish hurt and said, "Which breast?"

"What?"

"Which breast?"

"God, I don't know. Probably both at this point. Does it matter?"

It did, it mattered to me, because I could still feel Peewee Walcott's fingers digging into my right breast. Which meant he'd grabbed Carlotta's left breast. And although it made no sense at all, I knew he had damaged her, had planted something in her that would, twenty-five years later, mutate her cells, turn her body against itself. It was impossible, but it was true.

Her kids were eleven and eight and six. The treatments were going to be brutal, an aggressive poisoning of every cell in her body.

It worked, somewhat. Her hair even grew back afterward. But now, a year later, she was sick again. The cancer had metastasized, and Fran had set up a second crowdfunding page. The kids were now thirteen and nine and seven.

There had been a shift, a few years back: For a long time, when any classmates from high school or college passed away, it was a sudden accident, something fast that left no space for suffering, just for the shock of the survivors. But then a college friend had died a year back from leukemia, and then another from a brain tumor, and another from drawn-out COVID complications and a weak heart. And here was Carlotta, her skin waxen in photos, her life stretched thin like the last impossible pull of Silly Putty before it finally turns to air. I knew that in thirty years, there'd be a steady stream of regular obituaries describing lives well lived. But this middle phase, these deaths of people in their early forties, felt the cruelest. Maybe because there were always kids involved, ones far too young to leave behind.

Carlotta wasn't going to make it. I'd known it for weeks now, I'd felt it as a dull ache, but then Sakina confirmed it as we walked back to the inn that night. And Sakina knew what she was talking about.

I'd been right: I'd found out eventually from Carlotta herself, it was her left breast. Well, now it was everywhere, in her bones and liver and lungs. But it had started in her left breast.

9

Early the next morning, before they were due in court, I met for practice testimony with two of the assistant defense counsel in the "Blue Ballroom" of the Calvin Inn—a room that resembled a ballroom only in size. Its blueness came from an elaborate paisley carpet that must have camouflaged a few decades of stains. They'd pushed banquet tables together, and we sat on padded white-and-gold chairs with high backs, ones clearly meant for weddings.

We'd originally thought I might testify that afternoon, but the state was taking far more time than anticipated to cross-examine each witness, and now it was likely I'd go late tomorrow. More time to second-guess every word I planned to say. Britt would take the stand today, I knew from Alder's texts, and speak to the discovery of the blood evidence. I'd told Alder he could let me know who was testifying, as long as he didn't report what they said. He was also allowed to tell how the judge seemed (*Looks like a serious dude who's secretly a fun grandpa*, Alder wrote, unhelpfully. *Wish I could read his mindddd*) and how Omar was doing (*Hard to tell. He's not supposed to react . . .*), but I'd get to see both those things for myself soon.

"Amy wanted me to remind you about sequestration," the younger attorney, Hector, said. I cringed, assuming I was in trouble, but he handed me a sheet from a pile, one with the judge's orders typed out in bullet points. It wasn't personal. "It's a small town," he said, "so it'll be hard, but just don't do anything that would look bad, okay?" Hector was right out of law school, with a trace of what I'd learned was a Colombian accent, and pained, intelligent eyes. He came across as nervous in person as he had on Zoom, every sentence quavering out like he was onstage and hated public speaking.

The older one, Liz, looked like Lisa Kudrow. Liz, who would be playing Amy for the session, launched right in. Hector recorded everything on his phone for Amy to review later. Easy questions first: my name, my job, the dates I attended Granby, the dates I roomed with Thalia. Then some tougher ones about my time on campus in 2018, my role in the podcast, my role in the discovery of the blood.

Then: "Defense Exhibit 58 is this Granby planner for the 1993 to 1994 school year. Do you recognize this planner?" In this instance it was only a thin stack of colored Xeroxes, but I nodded, then remembered to say "yes." I explained the color-coding system; it was good for me to practice aloud.

We went through the '94–'95 planner next, me offering my interpretation. Which was still, I knew, just an interpretation.

Liz asked, "Do you have knowledge of anyone Thalia Keith had sexual relations with, aside from her boyfriend, Robbie Serenho?"

"I had, and still have, strong reason to believe that she was romantically, if not sexually, involved with the school's music director, Dennis Bloch." (Had I practiced that wording many times? Yes, I had.)

"What reasons do you have for that belief?"

I started with the Bethesda Fountain incident, the most specific, the most blatant. Then I detailed the time she'd spent alone with you in your classroom, the times she'd lingered after rehearsals. I talked about her yearbook entry. I was grateful that it was 2022, glad that any reasonable judge would understand how inappropriate this kind of contact was. Or at least the judge in my head understood it.

When I said these words in court, when I named you, it would be the first time I'd said as much in public. It would be the first time the public heard these details, the bread crumbs that had led me to you. I wondered if it would be a matter of hours or minutes or seconds before your name was all over the internet.

"Did you speculate with other students about this relationship?" Liz asked.

"There were at least three friends I specifically spoke about it with, at that time."

"Did they state that they shared your suspicions?"

"They did," I said.

That was the easy part. The difficult part was when Liz turned into a cross-examining prosecutor. In that role, in a harsher voice, she asked, "Did Thalia ever tell you what her system of dots and Xs meant?"

"Only the red dots. But the rest—"

"So you have no direct knowledge of what any of these colors or symbols means."

"No."

"These Xs could, for instance, indicate homework assignments, as far as you know."

"Yes." It didn't feel worth it to quibble, to protest that I was sure, pretty sure, kind of maybe sure.

"Ms. Kane, did Thalia Keith ever tell you she was romantically or sexually involved with Dennis Bloch?"

"No."

"To your knowledge, did Thalia apprise anyone else of a relationship with Dennis Bloch?"

"No."

"Ms. Kane, to your knowledge, what is the age of sexual consent in New Hampshire?"

"Sixteen. But Granby had rules about—"

"So although you're accusing Dennis Bloch of breaking Granby's internal code of conduct, you're not implying that he broke any law."

"Besides maybe murder."

She broke character for a second. "You cannot say that."

"Right."

"Did you ever see Thalia and Dennis Bloch kissing?"

"No."

"Holding hands?"

"No."

"Engaging in sexual intercourse?"

"No. But as I said, their ankles were touching at the fountain." It sounded so feeble.

"Have your ankles ever touched the ankles of anyone you were not sexually involved with?"

"Not in that particular way," I managed.

"And what was that particular way?"

"Their legs were . . . entangled. And they were leaning together."

"And based on this one incident of their ankles touching—which you perceived from across a crowded public space—you assumed a sexual relationship?"

"That was one of many indicators." My voice was thin. It dawned on me, sickeningly, that my saying your name in court might make absolutely nothing happen. Whatever fire I started might be immediately squelched.

"So based on this assumption, and based on your theory of these small marks in Thalia's planner, you feel you could have contributed more to the initial investigation?"

Could I have? Would I have managed, at eighteen, to say any of this to investigators—about periods, about sex with a teacher? Would I have implicated you, my favorite teacher, in a murder? But I knew the correct answer: "Yes."

"In fact this hearing has a lot to do with your intervention in the case, does it not?"

"I can't speak to that."

"You've certainly spoken plenty about the case publicly, haven't you?"

Liz was leaning into this, to the point that I was starting to think she genuinely hated me, that she'd never believed a word I'd said.

"What I've spoken about publicly, and here in court, are the same

things I knew in 1995, and these are the things I would have told investigators had I been asked." I said this with a good show of the certainty
I lacked.

"That's good," Hector said. "Remember how you phrased that."

"But you were not asked," Liz said. "Did you approach investigators
with the information?"

"No. I was sent to meet with them because I'd been Thalia's roommate
the previous year. But they didn't ask about her love life. And I never saw
the planner. Their focus was entirely on whether I knew anything about the
night she died. And I hadn't seen her that night, except onstage."

Hector nodded vigorously.

Liz said, "It was on your suggestion that Britt Gwynne instigated the
search of the athletic equipment shed on the Granby campus, was it not?"

"Yes."

"That's awfully specific. Did you suggest any other place to search?"

"I suggested the equipment shed, the press box on top of that same
building, and the bleachers serving the track and the lacrosse field,
which used to be the football field."

"Those are all quite close together. You just happened to suggest that
they look in the one place where there was indeed blood evidence?"

My mouth fell open. I said, "Are they really going to do that?"

Liz shrugged. "They could."

"But if they imply that I had some knowledge of what happened,
wouldn't that mean they *definitely* should have questioned me back in '95?"

"They could imply that the evidence was planted there later. Staged."

"That makes no sense. Does it? Is that even possible?"

"All they need to do is vaguely suggest it. They're likely to paint you
as a nosy person, overinvolved, trying to make a name for yourself. Their
goal is to get the judge to dislike you."

It would be easy to do, I imagined: Just look at her smug little face,
this meddling fame whore. She barely even knew these people.

Liz asked if I wanted to take a break. Yes, I did. I very much did.

10

I'd been planning to drive up to campus to see Fran, but I was physically and emotionally exhausted, so I got her to bring the boys to the hotel to swim. A decent-sized pool and a hot tub only half filled the enormous solarium space that jutted out onto the inn's back lawn. Three walls were glass, as was the gently sloped ceiling—but a thick, green glass that filtered the light softly, trapping the humidity and warmth and the smell of chlorine around us in a blanket of false summer. Fran had bought the boys Cheetos from the vending machine, but now that they were cannonballing into the water, she and I picked at the remaining pieces, staining our fingers orange. I hadn't had Cheetos in decades. If I let myself eat whatever I wanted, I'd have them every day.

I filled her in on my morning—no harm, since she wasn't on the witness list—and told her about seeing Sakina and Mike last night.

"What if," Fran said, pointing a fat Cheeto at me, "what if Mike Stiles left his wife for you and you two got married in Old Chapel?"

"My standards have gone up," I said.

"The Choristers could sing! Your bridesmaids could wear green and gold!"

"You're my matron of honor," I said, "and I need you in head-to-toe green taffeta."

One of the most delightful pieces of news I'd received in the past few years was that my Granby housemate, Oliver, had married Amber, the sweet young Latin teacher. And Oliver had landed a job at Granby. Fran passed along an invitation to a party at their place on campus the next night, Friday—a celebration of the fact that people could gather, however

short this window in the pandemic might prove. It sounded like something the attorneys would object to, but I couldn't think why. It was just
a party, albeit one remarkably close to the scene of the crime.

Three other kids had joined Fran's boys—two boys and a girl—and
their mother jumped gracefully in to swim a couple of laps. She was our
age, irritatingly cellulite-free.

Fran cleared her throat, looked meaningfully over my shoulder. I
turned to see, across the pool, a man in blue swim trunks, his belly soft
but his arms and legs muscled. I took in his face: This was Robbie Serenho. This was his lovely wife. These were his kids. He was blowing up
a floatie. The wife emerged from the water, wrapped herself in a towel,
grabbed a key card from him, and left.

I spent a panicked moment wondering what to do—diving under the
water and staying there seemed out of the question—before I remembered the choice had already been made for me. I wasn't *allowed* to talk
to him. At least not about the hearing, but that was excuse enough to
stay planted. I raised a tentative palm from my leg as offering. He squinted,
confused, at both of us. His hairline had receded dramatically.

"I'll go say hi," Fran said, before I could even ask her to.

She rounded the pool, pausing to tell Jacob not to splash water in
Max's eyes.

Had I built Robbie up in the past few years into some towering, sym-
bolic figure? Or had he lurked like that in my imagination since high
school? Or was my blood pressure rocketing for other reasons: my guilt
at upending his life, my fear that he hated me? There seemed to be no
oxygen in the room, only gaseous chlorine.

Fran was beside him now, her hands moving as she spoke. I couldn't
make out her words through the thick air. Robbie laughed at something,
she laughed at something. One of Robbie's boys clambered out of the
water, dripping, stood whining. Robbie put a hand on the boy's head,
made him wait while he talked to Fran. I remembered that I could pre-

tend to look at my phone, so I did that until Max, clinging to the gutter, lost his kickboard; I knelt and reached over the water and sent it sailing to him, then tossed him rings to dive for.

Robbie's voice grew loud, traveled across the pool. He'd turned in my direction. "I know I can't talk to Bodie," he half shouted, "but I hope you'll tell her it's good to see her."

Thank God. I laughed, shrugged, waved again.

He said, to the middle of the room, "Please tell her I think she turned out pretty cool. No hard feelings. Tell her my wife's a big fan!"

He turned his attention to the younger boy, who looked about seven. As Fran walked back to me, he picked the boy up and swung him—a giggling sack of potatoes—into the water. Robbie backed up, ran to the pool edge himself, grabbed his own legs in a cannonball, flew.

At 11:45, a text from Alder: *Shit shit shit.* I resisted answering.

At 11:47: *Very not good.*

11:50: *Can I not even tell u why??? It's bad. Britt still on stand, state bringing u into it on cross.*

I was at Rite Aid, buying the dental floss and antacid I'd neglected to pack.

11:52: *Flipping out. They're doing the timeline of when u got involved and they're going, was this the same week her husband was in the spotlight, was this before or after she got backlash for the following tweets. Batshit omfg*

11:55: *Like, they're trying to say u did all this to get attention off u and husband?*

Fucking Jerome.

If Jerome and his antics and my poor reaction ended up being the reason we lost, I'd never forgive him. Or myself.

I'd stopped in the digestive aisle, by the rows of Pepto-Bismol. I should tell Alder to stop texting, but didn't I need to know this?

11:59: *Making u sound like this desperate person. Amy objecting to like every word but judge allowing??*

It was everything I'd once feared—looking like a desperate interloper—but now I cared far less about that than about what this might do to Britt's testimony, or what it might do to my own testimony tomorrow. Omar did not deserve this.

12:20: *So they've been in bench conference forever, I can hardly even hear anything ughghghghgh*

I was at the checkout counter; I was walking down the icy sidewalk; I was drinking my bottled Frappuccino on the corner like a wino.

12:45: *They got like 2 more qs out and now another bench conference*

1:15: *Can't believe I'm missing class to stare at these lawyers' backs*

The call from Amy March came a little after five. I was lying on the bed in a sandpapery hotel robe, my hair wet, unable to nap because the elevator was too loud through my wall. She said, "I know you might have heard some things today. I don't want you to worry. Listen, though, nothing's for sure yet, but we might—we're reevaluating if we want you on the stand."

The smoke detector on the ceiling blinked red—a tiny, constant test-warning.

She said, "It seems their whole tack is to centralize you in all this, to cast doubts on your honesty and intentions."

"So shouldn't the judge see me so he knows that's not true?"

She hesitated. "We do want that testimony about her planner, but putting you up could backfire." She sounded so apologetic, as if the issue were my ego rather than the case. "We genuinely have enough with the blood. That's the core of our argument. You're one person who should've been interviewed, but we have others. They're building up to hitting you hard on cross, and if we don't put you up, it signals we have plenty without you."

I said, "That makes sense." It did, but I could hear the devastation in my own voice and certainly Amy could, too. I said, "We won't have a chance to name Denny Bloch, then."

"I know, I know," she said. "But at this point, I think it dilutes the case." She sounded so careful, so conciliatory. Not for the first time, I worried Amy thought I was hung up on my own agenda.

I said, "Can I come watch the proceedings, then?"

I already knew the answer: I'd be a distraction there, too. What she said, though, was "You're still on our list; nothing's definite. If you can stay in town that's great, and you're still sequestered."

"Right."

"We'll probably rest late Monday or early Tuesday, and then you can go."

I calculated that I could use the next few days as a writing retreat. I was deep into my research on Marion Wong and the Mandarin Film company. I could lose myself in that all day. But writing time was a sorry consolation prize. All I wanted was to be on the stand.

Your name had been sitting in my throat for four years, waiting to get out. I'd been waiting four years to see Omar, to look him in the eyes. I didn't want or expect anything from him; I just wanted to see his face.

I lay on the bed a long time, listening to the elevator let people off on other floors.

12

I sat on my cracked balcony chair in my coat that evening, staring out at the long, snowy lawn and the river it sloped to. A gazebo partway down, one that might have been used for weddings in summer, sat desolate—a place to break up with someone. The sun was setting, lending every-thing a golden glaze and a flimsy illusion of warmth. Jerome had texted to wish me luck tomorrow, and I didn't know how to explain that I was out here for nothing. Yahav, following the case closely via Twitter and getting updates from Alder, didn't need to be told; not long after I hung up with Amy, he'd texted, *They might feel it's a risk now to put you up there. Any word?*

I was thinking of going inside when a man came into view, pacing by the river and talking on his phone. I was fairly sure it was Geoff Richler, although this person strode confidently, with purpose, and didn't slouch like the teenager I'd known. He wore a fleece, but his shoulders seemed built for a blazer. They were architectural supports that something ex-pensive ought to hang from. When he returned the phone to his pocket, I called out and yes, it was Geoff; here he came leaping up the lawn. He jumped and tried to catch the lower rim of the balcony, which didn't work the first time but worked the second—and then he was hauling himself up, getting his whole body not over the railing but outside of it, so he stood face-to-face with me, the railing between us. I put my hands on his shoulders and squeezed. He couldn't hug me back without letting go of the railing and plummeting to the ground.

I said, "Look at you!"

He said, "Look at *you*!"

Social media had made him enough of a presence that it didn't seem possible I hadn't seen him since 1995.

He said, "Fill me in!"

"On . . . the case? My life?"

"Start with the hearing."

I shook my head. "I'm sequestered, but I don't think they're actually having me testify."

This was not the devastating news to him that it was to me. He said, "They're not putting Denny Bloch up there? That's all I wanted, was for them to subpoena him. Why can't they?" Geoff had developed the variety of crow's feet that made him look kind and wise and mischievous. He'd kept his freckles.

"I know," I said, "I know. But the strategy—the thing is, if they get him on the stand and ask, *Hey, were you sleeping with Thalia Keith?*, he goes *No, what the hell*. They say, *Some kids thought you were*. He goes *No, never*. And he comes off sincere and gentle. End of story, and it looks like we're grasping at straws."

"Sure. Okay. As long as I get to knock on his door when this is over and punch him in the face."

While we'd been cagey on the podcast about what we knew, what we suspected you of, I'd told Geoff everything. Geoff believed you were involved in Thalia's death even more than I did—which is to say one hundred percent to my ninety-five. And while I felt some combination of betrayed and horrified when I considered you taking her life, Geoff seemed filled with a more primal rage.

The sun was sinking fast, almost gone. I said, "Are your fingers going to freeze to the railing?"

"It would be a noble death."

I filled him in on Carlotta—he'd only known bits of it—and he closed his eyes against the news. He said, "I was always in love with her."

"I know."

"What it was, I had a crush on the two of you together. Not in a porny way, not like—it was the two of you as a duo. You were always having so much fun."

I understood, even if I didn't want to: Geoff and I would banter for hours, make each other laugh, but I was an oily-faced schlub and couldn't flirt in the slightest. Carlotta would strum her guitar and look stunning. Together, we filled all his needs.

"We were never a duo," I said. "There was Fran."

"Sure. Fran was who I talked to about it."

I said, "You know my absolute favorite memory of Carlotta?" I told him the story, which he'd surely once known: I'd been hanging out in the art studio as she finished a clay bust of Frida Kahlo, when Dorian Culler invited himself in, sat on the edge of the big metal table, tried juggling some of the thick acrylic paint tubes. We ignored him as we'd ignore a mountain lion we met in the woods, hoping our silence would cloud our scent.

"Carlotta," Dorian said, "if I may call you that. I'm worried about our friend Bodie. You see, I'm in a serious relationship now, and I'm not sure she can handle it. True fact: That's not even eyeliner around her eyes, she's just been crying over me."

While I stood frozen, Carlotta reached under the counter for a tube of blue oil paint. She squeezed some onto a brush and, stepping toward Dorian, painted a thick blue streak down his forehead and nose.

"Jesus!" he said, and hopped off the table and wiped at his face with his sleeves, but now the paint was all over. "You fucking psychopath." He left the studio.

Carlotta said, "The best part, he's gonna wash that with soap and it won't work." She laughed loud enough that he could surely hear it all the way down the hall.

At dinner that night, he was still pale blue.

"He looked like a Smurf," I told Geoff.

Geoff laughed gleefully. He said, "That guy had *issues*. Miserable little dude."

I was kind of stunned by the idea. Specifically: the notion—it should have been obvious—that Dorian's harassment wasn't about me. It had nothing to do with who I was or what I looked like; I was just a convenient prop, someone who wouldn't bite back. It should not have taken me this long to realize. It should not have taken Geoff pointing it out.

Behind Geoff, someone in a puffy red parka had walked to the gazebo and now circled it slowly, holding an iPad in front of his face. As far as I could tell it wasn't Hector or anyone else from the defense team. Not that it mattered—Geoff wasn't a witness—but it might look odd that I was playing out some awkward Romeo-and-Juliet scenario in back of the inn.

I said, "You want to come in? Over the railing?"

He shook his head. "Believe it or not, I still have two conference calls tonight. But let's do breakfast. And then—I dug up the stuff I promised your students. Well, your former—"

"Stuff?"

"They'd been bugging me for photos, but it was all in my mom's house. Old concert programs, whatever. I used to save things. I'm allowed to see them, right? Your students?"

"You can do whatever you want. You can talk to them, but only individually, because Britt's a witness and Alder's recording for the podcast, so he's press. And you can talk to me. But none of us can talk to each other."

"This puts me in an interesting position of power," he said, and grinned. "How shall I abuse it?"

I put one pointer finger on his forehead and said, "Should I push you? *Noted economist plummets to untimely end.*"

He reeled his head back, fake-flailed with one arm, then angled toward the lawn and jumped, landing hard enough that I worried he had hurt himself. The man in the red parka turned to see what happened, hustled a few steps closer and into the lights of the hotel. But Geoff was fine. Geoff was already bounding off, calling that he'd see me at breakfast.

Then I saw: The man in the red parka was Dane Rubra. He looked up at me curiously. He was taller than I'd imagined, his stringy hair hidden under a gray winter cap.

The moment he recognized me back was a clear jolt; he went from looking up to staring up, stunned.

He did nothing, said nothing—just stood, six yards away, and for a moment we were two figures in a geometry problem. The dead girl's onetime roommate is ten feet up on a balcony. Her YouTube avenger is eighteen feet from the inn and a little downhill. Solve for the line of their awkwardly locked eyes.

To put him out of his misery, I said, "You're Dane." I beckoned him closer.

He started to hold his iPad up in its thick green protective case as if to film me, then thought better, lowered it. This was a man who, in recent videos, had grudgingly thanked me for my work, but had also taken every opportunity to point out where he thought I or Alder and Britt had erred.

He said, "So we meet." As if I'd been waiting for him. As if he and I were the two main characters in this drama. He was right below me now, nostrils flaring the way they flared on-screen when he thought he was onto some new lead, or when he talked with palpable hate about Robbie.

"I figured you'd be lurking," I said, not unaware of my word choice. "You finding good stuff?"

"Sure. Maybe. Hey, you're testifying about the dots, right? What are you planning to say?"

"You know I can't answer that. Plus, I think you're recording."

He looked bewildered, then glanced at the iPad, still gripped in front of his crotch. He said, "No, I—" and flung the device across the frozen lawn like a Frisbee. It landed against one of the icebergs of old, brown snow.

"I'm still not telling you," I said.

Seeing the iPad lie there, I realized I had an unprecedented opportunity—speaking to Dane in person with no email trail, no recording phone. There were other ways, besides the witness stand, to get information into the world. There were other ways to blast out your name, in time for some relevant person to hear it and come forward. And whatever I told Dane could make it online by tomorrow.

I sat down cross-legged, so my face was closer to his. I said, "Can I give you some advice, though?" He seemed to brace for something, like I was going to tell him to get a life. I added, "A lead."

"Be my guest."

I said, "I was never the biggest Robbie Serenho fan. He was that guy we all knew in high school, the big shot. And he wasn't a great boyfriend to Thalia. But that doesn't mean he did anything. You're missing the obvious."

Dane laughed awkwardly. I could tell he wanted to defend himself against such an accusation, but didn't want to blow his chance of hearing what I had to say. He said, "I'm listening."

"I hinted about it on the podcast, but the lawyers wouldn't let me say the name. Dennis Bloch, the music director. He was definitely having sex with her. You have a guy whose marriage is on the line, whose job is on the line. Thalia's about to graduate, maybe he can't handle that. There's something off about him to begin with, right? Not so much in being attracted to her"—I added because Dane was, himself, clearly a man in his forties with a thing for an adolescent Thalia—"but to manipulate her like that, take advantage of her, break every rule. He ruined her life. Chances are he took it, too."

It was a melodramatic speech, to be sure. But I knew by then the way Dane talked, the way he thought.

I said, "The worst part is, he's still teaching. He's spent the past twenty-seven years out there, moving on to other kids."

Dane cleared his throat. "I think," he said, "that speaks more to the kind of cover-up Granby is okay with than to that particular individual. I've looked into Dennis Bloch, don't think I haven't. The school has covered up dozens of guys like him over the years. They give a letter of recommendation and send them on. I'm sure he was a creep, but this crime was *juvenile*. It's a fit of rage, it's sloppy. Put her in a bathing suit and maybe they'll believe she drowned. That's not a grown man thinking."

I said, "Most killers aren't Agatha Christie villains."

"Well," he said, and he turned in the direction of his iPad, "I thank you for your input."

I couldn't lose him. I couldn't lose this chance. "There was a phone in the gym lobby," I said. I didn't even know where I was going with this; I just needed to keep talking. "You could pick it up and hear whatever someone was saying on the pay phone in Barton, one of the boys' dorms. No one will believe this, which is why I haven't told anyone. Not even the lawyers." I felt myself about to lie, felt myself stepping over a line. But it was in service of a greater truth. And if I wanted Dane to latch on to it, I needed to give him something he'd never heard, something he felt was exclusive. "I overheard all kinds of things. It was also the dorm where Mr. Bloch had evening duty once a week. And—listen, I probably shouldn't tell you this. But I still think about it. It was threatening."

"He threatened her?"

"He was saying, *You have to say yes, you have to say yes.* It was a week before she died. He was like, *You can't do this to me.*" If I'd had time, I could have thought up better dialogue. "The thing is," I said, "the threat was in his tone, not his words. It was subtext. It's not something I could testify about. He didn't say, *If you don't do it I'll kill you.* But it was—you know that voice alpha males get, just telling the world what to do?"

I figured Dane for a person who put great stock in the power of alpha males. And indeed he nodded, eyes intensely focused.

How funny, to think of you as alpha anything.

I said, "But they're not about to investigate some guy just because I got a vibe. Plus, how easy would it be for them to say I'd misidentified the voices? And who would believe me about the phone thing to begin with? It would damage my credibility."

Dane said, "It's called a bridge tap. If a pair of stripped wires touch in the crossbox, the signals get mixed."

"I—oh. Huh."

He said, "I believe you."

"Well, good. I'm glad. I was starting to think I was crazy."

"Why are you telling me this?" he said. "Why me?"

"I figured you were the one person who could do something. You're not Granby, you're not the courts, you're not a witness, you're not the police. You're allowed to tell the truth." Yes, I laid it on that thick. I felt like a bit player in the hero origin story of Dane Rubra's life. "Please don't give those particular details. Please don't bring me into it. But I know you can do something."

He nodded solemnly, fingers working the edge of his hat. He was itching, I could tell, to run after his iPad. He asked if we could chat again and I said we shouldn't, I'd already said too much.

A thousand pounds left my shoulders. I imagined those weights taking flight from the balcony to find you, to settle around your neck.

Were you on some pleasant trajectory before I interfered?

Did I expedite your karma?

I will not apologize.

The Calvin Inn had an elaborate breakfast setup, one I'd avoided the day before. You chose a table on the glassed-in sunporch, or the extra sunporch off the first one, and circled your selections on the day's menu, one thing from each of seven categories. I asked for just oatmeal and a latte, but Geoff got brioche French toast, bacon, yogurt, fruit salad, poached eggs, a croissant, and a coffee, brought to the table in absolute random order. I'd have wondered how he could ingest so much if he weren't constantly moving every muscle of his body. I'd forgotten that about him. Or maybe, rather, it had seemed normal on a teenage boy and was more idiosyncratic on a grown man.

Geoff was the one to face the rest of the room from our corner, leaning back in a chair that might tip at any moment. I was glad to face only him, not to deal with the entrances and exits of the stage play behind me.

He said, "Ninety-four was the last good year for pop culture. Like, think of the music: We had the Cranberries, we had Bush, we had Veruca Salt and Smashing Pumpkins. The next year, what do you get? Dave Matthews takes over. Oasis and the Gin Blossoms. Straight downhill. Even the class after us, remember how *shiny* they all were? They were so peppy. I look back and—they were the first millennials, right?"

"I just remember not liking them," I said. "They seemed—yeah, too happy or something."

"They had this baseline optimism." And then he said, "Oh, wow, that's Beth Docherty."

I started to turn, stopped, reached for a jam packet so I'd have something else to do. I could forgive her for being mean, for willingly dating Dorian Culler, for probably sending me that weird note on Facebook asking who I thought I was. The things I couldn't forgive, the reasons my ribs had just tightened like a corset, were (a) she'd been the first to suggest Omar to the police; and (b) she'd been the one who'd dubbed me the Masturbator, and decided this was worth repeating for a year. Those are on a vastly different scale, I'm aware. I'd have endured a thousand hurtful nicknames to buy Omar one hour of freedom. I'm just saying I couldn't forgive her for either. I whispered: "Wait, is she testifying today?"

Geoff waggled his eyebrows. "She already did. Yesterday morning. Do I suddenly know more than you?"

"I'm not that clued in, believe it or not."

I could tell where she was in the room by where Geoff's eyes followed. He said, "She'd never recognize me. I could mess with her so bad."

"Please do. If she went yesterday, why is she still here?" I could answer my own question, though: possibility of recall, a return flight she'd scheduled cautiously late, the promise of the world's worst high school reunion, a chance to spend one more night away from home and kids and work. But I knew she wasn't here eagerly. Unlike Sakina, Beth had not volunteered for this. Getting called out for underage drinking twenty-seven years after the fact, being asked why she hadn't told the police about her backstage flask, getting grilled by the defense over why she'd named Omar—none of that would have been pleasant even without the media circus. Beth was one of the only Granby students to testify at the original trial—and who knew what being here now was bringing up? If I were her, I'd be long gone.

Geoff said, "I heard her husband is the guy who started that—what's the tech thing with the beaver logo? No, not a beaver, an otter?"

"So how did she do?"

"You haven't even listened to your own podcast? Last night's episode was about her and then all about how they tried to crucify you up there with Britt. Which was such desperate bullshit."

I said, "I suspect I'm here as a decoy now. If I stay in town, the state will keep focusing on me, but then, surprise, I never get up there."

Geoff said, "Okay, she sat down way over by the orange juice station. So, yeah, it was mostly about the flask. She doesn't remember Thalia drinking, she only admitted to passing the flask around. And then they basically took her back through what she'd told the police in '95."

"Oh. Wait, no, I didn't want you to answer that. I can't—"

"Shush shush shush, you're not listening to a podcast, you're not talking to another witness. You're just eating oatmeal. Look at you sitting there, eating the hell out of that oatmeal."

I shoved a spoonful in my mouth.

"She didn't come off well. The defense, like—honestly, they made her look pretty racist, or at least classist. Her whole thing was 'everyone knew' about Omar, and they go, *So you're saying you put a lot of stock in rumors.*"

I said, "They're broadcasting the actual testimony?" The last I'd talked to Alder, he hadn't been sure if he'd be allowed to, or if he could even pick up the sound well enough.

"The juicy parts," Geoff said. "You ever sat through one of these things? It's ninety-nine percent tedium."

I said, "Okay. I'm taking one more bite of oatmeal. Just tell me if anything completely shocking came up. Like, anything you think I don't already know."

"Doubtful. Oh, they were asking if she'd ever been in the equipment shed, if she knew other kids who'd been in there. Because you know the state, in their opening, they argued the location change didn't matter since Omar would've had a key to the shed. Did that door even *have* a lock? She's, uh—shit." He looked down at his plate, suddenly interested in the syrup-soaked dregs.

I glanced back in time to see Beth Docherty striding toward our table. She'd aged like someone who spent every vacation at a yoga retreat on an island. Her face was weathered, but *rich* weathered. No sag to it, just fine lines she could have Botoxed away but was confident enough not to. Her blond hair was short, tucked behind her ears, still beauti-fully highlighted. She barely paused beside our table, a kid in a John Hughes cafeteria. She said, "What a shocker to see you here."

I should have smiled and said it was lovely to see her, too, but before she could finish walking away I said, "I'm here as a witness. Just like you."

Beth wheeled around, sucked her tongue against her teeth, let out two small puffs of laughter. She said, "You didn't witness jack shit, Bodie. This whole thing is the most pathetic attention grab. You have a book deal yet?"

Geoff said, "No, but her album drops Tuesday."

Beth squinted at Geoff like she was trying to place him but didn't care enough to think too hard about it.

He said, "I'm pretty sure this is witness tampering."

Gratifyingly, Beth looked alarmed. She didn't know if he was a law-yer or what. She wiped her hands on her sweater, as if that would get rid of us, and left without saying more.

Lord knows why I felt the need to defend Beth Docherty in that moment—Beth, who saw me as no better than Dane Rubra—but I said, "I imagine she might still be close to the Keiths."

"She's close to the pole up her ass, is what she's close to. Listen, I can text from the courtroom if you want." Geoff was ready to join the crowd in the gallery at ten a.m., a crowd that had been packed with journalists and onlookers in the first few days, but had thinned somewhat for the long haul.

I invited Geoff to join me and Fran at the party on campus that night, and he grinned. "I'm forty-five years old, but the idea of freely drinking alcohol on the Granby campus thrills me."

"I think they let you do that at Alumni Weekend."

He said, "I'll go back when they invite me as a paid speaker."

When I passed the lobby desk, the teenager who'd checked me in was arguing, loudly, with two young women holding video equipment. It wasn't labeled; they weren't, as far as I could tell, a news crew. They looked young, like students themselves. The teenager stammered about them needing permission to film, about stepping outside until he could locate his manager. I scuttled past, hurried onto the elevator, jabbed the button to close the doors fast.

Something Amy March told Alder, and Alder texted to me:

Every morning, Omar was woken at six a.m. at the State Prison in Concord and given a quick, cold breakfast, then put into a Sheriff's Department sedan for the hour-long drive to Kern, where he was stuck in a holding cell until court began at nine.

Amy had to get permission from the bailiff to bring Omar some lunch, and every day since the hearing began, the bailiff had said no.

(*Why????* I texted Alder, and he sent back a shrug emoji.)

The hearing wrapped up each day around four, and Omar would be back at the State Prison by six—but dinner was over in the prison by then.

So for the full week since the hearing had started, Omar had been subsisting on one meal a day. It was a meal of a set size; there was no asking for extra food.

According to Alder, Amy was worried not only that Omar would pass out in court, but that the woozy, vacant look in his eyes might come off a certain way to the judge. Every day she argued her case to the bailiff, and every day the answer was no.

There's a women's clothing shop in Kern called Delilah's that I occasionally shoplifted from in the '90s. I decided to spend apology money there.

The place still smelled like patchouli, and the clothes looked no different. Linen dresses, chunky sweaters, bead jewelry, clogs. The silver-maned woman at the counter might have been standing there unchanged the whole time, too.

I'd picked a few dresses to try on behind the tiny blue curtain, and right as I struggled to get a too-small one back over my shoulders, my phone rang. When I finally answered, it was Defense Team Hector letting me know it had come to his attention that I was seen speaking with other witnesses in the hotel, and just to be on the safe side, could I please avoid all direct contact with other witnesses. It was ten minutes till testimony started, and this was how he was using his time.

"But I don't even have the full witness list," I said.

"So," he said, "I guess just avoid everyone you don't know for sure is *not* a witness." The hotel, he added, had agreed to make bagged breakfasts for those who needed them, and I could pick mine up at the front desk. "You don't have to hide in your room," he said. "Just be careful." I understood; this was less about actual sequestration than about me looking like some manipulator who scurried around town intimidating people.

I emerged from the stall, having decided to buy earrings instead, and came face-to-face with a woman I recognized from the pool yesterday as Robbie Serenho's wife. She had a couple of shirts draped over her arm, and up close she looked tired. We stood recognizing each other for an awkward moment before she extended her hand.

"I know who you are," she said. "I'm Jen Serenho."

"Oh, I—yes, hello."

"It's okay if I talk to you, right? I know Robbie's not supposed to talk to anyone on the list, which—you know Robbie, that's not easy for him. But Mike is here, and I've always loved Mike. He was in our wedding! I'm so fond of the Granby people I know." Jen Serenho was either the kind of person who always talked nonstop, or the kind of person who talked nonstop when she was face-to-face with the woman who'd ruined her husband's life. She looked anxious, was leaning in too close, and I was glad for my face mask. I couldn't imagine Hector would approve of this conversation, but then there was no possible way Jen was a witness.

I stepped to the side just to put the dresses back on the rack, but she touched my arm as if to stop me fleeing the store. "You know, it was the hardest thing in his life," she said. "He told me so on our first date. I asked about the worst time of his life and the best time, and he told me about losing Thalia. He's someone—he takes things hard. These past few years, especially, it's brought everything back."

It dawned on me that she wanted an apology. Instead I said, "This must be a lot for you."

"Oh! Well, yes. But the great thing about Robbie testifying, he can clear it up. We've been getting emails, phone calls. We took down our Facebook. Any package that comes, we have to double-check it's something we ordered. I know people only want justice, but they're so confused. You know, I saw someone with a T-shirt once that just said *The Husband Did It*, and I asked what it meant, I thought maybe it was from a TV show, and she said it meant when a woman is murdered, it's always the husband or boyfriend. We've been trained to think that way."

I wanted to tell her the shirt wasn't wrong; the issue was that Thalia had more than one boyfriend. And I wanted to tell her that whatever suspicion Dane Rubra had sent their way, I'd hopefully just made things better.

"The stress is so much for him," she said. "I know he'll be better once we just get through it. You know, we got here yesterday because they thought they'd call him before the weekend, but oops! I know what they want to ask him, they want to know why he wasn't investigated more, and you know what his take on it is? He *should* have been investigated. He's going to say that. They should've given him a polygraph. And then we wouldn't have this cloud of suspicion. They should have looked at him and at that guy, you know the rumors about that guy living in the woods. They should have looked at other kids, the girls even. Some of those kids, my God, do you remember this kid Peewee Something, he's been arrested for domestic violence more than once. And he wasn't at the party with them all! Did they ever ask where he was?"

"He gave my friend breast cancer," I somehow said aloud.

"I'm sorry?"

"Nothing. I'm glad you understand. The issue is they barely looked at anyone. They picked a guy, they said he did it, and they put their blinders on."

"That's it," she said. "That's it. And when you get up there, when you testify—you haven't gone yet, have you? That's what you'll say, I know. Maybe you can even say something about how you knew Robbie, how—"

My alarm must have shown in my eyes, because she stopped.

She said, "I shouldn't be talking your ear off. Can I give you a hug? Robbie's down the street getting the kids lunch, and I should go find them, but I just want to give you a hug."

I let her envelop me in the sleeves of her wool maroon coat, in her delicate perfume, her curtain of honey hair.

Jen started to leave, but turned back a few feet away. "I think I would have liked her," she said.

"You would have."

"I don't know that she'd have liked me." She laughed. "I was so uncool. I wasn't sophisticated, just a bookworm. Public high school in Nowhere, New York. But I'd have liked her."

I said, "Everyone did."

After she left, I picked three pairs of jangly tin earrings and a pewter necklace. I paid cash, and when the woman's back was turned I left the twelve dollars in change on the counter, hurried out before she could stop me.

I felt sick to my stomach about Jen, but still: I did find it delightful that Robbie Serenho had married the overtalkative nerd of her rural public high school class.

I was leaving the store when my phone pinged with a text from Alder. It said, *Ur boyfriend is going bananas. U will love.* Alder thought it was funny to call Dane my boyfriend. There was a link to a YouTube video. I stood on the sidewalk in the wind and waited for it to buffer.

Another message from Alder: *We're starting with a bench conference, kill meeeeee.* Then a GIF of a cat staring at a clock.

I fished my AirPods out of my purse and ducked inside a coffee shop.

"Major news here in Kern," Dane Rubra was saying. He was breathless, sitting on a bed with a dark hotel window behind him. He must have filmed this last night, after we talked. "I have exclusive sources, so you'll have to trust me here. This is why, listen, this is why you have to travel, this is why you have to be on the ground. I'm gonna phrase this carefully, but I have reason now to believe that we've been overlooking something huge. As I've mentioned a few times, there was a music teacher at Granby by the name of Dennis Bloch. Born April of 1962 in Olivette, Missouri. Most recently teaching in Providence, Rhode Island, but seems to have left that job a couple years back. I'll be posting some relevant links in the comments, and I know you all love to dig.

"All I'm saying for now is Dennis Bloch might know something significant about this case, something he should have revealed twenty-seven years ago. This is a guy who's stayed in education, he's gone on and worked with other kids. Some of them out there, they might know something. And look—" He leaned closer to the camera, shook his head slightly, clenched his jaw, gathered himself, continued. "He might be having relationships with young girls, he might've been doing this unchecked for decades. Here's what we want: employment records, any complaints filed against him, current contact information. In particular, we want anything any Granby student knows. Not rumors, okay, not hearsay, but did you witness something, did you see something, do you know something."

I realized I'd been standing numb, just inside the coffee shop door, without approaching the counter. I joined the short line, kept staring at my phone as Dane cautioned his followers not to approach you themselves, not to take matters into their own hands, to stay within the bounds of the law, to keep records.

"It's for your safety," he said, "as well as the integrity of the investigation."

Behind him, jumbled heaps of clothes on the hotel bed. The alarm clock blinked 12:00.

16

Fran picked up both me and Geoff that night to ferry us to campus for the party. Geoff cracked himself up playing "Radio Ga Ga" on his phone; it was the song we used to put on repeat in Fran's mom's car when Fran would sneak us off campus midday to Frogurt Bar.

Over the past four years, it would hit me hard as I headed to a dinner, stepped out for a run, boarded an airplane, that I was doing these things and Omar was locked in a cell. During lockdown, friends complained about having nothing but their jigsaw puzzles and sourdough starters, and I would bite my tongue—or not. But riding to a party so close to the happenings at court felt particularly egregious, even if the Omar I had known would've hoped it was a rager.

When the song ended Geoff said, "I'm not allowed to tell Bodie what happened in court." He was talking over his shoulder, to where I sat in the back. "But I need to tell you that it was disturbing to see Omar. He—for one thing, he's cuffed. Wrists and ankles, and his wrists are attached to this chain around his middle. So there's no way he can move normally. But you remember how he was always springing around, he was always—he was an *athlete*. He's so stiff now. He looks like he's in pain. He had to turn to the attorney and he turned his whole body, like he couldn't turn just his head."

I'd thought a lot about the hard beds, the physical violence, the cold. But it occurred to me only now that the last thing they'd let you see a doctor for in prison was chronic pain, some chiropractic concern. A small thing, but a huge thing.

Geoff said, "Holy shit, we're on campus. Did they shrink it? Fran, how did they shrink everything?"

Confoundingly, Oliver and Amber had wound up living in the same Singer-Baird apartment where they'd met, which had once been Fran's childhood apartment. A sociologist could write a hell of a paper on communities in which people are constantly moving into each other's homes.

I found myself standing in what was, for me, the third iteration of the Hoffnung kitchen. The fridge was covered with cheesy rest stop magnets from all fifty states, but otherwise the aesthetic was sleek and spare, a black leather sectional dominating the living room. Both Oliver and Amber hugged me and offered drinks, and I was thrilled to learn that Amber was expecting.

Two women I didn't know stared at me from the corner. It's funny: Because Fran had forgiven me, I hadn't particularly considered that I might be walking into hostile territory tonight. Fran had assured me that admissions numbers were fine. This might change, I thought, if any cover-up on the part of Granby came to light, but I didn't bring that up. The women leaned together to talk, and I assumed it was about me. But maybe I was being paranoid. Maybe it was just that I'd traveled from out of town and although I'd worn my mask in the door, I'd taken it off to drink and snack. Whoever brought the glorious pimiento cheese dip four years ago had made it again.

"You're gonna send your baby to Granby!" I said to Oliver. I was already a little buzzed from the glass of whiskey I'd had in my hotel room. "You came here like *What the hell is boarding school*, and now you'll have little baby Dragons!"

Oliver was teaching programming and web design. He told me about a programming student from Botswana, one who'd just gotten into Stanford. He was beaming.

I said, "Look who drank the Flavor Aid."

Geoff had made himself at home on the couch, chatting it up with my erstwhile host Petra. She looked riveted, and I tried to remember if she was single, tried to figure out if Geoff was flirting. I took him in through her eyes: handsome and successful and funny, with no trace of the awkward adolescent I could still see in him. Petra hadn't said hello to me yet, but at least she wasn't scowling, either.

The young English teacher who'd told me to read Shirley Jackson asked if I'd managed to. I said I had, and we gushed about *We Have Always Lived in the Castle*, and he poured me a celebratory cocktail despite the glass of wine in my hand. He told me I had to come back in April for the musical, which he was helping with. "Maybe I've just been living in the woods too long, but these kids are *extraordinary*," he said.

Dana Ramos came right up and hugged me. I told her Silvie was learning leaf shapes in fourth grade science, and she gushed. "Children are zoochauvinistic, is what I like to say. All animals, no plants. It would be far more useful to understand plants first!"

Geoff was telling the story of the kid who kept an elaborate glass hookah in his dorm room for a whole year, simply perching a small lampshade on top; no teacher ever looked twice. Petra found this hilarious, rocked her head back to expose her long neck.

Priscilla Mancio walked into the party with a bag of chips. I didn't know how she felt about the hearing, or if she was still in touch with you. If she came near me I'd just ask about her bulldog. But the moment she saw me, Priscilla put the chips down, said something to Oliver, gestured at her phone, walked out. A made-up emergency. Well, perfect, and now we could eat her chips.

Anne introduced me to the new director of development; he said, "I'm familiar with your work," and walked away.

It occurred to me that I might actually be ruining this party.

My phone buzzed with a message from Mike Stiles: *You won't believe where I am*. There followed a photo of the Samuel Granby statue. Then: *I was hanging w my nephew and now I'm walking around in a daze.*

I wondered why he'd texted me and not, say, Robbie, but I didn't dwell on it long; this could be my ticket out. I wrote back, *I'm on campus too!* and asked if he wanted to meet on the Lower Campus quad in twenty.

I showed the texts to Fran, who found them hilarious. She said, "I'm giving you my master key! Knock yourself out." As if Mike and I would go make out in the senior lounge. But Fran was tipsy and insistent, wresting a key from its ring.

17

Mike stood in a pool of light in front of Old Chapel, breathing into his cupped palms. The temperature had plummeted in the past hour, so while I'd thought we would take a walk, the first thing I did was show him the key. We let ourselves into the darkened sanctuary, saw our way around by the exit lights. It was a quarter the size of New Chapel, built for a school of a hundred undernourished boys, the benches puritan-narrow and puritan-hard.

"Let's look at the dead kid plaques," Mike said. There were, I'd forgotten, twenty or so small memorials, engraved brass on wood, lining the side wall. All for boys who'd died while students, none more recently than the 1920s. Mike turned his phone flashlight on to read them. Three had died in the same dormitory fire in 1840. Two different boys, fifty-some years apart, had both drowned in the Tigerwhip on the nights of their graduations, presumably drunk.

"You're gonna think I'm weird," Mike said, "but these were the first things I loved about Granby. On my eighth grade tour."

"Maybe more morbid than weird."

"It felt so legitimate. I knew I wasn't getting into Deerfield or Exeter, but these made the place feel old and serious."

I said, "I'd definitely never heard of Exeter or Deerfield when I got here."

"Oh—Iowa, right?"

"Indiana."

"My dad and brother went to Exeter. Honestly they might've let me in just because of that, but I was too scared to risk it. My grades were crap."

"They were?"

"Dyslexia. Took a while to work that one out. This guy here," he said, illuminating the plaque for Louis Stickney, deceased in 1890, "this was an initiation ritual gone wrong. They dumped cold water on his bed every night for a week and he got pneumonia."

"Initiation into what?"

"One of those stupid things."

"A secret society? Lola implied that you were in one."

Mike coughed out a laugh. "We *thought* we were a secret society."

I was surprised he was willing to say this much, although I suppose the charm of adolescent hijinks had long worn off.

"I can't tell you which," he said. "It was honestly dumb, like a bush-league frat. You got initiated, that was about it. Sometimes we'd all wear blue, but no one even noticed. Once a year they'd have a Heritage Day thing where we busted out of the dorms at night." He glanced at me. "It wasn't March third, don't get ideas."

"But you'd swear loyalty?"

"Sure."

If a significant number of boys on campus had sworn an oath to protect each other, that would be useful information for the defense team.

"Who else was in it?" I asked, and he laughed.

"Not Serenho, if that's where you're going."

"I wasn't! I'm—I hope you don't think I think that. About Robbie." I didn't add that this was more because of his incapacity for time travel, and what I knew about you, than any great admiration of him—but it was still true.

"Right," he said, and visibly relaxed. "A lot of people do. He's been in the shit. I'm not blaming you at all, but these people online are nuts. Did you know his kids had to switch schools?"

I shook my head.

"Some whack job kept calling the school office. It was this little private school without security, so Robbie and Jen pulled them out and put them in public. I mean, it might've been a financial decision, too. He's lost business. Like, a *lot* of business. They had just bought this house, and—I don't know."

"Oh God," I said. "Fuck." Jen had shown more restraint than I'd realized that afternoon. Maybe she'd wanted to spare me the guilt.

I felt like retching, but instead suggested we see if Fran's key worked for the clock tower. It did, and we climbed the wooden stairs, steep as ever. I'd gone up there with crew friends once, to pass a Johnson's Baby Shampoo bottle our cox had filled with Jim Beam. (She kept it in a shower caddy; teachers wouldn't think to smell your shampoo.) And I'd gone on my own, with Radiohead on my Discman—the only thing to listen to in a puddle of teen angst inside a clock tower.

We might have just stood awkwardly in the dark, but I decided to sit on the floor near the big gearbox, and Mike joined. The backs of all four clocks, each one five feet tall, surrounded us, their opaque glass glowing from the outside lampposts and the moon. A filmmaker scouting locations on campus would die of joy. But the floor was dusty, and it was almost as cold in here as outside. I wondered about bats. I wished we had booze, at least. A bottle of good old baby shampoo. Both of us hugged our knees.

Mike said, "So who's watching your kids? Aren't they still pretty young?"

"I left them in front of the TV with some canned goods and pepper spray."

He looked stupefied. "You're kidding, right?"

"Probably."

He said, "I've been meaning to tell you I changed my mind about something. When we first talked, I told you it was about the process for me. My original view was, Omar probably did it, but they investigated wrong, they prosecuted wrong, he didn't have adequate defense. That's my professional take. I think I even said to you I was still pretty sure he did it."

"You said something like that."

"Then when he was on the podcast, I don't know. I listened to that one episode five times. It's a gut instinct, but I fully believe him. My *personal* take, I'm listening and I'm thinking, my God, this guy didn't do it. Either he's the craftiest actor in the world, or he had nothing to do with that night."

"That's gratifying."

He said, "Do you have any pot?"

"*With* me?"

"I don't know, you're from California."

"Exactly. I flew here on a plane."

"Shoot. I thought you might."

"Is that why you texted me?"

He looked embarrassed enough that I guessed it was at least half true. He said, "We legalized last year, in Connecticut. It takes some of the fun away, actually. I miss that thrill of sneaking around."

I said, "And why would Omar meet her in the shed?"

"Huh?"

I realized it was a non sequitur. I was still half-drunk, so cold my brain was shrinking.

"Omar's an adult with an office and a car and an apartment. If she comes to meet him for sex, why would they go to this dusty place with old sports equipment? There were mice, remember? If you're meeting someone you're involved with, you go somewhere warm and private, or at least somewhere romantic, like here."

Mike blushed—even if I couldn't quite tell the color of his cheeks, I could see it in his eyes, the sudden downward tilt of his head—and I might have said then that of course that wasn't what I meant, I wasn't talking about us, about now, but instead I kept going.

"The only reason Omar, who has an office with a couch, takes her to the shed is if it's premeditated. But that doesn't fit with anything else. Not with putting her in the pool, which is a panic move. Not with the state's theory that it was some fit of rage."

Mike said, "I wish they could settle how that exit opened, what key and everything. It kills me they didn't document every inch of that door in '95."

Something else started nagging at me: Why would *you* take her there? Your home was off-limits, obviously. But your classroom? The choir room? You, like Omar, had a car. The shed was dirty. It wasn't the first time the incongruity had occurred to me: you in your neatly pressed khakis, clearing your way through cobwebs and broken track hurdles. Did Thalia lead you there? Did she show you how to open the door? Pure darkness and the smell of dust. She didn't understand what a gift she'd just handed you.

I said, "I'm really fucking cold. Let me bring you to this party. They have good drinks."

18

My hangover plus the warning from Hector were reasons enough to hide out in my room all morning. I went down only to grab the bagged breakfast (unsliced cold bagel, one little packet of cream cheese, flimsy plastic knife), then returned to bed to watch HGTV. It was Saturday—no action at the courthouse, nothing to wait for but any buzz about Dane's video. So far, the comments beneath it were all from Dane fans, agreeing or disagreeing, gossiping about what little they could find online. They were excited—but there was nothing yet from anyone who knew you.

I'd fallen asleep again when someone started knocking on my door despite the Do Not Disturb sign. It was one in the afternoon.

I saw Alder through the peephole and wanted to yell at him to go away, but also didn't want to yell, so I opened the door and pulled him in by the arm.

I said, "You're nuts."

"I'm not even here, though!"

Alder wore a sport coat over a *Purple Rain* T-shirt, and he'd grown even taller since I saw him last. I always forget how late boys keep growing.

He said, "You *have* to see this," and he sat on the end of my bed, poked at his phone.

I said, "This better be a YouTube video of kittens."

"It's the lead investigator for the Major Crimes Unit, from the State Police. Yesterday's last witness."

"Dwight Boudreau?" I looked at the paused video. The man was ancient. Old enough that I calculated he must have been nearing retirement when I'd spoken with him so briefly at Miss Vogel's kitchen table. I said, "You can't show me that."

"That's why I didn't send it! That's why I'm here in person!"

"Can you just summarize it?"

"Mostly, but there's one part you have to hear because it's hilarious. Okay, Amy's going through the investigation beat by beat, starting with the medical examiner contacting him. Most of it's excruciatingly boring. Like paperwork, but out loud. So then she goes through the interview transcripts, all these things he never followed up on. Some teacher said Thalia's grades were plummeting and she was like, *Did you obtain her grade records?* and he hadn't. Stuff like that. There were a million of those, so it added up. If I'd been the judge, I'd be like, *Oh, dang*."

"Anyway. I'm gonna put this kitten video on right over here, and if you happen to overhear anything, that's just bad luck."

He pressed play, laid the phone on the bed. I half sat on the dresser, a few feet away, as if a yard of distance would let me off the hook.

Amy March's voice: "You had a meeting on Wednesday, March 8, 1995, with Dr. Mary Ellen Calahan, Granby's head of school, is that correct?"

An old man's voice, thick and phlegmy: "Yes."

"And these are your notes from that meeting?"

"Yes."

"Could you read these highlighted lines out loud? We have magnification for you."

"I can't read that."

"Okay, if the court will allow, I'll read it." A mumble from the judge. "It says, *Dr. C suggests we look at community members strong enough to heft a struggling body into the pool. Not students, not faculty.* Do you recall writing that note?"

"If it's in my handwriting, I wrote it."

"Did you follow that advice from Dr. Calahan?"

"I wouldn't say that we took our direction from her, but sure, we're certainly looking at who could carry a teenage girl, who could wrestle her into that bathing suit, assuming it was put on her, and who could get her in that pool."

"Detective Boudreau, how much did Thalia Keith weigh at the time of her death?"

"I do not recall."

"Thalia Keith weighed 110 pounds."

"Okay."

"That's quite thin for her height. She was significantly underweight."

"In my experience, human bodies are cumbersome."

"So you'd need to be incredibly physically fit to lift a 110-pound girl."

"Yes."

"Can you give me an example of someone who's fit enough to do that?"

"An example?"

"What type of person could lift a body of that size?"

"An athlete. Someone large. Not your average fifteen-year-old boy."

"Would you say an eighteen-year-old Olympic skiing prospect could lift 110 pounds?"

"Perhaps."

"Would you imagine a thirty-year-old English teacher who also coaches football could lift 110 pounds?"

"That would depend on the person."

"Would you say my co-counsel here could lift a 110-pound woman?" I assumed she was referring to Hector.

"I have no idea."

"I weigh 160 pounds, significantly more than Thalia Keith. She and I are the same height, five foot six. Shall we get him up here and see if he can lift me?"

"I'd like to see that," he said. The state objected and the judge sustained it, but he sounded amused.

Amy said, "Hector, I'm afraid we'll have to test your strength another time. Detective Boudreau, you're saying that *independently* of this pointer from Dr. Calahan, you decided a student or faculty member was unlikely able to lift Thalia Keith?"

"It would be hard. When I investigated this case, I remember thinking, I couldn't lift that myself."

"So you allowed your own lack of fitness to guide your decision-making."

There was an objection, and Alder stopped the video and dissolved in laughter.

He said, "Okay, so *then*, they break for recess and after the judge leaves everyone's trying it out, everyone's lifting other people up. There's no way the judge doesn't try that out on someone, too."

I said, "That was one fantastic kitten video."

"Right?"

From what I'd heard of Omar's defense at his first trial—we'd obtained the audio for the podcast—the Boston lawyer sounded like someone doing an uninspired table read for a dull legal procedural. Amy was a huge improvement.

He said, "And I don't know what got into your boyfriend, but after that video the Denny Bloch thing is finally getting traction." Instead of answering, I swallowed. Alder and Britt weren't as fixated on your guilt as I was—Alder had become more focused on Ari Hutson emerging from the woods to kill again—but we all agreed that any suspect besides Omar was a help. "Have you seen this?"

He showed me a new Facebook page called "Dennis Bloch Thalia Keith 'Unsolved' Murder Reward." There was one administrator post: *Denny Bloch, where are you? Interested parties are willing to pay for a polygraph for both you and your wife Suzanne Hamby Bloch. The world wants to know, what are you hiding Denny Bloch? Relatedly, we are offering a $10,000 reward for any information regarding Dennis Blochs involvement* *in the death of Thalia Keith. Is your wife Suzanne Bloch hiding information as well? Come Clean Dennis Bloch. DM us with any information regarding the involvement of D Bloch in the 1995 murder of Thalia Keith.*

There were already a thousand followers.

"That's wild."

"Things are moving!" Alder said. "Things are shaking."

I said, "I don't want you to get your hopes up."

Alder stood, brushed off his jeans. He said, "I'm a Black man in America. My hopes aren't up."

19

I figured the safest place to exercise was the fitness center, which had been empty every time I passed its glass door. If I went to the pool, I might run into the Serenhos again; walking or running in town, I might come across any number of witnesses and be "seen" with them in some problematic way.

It was a tiny room, one wall all mirrors. Two elliptical machines, a stationary bike, some free weights. Overhead, a TV blasted CNN—bombs in Kyiv, bombs in Kharkiv, loud men with loud opinions about it all. It took a few attempts of smashing the remote buttons to turn it off. I was ten minutes into my elliptical workout, and ten minutes into my show about a Parisian talent agency, when Beth Docherty came in.

Or rather: She entered, saw me, wheeled around, left. Seconds later she was back, storming to the other elliptical, just feet from mine, slamming her water bottle into the cup holder. She went at the machine like if she pumped the handles fast enough, she could lift off in rage-powered flight. She tried to turn the TV back on, but the remote wouldn't work for her. Beth was muscly and thin, the kind of fit only sustainable in your midforties with near-constant exercise. She was tan, too. In March.

I had every reason not to talk to her, and that was my plan, but then she appeared to say something, so I removed my earbuds.

"I'm sorry?"

"I wasn't talking to you," she said. "I was swearing."

"Oh. Okay."

"You can go back to ignoring me."

I said, "I wasn't trying to be rude. We're just not supposed to talk. I haven't testified yet."

She laughed bitterly. "That's so convenient. You shoot your mouth off in public when it suits you, but if there's an actual human affected by your actions, you're suddenly some big rule follower."

"I'm sorry if you feel my actions have affected you," I said, hearing my phrasing, recognizing it as the syntax of bad people. But I didn't care. I was not sorry about inconveniencing *Beth Docherty*. "You don't even have to be here still, do you? They're not gonna recall you. Can't you just go home?"

"My husband is picking me up in an hour. I should've just fucking walked home. I hate this. I hate seeing these people. I hate reliving the worst years of my life."

It took me a second to register that she hadn't said the worst moments of her life, but the worst years. Plural.

I said, "You're—no longer a Granby fan?"

She snorted. "Every moment of that place was a nightmare." She jabbed a button on the machine and it beeped, displayed her brief workout results as she dismounted.

I thought she was going to leave, but instead she unfurled a purple yoga mat from beside the weights and sat, legs crossed, hands on knees, staring into the mirror. She breathed with great, loud control. I could see her reflection without turning my head much, and I watched her like I'd watch an encroaching wildfire. I didn't put my earbuds back in, kept the show paused on a small dog emerging from a bag.

Beth said, "I was worried they'd ask me about Mr. Bloch." Her voice was smaller. And something seemed to be wrong. It merited my stopping the machine, getting off. I stood beside her, sweating, hands on hips, made eye contact with her in the mirror.

"Would that have been a problem?"

Her face was a dying star. She said, "I don't want to deal with any of this. I testified in '97, I had to leave college to come up here, I never wanted any of it." Unexpectedly, inappropriately, I wanted to hug her. She seemed so small on the floor, an already tiny person making herself still as a pebble. She closed her eyes. I sat beside her as quietly as I could, folded my own legs, looked straight ahead in the mirror, as if we were attending the same yoga class, awaiting instruction. "They wanted to know about my flask, and why would I even remember? And then they're asking the same things as last time. If they want me to be a broken record, can't they just read what I said before? My memory hasn't gotten any *better*. And Jesus, they're trying to make it look like I personally framed him. The police *happened* to talk to me first, but we were all saying the same thing. Somehow I'm the problem. And listen, we were *right*. There was DNA. Maybe I'd feel different if what we said was the only evidence, but it wasn't."

I managed not to argue.

When she opened her eyes, I said, "They just want to prove no one else was investigated."

"What's funny," she said, "is I could have told them about Mr. Bloch if they'd *asked*."

"About him and Thalia?"

"He would stand behind you and put his hands on your stomach, like he was checking your diaphragm for how you were singing. Or he'd stand in front of you with his hands on your shoulders, to show how you shouldn't move your shoulders when you breathe, but he's so close his breath is in your face. This horrible coffee breath."

I said, "Oh." Why was a small part of me surprised? I'd expected to hear from someone you'd preyed on in Providence years later, maybe someone who looked like Thalia. Maybe I'd assumed you picked one girl every once in a while. Not that you had your hands all over everyone. It was dense of me. The fact that you never bothered *me* didn't mean you were monocular in your fixations. "Did he ever do more than that?"

"You were supposed to be flattered. Sophomore year, his first year, right? He was so into that senior, you remember Erin Dominici? She was *gorgeous*. Then that spring he starts paying me all this attention. And it's weird, but I'm not in the same league as her so the flattery is intoxicating.

Everyone thinks he's cute. He had—when you think back, he had a young look, which was more attractive to teenagers than if he had some big beard, you know? He wanted to meet more, one-on-one, to practice. He literally called my house that summer. It was lucky I was the one who picked up, but maybe he'd tried before and hung up when he got my dad. He said he wanted to check if I was singing. Then he's telling me how lonely Granby is in summer."

She was speaking, I realized, with the practiced self-awareness and the monologuing capacity of someone who'd gone through a lot of therapy.

"We get back in the fall, and Thalia's new, and I'm the one who convinces her to try out for Follies. Right away, he's obviously infatuated. What's fucked up is, when it was *me*, I was okay with the attention, and suddenly it's her and I find it disgusting. Which then, I think I must be jealous, right? Thalia's so beautiful, I was dumb to think he liked me, blah blah. But it bothers me, how she's falling for it. That's how I think of it, that she's falling for some scam he pulls with everyone.

"And she let it go so much further than I had. I remember once that fall we went shopping and she was looking at all this sexy underwear, these black lace things, asking if I thought he'd like them. I was like, *But he's never going to see them, right?* and she goes, *He likes to keep the lights on.*"

I said, "Oh my God." I watched my own face, surprised it didn't burst into flame. I needed to call Amy March, needed to tell her to recall Beth, but first I needed to breathe.

"Did you know I fixed her up with Robbie?" she said. "I worked so hard to get them together. To get her away from Mr. Bloch, which didn't work. And then Robbie was such a little dick to her. And I—for years, I told myself I must have just wanted the attention all to myself. But sometimes when we're young, we're smarter than we think. Maybe it didn't bother me because I was jealous. Maybe it bothered me because it *bothered* me."

She paused long enough that I thought I should say something. "You had good instincts," I offered.

"We were on that opera trip, and she kept vanishing with him, even though Robbie was there. And I kept trying to get her to do stuff with me, just to keep them apart, and we had this huge fight. We didn't talk for weeks."

I thought I'd been so observant, and all this had gone right past me.

"I don't want you thinking that was the reason I hated Granby. The girls were awful. The *boys* were awful. Freshman year we had to take some stupid anonymous sex survey in that health seminar, and fucking—I'm not even gonna say who it was, but someone found the pile of surveys and took mine, because I was the only one who said I'd had sex. So she shows it around the whole *school* before I even find out why everyone's whispering about me. And then I have two choices: I can skulk around and be embarrassed, or I can own it. I tried to drop out, but my father—I don't know. I stayed."

Humiliatingly, I remembered. Donna Goldbeck—that's who it was—had showed the completed survey around the dorm, along with a message Beth had once jotted down for her from the pay phone. She needed a lot of opinions, every single person's opinion, on whether the handwriting matched.

"You know what's ironic? I hadn't even had sex. I'm in a new school, these kids all seem so sophisticated, and I'm thinking, I'm probably the only one who hasn't done it. At fourteen fucking years old. So I put yes to all these things, because I'm afraid of someone looking over my shoulder and thinking I'm a prude. And it backfires just spectacularly."

I said, "I'm so sorry that happened to you. And I want to be honest here, I'm sorry I took part in that. I talked about it. I don't want to pretend I didn't." It wouldn't have occurred to me in infinite lifetimes that I'd had a hand in bullying Beth Docherty.

"I don't blame anyone for believing it. Even now, with my own kids, it's confusing as hell. I tell them not to believe rumors, and then my daughter is like, *But rumors are how we know if someone's an abuser.* She has that vocabulary at twelve, which blows my mind. So I'm supposed to say, *Yes, believe those rumors, but not the other ones? Only believe rumors about men?*"

"Well," I said. "Believe women. It's not perfect, but maybe it's a start."

Beth snapped her head to look right at me for the first time. "Sorry, but didn't your husband get totally me-tooed?" She was back to her sharpest voice. As if the whole conversation had been a trap, just like "Nice top" had once been.

I said, "Someone had some issues with him."

"So you're one to talk. You don't believe *that* woman, but you believe women when it suits you."

"I don't think that's fair."

Beth returned her gaze to the mirror, recalibrated her breath. We were back in yoga class.

"Anyway, I read all about it."

"Yes," I said, "he has a high profile. But my point was, I'm sorry that happened to you."

"You remember I dated Dorian senior year? We broke up partway into my first semester at Penn, but it was a year of my life. He treated me—everything was a joke. He was all the worst things about Granby in one ball."

Beth and Dorian broke up and made up so many times that we'd laugh about it, a running gag. She'd show up to class with puffy red eyes, and Fran would pass me a note: *Trouble in Loverville!*

"We were at Mike Stiles's ski place in Vermont, and there was a security camera set up on their front porch. So Dorian somehow moved it into the bedroom, and then he brought me in there. He'd told everyone else to watch on the monitor, and I had no idea."

In the mirror, my eyes widened, my mouth searched dumbly for words.

"That's horrible."

"They all sat there and watched what we were doing. Which wasn't even anything I wanted to do. Dorian thought it was hilarious."

"That's *horrible*." I was doing a mental inventory of who'd likely been there, who might have sat watching, laughing. Mike Stiles, for one. Robbie. I couldn't imagine Thalia sitting through it. She'd have told them they were being disgusting, left the room.

"It's so hot," I remembered Donna Goldbeck saying to me, about Beth and Dorian. "The way they fight. It's, like, steamy. They were screaming at each other at Stiles's house and then, like, five minutes later they're upstairs fucking."

And I took her word for it: that it was hot, that it was enviable, that it was some level of relationship I could only aspire to.

"You don't understand, though," Beth said. "You say it's horrible, and you have no idea. You were *safe*. You were never in that position."

"I was safe?" I tried to comprehend this.

"Jesus, Bodie. You were weird. You were intimidating. You were always rolling your eyes at everything we said, like you thought we were the cheesiest people in the world."

I couldn't disagree. I could have told her things about my own life, my childhood, could have reminded her that she named me the Masturbator. But I'd learned long ago not to counter people's trauma with my own. I said, "I am so sorry you went through that. I had no idea, and I'm really fucking sorry."

"And I'm sorry to hate you this much. But, Bodie, I hate you *so much*. You set this all in motion, and now I have to face these people. My husband is having surgery this week, and I should be focusing on that, and instead I'm here. I'd like to just keep living my life. I hate you for bringing me back here."

We were still looking only into the mirror, two women of the same age sitting in the same position. Her smallness had seemed such currency to me at Granby, when I believed the smaller you could be, as a girl, the more the world revolved around you. Next to me now, two-thirds my size, she looked like someone overwhelmed by a too-large world, someone never allowed more power than a little girl.

I said, again, "I had no idea."

She stood without using her hands, just lifted weightlessly up. She said, "I am so fucking happy to leave this place."

20

Dane Rubra was breathless.

He'd found you. Or someone from his "community" had. There was a D. Stanley Bloch in Silver Spring, Maryland, aged fifty-nine, working with a community youth orchestra. I was skeptical for a minute (Stanley?), but Dane's people had done their due diligence.

"Look," Dane said in his newly posted video. He stood in a parking lot for this one, birdsong and traffic noise around him. "Having someone's location doesn't mean we show up in a mob. It means we reach out to people *near* him, people who've had contact since 1995, employers, coworkers, former students. I can't emphasize that last one enough. *Former students.* This guy, you find him on the street, he's not giving you anything. But little Sally the flute player who, you know, he made her sit on his lap, maybe she has a story to tell."

I was equally nauseated at the glee in his eyes and at his use of the name Sally, the clichéd innocent girl who was for some reason from 1955. Little Sally and her brother Timmy.

Still: He was useful. His followers were useful. Who knew what else they could find?

I had started three times that afternoon to text the defense team, telling them to talk to Beth again, but each time I'd deleted the words. I'd be telling them about Beth's own abuse, not just Thalia's, and without her permission. And if the defense didn't need my accusations of Mr. Bloch, did it need Beth's? If she'd already testified and then they called her back up there, would it look like she'd been coerced? What if the state asked if she'd spoken to me between testimonies? It should be

Amy's call, but still, I had to think it all through. And it was only Saturday; I could call Amy tomorrow.

In the meantime, this—Dane's lackeys following the bread crumbs—this was exactly what I'd wished for.

"The other thing we want," Dane said, "we want to keep an eye on him. This guy changed his name at least once. We don't want him skipping town."

I wondered how many of them were heading to Silver Spring right that second, how many were hacking your email. How many planned something bigger than that.

With a chill down my neck, down my arms, I remembered the guy who'd gone into a pizza place with a gun, looking for the nonexistent pedophile ring in the basement. I remembered how many people in America had guns.

I was shocked to discover a very, very small part of me still loyal to you, a part that wanted to send you a message: Get in your car and drive. Change your last name, too. Don't look back.

I tried to distract myself with a movie, but since the Calvin Inn wi-fi was too fatigued to continue the day, I was beholden to the offerings on my room's bulky Panasonic. Here was *Bus Stop*, a movie I hated. *Bus Stop* is what happens when no women were involved in the writing process. We get, for instance, a woman who, when Marilyn Monroe sidles up to her on the bus and says she's been kidnapped, replies: "It wouldn't be so bad if you were in love with him."

I turned the TV off and checked email. Someone I didn't know had sent a clip from a Boston station—part of an interview with Brad Keith, Thalia's half brother. He'd gone gray in a thick-haired, dignified way. He wore a powder blue sweater. Last I knew, Brad Keith was a commodities trader.

"But in the interest of justice—" the reporter across from him said.

"Justice *was* served. He got his day in court, he got it again on appeal. I understand the right to a fair trial, but three trials? Four? Five? Where does it end? You can't just keep rolling the dice till you get what you want."

The reporter didn't point out the difference between a hearing and a trial. She said, "There's been new evidence. We know now th—"

"Nothing's new. We have her old roommate with some baloney about *dots*. We have blood evidence that just moves the assault a few feet to the left. Omar Evans ruined all our lives, not just Thalia's. And every time we get dragged back, he destroys us again. We've been through enough."

"Your sister Vanessa disagrees."

He shook his head, resigned. "She was so young when this happened."

Below the video link, the email read: *Look what you're doing you unconscionable bitch.*

Geoff had ordered pizza for dinner, and we ate at the little table in his room. Geoff, who used to accept dares to mix chocolate milk, hot sauce, ranch dressing, and orange juice in a dining hall cup and drink it down, had ended up with sophisticated taste. He'd managed to order a very specific herb pizza via Grubhub from Hanover and get it delivered still hot, along with a bottle of excellent Syrah from a completely different place. We were planning to go through the hoarded Granby junk he'd brought for Britt and Alder. But first, carbs and cheese and wine. I decided to let myself eat as much as I wanted.

He said something I didn't get about the Calvin Inn being the place where you got whatever you deserved, and then had to explain that it was a joke about Calvinism. "Oh, one of *those*," I said. "I love a good Calvinism joke."

He asked if I thought Carlotta was going to make it, and the cheese turned gluey in my throat.

Alder joined us at nine. I'd decided to give up on staying away from him—what difference could it make if someone who was never going to testify spoke, privately, to a member of the press?—but I hadn't told him yet what I'd learned from Beth. Alder was not the best keeper of secrets.

Geoff wheeled a roller-board suitcase out of the closet, opened it in the middle of the floor. "I had to get my mom's nurse to dig all this up." The suitcase was stuffed with yearbooks and papers and photos and *Sentinel*s.

I said, "How much did you have to pay the airline to bring a two-thousand-pound suitcase?"

We sat cross-legged on a carpet that probably wasn't completely clean.

I plucked our senior *Dragon Tales* off the top of the mess, opened it to the autograph pages, pretended to read: *"Dear Geoff, I want to confess to a murder that*—my God, Geoff, you've been sitting on this for twenty-seven years!"

"Dr. Calahan!" he cried. "All along!"

We spent three hours sifting through things, sometimes sorting them into well-intentioned piles, sometimes reading aloud and dissolving in laughter. Geoff used to review movies for the *Sentinel*, and in 1994 he'd deemed *Pulp Fiction* "an iconoclastic piece of cinema, one that would be destined for the halls of greatness had it not already achieved that excellent canonical designation."

"You're free to use that in any future lectures," he said. "Feel free to just quote the hell out of that."

Alder wanted gossip about every student with an interesting haircut. He loved the youthful pictures of people like Priscilla Mancio. He said, "They had a *web surfing club*?"

"It was only the biggest nerds," I said. "I hope they're all billionaires now."

By midnight, we were slaphappy and exhausted and would have finally gone to bed, but, to Alder's glee, we'd just found the full roll of Jimmy Scalzitti's photos—*Camelot* and the mattress party and, finally, Jimmy's dorm room floor. There were more than thirty-six prints in the white business envelope, but then some were doubles. I was amazed that the negatives were still tucked in there; another thing the State Police hadn't asked for. There was nothing new, alas; these same shots were all online—but still, we got caught up in laying them out in order on the bed.

In late 2018, there'd been great interest online in seeing if anyone's sneakers were visible, in hopes of identifying the toe print on the equipment shed door. That timeline made no sense, unless someone from the mattresses had gone over later to help clean up the mess, but to those convinced of Omar's innocence it was still worth a shot. A matching shoe might be a tiny wedge in his case. But the only shoes you could see clearly enough to identify were Asad Mirza's duck boots.

"You know who would absolutely orgasm over these," Geoff said, placing a picture of Beth and Fizz on the bed, "is that pasty YouTube guy."

"I worry that's literally true."

We laid them in rows, referring to the negatives to establish chronological order, stacking identical prints. First were twelve shots of *Camelot*—awful ones, as Jimmy wouldn't have been allowed to shoot with flash—and then a blur of legs and someone's blue North Face jacket in the dark in the woods (he must've used his flash this time), the timestamp suddenly on: 9:58.

Then came the 9:59 shot with the infamous "blood spatter" that was so clearly just mud up the back of Robbie's sweatshirt. The framing was slightly wider than the photo I'd seen online. Five kids, three with their backs turned. Two faces—Sakina John, Asad Mirza—glowed in the beams of the flashlight bonfire; the camera had given both red devil eyes. We named everyone for Alder, but he already knew.

Next: the 10:02 photo of Robbie with his arms around Beth and Dorian. Here was his face, not just his back; this was the photo that easily proved his alibi, the one most prominently discussed online. Reddit users had whole threads on it. (*How accurate is a random 1990s camera timestamp anyway? This isn't like a smartphone syncing with GMT. Could be off by a lot. Time zones, DST, etc.!*) But even if it were off, the photos spanned forty-one minutes, down to that last one of Fizz drinking a beer—and unless these kids all flew back to their dorms, the right amount of time is accounted for. It would've taken someone smarter than Jimmy Scalzitti to change the clock setting multiple times.

I was looking at the last three shots, the ones of Jimmy's dorm room floor, feeling satisfied that all thirty-six photos were accounted for, when Alder said "Huh."

Just that, like a small, dull bell.

I peered over his shoulder and tried to see what he was looking at. He picked it up: the mud photo, the kids' backs.

Alder said, "That's Serenho, right?" He pointed with a pinky to Robbie's back. That was him, his floppy hair, the back of the same gold Granby ski sweatshirt he'd been wearing in other shots, the same baggy jeans.

I said, "Yeah. It's *not* blood."

"No, I know." Alder popped his lips.

"It's just dirt."

"Right."

He took a photo of the photo with his iPhone, adjusted the contrast to its most extreme. He zoomed in on the back of Robbie's sweatshirt. The splatter of dirt ran straight up the middle, a pattern wider at the bottom, narrower at the top. There were a few more millimeters to this print than to the online photo, so you could see more mud going farther down. But it still wasn't blood. "Here's what I'm thinking," he said. "That's from a bike. That's from riding a bike through the mud."

I had no idea what Alder was getting at, but I couldn't breathe.

"No," Geoff said. "No one had a bike. Can you even ride a bike on campus *now*? There's no point."

But Alder was right. This was how the backs of Leo's T-shirts looked when we visited Jerome's family in Wisconsin and he rode around their farm.

Alder zoomed in as far as he could, as if some answer would be written in the dark spatter. He said, "It's from a bike."

"It's from a bike," I repeated dumbly.

Geoff said, "Yeah, but who had a bike?"

"I mean—little kids," I said. "Right? Faculty kids." I remembered Mr. Levin's son Tyler riding his kid-sized BMX around and around the all-weather track. It would've been idiotic for students to try to navigate campus on wheels, but if you had a five-year-old kid, you still bought them a bike. They had to learn somehow.

Geoff said, "He probably had one at home."

Alder said, "He rode a bike at home in Vermont over Christmas? In the mud? And brought his sweatshirt back and didn't wash it for three months?"

"Maybe," I said. "Or Feb Week. It doesn't sound right. Why is my heart racing?"

Geoff, staring at the photo, said, "Jesus," as if he'd just figured it all out, too, and I was the only one in the dark.

Alder said, "Talk this through with me. Talk this through." He sat on the edge of the bed, the other photos sliding together.

It took me so long. It took me a stupid amount of time. And yes, most of the problem was that I was so fixated on you, so laser-focused on your alibi, your motives, your sins, your lies, that what I should have seen as illumination, I saw as a blinding glare. I could only look around the edges of it, like an eclipse.

I said, "He rode a bike because—okay, he rode a bike to get to the party. Everyone else walked, but he rode a bike?"

Geoff was pacing, his hands on his head.

Alder said, "He left *Camelot*. And they started walking. And so—so they walk there, they stop at the dorms first, maybe they leave at nine. It takes them half an hour. They walk slow because of Mike Stiles's leg, right?"

And still I didn't get it.

"He wasn't *with* them," he said. "Not at first. They're in groups, there are nineteen kids, they're not taking attendance. Half are already drunk."

I said, "He wasn't with them," or at least I mouthed it. Was that even possible? There was math involved. I grabbed a Calvin Inn notepad and pen from Geoff's desk and wrote:

> *8:45-ish? Camelot ends*
> *9:00 start walking*

9:30 mattresses
9:58 first mattress photo
9:59 first photo of Serenho
10:45 leave mattresses
11:05 back in dorms

Geoff took the pen from my fingers and drew a circle around the first five items, everything from the end of *Camelot* to Robbie Serenho's first photo. Next to it, he wrote *1:14*. It was so much time. Even if the show had ended a few minutes later.

He said, "How long do you think it takes to bike from the gym to the mattresses?"

"It was muddy," I said. Only the dumbest of my thoughts were processing fully. I said, "Alder, you're not recording this, are you?"

He shook his head. "Should I be?"

"No."

Geoff said, "I ride a five-minute mile when I'm lazy. Let's say pedaling fast over 1.4 miles of muddy terrain, maybe on a kid's bike, let's say conservatively ten minutes. *Extra* conservative, fifteen minutes. Even though we're talking about a teenage athlete with a ton of adrenaline."

I said, "He's still got almost an hour."

My face was in my hands, because my face was hot and my hands were ice-cold.

Alder slid down to the carpet, lay on his back, stared at the ceiling. He said, "Are we nuts? Maybe we're nuts. So wait: He picks Thalia up backstage. Maybe he tries to get her to come to the mattresses. Maybe he's told his friends he's coming, right? They start fighting, they head toward the gym. Whatever happens, happens. He freaks and realizes he needs an alibi. If he goes back to the dorms, he won't be accounted for over the past forty-five minutes."

"Plus he probably wants a drink," Geoff said.

"Right. And he wants his friends. So he needs to get to the mattresses fast. He looks around and sees a kid's bike, or maybe there's some faculty bike, whatever. He rides up, ditches the bike in the woods, and as soon as he's there he makes sure they see him. He pretends he was there the whole time."

"They don't see him come up?" I said. "They aren't like, *Where'd you come from?*"

Geoff said, "Okay, so maybe they don't notice, or maybe they forget. Or maybe they cover for him later. But he sees that Scalzitti still has the camera. The pictures don't even start till he's there. Maybe he grabs the camera and turns on the timestamp."

Alder, still on the floor, said, "Oh my God oh my God. Can I call Britt?"

I said, "I just—that's a lot of crafty thinking for a drunk guy."

"Who said he was drunk?" Geoff said. "Maybe he was stone-cold sober. Or sure, maybe he was wasted the whole time. Those aren't sober actions. Doing it to begin with. Throwing her in the pool. Stealing a bike and plowing through the woods."

I said, "You're using circular logic. We're going off a streak on his sweatshirt. It *could* have been months old. He's a teenage boy. It could've been from something else. That could be someone else's sweatshirt."

"Right," Alder said. "And this is not particularly useful in court. Robbie had a dirty sweatshirt so Omar's innocent. That's not—" He finished the sentence by rolling over onto his stomach, his face on the carpet.

I said, "It's not a thing."

But still: I felt my edges blurring.

I'd believed for so many years that it was Omar, that it was settled, even as my doubts about the case against him—and my suspicions about you—started pecking at me, a bird ready to escape its shell. And then the shell cracked, it fell to pieces, and the only plausible explanation was it was you.

It was you, it was you. Everything fit. You had motive, you had opportunity. You'd done one terrible thing, so you must have done another.

The most moronic thought: It couldn't have been Robbie, because look at the carefree way he'd jumped into the pool the other day.

Alder and Geoff were staring at the photo again. Somewhere in the same building, Robbie and his family slept. Somewhere out there, so did you.

There was once a man they caught because he claimed he hadn't left the state—but the dead bugs on the windshield of his rental car could only have come from outside California.

There was a man they caught because he'd ordered the knife on Amazon.

There was a man they caught because his name was on the Starbucks cup in her trash.

There was a man who was told that his wife's body had been found in the woods. He arrived on the scene and instead of running toward the police tape, he ran to the exact spot where he'd left her body.

There was a guy whose claim of earlier consensual sex fell apart because his semen was in her body, but not in her underwear or pants. "Because dead women," the prosecutor explained, "don't stand up."

There was a woman who managed to cut her captor's driver's license into twenty little pieces and swallow them so when they found her body his ID would be in her stomach. And they arrested him. They brought him in for questioning. But they never pressed charges against him.

Back in my own room, I lay in bed trying to think. If Robbie killed her, if Robbie lost his temper and became violent, it was likely over you. What else would make him that angry? Well: Some people have rage right below the surface, and an overcooked potato is enough to incite domestic homicide. As far as I knew, that wasn't Robbie. She'd never gone to class with bruises on her face. She was coming from your show. Had he seen something between the two of you?

I remembered the seed of my own initial unease: the way Thalia turned her head offstage, the way she mouthed *What?* as if someone were back there, waiting for her, upset with her. You were in the orchestra pit, conducting. Omar's presence in the theater would have been noted. Whereas Robbie Serenho could slip backstage, could walk straight through the clusters of waiting actors with no more than a whispered *"Robbie, you're not supposed to be here!"* Their fight could have started when she came offstage and told him to leave. Or maybe he was back there because the fight had begun hours earlier. Maybe he was coasting on hours of rage. Maybe he knew exactly what he was planning.

I slept, but my dreams only rehashed things. The photos on Geoff's bed, the math problem of the bike in the woods. *A train leaves Kansas City at 9:00 p.m., headed for the gym. How angry is the driver?*

In the morning, I texted Fran: *I have a quest for Jacob and Max.* Could they time themselves, I asked, riding bikes from the gym to the old mattress spot? Could they avoid any newer paths? I didn't explain.

Fran wrote back: *Who on earth had a bike?? But sure! They need exercise!*

It was cold now, and muddy, only a little snow. The conditions were about the same.

We had decided at the end of the night that Alder would fill in both Britt and the defense team. We knew it was a reach—we'd probably sound like lunatics—but Robbie had yet to testify, so maybe they could make something of it. And meanwhile, those of us who had nothing better to do could at least dig harder. I had ridiculous visions of finding a rusty bike in the woods, Robbie's fingerprints and Thalia's blood still on the handlebars.

The image I kept returning to was of a tangled necklace chain. In one of the more normal moments of my later childhood, my mother taught me to rub a chain with olive oil, then take a long, straight pin and start working on the tiniest of gaps, the place with the most give. Once one thing loosened, another could loosen, another. I always felt claustrophobic at the start. But over time I'd learned patience, learned the reward of breathing through my discomfort.

What I knew was that we'd found a gap in the knot. I didn't know what else it would loosen up, and I didn't want to pull too hard, but I knew if we finessed it, wiggled it gently, other things would follow.

Midday, Geoff and I took our laptops to Aroma Mocha and sat looking through the 1995 interview records for any details of the mattress party timeline, any mention of Robbie being there the whole time or of who walked together. The kids who'd been there listed all nineteen students at the mattress party, confirmed that they'd been drinking, talked about when they'd last seen Thalia. Nothing about how scattered they'd been on the trail.

The only time it came up, either as a question or an answer, was the State Police asking both Sakina and Bendt Jensen whether Robbie had been there the whole time. Sakina said that to the best of her recollection, he was. Bendt said that he assumed so. They asked Sakina if he could have left early and she said no, because she remembered him helping Stiles walk home on his bad leg. Mike Stiles, in his own interview, talked about Robbie and Dorian helping him back.

"It's amazing," Geoff said, "that they thought to ask if he left early, but not if he got there late."

"Right. Because bad stuff happens late at night. Bad stuff happens *after* you've been drinking, not before."

Alder texted: *LOL, Amy was like, uh, thanks for the theory. She at least agreed it looked like bike mud!*

Just as we were leaving, setting our empty cups on the counter, Fran texted back: *Nine minutes for Jacob, twelve for Max w/ training wheels, if I got the spot right. J says he could do it faster if it weren't so wet.*

25

I deployed myself that night as a weapon. A spy, in the grand tradition of women who trade sex, or the promise of sex, for secrets. Only I was wearing pajama pants and a USC sweatshirt, and all I did was text Mike Stiles. *I'm stir-crazy,* I wrote. *Need to talk to someone not on the fucking witness list. Drinks on balcony? It's not too cold!*

When I opened the door he looked composed, but as he stepped inside he flushed. He was aware, at least, that he was a married man entering a woman's hotel room at night. We sat outside and drank whiskey out of the two ornate glasses from the ice bucket tray. We talked about Lola, about his tripping over their pronouns (he was working on it) and how they were doing at Baylor.

I couldn't get out of my head the idea of Mike being there at that ski house when Dorian put Beth on the monitor. Mike maybe showing Dorian where the security camera was. Mike being part of the "all of them" who'd sat and watched. I couldn't imagine it was something he was proud of. I wondered if he ever thought of it at all.

I waited till he'd refilled his glass to say, "This hearing is bringing up so much for me. All my adolescent insecurities. I wanted to leave that kid behind." I felt guilty that I was basically quoting Beth here, but I'm not a creative liar.

"That's funny. I never knew you were insecure. You weren't trying to play the game, from what I remember. I mean that in a good way. You weren't doing the whole teen magazine thing."

"I don't know what that means."

"Just—the girls who'd all get the same haircut and try to sit on your lap in the library. They were insecure. You weren't like that."

Under most circumstances, I'd have called a man out on using "You're not like other girls" as a compliment, but this wasn't the moment. I looked straight at him and said, "I've always known what I like."

An unoriginal line, but yes: His ears reddened, he started to say something and stopped.

It was too cold, so we moved inside—Mike in the flowery chair, pulled close to the bed so he could put his feet up in their woolly socks. I reclined on the too-many-pillows that the Calvin Inn provided and took my sweatshirt off. I'd put thought into the tank top I wore beneath.

"I bet you're the only person from that ski crowd doing actual useful work now," I said. "Isn't everyone else basically just turning money into more money?"

He protested, but was clearly flattered. He swished his whiskey and said, "It's hard to break that pattern of what your parents want. You think you have to earn at least as much as them. Then there were kids like Serenho who didn't grow up with much. My grandfather and my dad worked their asses off and I get to have this comfortable life in academia, but there's always the safety net."

"Wait, I thought Serenho was loaded." I took a sip to hide my shoddy acting.

He leaned in, secretive. "No way. He was on massive aid, and the last two years Rachel Popa's family paid for him."

"Why would they do that?"

"Because they could. I don't know; he's just a great guy. And he knew how to charm it up with people's parents. Moms, especially. We'd rag on him, how he was suddenly so polite, like, *That sweater really suits you, Mrs. Stiles.*"

I could see it. He'd been so good with teachers, had the kind of casual relationships with them that meant when I'd show up early for ninth grade English he'd already be there, asking Mrs. Hoffnung how he could get this chocolate ice cream stain out of his favorite oxford.

"Wasn't he always going on vacations with you all?"

"Sure. But we'd pay. We'd find ways, like a few of us would gather money for the keg and make sure he didn't get hit up."

I said, "I guess Thalia knew, obviously. That he was on aid."

"Yeah, but he also never took her home to Vermont, you know? And her showing up later, she didn't see him when he was wearing crap clothes and cheap skis. She only met him after he had all the stuff we'd given him."

This stung. I'd never noticed that Robbie had dressed badly, maybe because he was a boy, and because even his "crap" clothes were still a step up from Indiana. That he'd undergone his own transformation, parallel to my raiding of Fran's sisters' closets, hurt. I couldn't figure out why. Maybe I felt for him, or maybe I hated that his friends had elevated him to social stardom, when my own transformation, liberating as it was, had only distanced me further from most of my peers. But hadn't my own friends held me up? Hadn't I done fine?

"I had no idea," I said. I poured us both more whiskey. "You must've felt protective." I worried Mike would snap into defensive mode, but he leaned back in the floral chair, feet close to mine. He had an impressive five-o'clock shadow. "When everything happened with Thalia, I didn't realize how vulnerable he might have been. It's one thing if a rich kid gets accused of something and they can lawyer up, but if they'd blamed Robbie he'd be in the same position as Omar." I didn't believe that was true for one second. "He must have been terrified."

"He was." Mike's eyelids were drooping. I needed to keep him awake, happy, talking.

I said, "I remember Scalzitti got those photos developed, like, *right away*. When usually the last thing you'd want proof of was drinking on campus. I always imagined that was to protect Robbie. Or maybe Robbie asked him to."

Mike pointed at me. "That's exactly it," he said. "Scalzitti wanted to destroy the film. I was there in Lambeth and they had this blowup. Serenho was like, *They're gonna say Thalia was with us, and we'll all get blamed. If we get the pictures developed they'll see she wasn't there.* Scalzitti was still chickenshit so I literally walked him over to the darkroom to see that little—what was that guy's name? Ritter? Otherwise I think he would've dumped the film in the creek."

I said, "There were the timestamps and everything. That was a life-saver for Robbie."

"For all of us, probably."

"Right. Because no one who was there could've done it. Which—that wouldn't have been obvious for a few days, right? It took a while for them to get the cause of death, and the time of death. You figure, at first it might've looked bad. These are the kids who were out drinking, and they were sneaking around campus, so who knows what else they did."

Mike looked confused, thick brows coming together. "I guess the point was she wasn't with us."

"But it's funny," I said, "that Robbie took that risk."

"He knew he had nothing to hide. That makes it easier."

"I know from Sakina that you guys got to the mattresses in clusters," I lied. "I mean, that only makes sense. You were probably slower than everyone else with your leg. But when they ask about it, you just—you simplify it, right? If you all walked there together, it gets the gist across better."

"Wait, is that what she said on the stand?"

"I doubt it. I mean, if anything, they're interested in when people *left.*"

"Right." He relaxed back in his chair. "I don't know. In the days afterward, we kept checking with each other, making sure we had our story straight. Not like we were making it up, but just things like whose idea was it, how long were we there. Honestly, we decided together to say it was only drinking and cigarettes. There was definitely some pot, but that wasn't in the photos, so why bring it up?"

"Right," I said. "Why would pot be relevant?" But he didn't seem to catch my sarcasm.

I refilled his glass, even though it wasn't empty. I topped mine off just a millimeter. I'd barely drunk any. As I leaned back on the pillows, I stretched my arms overhead, a move I'd learned men took as egregious flirting even though I never meant it that way; I just had tight shoulders. But I lingered with my arms up, stretching to the right and the left.

In the aftermath of my latest Yahav relapse, I'd had the unflattering realization that I had never once, in my life, gone after a man who was fully available. In my early twenties, I honed my skills on married men, men whose rejections and eventual departures it would be impossible to take personally. Even Jerome wasn't someone I ever possessed completely, or wanted to. And look who I'd pined after at Granby: the hottest guy on the ski team, and Kurt Fucking Cobain. Men who could never hurt me, because I could remain invisible to them. ("Do you think this might have to do with your father and brother?" asks every new shrink, tentatively, as if it weren't glaringly obvious.)

Now I said, to the boy in whose honor I'd once borrowed a library map of Connecticut just so I could look up the precise location of his street in New Canaan: "You know what the clock tower made me think of, the other day, was all the spaces people used to go to make out. Or smoke."

He laughed, wiped his mouth with the back of his hand. "Oh, man. I was never a smoker, so I wouldn't know about *that*."

"Right. You only knew the make-out places, and I only knew the smoking places."

"You never got busy on campus?"

"Not once." It didn't sound pathetic, the way it might have if I'd said it at eighteen. "Where were the big spots? I'd catch people in the theater all the time."

He said, "Aw, man, that's not even creative. There was this guest apartment at the back of Jacoby. That was a good one if you had the key. But in spring they'd put up people interviewing for jobs, so that was out."

I said, "I remember certain couples had spots that were, like, *theirs*.

You'd never go to the Quincy balcony at night, because Sakina and Marco would be there."

"Man! I forgot that. It was so territorial. Can't you imagine a David Attenborough narration? *The adolescents have staked out their breeding grounds.*"

I laughed. "Totally. Angie Parker and that short guy, Steve whatever, they were always up in the English hallway."

"Dorian," he said, "when he dated Beth, they'd get a full-on hotel room in town. The rumor was she made him, she wouldn't sleep with him on campus."

"That tracks." I laughed, this time not genuinely. Good God, I didn't blame her, given what his friends had all seen. I said, "Where was— Robbie and Thalia had a place, right?"

He blanched, actually blanched, to the point where I couldn't just play it cool; I had to say, "Why, what?"

I hoped he was drunk enough. I knew what I wanted him to say, and he just needed to be drunk enough to say it. He wasn't. I could see his wheels turning, but he said nothing.

So I said, "Oh God, was it—was she waiting for him that night, you think? In the shed? I bet she was there looking for him, when someone— oh, shit." Mike didn't deny it, so I pressed on. "That makes sense, then, why you'd need to back up his alibi. Even before we knew it happened in there—it was so close to the pool. God, can you imagine? If the police had tried to put him right there by the pool?"

He said, quietly—as if lowering his voice would keep this just between us—"This is why he's always felt responsible. They got their signals crossed, somehow. He thought she was meeting him at the mattresses, and she thought he was meeting her at the shed."

"So you all knew she was at the shed. I'm not—don't get me wrong, I'm not accusing anyone of anything, but that's got to be heavy, that you all didn't mention the shed to the police."

"We didn't know it happened there."

"Sure, no, of course. But if the police had looked there, if they'd found the blood, it might have changed things."

He shook his head. "Right, it might have changed things just by putting a different innocent person in prison. I'm not saying I value Robbie's freedom over Omar's, but there's no telling what else they would've gotten wrong."

There were several things I wanted to scream at him. One was the fact that he clearly *had* put Robbie ahead of Omar. Another was that he didn't even seem concerned about justice for Thalia, about the fact that maybe she wasn't resting in peace, and maybe the person who did this had gone on to hurt more people.

Instead of screaming, I tucked a bolster pillow between my shoulder blades, stretched my shoulders back and pushed my boobs out.

I wondered whether Mike would testify to any of this—whatever his professional convictions, his personal ethics. My phone had been recording the whole time, just in case. I'm not an idiot.

"It makes so much sense, then, that you'd all get your stories straight. He was vulnerable." I swallowed all the spit in my mouth and said, "Even if Robbie had shown up a little late at the mattresses, you'd have to say he was there from the beginning, right? Otherwise they're off on some rabbit chase. Maybe they'd fully pin it on him."

I expected Mike to look alarmed, but he shrugged. "He was there, though."

"You remember walking with him?"

"After all this time, I mean—but he was in the pictures from the beginning. That's rock-solid."

"Oh, right," I said. "He's in the first one. Knowing him, it was probably his idea to take photos in the first place."

"Right? If we were kids now he'd be the Instagram king. He always wanted everyone to remember how much fun they'd had."

"That's really sweet," I said. "He's a sweet guy."

"He's a sap. He used to listen to *Phantom of the Opera*. I could never figure it out, how does a guy get away with listening to *Phantom of the Opera* and not get ragged on? No one questioned his sexuality."

"So if they asked you on the stand," I said, "whether he was there from the beginning, you'd be positive? Because I'm having this crisis of confidence about testifying. Like, how do you remember things? It was so long ago."

"I think for us, it helped that we talked about it right away. We're sitting around listing who all was in the woods, we're making sure we know what time we got there."

"Was that all from Robbie? It seems like he was so smart about it, developing the photos and everything."

I sipped my whiskey and intentionally spilled some down my chin, onto my tank top, so I had to paw myself dry.

Mike kept his eyes studiously above my head. "Yeah, actually," he said. "He was the one who gathered a bunch of us. Or maybe—I guess we were in his room to check on him. It was the day after they found her. He started writing everything down in a notebook, who was there and what time we left the theater. It helped him process it all."

The motherfucker. That entitled little floppy-haired motherfucker.

"For sure," I said. "And I bet he was terrified. Of being blamed. I mean, what if he hadn't been there? Or what if he'd joined you all later, or left earlier?"

"But he didn't," Mike said, and it felt like I'd hit a trip wire. He looked irritated, checked his phone. "Jesus, it's late," he said.

I threw a pillow at him. "No kidding! Get out of here and stop keeping me up!"

And there he went. There was Mike Stiles's back as he left my hotel room like a lover departing after a tryst. The teenager somewhere in me, watching from 1995, was bewildered by it all.

I whispered to her: "It's not what you think."

26

I have some questions for you.

Did you know it was Robbie? Did you at least know it wasn't Omar? Did you hear the rumors about some older guy and realize, when they arrested him, the bullet you'd dodged?

Did Robbie see something? Did he walk in on you and Thalia? Did she tell you he was growing suspicious? Did she tell you he knew? Did she tell you that one night, early that spring, she'd confessed it all to Robbie— or at least confessed that she was seeing *someone*, even if he didn't know it was you? Did she tell you he was angry? That she was scared of him?

When they came around asking questions, did you refrain from implicating Robbie, from mentioning that he might have a motive, because if you fingered him, he could finger you? Did you work it out with him, even? Make meaningful eye contact across the dining hall, the kind that said *We'd both do best to keep our mouths shut*?

Did you accept that job in Bulgaria before Thalia died? Did you take the job and tell her and she was mad that you were leaving the entire country, and let something slip to Robbie? Or did you conduct a frantic job search the week after her death, knowing if you stayed the rumors about you might accumulate, stick?

Before they arrested Omar, did you worry they'd get you? Did you lie awake thinking about yourself, rather than what had happened to Thalia? Did you thank God for your alibi, for chatting with me as you rolled the timpani away? Did you make sure your wife remembered what time you came home?

Have you thought what would have happened if you'd come forward? If you'd sacrificed everything to help Omar? To find justice for Thalia, whom I'm sure you believe you loved? It's a big ask, I know. It would ruin your marriage, your career. (Careers and marriages have been ruined for less.) But you could have told your own version of the story. She wasn't there to contradict you.

Have you thought about the cavity searches that happen in prison? Have you thought about the way prison guards exact their own arbitrary justice, kicking a guy's teeth in because he didn't show enough respect?

Have you considered how things might have turned out had the adult closest to Thalia at Granby been a voice of wisdom, someone she could confide in, someone who would notice that she was miserable with Robbie, that she wasn't eating, that he was angry and controlling?

If you had done the difficult work of adulthood and intervened—what then? Would she have lived?

Do you sleep well?

Do you dream?

Is there forgiveness, in your dreams?

Monday morning, I gave up on a frustrating Google search and texted Yahav to ask what would happen if new evidence were discovered this late.

What kind of evidence? he wrote.

Well, that was the problem. It wasn't really evidence. And it wasn't really new. And Amy March wasn't even particularly interested. I wrote: *Let's say evidence that destroys another viable suspect's alibi.*

If the state withheld it, he wrote, *that's a Brady violation.*

No, nothing like that. More like—if sthg new came up or a witness changed their story. Wishful thinking. Even if I could crack Mike—and I wasn't sure there was anything more there to crack—he wasn't on the witness list, which complicated things further. Sakina had never changed her story. And Beth was gone and hated me. What was I going to do, track down Bendt Jensen in Denmark and ask if he happened to remember who arrived in what order twenty-seven years ago?

Geoff was in touch with a few other people who'd been at the mattresses, and he planned to spend the day contacting Jimmy Scalzitti and Fizz and a skier named Kirtzman whom I remembered primarily as a loud sneezer. He'd see if he could find anything concrete.

Yahav wrote, *Is defense still presenting? Defense could still call whoever. Or if they already testified, could recall during rebuttal after state closes. What happened???*

Really nothing, I answered, more accurately than I would have liked. *Just curious.*

A correction: Beth was gone, but, I discovered, not far. On her Instagram, she'd posted a photo of herself and her handsome husband at a fire pit on a restaurant terrace. She'd labeled it #selfcare and #r&r, and had tagged a ski resort in Stowe, Vermont—one that looked, from its website, to offer luxury spa services and locally sourced food. It clicked now why she'd waited for her husband to pick her up; they were having a nice weekend before his surgery.

I scrolled through her older photos: Beth on a footbridge, Beth's husband in a tux on a crosswalk, Beth's kids sprawled across her bed in what looked like a magazine shoot, and possibly was. One photo showed her getting vaccinated last spring, blue eyes welling with happy tears above her mask.

I didn't know what I was looking for. I didn't know if she'd be able to help, or willing, and nothing here would answer those questions. But I had to try. If I ruined her weekend, I ruined her weekend.

Alder was back in court, but Britt was not—and Britt could be trusted with discretion. She was the one I called to ask if she'd drive me to Vermont. The sequestration rules were my last concern. Britt had driven here from Smith, and she picked me up in front of the Calvin Inn in her Kia.

As we drove, Britt said, "If we're right—I bet that's why Robbie brought his family. Don't you think? He was scared of something like this happening. He wants to look good." Britt was convinced by Alder's theory, even if the defense team wasn't. They weren't about to discuss it on the podcast yet, but they could always do that down the road, if need be.

The drive took us two and a half hours—the roads, as we got up into the mountains, still packed in places with opaque gray ice.

I asked Britt if she was seeing anyone at Smith and she said, "I'm still with Alder."

I was glad she was looking at the road and didn't see my gobsmacked face. To the extent that I'd considered it at all, I'd assumed both of them were interested in the same sex. And I'd never had the slightest hint that they were an item.

"That's so great!" I managed to say after too long a pause. "How long has it been now?"

She shrugged. "I guess since your class, basically. The long-distance thing has been chill."

Asking more seemed invasive, so I dropped it. But the news delighted me. Proof that it wasn't only a trail of chaos I was leaving behind.

Britt said, "I've been feeling optimistic. Even before today. The problem is, that's usually a bad sign."

"I know what you mean." I've always preferred to hedge against optimism. But hope—wasn't that how Omar was staying alive? Knowing hell might one day end?

All day I'd been filling with hope for Omar. I'd imagined him stepping out into the wind of a spring day. I'd imagined him moving in with his younger brother, and the new, soft sheets his brother might buy him. I imagined him eating all the foods he wanted. Ice cream, hot bread, a beautiful salad. I imagined him getting a massage, getting acupuncture, seeing a chiropractor, lighting up a joint. I imagined him moving through space the way he used to, graceful and muscled, on springs. Getting in a car and driving fast, fast, fast.

Of course, even if his conviction were vacated, it might be two or three years until a new trial. Maybe longer, if there were more waves of COVID. In the meantime, the state could appeal and the New Hampshire Supreme Court could reverse the judge's decision, just like that. It was unlikely that bail would be granted, since it wasn't granted back in '95. And all of this was the best-case scenario, the pipe dream.

We arrived, finally, at a resort much larger than I'd anticipated, a parking lot teeming with out-of-state SUVs.

"God, I didn't think this through," I said. I'd had some vision of staking the place out all day, but it was already three p.m., and I didn't want to make Britt retrace these mountain roads in the dark.

She messed around on her phone, then put it on speaker, deftly navigating the phone menu of the resort spa until she reached a silken-voiced woman. "Yes," Britt said, "my name is Beth Docherty. I believe my husband made an appointment for me today, but he forgot to tell me what time."

Shuffling and confusion on the other end, and the woman said, "I have you as already checked in for your 2:30 facial. Are you not—"

Britt hung up on her and tossed me her phone like a hot potato, and we sat gasping with laughter.

I said, "My friends and I could've used you at Granby. We spent so much time pranking people on the dorm phones. You never knew who'd pick up."

29

I waited on a cushioned bench outside the second-floor spa, a place called Seasons! that emanated a soothing shea butter scent even through its marbled glass doors. Britt had sauntered into the business center like she lived there and headphoned up to work on edits.

Something I wish I'd figured out earlier in life: Walk into any place like you belong, and you will.

I killed time watching a video Jerome had sent of Silvie jumping rope on our driveway. Her legs were so strong, her face so jubilant with concentration and success. She jumped normally, then crossed her arms, then normal, crossed, normal, crossed. A new trick.

I thought of a friend in LA who'd said recently, of her own daughter, "It feels wrong to give her all this happiness and confidence when we know what's coming. Seventh grade's gonna hit like a wall. It feels like fattening a pig for slaughter."

But what was the alternative? Starving the pig?

Beth emerged from the spa looking down at her phone. She was makeup-less, her face raw but glowing, and she wore spa-issued green foam flip-flops, cotton between her freshly magentaed toes. She carried her shoes in her hand. I stood from the bench with enough urgency to attract her attention.

She looked me fully up and down, as if the bottom half of my body might explain what I was doing here. She said, "What. The fuck."

I had considered whether I'd explain or apologize or try to pretend it was all a coincidence, but what I'd settled on was "I'm going to buy you a drink downstairs and then I'll get out of your hair forever. But you need to come with me right now." When you're kidnapping someone, it's best to be assertive.

And despite muttering to herself and sending a voice message to her husband that "some incredibly stupid shit just came up," she did follow me down the long hallway, down the grand curving staircase, and into an oak-and-red-leather bar lined with photographs of celebrities who'd stayed at the resort over the years.

We sat at a small, sturdy table under a signed picture of Bing Russell in a cowboy hat. A waiter was immediately upon us, filling glasses with ice water and telling us they were short-staffed but he'd be right back, which Beth seemed put out by; it implied we were staying more than thirty seconds.

She said, *"Well?"* Her eyes were the crystalline blue of a movie villain's; her pupils had shrunk to pinpricks.

"Okay." I placed my hands palm-down on the table and then, thinking about body language, turned them faceup. "I appreciate how open you were the other day. I was thinking about it afterward, how awful that must have been for you—the thing about Stiles's house. That was assault."

"Sure."

"It was assault from *all* of them, from everyone who saw it."

"By modern standards, sure." She brought her ice water halfway to her lips but put it down again.

"There was such a code of silence around things like that. All those boys. They made an impenetrable wall together, wherever they went."

She shrugged. "Well, the girls, too."

"I was thinking," I said, as if I'd been driving by this resort and it had just occurred to me. "The night of March third. You were there in the woods."

"You want to ask about *that*? Yes, I was in the woods. I was not in the pool with Thalia or whatever the fuck you're thinking."

"It's only one thing, hang on. You remember walking back with Robbie at the end of the night, along with everyone else."

"Sure."

"Do you remember walking *there* with him? Like, do you have specific memories of him being there on the walk out?"

She squinted at me like I was crazy, then looked up at Bing Russell's photo.

"What I remember," she said, "is he jumped out from behind a tree and scared the shit out of me."

This was new.

"How so?"

"Like—we were all up there, drinking, and suddenly he's jumping out at us, like, *Ha ha, I was hiding back here and you didn't even know, what if I was an axe murderer, blah blah blah.*"

"So he just appeared?"

"That thing—you remember how in middle school, boys were always riding their skateboards straight at you, and at the last minute they'd swerve and laugh at you for being scared? Or they'd cover your eyes from behind and if you didn't find it funny you were frigid or something? You just have to roll with the abuse, otherwise you're a crazy bitch."

"So, how long, would you say? Before he popped out?" My heart was an entire percussion section.

"Long enough that it was weird and funny. Not five minutes. Like half an hour."

"And you hadn't seen him up there before then?"

"No. That was the joke."

I said, "Okay. Okay."

"Why. What."

"Let me show you something," I said, and I brought up the photo of Robbie's sweatshirt back, zoomed in on the streak of mud splatter, explained Alder's theory and what that would mean for the timing.

She said, "I see what you're seeing, but I think you're grasping at straws."

"You don't think this might be interesting to the defense team?"

"Jesus."

"I don't mean—"

"Jesus. You're not, like, recording this, are you?"

I wasn't, this time, but just to prove my point I set my phone on the table, pressed the side button till it powered down.

She said, "What I do *not want*, Bodie, is to be, like, a key witness or something. I wanted nothing to do with this. I would like to forget those entire four years completely. You know that movie where they erase people's memories?"

"No one asked for this. No one asked to be a witness."

"Well, *you* kind of did."

"Absolutely not." I felt the need to explain myself, but also felt like the less I said, the better. What I did say was, "Between us, I remember Robbie being awful to her, too. When I roomed with her, I noticed a lot. Or at least, I look back as an adult, and I notice things."

Here was the waiter, and I ordered us both glasses of Malbec as Beth gazed over my head.

When he was gone she said, "He was always accusing her of stuff. He'd wait outside her class and walk her to her next one, and everyone thought that was so cute. I did not. He always had one hand on her. He stole her retainer."

"He what?"

"You know how she was supposed to wear her retainer at night? She was planning to go with some of us to Anguilla for spring break junior year. Puja's family invited everyone. There were other guys going, Dorian and Kellan and all them. But we had to pay for the flights, and Robbie wasn't going to be able to pay. So he took Thalia's retainer and told her if she went, he was keeping it the whole time. She'd come back two weeks later with her teeth all fucked up. And she was scared of what her orthodontist would say."

"So she stayed back?"

"Yeah, I think she went home instead. It's not even like she was with him, she just wasn't with *us*."

"I'd forgotten," I said, "but I remember you all talking about Anguilla. I'd never heard of it, and I thought you were saying Aunt Willa. Like, you were going to Puja's Aunt Willa's place."

"That's so funny," she said without laughing. "You're from the Midwest, right?"

I thought, pointlessly, that Indiana was closer to Anguilla than New Hampshire was, but I knew what she meant.

She said, "This other time, senior year, he threw out all her photo collages. Those ones she had up of her friends back home, he was jealous of some guy in the pictures. She came back to her room one day and they were gone. She knew it was him. She even went through the trash in his dorm hall, nothing."

I remembered the collages—she'd had them junior year, too. And I wondered, suddenly, if she might have circled various campus dumpsters, searching for them. If she might not have run out in her pajamas, looking dazed, even drugged, in her disbelief.

I asked, "Did he ever hit her?"

"Imagine if I'd said all this up there on the stand. The hearing would go on forever. They'd be dragging Robbie up. I'd be testifying for days."

"Well, you wouldn't just randomly be saying it, you'd have gone to the defense team and they'd have a chance to figure out how to frame it all and they'd disclose it to the prosecution and so on."

"Which is all a moot point, because I'm done."

"Listen, it could seriously help Omar's case. It would be tricky because they'd have to get the judge's permission to recall you. There's a ton of red tape, but it's so important. Don't you think?"

The waiter arrived, not only to give us our wine but to ask where we were from, if we were enjoying our stay, if we were disappointed there wasn't fresh powder out there. "I've never skied in my life," I said, impatiently enough that he left us alone.

When I looked back at Beth she'd closed her eyes, was holding the stem of her glass meditatively between her thumb and middle finger.

She said, "He went around to us all, after they found Thalia. He made sure we remembered him being there, at the mattresses. I was like, of course I remember, you popped out and we screamed. I might've been a little drunk, but I remembered that. It made sense that he was afraid of being blamed. And I've never thought for a second he had something to do with it." Her eyes widened, blue blue blue. "He couldn't, right? This stuff you're saying, it's all—this is just that they should have looked at him."

I shook my head as slowly as if I had something balanced on top.

I kept looking at her, until her gaze fell to the table.

She mouthed, *Oh.*

I said, "Do you think anyone else would remember that, his popping out at you all, his showing up late?"

She shrugged. "You asked if he ever hit her. You know what's funny, she *told* us he slapped her across the face, but then Puja was talking about reporting it to the counselor and Thalia said we didn't understand, she hit him, too. She'd slap him and he'd slap her back or something. It seemed like one more adult secret. Someone's abortion, someone messing around with a teacher, someone's drinking problem. You remember that show *Thirtysomething*? It was so naïve of me, but those were my markers of adulthood, like you're not an adult till you have prime-time drama problems. You know what's sad, it was one of the things we fought about after she died; Puja wanted to tell the police about it, but, like, we'd all agreed—" I waited for her to continue, but she was lost in some fog.

"And you haven't mentioned that to the lawyers. You didn't say that in your statement or in your testimony?"

"They only wanted to know about the flask, and they wanted me to rehash everything about why I'd brought Omar up to the police. But there was no one else it *could* be. I mean, Mr. Bloch would never do that. Can you imagine? He was a perv but he was so, like, bookish and weepy. He cried in front of me once. Not that a person who cries can't kill someone, but it just never seemed likely."

I nodded a vague agreement.

She said, "If Omar—you really don't think he did this?"

"I don't blame you for bringing up his name. None of this is your fault. But I genuinely believe Omar had nothing to do with it."

"I don't like to think of myself as racist. And then what if I—" She put her head in her hands.

I wasn't going to contradict her, but I said—carefully, appeasingly—"You were a kid."

She didn't move.

I said, "If you're willing to talk to the defense team about Robbie—about his hitting Thalia, about his maybe getting to the mattresses late—we have some other stuff, too. You'd only be telling the truth. It was so unfair, that teenagers had to deal with this. But we can fix it now."

"I have a life. I don't want this to be the first thing that comes up when someone googles my name. Or my *kids'* names. Christ. I don't want to deal with any of this. I want to go home."

"I know," I said.

She said, "Bodie, can you leave me alone? Just—listen, you can leave me your number or whatever. I just need to be home with my kids."

30

It was the one where she used her umbrella as a shield.

You remember, right? Nancy Grace covered the trial.

Think hard, Mr. Bloch, because I'm sure you remember.

It was the one where after she threw hot water at him and escaped, no one believed her. She was probably looking for attention. She had psychological problems, after all. Those panic attacks she kept having: evidence she was unwell.

What you likely saw on TV was the part about how her own brother invited the guy over, told her to apologize for dragging his name through the mud. And she did. She apologized.

The next night, he came back and he stabbed her.

This was the one where people had a hard time taking her seriously because her name was a stripper name. Jay Leno made jokes about her, about her name.

This was the same year Lorena Bobbitt cut off her husband's penis. It was right after sophomore year at Granby. Leno made a joke about both this woman and Lorena Bobbitt: something about their names, something about knives.

She survived the stabbing. She was the one who went on *Oprah* with scars on her neck, scars on her face. She was the one who sat down with Barbara Walters. Barbara leaned in close and asked if she had it in her to forgive her attacker. He'd just been released from his two-year prison sentence.

Here's what I remember: This woman, still so young, looked back at Barbara Walters and said, "Am I supposed to? I guess that's what you're supposed to do. That's how you move on."

It didn't stand out to me at the time. This seemed the kind of thing people said. But ten years later, I woke in the middle of the night suddenly remembering that interview, wanting to scream.

I googled the woman to see if she'd changed her mind, if she'd spoken out again.

She'd died six years earlier, shot by a different man. One she'd forgiven again and again, just like she was supposed to.

#9: ROBBIE SERENHO

There are things I'll likely never know: If it was planned, if he was drunk, if he told anyone, if he knew what he was doing or only understood once it was done. If he had that bike waiting, or found it—a sign from above that he was meant to survive this, to ride away unscathed. If he was shaking, terrified, the rest of that night, or pleased with himself. If a friend helped him scrub up the equipment shed the next morning, while Thalia still floated, unnoticed, unmissed, in the pool.

The way he treated his wife all these years—maybe holding things in, maybe never hitting her—but still the man capable of that violence. Or maybe hitting her. Maybe worse. Maybe—it's not impossible—living a model life, as if doing so would pay a cosmic debt. Maybe running forever from that teenage boy and his sins.

There are things I can assume: That he drank his way through college, trying to forget. That he justified it to himself—not that Thalia deserved to die, but that Omar's life was more expendable than his own. Maybe he told himself how far he'd come in the world already. Maybe he told himself it would kill his parents if they knew, and wouldn't two more deaths be worse? Maybe he convinced himself that Omar, surely selling drugs, was bound for prison anyway. Maybe he managed to forget Omar entirely.

There are things I can't stop imagining: Robbie's face turning red with rage. His pupils, dilated huge in the dark. The sound of a cracking skull. The look of horror and desperation on her face. The weight of a body, even one that thin. Her regaining a moment of consciousness when he dropped her in the water. Her knowing this was it, this was the whole world leaving her.

The few things I know: She was facing him when he slammed her head back, more than once; they were eye to eye. (I can see it, clearer than I could ever imagine Omar snapping, clearer than I could ever see your hands on her neck.) She didn't have time to defend herself. There was a moment when she understood this time was different. She took several breaths in the water. Conscious or unconscious, it took her a long time to die.

I know that Robbie showed up for brunch the next morning. He skied at the Granby Invitational the next weekend. Everyone said how strong he was to hold it all together. By May, he was spending time with Rachel Popa. He received the Senior Spirit award. He graduated with a 3.5 GPA.

31

Back at the Calvin Inn, in the empty solarium, I jumped into the pool, sat as long as I could on the bottom. It was bracingly cold.

On the drive back, I'd texted Yahav asking him to call. I wanted his legal advice, and I also wanted to unload everything Beth had said. If nothing else, he was still a good friend. And, there *was* nothing else. I had to accept that people fundamentally slide past each other in this world. I couldn't make him stay, couldn't shake him by the shoulders, couldn't let myself be overtaken by any atom of the possessive force that made Robbie grab on so hard to Thalia.

It was easier to see that from the bottom of the pool.

The light filtered through in solid beams, made the water a cathedral.

I wanted to breathe, but I didn't want to rise to the surface. I wanted to breathe in water, to discover that I had gills.

I'd watched video of Jasmine Wilde's Washington Square Park piece, the one where people brought her the things she subsisted on. When no one brought her food, she didn't eat. When no one brought her water, she didn't drink. At one point, deliriously sick and dehydrated, she'd pulled up clumps of grass to chew on. "There's life in here," she said to the camera, or whoever was holding it. "The roots hold a lot of water. Sometimes you have to take."

I had no idea what it meant. Wasn't this the problem, all along? All we did was take from each other and from the earth and from ourselves. Maybe her point was that we couldn't help it. Right now, I needed to take from Beth, who didn't deserve it; and from Robbie, who did.

My survival instincts kicked in, and without deciding to I rose to the surface, gulped in oxygen for every cell of my body.

My phone, on the side of the pool, showed a voicemail alert from an unknown number.

I dried my finger on my towel so I could hit play, and Beth's small voice filled the room. She said, "I still can't believe you drove all the way to Stowe." And then she kept talking, but it was there in her voice from the beginning, in her tone of relieved resignation: That she would do this, she would talk to Amy. That she had realized she'd been waiting for decades.

32

A full day passed.

Across from Aroma Mocha, where I sat with my laptop and a latte, across a street that had been a street since it was cobblestones and dirt, was a soft-serve ice cream place. Robbie and Jen Serenho were unmistakable, Robbie in a dark blue parka, Jen in her maroon coat, the kids bouncing like rabbits.

I was waiting for Amy March, who—after my ridiculously long voicemail—had stalled all day in court, taking far longer than needed to examine the second State Police detective. (*She practically asked his shoe size*, Geoff texted. *She's like, can you read this entire ten-page document aloud?*) And I was waiting for Beth. They were both due here at 4:30, once Amy was done for the day. It would be just the start of a bunch of dominos falling. Rather than wait and recall Beth after the state presented its case, they could use Beth's husband's upcoming surgery and petition the judge to let her be recalled out of order. That way, by the time Robbie took the stand—although he'd know what was coming— Amy could ask him directly about Beth's testimony.

I watched as, across the street, Robbie picked the youngest up, swung her by the armpits, set her down.

The universe stood still. I wondered if I could at least jump off.

Here was the person I'd been looking for, all these years. A person I couldn't wait to destroy. Here was the person living the life Omar deserved. The life Thalia deserved.

Here, also, was someone with young children who loved him, with a wife who loved him. (I know, I know. I know.)

It was the kids I thought about. Even if Robbie was never put on trial himself (the chances were slim), even if he kept his job, even if he kept his marriage together, his children would grow up in overwhelming shadow.

Not like my kids, who might or might not fully become aware that someone had made an art piece about their father, might dismiss it or embrace it, might accuse or defend him.

This was murder, it was strangulation and assault. He had bashed in her head and left her to drown. This was an abuse of privilege that the world would eat up: a boy at a fancy boarding school, an athlete and star, a stock character. For a reason. A guy we'd seen before because we'd seen this guy before.

To be absolutely clear: I'm not saying *What a fine young man, let's not ruin his future.* I'm saying, I looked at him and knew I was looking at, among other things, a murderer. And the chill I felt, I expected it. But I didn't expect to feel like a killer myself, like someone reaching out to end something.

Not a single cell of his body was the same as it had been in 1995. But he was still himself, just as I was still, despite everything, my teenage self. I had grown over her like rings around the core of a tree, but she was still there.

Robbie's daughter had a pink swirl, maybe strawberry. One son had chocolate, one son had vanilla. He swung the little girl again: left, right, left, right.

I was wrong about you, too, Mr. Bloch, but I still don't feel that wrong.

To put it another way: I was mistaken, but I wasn't incorrect.

At freshman orientation, they had us do that embarrassing game where someone pretends to be a machine part, and someone else joins, making a different motion, a different noise, then someone else, someone else, till we were all one big hormonal machine in the middle of the hockey field.

My point is, you were a part of the machine: an arm, a leg. You drove the getaway car. You threw bricks through the window and someone else grabbed the jewelry. You distracted the feds while the spies got away. You held her down while someone else beat her. You shot the deer and wounded it; when the second hunter came along, the deer could no longer run.

Dane Rubra stares into the camera a long moment, blinking. His eyes are bloodshot, but the irises remain a reptilian amber.

"Ladies and gentlemen," he says, "and others. I am—I don't even know what to say. As you've doubtless heard, we had the kind of bombshell today that could upend this whole hearing.

"I'm speaking to you from my hotel room on the evening of Wednesday, March sixteenth. Here's what we know so far. Today, the defense was able to recall their witness Elizabeth Docherty, who testified that Robbie Serenho was not provably at the mattresses until 9:59 p.m., and that Thalia Keith confided with her on more than one occasion that Serenho had physically assaulted her. To which I say: *whooooo, boy*.

"I'm happy that my gut instincts were right, my very first instincts. If you're wondering how Denny Bloch fits into all this—and if you haven't watched Episode 46, please give it a moment of your time—what I recently discovered is *not* irrelevant. Robbie Serenho did this thing. Dennis Bloch was the motivation. Ms. Docherty spoke about Bloch today in court, and it seems the defense will use that in some way going forward. Thalia sleeping with her music teacher, that's a death penalty offense according to young Mr. Serenho. We now have means, motive, and opportunity for Serenho. That makes him a viable suspect, a *more* than viable suspect."

Dane stops here, takes a long sip of water from a fingerprint-smudged glass.

"Serenho is entitled to get himself legal representation, which, duh, he will. He's on the docket for tomorrow morning, which should be incredibly interesting.

"I have seen Robbie Serenho in town with his family. At the time I sighted them, I was more interested in the new information about Dennis Bloch; otherwise I might have been tempted to confront him. One of many reasons I'll be staying in Kern a while is to see if I can find him before he leaves."

Dane leans in to stop the recording, his nose too close to the camera.

Geoff, watching the video with me Wednesday night, had already filled me in on the day. He'd told me how Mike Stiles had raced out of the courtroom right after Beth's testimony, before the cross-examination. Presumably to tell Robbie everything that had happened.

Geoff said, "You got what you wanted. I mean—with Bloch, his name going on the record. You still wanted that, right?"

Yes. I did.

I said, "I don't want them to kill him. I don't—"

"No, I know."

I said, "It's out of my hands now. Which feels good. Or at least it's supposed to feel good."

Geoff pulled me onto him, stroked my hair.

For context, I suppose I do need to explain here that Geoff and I had found ourselves in my bed. I don't feel like telling you more than that. It's none of your business.

Geoff said, "What do you think the Serenhos are doing right now?"

I couldn't imagine. All I knew was that Robbie had lawyers, and probably his lawyers had lawyers. He was well-connected, after all. A Granby alum.

35

When I arrived for freshman year in August of '91, Severn Robeson walked me around the unchanged parts of campus. The dining hall, Old Chapel, New Chapel, the library. He walked me into Couchman, his old dorm, to my excruciating embarrassment. Surely I wasn't allowed in here. But no one looked at us twice; maybe they assumed I was dropping off my brother.

The broad wooden window frames in the Couchman common were carved within an inch of their lives—initials, dates, names. With visible pleasure, Severn found, in the corner of one frame, the initials SDR. "There I am!" he said. "Ah, that's gratifying. Like I never left."

I'd seen plenty of graffiti back in Indiana, but that was the vandalism of the bored, the desperate, those trapped in a horrible town and ready to desecrate it. *This*, though—this was a thing of beauty, these lasting marks. Like someone had summitted a mountain and wanted to leave a mark, to say *I was here*.

I think about this a lot. When someone asks if I liked boarding school, I can no longer base my answer, my judgment, on the people I knew. Once, I might have thought of you. I might have thought of any number of people who weren't what I once believed. But I can still love the place itself, as a *place*, as smells and echoes and angles of light, as surfaces etched deep with their own history.

If Mike Stiles first knew he belonged at Granby when he saw those memorial plaques, I felt something similar in the Couchman common. It wasn't destiny I felt—just that this was a place where someone could claim a small corner, a place where, by the end of four years, I'd be able to say I was part of something. Somewhere on campus, I'd find a place to leave a piece of myself.

I was here.

I was here.

Alder and Britt and Geoff all individually related the bizarre scene that had rolled out Thursday morning, the same morning I'd spent lying in bed staring at CNN, at global calamities that made the entire state of New Hampshire feel microscopic.

Robbie, his face pale and swollen, had taken the stand with his lawyer right behind him—"hovering over him like a puppeteer," Geoff said. Britt said, "I had no idea they could do that. This guy was just *telling* him what to say."

Robbie had apparently looked to his attorney after every question, even the ones about what years he'd attended Granby, whether he knew Thalia at all. For those questions, the attorney nodded and Robbie answered. As soon as Amy asked if his relationship with Thalia was sexual in nature, the attorney shook his head, and Robbie said, "I exercise my Fifth Amendment right not to answer." And then the same, again and again, for every remaining question.

On cross-examination, the state asked only "Were you responsible for the death of Thalia Keith?" to which Robbie responded, loudly and forcefully, "No."

Geoff said, "The fucker's gonna get away with it. Even if Omar got off, they're never going after Serenho. I don't see it."

Yahav said so, too, on the phone. He said, "There's no case against him."

I said, "But there was no case against Omar, either."

"Yes. Well."

There was a man who got off the hook because he married the only witness very quickly; she couldn't be forced to testify against her husband. She was the victim's mother.

There was a man who got away with it because the defense made the girl's best friend, now thirteen, testify that the dead girl had sneaked into R-rated movies. This apparently meant she was mature enough ("sexually active," they said) at twelve that anyone could have killed her, not just the bus driver who had the nude photos.

There was a man they let out on a technicality (a paperwork error) who went free in just enough time to show up, to her family's horror, at the graveside service of the girlfriend he'd strangled.

There was a boy who was not charged with involuntary manslaughter for pushing his father off a restaurant deck—because the system worked for him as it should work for everyone. When they brought him in for questioning, they gave him a blanket and hot chocolate. They understood that he was a child.

There was a man who got away with it because five Black, trans women found dead in the same park in one year must have been coincidence, a sign that it was a seedy park. They never even looked for him.

In the '90s there was a case where the state declined to press charges against the family friend whose semen had been found in the mouth and vagina and anus of the murdered eleven-year-old. The state's attorney didn't feel there was enough evidence. The girl might have been sitting on a bed where he'd previously masturbated, and eaten some popcorn there, and gotten his semen in her mouth. "This is how we get colds," the man said. "We touch something, we touch our face. And then a little girl goes to the bathroom, and what does she do? She wipes herself, front to back, like this." And on live TV, in some marbled court hallway, he squatted low, swiped his hand between the legs of his suit pants.

The defense rested after they questioned Robbie, and the state introduced no witnesses of their own. They spent the following day making arguments, the state again saying I had influenced people, this time manipulating Beth. I would have been allowed into the courtroom for the closing arguments, but Amy didn't think that would be a good idea; she told me to fly home, and the whole thing ended when I was in the air somewhere over the Rockies. When I landed, I had a voicemail from Amy telling me she thought it had gone very well. Now the judge would take it all "under advisement," and in one to six months, Amy thought, we'd hear if he'd decided to vacate the original verdict.

The day I got home, I checked my email and found a note from a young woman in Salem, Oregon. You knew her when she was a student in Providence. Paula Gutierrez; I'm sure the name rings a bell. She was hoping I could get a note to Beth Docherty, thanking her for what she'd said about you on the stand. *It sounded so eerily familiar,* she wrote to Beth. *Like you were talking about my own life.*

A week later, Dane Rubra forwarded me an email from Allison Mayfield, who'd attended the school you came to Granby from. Do you remember her? The one who dropped out junior year after she cut her wrists with fingernail scissors?

How about Zoe Ellis? She really thought the two of you were in love. She hadn't reexamined it until a friend sent her news about the hearing. God bless Zoe, she was ready to go public, to write about it all.

How about Annie Mintz?

Do you still have a job? Do you still have a family?

It's hard to tell online.

In April, I flew back east to see Geoff. We spent a week together in New York—we lay around in bed, I worked on the book, we ordered food—and we made plans for him to come out to LA that summer. I was very happy about it. I'm still happy about it.

I lied to Fran that I was in New York for research. I was holding out for the right moment to tell her, the right moment to hear her shriek "I've been waiting for this for *thirty years!*"

From New York, I took the Amtrak up to Manchester, where Fran picked me up and brought me to Granby; I'd stay with her for two nights. We had something important to do, something I don't want to tell you about quite yet. The next day, we'd go to the matinee of the student musical, the one the Shirley Jackson fanatic wanted me to see.

Late that first afternoon, as Fran and I walked her golden retriever around the lacrosse field, my phone buzzed with three messages in a row, from Britt, Yahav, and Alder: *Bad news* and *Motion for retrial denied* and *Fucckckck*, respectively.

My breath stopped with disbelief more than shock. Wasn't it too soon? It had barely been a month. This was surely a mistake, some minor legal hiccup I didn't understand. But it was real.

Yahav wrote again: *He can appeal, altho that's an even longer shot. I'm so sorry, Bodie. I hope I didn't give you false optimism. I tried not to. These things never come through. They're designed that way.*

I showed my phone to Fran, my hand shaking. Boris tried to jump up to sniff it, this thing we were both so interested in.

Fran asked if I wanted to be alone. I didn't answer, just numbly followed her home.

I wondered how long it would take for Omar to get the news. He might not know yet. I wished him one last night of hope.

In Fran's guest room, in the dark, I watched the video Dane Rubra had just put up. I'd become strangely fond of him. If nothing else, I could let him feel all the emotions for me.

Dane said, "Ultimately, no, it's not a shock. This was not actually exculpatory evidence for Omar. You can believe Robbie Serenho beat the tar out of Thalia every day and showed up late to the woods and still believe Omar was the one who did it. You'd be wrong, but there you go."

He said, "You know what to do, all of you in this incredible community we've built. Brand-new evidence could still be a game changer, and we know there's more to be found. The state is bound to dig their heels in. They'll never admit they were wrong. My strong guess, they're consulting with Thalia's family. And the Keiths have been dead set from the beginning on Omar Evans's guilt. If you've seen the video of the Keith family's statement, of Myron Keith outside his house today, you know what I'm talking about. These people won't budge. But we—everyone watching this, this whole army we have now—we're going to move *mountains*."

I felt strangely galvanized by his little speech. That, and I felt a wave of fury. Or rather, I felt my extant wave of fury grow tsunami-tall.

I was thinking of the moment Omar would learn this news; and I was thinking of everything we'd done, everything Beth had put herself through; and then I thought about the people out there—you, Mike, Dorian, not to mention Robbie—just sitting on what you knew.

I was thinking that if I had nothing to lose, I'd go find you myself. And if I couldn't get you to talk, I'd do the talking.

I was thinking: What *do* I have to lose, really? The things that matter aren't going anywhere: my kids, Geoff, the book I'm falling deeper into with every moment of research.

And maybe you're the missing piece of the puzzle. You, Robbie's motivation. You, who knew a lot about a lot of things and never said them. You, with a front-row seat to what went wrong. You, a big part of what went wrong.

Maybe I'm coming for you. Maybe I've been coming for you all along.

That was her flip-flop beside the van.

That was her comb in the ravine.

That was her bank card at the ATM in Kansas, but that wasn't her on the security footage.

Some leave more than others, to be sure; some leave trails and videos and yearbook quotes; some leave barely a trace.

That was her handwriting in the logbook.

That was her phone, tossed off the overpass.

That was her blood in the bathroom.

That was her hair in the attic.

We're lucky to find this much.

That was her laundry, still in the dryer.

This was her body, but she's long gone.

The show was *Into the Woods*, which we never could have pulled off in our day: complex orchestration, boys who could actually sing, a budget for mechanized trees. It had choreography well beyond the grapevines and box steps that had been my peers' entire range. It had a Cinderella from Nigeria and a Witch from Shenzhen and a Big Bad Wolf who, Fran whispered, was headed to Berklee in Boston for musical theater.

It was a worthy distraction. I've always been happiest when I can sit in the dark, when I can turn off my own life and watch a story unfold.

At intermission I met the couple next to me, retirees from Peterborough who said they never missed a Granby show. "We saw this one on Broadway in the '90s," the woman said, "and I swear this is just as good."

As the lights dimmed again, I said to Fran, "I'd never get into Granby now, would I?"

"Probably not," she whispered. "No offense."

Of course, we'd be different if we were growing up now. We'd still be idiots, still naïve. We'd be more stressed. Maybe we'd have ulcers. But we might have put up with less. And that would be something.

The kids sang and acted their hearts out; what better to do with all the concentrated emotions of youth?

There was, I remembered, a man released after forty-three years on death row who said the best thing about being free was singing in a shower where he controlled the temperature. He said, "I can sing opera in scalding water if I want."

There was a man they released after forty years, one rolled out in a wheelchair. He said on the news, "I can't think about the lost time because guess what, time doesn't work backwards anyway. I got what's in front of me, same as you." They invited him to Camden Yards and lifted him so he could feel the grass beneath his feet.

After the show, I went back to Fran and Anne's for an afternoon beer, which turned into three.

Fran was the one who showed me the video online from that morning: Amy March outside the State Prison, her face exhausted but her eyes fierce. She said, "The victory we've achieved is that Omar knows there are so many people who believe him. He told me that's what he's thankful for: the growing number of people who understand his innocence, who will continue to fight for his freedom. He's ready for the battle ahead. You have to remember that he's an athlete; he knows about endurance."

Fran rubbed my shoulders while I watched it. She said, "So we do it all again, right?"

I'd been foolish enough to wish Omar a few more hours of hope, but what else had he lived with all this time aside from hope in its purest, most undiluted form? Next to him, I knew nothing about hope.

The boys wanted to show me their backyard ninja course, and thanks to my buzz they successfully got me to try the zip line.

I decided to walk off the beer before Fran and I did the thing we had to do. I wanted to be sober for that.

I didn't particularly feel the need to circle the whole campus; it was all fresh from my stay in '18. So I walked over North Bridge, and back over Middle Bridge, and then halfway over South Bridge, where I stopped and sat with my legs dangling off, under the bottom rail. The tree branches were just barely unfurling the softest, smallest leaves, pale yellow-green, but down below, the forest floor was already lush and crowded—moss and shoots and creepers, a few violets and primroses—and the little creek at the bottom of the ravine burbled high with what must have been spring melt from the mountains.

I was thinking about Carlotta. Who knows if you even remember her. Maybe you remember her as a girl too prickly to close in on. Maybe she was forgettable background noise to your obsessions. In any case: She meant the world to me.

What I haven't told you, what I hadn't fully wrapped my mind around, is that I had come to Granby so that later that evening, Fran and I could sprinkle an eighth of Carlotta's ashes into the Tigerwhip. Carlotta had wanted this. She loved the place.

On the bridge, I told myself again that it had happened, that we'd lost her three full weeks ago. I couldn't let myself think about her children, not yet, but I could imagine her here with me, free now to go wherever she wanted. She'd been forty-five. Now she was seventeen again, too. Not in the horrible way Thalia would always be seventeen; remembering Thalia at seventeen was remembering someone on the steepest precipice. Picturing Carlotta young was picturing someone soaring through the sky, someone with everything to look forward to. Someone living more in genesis than aftermath.

I thought about how junior spring, Carlotta and Fran drove out to surprise me when we rowed at Kent on the Housatonic. As we passed, Fran cheered and chanted my name; Carlotta turned around and mooned me. I laughed and almost lost my rhythm, but I loved her for it.

Something I remembered only then: Maybe that day, or maybe another—Omar, there for icing and taping our joints into submission, turned up jogging along the very last stretch of the river. The water was a choppy mess, and we had two seniors out with the flu so a terrified sophomore was in the stroke seat for the first time, and we'd never rowed so badly. We'd fallen hopelessly far behind the competition, but Omar decided *he* was the one we were racing. As soon as we passed him, he started sprinting behind us; and although we were so slow that he likely could have caught up, he never quite did—slowing down, pretending to be winded when we struggled hardest against the unkind water. Five yards from the finish, he doubled over as if he couldn't go a step farther— the whole thing a silly, throwaway kindness.

Why on earth, despite the leaden sadness of yesterday and today, I felt profoundly light right then—ready to float away—I'm not sure. I'd had three beers, as I said.

These plants below were lucky, the early arrivals. The ones born later to a choked summer ravine would have to fight for sun and space. Plenty would make it. Everything green is something that's survived.

I could see Lower Campus from where I sat, could hear the shrieks that accompanied a cluster of kids tackling each other on their way down the quad.

I'd forgotten the names of most of the plants, but back in Dana Ramos's class I'd known them all. I only lived four years in New England, but I noticed more and learned more about what was around me there than I ever had in Indiana, and more than I ever would in LA, where there's constantly something new and impossibly technicolor blooming on my street. I could still tell you a few of them, the stalwart trees and ephemeral flowers of New Hampshire: painted trillium, bunchberry, hemlock, sheep laurel, white cedar, bloodroot.

Below me and above me and in the woods stretching thick and endless, their leaves made sugar out of nothing but light.

ACKNOWLEDGMENTS

First, a biographical note: I have lived for twenty-one years on the campus of the same boarding school that I attended as a day student in the 1990s. (For the curious: I met my husband in grad school and dragged him back to Chicago, where he applied for teaching jobs; the one he landed was at my alma mater. It was only weird for the first few months. No, I'm not a dorm parent and I don't teach there. I do live in a dorm apartment.) I'm forever grateful to that school for both a singular education and generous financial aid.

It should be obvious to everyone who knows that school that Granby is a very different place. It should also be clear to anyone who knew me in high school that Bodie is not me, and I hope it's equally evident that no one in the book is you. If I bent so far over backward on my characters that I accidentally came back around to any real-life similarities to anyone I know now or knew back then, it was in no way intentional. (The one exception: My class did, indeed, have an underwear thief.) You all know that if I wanted to write a book about real people I'd have a hell of a story, but it wouldn't be this one.

The hugest of thanks to Stephanie Hausman, a brilliant and passionate public defender in the state of New Hampshire, who course-corrected and fine-tuned the legal parts of the book, taught me about the New Hampshire penal system, and was generally a great reader.

Additional thanks: Paul Holes gamely helped with luminol and blood spatter. Liz Silver answered some legal questions early on. Becky Findlay and Suzy Vaughn helped with the crew parts. Dr. Ciprian Gheorghe helped with emergency medicine. Any errors on those issues are mine alone.

Jordyn Kimelheim named *Starlet Fever*. My kids named the Dragons and chose their colors. Lacy Crawford's brilliant memoir *Notes on a Silencing* (please read it!) shed light for me on institutional collusion. As I wrote, my student Rosemary Harp was also working on a boarding school novel (a brilliant one) that reminded me of the magic of a beloved space in the woods. The poet Kaveh Akbar gave a craft lecture that indirectly led me to the book's closing images. The writer Omer Friedlander solved a Hebrew emergency.

I'm grateful to the two dozen people who gave their names to characters in this book—something I offered in exchange for supporting an indie bookstore a few years back. They were all meant to be peripheral characters, but some of them came to life in unexpected ways, and I hope no one is horrified by the result. Names hold magic for me, and these ones inspired me in unexpected ways.

This book was started at the Ragdale Foundation—and later, when COVID canceled further residencies, I was grateful for the generosity of Barbara Nagel, Catherine Cooper and Marshall Greenwald, Catherine Merritt and Jack Wuest, and Lika Lopez de Victoria for letting me house-sit and make my own retreats.

Rachel DeWoskin, Gina Frangello, Thea Goodman, Dika Lam, Emily Grey Tedrowe, Zoe Zolbrod, Charles Finch, and Eli Finkel were fantastic early readers. Jon Freeman is no longer my first reader but he's still my last, and also my emotional support human.

My students and colleagues at StoryStudio Chicago, Northwestern University, and Sierra Nevada University have provided support and inspiration, especially as the world fell apart.

An Illinois Artists Fund grant helped support me in the last year of writing.

The hugest of thanks to my two editors on this book, Lindsey Schwoeri and Andrea Schultz, for a double ass-kicking and double support, and for editing under unusual circumstances—and to the whole ship full of Vikings: Brian Tart, Rebecca Marsh, Lindsay Prevette, Kate Stark, Allie Merola, Sheila Moody, Katie Hurley, Maddie Rohlin, Lucia Bernard, Elizabeth Yaffe, Christine Choi, Mary Stone, and Sara Leonard. Clarence Haynes gave the book a fantastically helpful authenticity read. Truckloads of gratitude to Nicole Aragi, Maya Solovej, and Kelsey Day. My assistant, Keaton Kustler, has kept my head screwed on.

Over the past couple of strange years, I've felt the support of independent bookstores more than ever. If you're reading this, please go buy yourself a present from one. You deserve it.

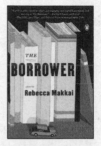

THE BORROWER

Children's librarian Lucy Hull has been helping her favorite patron, ten-year-old Ian Drake, smuggle books past his overbearing mother, who has enrolled him in weekly antigay classes. Desperate to save him from the Drakes, Lucy finds herself both kidnapper and kidnapped when she discovers Ian camped out in the library after hours, and the pair embarks on an ill-advised road trip. But is it just Ian who's running away? And should Lucy be trying to save a boy from his own parents?

THE HUNDRED-YEAR HOUSE

In this brilliantly conceived and deeply rewarding novel, Rebecca Makkai unfolds a generational saga in reverse, leading the reader back in time on a literary scavenger hunt as we seek to uncover the truth about a strange family and their vast, mysterious house. With intelligence and humor, a daring narrative approach, and a lovingly satirical voice, Makkai has crafted an unforgettable novel about family, fate, and the incredible surprises life can offer.

PENGUIN BOOKS

MUSIC FOR WARTIME

Stories

Named a must-read by the *Chicago Tribune, O, The Oprah Magazine, BuzzFeed,* and *The Huffington Post,* this collection of transporting, deeply moving stories—some inspired by her own family history—amply demonstrates Rebecca Makkai's extraordinary range as a storyteller, and confirms her as a master of the short story form.

THE GREAT BELIEVERS

It's 1985, and Yale Tishman's career begins to flourish, even as the AIDS epidemic grows around him. Soon the only person he has left is Fiona, his departed friend's sister. But it will be years before Fiona finds herself grappling with the devastating ways AIDS affected her life. The two intertwining stories take us from the heartbreak of Chicago in the eighties to the chaos of the modern world in contemporary Paris, as both Yale and Fiona struggle to find goodness in the midst of disaster.